The ENGLISH GIRL

BOOKS BY SARAH MITCHELL

The Lost Letters
The Couple

SARAH MITCHELL

The
ENGLISH
GIRL

bookouture

Published by Bookouture in 2021

An imprint of Storyfire Ltd.
Carmelite House
50 Victoria Embankment
London EC4Y 0DZ

www.bookouture.com

ISBN: 978-1-80019-692-6
eBook ISBN: 978-1-80019-691-9

This book is dedicated to Frankie, our golden retriever and family friend for fifteen and a half years. During the last months of her life she always positioned herself so closely behind my chair that it was difficult for me to move away from my desk – which is probably why I managed to finish the book on time.

'In the depth of winter, I finally learned that there was in me an invincible summer.'

—Albert Camus

The winter of 1946/47 is the snowiest, and one of the coldest, on record in the UK.

Chapter One

9 November 1989

West Berlin, West Germany

Tiffany lowers her rucksack onto the packed pavement of Friedrich-Strasse and listens to the sound of singing. Lusty serenades float across the rooftops, while on the streets crowds of young and old are gathering, strangers calling out to one another and hugging with abandon. People swarm past her like a river, laughing, crying, waving their arms. It's almost nine o'clock in the evening, and all around the night air thrums, jubilant and bright with shock.

In London rumours had been building for weeks. Swirling with the autumn leaves as she jogged beside the steely Thames. Gathering momentum from the updates on her radio. Reports of resignations, of capitulations, of demonstrations in East Berlin. Tales of a people's tide, about to turn a country on its head. And every hour made for fresh news. She listened while she ate breakfast on the counter that doubles as a table (trebles, occasionally, as a desk). Wondering, waiting, thinking of that address scribbled in her Filofax. And at long last, the dam burst. Today at the airport nobody bothered even to glance at her passport. Finally, Berlin has become the centre of the world. Today Berlin is focused only on itself.

Two young men are hurrying past.

Sofort! she hears.

Freiheit!

Delving into her coat, she pulls out an English-German dictionary. A soft-back book purchased late yesterday afternoon from a disgruntled shop assistant wanting to cash up his till. *How can it have been just yesterday?* The day before yesterday, she faced commuting in the London rain, persuading herself that selling artisan bakery products was the perfect job for a psychology graduate, and a steady and depressing stream of sympathy invitations supposed to lessen the pain of heartbreak.

Yesterday, however, everything changed.

Or rather, *she* changed everything.

She dug out the address (from her Filofax), packed a bag (the trusty rucksack), bought a flight (an open return) and left a message on the answerphone at work. (And how will *that* turn out when she gets back to London?)

Never mind.

She is here now.

Listening to history.

And history seems to be shouting in her ear. A male voice says, '*Freiheit*, it means freedom. And *sofort*, that means immediately. Right this moment. *Now!*' One of the young men has returned. He is smiling, beaming. His face is alight with happiness and crowned with soft brown curls that glow bronze in the streetlights.

She gestures at the hordes. 'Where are they going?'

'Everyone is going to the Gate!' His eyes are dancing. 'Do you want to come? Do you want to see it too?'

'The Gate?' The question is superfluous. She is shoving the dictionary into her pocket, hoisting the rucksack onto her shoulder.

'The Brandenburg Gate. The crossing to the East.' Already the human river is sweeping him away. Stretching forwards, he grabs her arm. 'Let's go, *sofort!*'

The roads are becoming busier by the minute. Everywhere people are chanting, singing, shouting. Cars are hooting, vehicles parked haphazardly, their drivers standing dazed and confused by half-open doors. Twice the young man turns to check she is following, pushing wire-framed glasses up the bridge of his nose and a hand, sometimes, through his hair.

All at once there is a street sign.

Invalidenstrasse.

Then spotlights. Cold and white and too many to count.

'The border!' Her companion points towards a passageway, a high-sided concrete alley that is beginning to fill with clusters of people all drinking and cheering. He shakes his head as though he no longer trusts his eyes. 'It *was* the border! Now we go where we want! East to West, West to East. Now there is one Berlin!'

He pulls her closer to the crossing, to the checkpoint, where before there must have been barriers, policemen, border officials, and now a succession of small squat cars is crawling steadily into the West. Some of the occupants appear to be crying. Some are waving, Others, more composed, looking tired and pale behind their steering wheels, make Tiffany want to cry herself. Fists bang a welcome onto roofs. Champagne drenches bonnets in cascades of foam. 'Die Mauer ist weg! Die Mauer ist weg!' *The wall is gone! The wall is gone!* Although her new-found friend is translating again, this time she doesn't need him to. The excitement is catching, like a fever. Now any fool can guess what the people are saying.

Someone nudges her arm. A bottle is pushed into her palm. 'Trink nach Berlin!' *Drink to Berlin!* The glass is cold, the champagne colder and tastes likes almonds, cherries and buttered toast all at the same time. Tipping back her head, she swallows again, wipes her hand across her mouth and passes the bottle to her friend.

'Trink nach Berlin!' Her first words of German.

He grins.

They are of similar age, she sees. And behind the glasses, behind the delight, a hint of earnestness, of dependability.

'Do you want to go into the East?'

'To East Berlin?'

He nods.

Tiffany stares. This is why she is here, after all. To go to East Berlin. But she didn't expect this. Not so soon. Can they really go now? Can they go *sofort*?

The concrete passageway is overflowing with bodies. As they watch, a woman climbs onto the shoulders of another, scrambles up the wall on the far side and jumps from a bulwark and straight into the East, hair trailing behind her like a flag. A great roar erupts. More bodies surge forwards. From nowhere four border guards appear. They glance at each other, as if for reassurance, before pushing the next in line back towards the western wall. In the glare of the lights the officials appear uncertain, almost scared.

The crowd edges forwards again. 'Lass uns rein!' *Let us in!*

The air seems to tremble.

Tiffany finds she's holding her breath.

'We go a different way. In one moment.' Her companion passes her the bottle of champagne, and as she drinks she feels the bubbles in her blood, the rush through her veins. He points towards the slow column of vehicles edging over the crossing, inching into freedom under the gaze of a full moon.

And here comes the next, small and blue on thin fragile wheels.

As the people part to let the car through he grabs her hand and together they race over the border ground towards the East. Her rucksack is bouncing on her back, the champagne is sloshing high against the glass. And in her chest her heart is thundering. She doesn't dare look around, doesn't dare look anywhere but at the outstretched arm of the brown-haired boy who is tugging her onwards and forwards until they have outrun the crowds and the furore and all there is about them is a dark and empty plaza.

He slows to a halt.

Both of them are breathing hard.

Tiffany shakes her hair, long and blond, out of her eyes. 'This is East Berlin?' She can't believe it.

'Yes.'

But nobody is here. Does anyone live in East Berlin? Do they know what's happened?

From deep inside her rucksack she seems to hear a rustling of paper.

All at once her companion spins around. 'Look! Over there!'

Tiffany turns and steps back in amazement. To their left the Brandenburg Gate is soaring above them. Bathed in a deluge of light, the monument looms ghostly and majestic beneath a sphere that is as full and as round as the sun. For a while, they both stand motionless. Tiffany tries to imagine what it would be like, *what it would have been like*, to gaze at the titanic columns and galloping chariot from this spot before tonight. The Gate so close, yet so utterly out of reach. Dropping her rucksack onto the ground, she fishes out her camera. Although she knows the lens will never quite capture the authority of the moon hanging low like a polished coin, the uncanny quiet of the square, or the fact that less than a mile away a festival is exploding at the border.

Nevertheless, a photograph is better than nothing.

Afterwards, she sits down on the plaza. The ground has a deeply frozen quality that immediately seeps through the lining of her coat. Her German friend squats beside her. Neither of them seems able to drag their eyes away from the silver-drenched pillars. Silently she sips from the bottle. Her fingers are freezing, her grip on the glass is becoming clumsy. Yet a sensation of warmth is swelling inside her chest, either from the alcohol or simply the thrill of being where she is, being alive on 9 November 1989, when the world is changing in front of her eyes and she's here in Berlin, witnessing the transformation for herself. She gives the champagne to her companion. For some extraordinary reason it doesn't seem particularly ridiculous to consider leaning against him, a boy whose name she doesn't know, or even to find his hand and slide her fingers into his. Maybe she is not quite as heartbroken, not quite as wretched, as she was three months ago. Perhaps, after all, she is moving on.

As soon as he finishes drinking, however, her new friend rests the bottle on the ground. There's a sense of finality to his action. 'Shall we go back now?'

'Go back?' She blinks.

'To the West.'

He must go home, of course. Now he has crossed the border and experienced the fallen wall for himself he has no reason to be in the East. She, on the other hand, has no reason at all to return. And every reason to stay.

She shakes her head and tries to hide her disappointment.

It's his turn to look astonished. 'If you don't come back, what will you do?'

'I will find somewhere to sleep.' She's surprised to sound so confident. Already her stomach is tightening at the prospect of such alien surroundings. But surely East Berlin must have some kind of hotels or guesthouses? And since the border no longer exists, since nobody can send her away, why shouldn't she stay in one? Before her courage has time to dip, she jumps to her feet, swings her hair into a ponytail and clips it high on her head with a band from her pocket. A sign she means business.

Her companion gets up more slowly. He slaps the dirt off the seat of his jeans and takes a moment adjusting his spectacles, even though they don't appear to have moved since he last corrected them. 'So, I will leave you now.' The sentence is poised between a statement and an enquiry.

Before she can react, voices interrupt them, shouting from the eastern end of the plaza. Two young women are hastening across the square, hurling questions towards them through the dark. *Die Mauer ist weg. Die Mauer ist weg?* The wall is gone?

Tiffany's companion calls back, 'Ja! Ja! Wir sind aus West Berlin!' *We are from West Berlin!*

There are squeals and screams. The women consult each other briefly before running in the direction of the border. The second they disappear, more people arrive. *Die Mauer ist weg.* They too sound incredulous. Soon the trickle expands in number and swells in volume until the hush of the previous minutes is evaporating amongst an assembly of stunned faces and rapid, eager German. Some of the crowd start to rush across the plaza. Others hang back as though the news must be a trap. Or a joke. As if their hopes have been dashed too many times in the past to dare to trust them again now.

'I must go.' Her German friend sounds worried. Tiffany can't tell if he's concerned about her safety or anxious his journey back won't be as straightforward as their one here. She's still wondering about that, about the thoughtful crinkle to his brow, as he thrusts out his hand. She hesitates. The handshake has a strange solemnity. She feels the fleeting grip of his fingers, a sensation of heat and the brief charge of interlocking eyes before he swings around.

'Hey?' She catches his sleeve. 'What's your name?'

'Ralp. My name is Ralp.'

'And mine is Tiffany.'

'Goodbye, Tiffany. Viel glück!' He leans forwards. 'It means good luck!'

She starts to walk, heading away from the border, against the steady current of people now negotiating the square, and only allows herself to stop and turn around when she reaches a road. Although her German friend is nowhere to be seen, she can still glimpse the green glass of the empty champagne bottle through a sea of legs.

She feels suddenly alone.

Alone and slightly afraid.

Ahead the Unter den Linden stretches long and dark with only the occasional yellow arc light to dilute the gritty gloom. Tightening the strap of her rucksack, she tells herself to get a grip. This is nothing, she reflects, compared to what my grandmother did when she was my age. But remembering her grandmother is less of a comfort than she might have hoped. Her grandmother would certainly not approve of Tiffany's current whereabouts. And if she knew what Tiffany intended to do next, she would probably be utterly horrified. She would never even have mentioned the existence of such a heartbreaking letter. Let alone shared the anguish of the writer with her impulsive granddaughter.

As she walks away from the plaza, the pavements get busier. People trickle from buildings and alleyways. All of them wear the same stunned expression of disbelief and the same style of dreary, functional clothes. There's a smell in the air too. An oily, fume-laden stench, and every so often her boot turns on a broken paving slab and slips into a puddle.

She almost walks straight past the Hotel Metropole. Most of the illuminated signage over the entrance isn't working; only the letters *tel* and *Met* stutter a lukewarm glow that makes little impression on the darkness. Tiffany hesitates. The concrete edifice is sooty and decayed and the windows are too grubby to see through properly. She's still dithering as someone nearly knocks into her. The woman running past is in hair-curlers and appears to have thrown on her coat over a baby-blue bathrobe. Tiffany watches her hurry into the gloom and only once the woman has disappeared does she take a breath and push open the door.

Inside the dirty, marbled lobby, two men dressed in jeans and leather jackets are slumped on a sofa. Both are smoking cigarettes while beside them an ashtray on a metal stand overflows with stubs. The receptionist is talking on a telephone, whispering into the receiver. As soon as she sees Tiffany, she stops and covers the mouthpiece with one hand. Although of similar age she's dressed in the type of shapeless skirt and jumper that Tiffany associates with her parents' generation, and her expression is one of naked astonishment.

'I was wondering,' Tiffany says quickly, 'if you have a room that I can stay in.'

The young woman looks at her wordlessly.

'A room…' She scrabbles in her pocket for the dictionary and thumbs through the pages. 'Ein Zimmer.'

'Ein Zimmer?'

'Yes.' She nods to reinforce the point.

The receptionist's gaze sweeps from Tiffany's kitten-heeled boots to her red-and-blue checked coat. 'Bist du aus *West Berlin?*' The emphasis on the last word is almost reverential, making the question obvious.

'I'm from London,' Tiffany says, and then reconsiders. '*Today* I came from West Berlin.'

'Die Mauer ist weg? Ist es wahr?'

'Ja!' she nods again. 'Die Mauer ist weg.' Speaking the sentence in German sparks a flare of triumph. And also of memory, the heady breathlessness as she ran with the German boy – with Ralp – across the border, and the sudden, intense serenity of the plaza in the moments before anyone else arrived.

The woman gabbles into the telephone and hangs up the receiver, then reaches beneath the desk and produces a key attached to a metal ball the size of a billiard. She seems quite mesmerised and unable to take her eyes off Tiffany, even when one of the men on the sofa says something and laughs.

Tiffany shifts uncomfortably. 'How much for *ein Zimmer?*'

There is another blank pause.

She pulls a bunch of American dollars from her purse and fans them into a semicircle. There must be a better way to do this, but she can't see any sort of price list and the information she read before she left London suggested dollars would be more useful than German marks. This appears to be true because at the sight of the money the young woman's face lights up. Leaning forwards, she plucks three ten-dollar notes from Tiffany's grasp and drops the key onto the counter as if the metal has suddenly become hot.

'Where,' says Tiffany, 'where do I go?' Although she can see the number 14 marked on the fob, she has no idea which floor the room is on. And she has probably paid far too much. The receptionist's attention has become entirely absorbed by the dollar bills at which she is staring incredulously.

Tiffany consults the dictionary again. 'Wo gehe ich hin?'

Briefly the young woman lifts her head and points to a staircase in the corner. Gathering her rucksack, Tiffany heads towards the steps. As she does so, she's aware of a burst of staccato German from the sofa and a rapid, impatient reply. Turning around, she sees the receptionist has donned her coat and has come out from behind the reception desk clutching the American money. One of the men gets up to block her way and their voices rise in an angry crescendo, the gist of which is plain.

Tiffany settles the rucksack on her shoulders and embarks upon the dismal stairwell. She can't get involved with the altercation in the foyer, she has to focus on the task in hand. Tomorrow she has someone to find. The fallen wall might have made her journey possible, but she knows the path ahead is still buried deeply – perhaps too deeply – beneath choices that were made long before she was even born.

Chapter Two

19 October 1946

Norfolk, England

The men arrive one dank afternoon when Fran is in the corner shop considering the relative merits of corned beef compared to potted shrimps. It takes a moment to notice her older sister standing in the entrance and wearing such an expression of suppressed fury that Fran knows why she's there before either of them say a word.

'You need to come now, or you'll miss seeing them altogether!'

Fran doesn't reply. There have been several false alarms before, with June insistent they must both go to witness the influx of foreigners, *the Hitler filth*, only to have to contain her passion and return home when the rumours didn't materialise.

'They've been spotted on the coast road. Apparently, the trucks didn't arrive so they're marching from the station.' Her sister's face darkens with intensity. 'This time it's *really* happening.' With that, she spins on her heel and disappears, leaving the door wide open so that the newspapers begin to rattle in their stands and a stray brown paper bag dances across the floor and blows straight out through the gap.

Fran hesitates less than a second before shoving both of the cans back onto the shelf. 'Sorry, Mrs Reynolds,' she calls, half-turning to the counter, 'I'll come back for them later.' Tightening her coat, she hurries after June. Behind her the door clatters shut, the chime of the bell jangling at her heels like the signal in a theatre that the show is about to start.

She doesn't have to go far before she can see quite a horde has gathered. The villagers have clustered a little way beyond the church where the last of the cottages accede to the empty mauve of heath to the south and the grey-green of the salt marsh to the north. Men and women are standing on the inland side of the road, sheltering in the lee of the flint-stoned walls that face the darkening shimmer of mudflats and the invisible pebble beach beyond.

Fran jogs to catch up with June, who is striding towards the crowd, head down, hands buried in the pockets of the same black overcoat that eighteen months earlier their brother would wear to school on wintry mornings. Recently, June has started to wear the coat at every opportunity. Despite the fact the garment drowns her slender frame and, together with her new, short haircut, makes her resemble a schoolboy herself. Now, though, Fran wishes she herself had something warmer than her ancient mackintosh, which is outmatched by the breeze that is whipping straight off the shifting North Sea and gaining in strength.

As they approach, Fran spots friends and neighbours among the jostling pack of bodies. There is a good turnout to observe the arrival of the Germans. Even if nobody wants them here, it seems that most people want to watch them arrive. The villagers haven't gathered together in such numbers since the end of the war. On those honeyed days in May and August, when the airwaves throbbed with the surrender of Germany and Japan, an impromptu band played until the sky broke with the dawn, dancers filled the tabletops of the Dun Cow, and for a short while at least some of them had been able to forget the terrible price the village had paid for their victory celebrations. It was more than a year ago now Fran realises with surprise. It's hard to believe the war has been over for a full loop of the seasons when rationing is worse than ever – even bread, since July – the beaches still blighted with mines and barbed wire, and the village is about to be inhabited by Germans.

Work on the old radar site in Purdy Street began a month ago. One dazzling day towards the end of September, when the heath was the colour of new copper, four military trucks appeared with sections of chipboard and wooden planks protruding over their backboards. As huts were patched up, buildings were added and new fencing built, rumours flew about that the site was to become a camp for German prisoners of war. Nobody was certain whether to believe the story or not until Major Toby Markham moved into a large Victorian house on the edge of the village and word got out that the camp would be opening in two weeks' time, and that Major Markham would be running it.

Fran, however, is more interested in Major Markham's wife than Major Markham. Nobody knew Major Markham even had a wife until she appeared the week after her husband, driving a very smart racing-green Ford Anglia with a little girl of about seven sitting next to her on the front seat. Fran has only seen her from a distance, hand in hand with her daughter outside the school gates, when the spectacular combination of creamy skin and rich black hair made Fran think, absurdly, of the chocolate éclair she once ate at a birthday tea some time long before the war. There was even gossip Mrs Markham might be French until somebody overheard her asking in the Dun Cow about the nearest bus stop; though her voice was reported to be rather beautiful, there was, apparently, no trace of a foreign accent.

Fran reaches forwards and plucks June's sleeve. 'Is Mother here?'

Her sister shakes her head. 'She decided to stay at home.'

'Why did she do that?'

'Why do you think?'

Fran pauses, although she can very well guess the answer. 'Because of Robbie.'

The words thicken into a paste. She used to call his name what, ten, twenty, times a day? Banging on the door of the lavatory, arguing about whether he had to walk with her to school, telling him to hurry, or shouting up the stairs that supper was ready and if he didn't come down right away she or June would get a second helping. Now she hates to say his name, and when she does the word sounds alien. Almost as if it's not, and has never been, her brother's name and a term of affection wrapped up together, but rather the prompt for a shadow to fall, a wretchedness to blight the conversation.

'Of course, Robbie.' June makes no attempt to conceal her impatience. 'Mother can't stand to contemplate actual Germans being so close, let alone want to see them in the flesh. I don't know how she's going to cope. I don't know how any of us are going to cope. I mean, real German soldiers living here in the village. *Our* village.' June shudders, and the movement is so blatant there seems to Fran something almost theatrical about it.

'They're not—' Fran stops.

'What?'

'Nothing.'

'What were you going to say?'

'*Nothing.*'

They have reached the edge of the waiting crowd. June comes to a halt and turns around. Her brows furrow into a V. 'Tell me what you were going to say!'

Fran finally draws level. Now she can see directly into her sister's eyes, the familiar storm-grey gaze that since Robbie died seems to have deepened almost to black. 'Only that they're not soldiers any longer, are they? The war is over.'

'Shh! Be quiet!' A man some distance away raises his arm above the sea of jostling shoulders. 'I think I hear something.'

A hush falls like a dropped cloak. Fran stands on tiptoe and tries to peer east along the granite ribbon of the coast road, but everyone else is doing the same and, however much she struggles, all she can see is a wall of backs and bobbing heads. Besides, at well past three o'clock visibility is dissolving in the weak October light and the faraway point where marsh and sky slide into one grey space has already been lost. The man ahead keeps his hand held high and perfectly still while the crowd stays silent. Fran strains to listen but all she can hear is the shuffling of shoes on tarmac and the geese calling out to each other in the impending dusk. Then all at once the air starts to vibrate. Within moments, rumours of noise bloom into the reality of shouted orders and the thrum of stamping feet, and seconds later a column of men appears in the distance.

The villagers surge forwards. Propelled by pushing limbs and elbows, Fran somehow finds herself at the front of the throng with nothing between her and the road upon which the men are fast approaching. Soon two long lines of German prisoners are in plain view, their shabby uniforms patched with black squares and their trouser legs splashed with one bright white letter – P. Beside them, British soldiers bark orders and nudge the slackers to pick up their pace.

Nobody is silent now. Some onlookers merely boo and hiss, but others shout. Fists are raised. Threats are yelled into the cold air. It occurs to Fran that the presence of so many soldiers might be to protect the prisoners rather than prevent them from escaping. A lump of phlegm flies by her ear and lands in a bead on her shoe. Amidst the indistinct roars of protest she hears the woman behind her yell, 'Bloody German filth! Friggin' murderers!' and is momentarily stunned when she registers that the voice belongs to June.

The cavalcade approaches, leather soles smacking against the tarmac. Soldiers flick occasional glances of pride and triumph at the villagers and their marching acquires extra zeal. By contrast the prisoners' gait is the stumbled step of the tired and fearful, and the eyes of all but one of them – a man in the column closest to the crowd – remain fixed on the safety of their own feet.

Fran's throat tightens. There is something outrageous and unexpected about the spectacle that is not the baying, angry

people or the shuffling foreigners who dare not lift their eyes. As
the lines of prisoners get close enough to make out the features
of individual men, she is shocked to realise they look the same
as British soldiers. Not vicious, not monsters. No different from
Robbie, in fact – except that Robbie had toffee-coloured hair that
fell into his eyes whenever he laughed and the same grey-brown
eyes as June, whereas the German men seem mainly to be fair.
Fran blinks back sudden tears, fumbling in her coat pocket for a
handkerchief.

She wants, she realises, to go home.

She turns to search for a gap through the crowd, but the woman
barring her way is too busy gesticulating to stand aside. 'Look!' she
is shouting. 'Look what you did!' For a confusing moment it seems
to Fran the vitriol is directed at her, but then she spies the dark
expanse of field behind the road and understands. The location of
the welcome party is no accident. By instinct or design the villagers have gathered in front of the same piece of grass that used to
be cut and rolled and crushed underfoot every summer Saturday.
Now the place is barely recognisable. With the wicket knee-high in
grass, the weeds unchecked, the object of the woman's frenzy has
disappeared. In better light a memorial would be visible, dedicated
to the local boys, many of them members of the cricket team, who
were slaughtered within moments of each other on the beaches of
Normandy. The wooden board bears ten names in total. And the
eighth one from the top belongs to Robbie.

As the soldiers draw level with the crowd the metronomic thud
of boots swells louder. Still Fran's escape from the spectacle remains
blocked. Now she can discern the individual orders being flung out
by the soldiers. 'Pick up your feet!' 'Keep bloody moving!' 'You at
the back, shut your mouth!' And the air is rent with the smell of
fear and trepidation, of sweat and dirt, of anxious men who haven't
washed more than their face in a good number of days.

Taking a breath, she makes herself swing around to face them. To her alarm, her gaze alights on the face of the one prisoner who is not staring at the ground. Eyes blue as a starling's egg lock onto her own and instantaneously the space between that moment and the next opens into a chasm wide enough to swallow her whole. At some point she realises the man is speaking and at some later point that he is talking to her.

'You dropped this, I think.'

Fran blinks. The German prisoner has stopped marching and is holding a handkerchief. Her handkerchief. She can see the letter 'F' in the corner, embroidered with tiny pink silk stitches she remembers sewing one winter evening to keep her mind from lingering on the dreadful news sputtering from the radio. The columns behind the stationary prisoner are forced to halt and the ones ahead stop too, craning over their shoulders to see what might be causing the delay. Surprise and curiosity still both the heckling of the crowd and the edicts of the soldiers.

A tentative silence arrives.

Fran doesn't move.

'It fell from your pocket. I saw it drop when you turned around.' His English is impeccable, the accent startling. The prisoner extends his arm towards Fran, his eyes latched onto hers. Spellbound, she leans forwards to take the cotton square but as she does so somebody smacks her hand away.

'Leave it. It's dirty.' June's voice is rough.

The handkerchief is barely smudged. Fran glances at her sister with surprise. 'I can wash it!'

'Dirt like that won't wash off!'

A second later she's yanked backwards, and her sister's arm is looped tight around her waist. She sees June glare at the blue-eyed German, who after a moment folds the handkerchief with care before slipping it into his pocket and walking on. As the lines restart and the prisoners shuffle forwards, Fran wills him to look over his shoulder so she might glimpse his face one more time. Just when it seems he won't oblige, at the very last point before the men behind mask him from view, he twists around and smiles at her and Fran forgets that he's a prisoner, or German, or different from any other man, and she smiles back.

Chapter Three

29 October 1946

At barely six o'clock in the morning, Fran is adjusting her hat for the third time. Staring at her reflection in the bedroom mirror is like an encounter with an older relative. The difference is not her face, which is the same smooth-skinned oval, the same cinnamon scatter of freckles over the bridge of her nose, and the same eyes that have turned green with the intensity of self-interrogation but will revert to their customary brown-gold as soon as her focus softens. The change is all in her clothes. While the skirt is her own, the jacket of shale-grey herringbone has been donated by a friend of her mother's and their uniform-like combination confers on Fran a competent, authoritative air she finds both disconcerting and exhilarating. It's similar to how she felt when she joined the Women's Land Army with June. Although the pledge card had been suitably rousing – *You have made the home fields your battlefields* – that challenge turned out to be less daunting than expected as they were both billeted to a farm only eight miles from home.

Before handing the borrowed jacket to Fran, her mother had made her pinch the fabric between her thumb and forefinger to appreciate the quality of the wool. 'The camp is bound to be cold,' she warned. 'Even in the office. At least this will help you stay warm and still be smartly dressed.' At that moment, the back door clicked. They both looked up and when June walked in fell immediately quiet, as if she had caught them with cups of gin or forging petrol coupons.

Yet again Fran repositions the hat, but the more she fiddles the worse the beret seems to suit her. In exasperation she removes the item completely and throws it onto the bed. A hat, surely, is unnecessary for her position at the camp, a position for which she doesn't as yet even have a job title.

The Saturday before, a week after the prisoners arrived, she had found herself standing at the counter in Mrs Reynold's shop behind a woman in a magnificent blue coat who was asking about the bus in a curiously urgent tone. Once it became obvious Mrs Reynolds couldn't help with the enquiry, Fran cleared her throat and tugged the blue sleeve. When the woman swung around, Fran's cheeks flushed with surprise. The wearer of the coat, however, appeared not to notice Fran's embarrassment and listened to her description of the differences between the weekday and weekend timetable with an electric, almost disconcerting, intensity. After Fran finished, there was a pocket of silence before Major Markham's wife began to thank Fran profusely and collected the shopping basket at her feet. She appeared on the verge of leaving but at the last minute put the basket down again, pushed a lock of coal-black hair away from her face, and asked if Fran might be interested in a clerical position at the camp because her husband had been complaining only the previous evening that the girl working for him seemed to be entirely overwhelmed. A moment later Fran was writing her name and address on the back of Mrs Markham's box of porridge oats.

Fran descends to the kitchen, which is practically dark. The dresser, the rocker in the corner and the large pine table strewn with pins and sewing patterns are all indistinct shadows, while outside the sky is the delicate pearl of an autumn dawn. As she flicks the single light above the Aga the day budding beyond the window reverts to night. It's too early for Fran's mother to be up, poring over her next dressmaking assignment, too early, really, for Fran. She's not required to report to the camp until eight, but the combination of nerves and excitement made further sleep impossible. More than that, she feels a compulsion to prepare earlier than necessary, as if any number of unexpected obstacles might threaten her punctuality. Taking a loaf from the breadbin, she slices a hunk and spreads it with margarine. Not until returning to the larder does she notice the fall and rise of the rocker and realise a split second later that June is curled upon the seat and watching her from beneath a blanket.

'How long have you been there?'

'Three, maybe four, hours. I couldn't sleep.'

Fran has been aware of June's nocturnal restlessness since Robbie died. The night-time visits to the lavatory, the pre-dawn creak of the staircase, the morning bruises beneath her sister's eyes seem if anything to be increasing. Fran has lain in the dark often enough herself, longing for Robbie's loud, laughing presence to spill like sunshine through the house, to understand the pull of the kitchen. Surrounded by the warmth of the Aga and the smell of baking, by the stamp of stability and the solace of memories, it's easier both to believe in miracles and to cope with their absence.

The margarine is still in her hand. As she opens the larder door, June's voice hauls her backwards. 'I don't know how you can do it!'

'What do you mean?' Fran directs her question towards the tins of spam and sardines, the carefully arranged rows of homemade chutneys and bottled fruit. She's playing for time; she knows exactly what June means and immediately the excitement in her gut sputters and wanes like a candle exposed to a draught.

'Take a job in the camp! With German prisoners of war!'

'It's not the Germans I'm helping, is it? I'm helping the British army to keep them locked up so the prisoners can work and be useful to us all.' The words are those of her mother, the argument she used when Fran, riddled with conflict and doubt, told her about the conversation with Vivian Markham. Fran isn't certain whether her mother is truly convinced by them, whether she wanted to make Fran feel better, or whether the extra money from the position at the camp is simply too tempting, given the modest income her mother's skill with a needle and thread brings in. And she doesn't know her father's views on the matter at all. Or even if his opinion has been sought.

'You'll still have to talk to them. You might even have to work in the same room. Apparently, some of the prisoners are given camp jobs.'

'Mrs Markham told me there was another girl in the office, and when I met Major Markham yesterday, he definitely didn't mention working with any prisoners.' Fran falters; the interview with Major Markham – if you could call it an interview – had been rather odd. Shortly after meeting Mrs Markham an unsigned note had been put through the letterbox telling Fran to come to the Dun Cow at two o'clock on Monday afternoon. Since the camp was tucked down a side road behind the pub, the location for the meeting was not terribly strange. The encounter with Major Markham, however, was not what she'd expected.

Fran had spent the morning practising what she might say if asked how she felt about the arrival of the Germans. *It might take some time to adjust, but she understood, given the shortage of local men, why they were needed.* Or what she had done to help the war effort. *She had been a Land Girl on a Norfolk farm. And although milking cows or feeding pigs was not office work, she was confident she could easily adapt.* However, Major Markham had merely asked her if she had achieved her school certificate and considered herself reliable. Then he had fished out a packet of Marlboro Lights and a box of matches from his top pocket and proceeded to light a cigarette.

Fran was in the process of assuring him that she was both reliable *and* hard-working when a shattering crash from behind startled her to silence. Twisting to look over her shoulder, she glimpsed Mr Graveling, the publican, on his knees surrounded by shards of glass and a lake of beer inching slowly across the flagstones. Major

Markham, she was sure, was in a better position than her to view the harassed landlord, yet when she turned back, she found him on his feet, swaying slightly and gripping the table with blanched knuckles, the cigarette dangling loosely from his mouth. Uncertain of what to do Fran set her gaze elsewhere, but when Major Markham eventually sat down he seemed to have lost concentration. He didn't respond to her answers, wrote nothing on his pad of paper and after a couple more minutes of stumbled, gap-filling sentences from Fran, he interrupted her to say that he would see her in the morning, got up and left.

'All the same' – June's voice brings Fran back to the kitchen – 'I don't know how you can bear it.'

She is genuinely perplexed, Fran realises. And perhaps her sister is right. Why would she want to spend her days in the company of German soldiers? *Hitler scum*, according to the locals. Men who not only killed her brother but brought such terrible, desperate sadness to everyone she knows. Maybe the reason she was given the job is because nobody else in the village would do it.

'Perhaps I won't take the position after all.' Fran tugs at the collar of the grey jacket. Standing by the Aga, the fabric is beginning to feel hot, almost oppressive, and her earlier sense of exhilaration nothing short of ridiculous. 'I could simply not go to the camp this morning.' She doesn't add that she's not one hundred per cent certain that Major Markham will actually remember he asked her to attend. He didn't even tell her what time she should arrive.

'You must go' – June narrows her eyes over the top of the blanket – 'and then explain to Major Markham you've had second thoughts and decided you can't possibly work in the camp after all.'

Fran regards her sister with dismay. The idea of a damp, chilly bicycle ride to inform the major to his face she doesn't want to work for him is worse than if she had never been offered the job in the first place.

June reads her hesitation. 'Go now. Get it over with. Before you change your mind. And' – she squints through the window at the unappealing morning – 'wrap up warm.'

Fran gathers her handbag and goes to fetch her coat from the hooks beside the back door. The pile seems lighter than normal and when she rifles through the assortment of fabrics, she sees Robbie's black overcoat is missing. She frowns in surprise, then with sudden insight looks at June. As if by way of answer, her sister shifts on the rocker and pulls the blanket, that is not a blanket at all, more closely towards her chin.

Chapter Four

Fran cycles east towards the village. To her left sits the marsh with the beach some distance beyond, a bank of shingle that after a couple of miles abandons the coastline and curls outwards into the sea. On visits before the war she, June and Robbie used to hike along the pointed finger of land to the very tip of the spit and watch velvet seals slide in and out of the water while terns and black-headed gulls strutted and dived in the shallows. Although the beach is still cut off by barricades and buried mines – defences against the invasion that never came – one day soon, she tells herself, she'll be back there again.

Though not, of course, with Robbie.

She pedals even faster, before standing up to let the wheels roll freely. The push and rhythm of the bicycle have warmed her core while in the distance gold-tipped clouds float low on the horizon surrounded by banners of peach and baby blue. Instead of Robbie, she focuses on the unexpected gift of sky. On the pink-footed geese, who are beginning to cruise the mudflats, drowning out the zip of her tyres with their early-morning cries.

And slowly she sits down again.

At the Dun Cow she gets off the bicycle and walks the last part of the journey so as not to arrive red-faced and out of breath. The gate is topped with two threads of barbed wire and guarded by a bored-looking soldier in army khaki who is plainly not expecting her but seems only too happy to leave his post in search of someone who might be.

The camp is unexpectedly small, and she can see most of the site from where she is standing. A churned-up parking area leads to a long, whitewashed building with steps to an entrance at one end. Further away about six Nissen huts and some wooden outbuildings cluster around a much larger brick structure which might be the cookhouse because crates of something like cabbages or cauliflowers have been left beside the door.

As she waits, three prisoners come out of the furthest Nissen hut. One disappears behind a wooden lean-to and reappears with a tin pail, sloshing the contents over the rim. Immediately, the men strip off their shirts and start to splash water onto skinny, pale torsos. Fran tries not to watch but her head keeps lifting, her focus lengthening, and with a bite of self-reproach she realises she's hoping to see if the blue-eyed German happens to be one of the three.

Minutes later the soldier returns, marching with renewed purpose towards the gate. He tells Fran that she is expected, though not perhaps this early. She has arrived before Major Markham, but that can only help to make a good impression. Now the soldier knows she's to join them he seems determined to be friendly, as if he's already aware there might be a divide between the camp and the village. He smiles as he speaks, revealing a gap in his front teeth that is accentuated by a long, pink scar running from the tip of his right ear to the edge of his mouth. As Fran follows, wheeling her bike across the camp's muddy turf, her spirits sink: she will hardly make a good impression when she informs Major Markham she no longer wants his job. She considers telling the soldier instead; however, before she can summon the courage, he has already pointed her in the direction of the whitewashed building and is returning to his post.

The corridor inside contains a wooden bench that looks like it came from a school gymnasium. Cubbyholes stuffed with envelopes cover one wall, while the door facing the bench bears a handwritten sign saying Camp Office. After Fran has been waiting at least half an hour, a soldier strides into the lobby and without breaking momentum attempts to enter the office. When the handle refuses to budge, he turns around.

'Major Markham not in yet?' The soldier's hair is slicked sideways and shines as if he has just stepped in from the rain.

She shakes her head. 'I don't think so.'

He peers more closely. 'Are you the new girl?'

Fran's chest stiffens. *Not for long.* She nods and holds up her identity card.

'In that case, welcome!' The soldier sticks out a palm, 'The major gets later every day, though don't' – he shakes her hand with good-natured energy – 'ever tell him I said that!'

With his departure the office seems quieter. Outside, however, the volume is rising. Men's voices weave a tapestry of noise. Although the lilt and cadence of the sentences seem familiar, when she listens closely the language is a mixture of English and softly guttural German, a sound she has only heard before on broadcasts from the wireless and newsreels of crowds saluting Hitler with unnerving synchronicity. The tightness in her chest intensifies.

All at once the abrupt cough of a motor engine provokes shouting and a burst of footfall and makes Fran get up and peer around the outside door. An army truck is reversing through the gate, the exhaust spewing fumes she can smell from where she is standing. As soldiers yell orders, prisoners stream out from the Nissen huts and gather together at the edge of the parking area. Fran watches the truck shudder to a halt. The engine cuts and the German men begin to scramble aboard, each of them bending down to proffer a hand to the one up next. She is so immersed in the scene that the sudden proximity of a female voice catches her by surprise.

'Well, that *is* something I would like to see. You lot playing football!' The woman speaking appears to be a similar age to Fran. Dark-blond waves of hair surround a wide face that might be at risk of plainness were it not for the evident good humour playing across it, the confident slash of cherry lipstick and the friendly gaze fixed on the prisoner walking beside her. Both of them are rapidly approaching the camp office.

The prisoner is smiling. 'We can play football. Better than you English!'

Fran darts back inside.

A second later the woman comes through the entrance. She stops when she sees Fran. 'You must be Fran. I'm Daisy.' She follows Fran's gaze through the open door, where the black-shirted man is walking away. 'And he, by the way, is called Hans.' She must catch something of Fran's confusion, because her brow furrows. 'We are allowed to talk to them in here, you know. The government regulations don't stop us from doing that. As long as we're inside the camp and doing our job, it's hardly fraternising with the enemy, is it?'

Fran colours slightly. She has too many questions bumping around her head to risk a reply. Instead, she watches Daisy reach into the back of one of the cubbyholes and extract a key from beneath a pile of brown envelopes which she slots into the keyhole of the locked door.

The office has been divided into connecting rooms. In the first, two wooden chairs have been placed each side of a functional desk obscured by a jumble of files and papers. The second, Fran spies, boasts a curved-back leather chair behind a large desk bearing a magnifying glass and telephone. A stench of smoke drapes the space like muslin. Wrinkling her nose, Daisy shuts the connecting door, marches to a window and throws it open.

'At least when the major's in London we get to choose whether we breathe and freeze our behinds off or simply choke to death. When he's here all day, I honestly think I'm going to suffocate.'

Fran stops in her tracks. 'Is he away then?' She's been worrying how long she would have to make conversation with Daisy, go through the motions of starting work, before the major arrived and she could explain that she couldn't take the job after all.

'He's gone to Whitehall for a meeting. I don't think he'll be coming in at all today. Didn't he tell you?'

Fran shakes her head.

Daisy squints at her and misreads whatever expression she detects on Fran's face. 'Don't worry, I can show you what to do. You'll pick things up in no time.'

Before Fran can open her mouth, she finds she has been ushered onto one of the wooden chairs and Daisy is leaning over her shoulder and selecting a dark-green folder labelled *Supplies* from the top of the nearest heap of documents.

'Ordering more food is the priority this morning. We don't want prisoners dropping dead from starvation. At least not while we still need them to de-mine the beaches.'

'How do I do that? I've no idea what to order!' Fran's sense of panic is growing. She can't tell if it's because she should by now be on her way home, because of the proximity of so many Germans, or because she doesn't know how to even start the job. Daisy is close enough for Fran to be aware of a sweet floral scent of perfume or talcum powder and the ruby contours of Daisy's painted mouth. All at once she's horribly aware of her blandly powdered face, her borrowed jacket.

'Here, this is what I bought ten days ago.' Daisy pulls a sheet of paper from the file. A handwritten list – *porridge (8 boxes), mutton (9–10 lbs), rabbits (18 approx), potatoes (2 sacks), cabbages (2 sacks)...* – fills the entire page. 'You can start with this, but the numbers have changed since then so the quantities will be different. You'll have to check how many prisoners arrived last week and how many are due to arrive and leave next week.'

'Wouldn't it be better for you to do it,' Fran says weakly, 'as you did it before?'

Daisy laughs. 'I have to sort out the vehicles – the trucks to get the prisoners to their place of work, petrol supplies, spare parts, that sort of thing. Then there's all the other equipment and knowing which prisoners are going where, which ones are clearing the beaches, which ones are doing the farms. Apparently a few of them are needed in the brickworks too. And on top of all that, someone has to type Major Markham's letters for him.' Her gaze narrows. 'Can you type?'

'Not terribly fast. What about you?'

'I used to be a typist at an RAF station. During the war, I mean. That's why I got given the job here. Well, if you do most of the ordering, I'm sure we'll manage somehow…' Daisy's voice trails off as if flattened by the weight of the tasks confronting them both. Then she adds with unexpected warmth, 'I'm so pleased there are two of us now. Apart from nearly suffocating and dying of overwork, it's been pretty lonely, to be honest. The major hardly spends any time in the office, and when he is here, well…' – her face clouds – 'the smoke isn't the only problem.'

'What do you mean?'

'You'll see for yourself.'

Fran looks at her.

Daisy hesitates. Then says quickly, 'Often he says he has meetings which don't seem to be in his diary. And if Captain Holmes is away the major works in *his* office instead, as if he prefers to be entirely on his own. Even though that room is really for meetings and the major doesn't keep any of his files in there. She throws a glance at the door, lowers her voice, 'Once I even found him sitting in the stationery cupboard.'

'The stationery cupboard!'

'Shh! Well, it's for general storage, I suppose, but even so… He pretended he was searching for something, yet when I walked in he was just sitting on a box and staring at the wall.' She must see something of Fran's alarm because she adds in a business-like voice. 'It's nothing to worry about, really. Honestly, it's got to be better to have a slightly barmy boss than one who shouts all the time. Look – we'd best get on or else we'll never get those orders in on time.'

*

Some time later Fran puts down her pen and glances at the clock. To her astonishment, nearly two hours seem to have passed. She has almost completed the new lists of supplies. After checking and cross-checking between each prisoner's dossier and a separate file that contains authorisations for transfers between camps, she's confident there are eighty-three prisoners currently at Salthouse, with another four expected by the end of the week. Given that Daisy based her previous order on an occupancy of sixty-six, Fran has decided to increase the quantities by another third. The level of attention required to chase up prisoners' details has proved much more gratifying than she anticipated, particularly since it quickly became apparent how badly the paperwork was organised. On more than one occasion she caught herself thinking she would suggest to Daisy they create a more efficient system, before remembering that at the first opportunity she was supposed to tell the major she was leaving. Admiring her neat columns of figures on the page of calculations, she wonders if perhaps she should offer to stay until he finds a replacement.

'Time for a cuppa?' Daisy cuts into her ponderings.

A small table in the corner boasts a kettle, two chipped porcelain cups and a caddy bearing a picture of a Scottish golfer so worn that patches of tin shine from the lid. When the kettle boils, Daisy pours water through a strainer into each of the cups. 'No teapot, I'm afraid. Or milk, for that matter. Here – take your pick.' The tea poured first is a much deeper colour than the second.

Fran selects the weaker option, curling her fingers gratefully around the heat of the china. If the window is going to be open regularly throughout winter, she must remember to wear fingerless gloves.

'They're not all beastly, you know,' Daisy says suddenly.

It takes a moment or two for Fran to realise Daisy is referring to her conversation with Hans. Or more accurately, to Fran's reaction. Despite the temperature of the room, she feels her face start to smoulder.

'These German prisoners probably hated the war as much as we did.'

Fran swallows. 'Well, they started it. And kept fighting it. And they killed our soldiers. Thousands and thousands of them.' She stares into her tea. The dark hollows of her cheeks and eye sockets are reflected in the amber liquid. It's like looking at a pencil drawing of a skull.

'Maybe most of them didn't have a choice. Not a proper one anyway.'

Fran doesn't reply. This is the perfect opportunity to tell Daisy she can't possibly work alongside so many Germans; that her sister has convinced her accepting the job was the wrong thing to do. She should simply hand the completed order list to Daisy and leave. She wouldn't even have to put on her coat since the room has been too cold to even consider taking it off.

Instead a second, then two seconds, slip by and she says nothing. Gradually, the distant business of the camp begins to seep into the silence.

Daisy says gently, 'Who did you lose?'

Fran's gaze stays fixed on her cup, the rim swimming slightly out of focus. 'My brother.'

A pause.

Fran thinks of saying his name. Robbie, she should tell Daisy. His name was Robbie. She opens her mouth. Takes a sip of tea.

'How long ago?'

'It happened in June 1944, on D-Day. Although we didn't find out for several weeks. Not for sure.' At the time everyone had said the agony of not knowing, the uncertainty, must be the worst thing of all, but it hadn't been. Uncertainty had meant hope, seconds, sometimes even whole minutes of time when they had convinced themselves he was still alive. The worst thing had been when the letter finally came, hearing the wild sobs of her mother behind her bedroom door, a racking, animal-like keening that sounded unlike anything Fran had ever heard before.

And the loss doesn't feel any smaller now merely because two years' worth of days have passed. Robbie's continual absence presses upon them far more than his taken-for-granted presence would ever have done. It feels like a gale perpetually raging against the flimsiest branch of a tree. Sooner or later the wood must snap, Fran thinks, and then where will they be? Her wrist quivers, and she lowers the cup onto the desk. 'What about you?' she manages. 'Do you have a brother?'

There is a fractional gap before Daisy answers.

'Yes.'

Fran lifts her gaze.

'He didn't fight in the war.' Another hesitation. 'He has a heart condition.'

'Oh,' Fran says, then, 'I'm sorry.' Yet she still can't prevent an instinctive snap of bitterness that if Robbie had had a problem with his heart, he would still be alive too.

'We didn't realise until he failed the medical,' Daisy continues. 'I know you must think he's a lucky bastard, but it hasn't been… it isn't as easy for him as you might imagine.' Although her tone stays level, something desperate flits over her wide brown eyes.

Fran remembers now, a snatch of conversation she overheard in the village shop: *The lengths a man will take to avoid doing his duty*, a woman had said. And the gossip about the *draft dodger* that seemed to surface whenever the village suffered a new death, a fresh ambush of grief. Even at the time she found the rumours unpleasant. However, her family was then so new to the village, she had no idea who they were talking about.

Fran frowns. 'Is he very ill?'

'No, it's not that.' Daisy drains her tea and places the cup with a jolt. 'He can't forgive himself for not being able to join up, and it seems that nobody else can either. I know he's alive, but I honestly believe he'd rather have taken his chances with the others than spend the rest of his life feeling a failure—'

'He's not a failure.' Fran feels bad now, for her earlier flash of resentment. 'He can't help having a weak heart.'

'That's what I keep telling him.' As Daisy gathers up the dirty china, her expression dips from Fran's sight. 'But it doesn't seem to help very much.'

The rest of the day passes at the same startling speed. At about half past twelve Daisy extracts a brown paper parcel from her bag and unwraps an egg sandwich. Fran watches in mute embarrassment, wondering how she managed to entirely overlook the matter of her lunch, until Daisy grins and passes her the second half of her own. As if by silent agreement they talk about themselves, rather than the war. Daisy is twenty-two, the same age as Fran. She laughs more often than anyone else Fran knows, tipping back her chin as she does so to reveal her pearly white throat. She is more curious too, firing questions in such quick succession that Fran barely has time to ask her own. Still, by the time they have brushed the crumbs from their laps and drunk another cup of tea, Fran has learned that Daisy likes films, that she gets bored easily – *I absolutely must have a job of some kind, I can't possibly stay at home all day* – and that although she's desperate to drive a motor car, her real passion is dancing. 'You must come to my house,' she tells Fran. 'We live in the next village. One day after work. I'll teach you how to jitterbug. And then,' she adds so easily that Fran almost misses the slight inflection in her voice, 'you can meet my brother, Martin.'

At four o'clock Daisy announces that this is when she normally finishes and besides, today she has to take care of Major Markham's little girl after school. She slips the cap back on her fountain pen and gets to her feet with one eye on the clock. For an instant her face clouds. 'To be honest, I think it's a bit of nerve, asking me, but I could hardly say no.'

'Where is Mrs Markham?' Fran asks. 'Is she in London too?' An image of the beautiful Mrs Markham draped in fur, sashaying across a banquet hall on her husband's arm, comes to mind.

Daisy shrugs. 'No idea, but I'm hoping this won't become a regular request. I've no intention of becoming a nanny.' She beams at Fran from the doorway, her good humour evidently recovered. 'See you tomorrow, then? Don't forget to lock up.'

Fran packs up her belongings more slowly than Daisy and is careful to leave the key in the same cubbyhole Daisy took it from that morning. Already, the long wait on the bench seems to have happened months ago. As she crosses the camp, the sky is heavy with cloud and impending darkness. From one of the huts, she can hear two prisoners talking. For a minute she stops and makes herself listen to the soft rise and fall of the alien language. Tomorrow, she supposes, she must face the task of telling Major Markham that she doesn't want the job. Not for the long-term anyway. As she engages the dynamo to the back wheel of her bicycle and climbs aboard, she experiments with the phrases she might use to explain her resignation. *I can't work alongside so many Germans… My family doesn't approve…* They are beginning to seem like words from a theatre or radio drama, she realises. Sentences learned for a character she's no longer certain that she's willing to play.

Chapter Five

Vivien Markham is not gliding across a banquet hall. Instead she's sitting on a bus to Sculthorpe with her handbag gripped securely on her lap. Dressed in her tailored blue coat and matching felt hat she's very well aware that everyone is looking at her. Not staring exactly but stealing sidelong glances in a way that is meant to be, but is not, discreet. Even as she climbed aboard, she felt the gaze of the woman in the front row snag for a split second on her ankles and the real silk stockings that encase them. She should, she supposes, have made an effort to be less conspicuous, but Alex likes her in blue.

And he particularly likes her in silk stockings.

She shivers with anticipation – and a transitory flash of guilt that causes her to glance awkwardly at her fellow passengers. She decided not to take the car in case anyone should spot it outside the base but, given the level of interest she seems to be generating, perhaps that would have been preferable. At least Toby will be unlikely to ask her too many difficult questions this evening. His meeting in London means he's bound not to arrive back until late; and even if she should get home after him – Viv closes her eyes in a little prayer of hope, knowing exactly what returning so late would mean as regards her meeting with Alex – she will simply say that she decided to go exploring and got herself a little lost.

Outside the window the countryside is drear. Hedges, trees and grey flint cottages rattle indistinctly past the filthy glass. She should probably have left earlier but reasoned that arriving later in the morning might increase the chance Alex would be able to have lunch with her, perhaps take the rest of the day off. There might even be the possibility of spending the evening together. At least that's what Viv suggested in her letter and Alex hasn't replied to say that isn't a good plan. Or, for that matter, to say it is a good plan. Or, even simply to say that he's looking forward to seeing her.

Viv makes herself breathe slowly – in and out, in and out, the same relaxation tips the doctors recommended during the war – to suppress the surge of panic that erupts whenever she confronts the fact that she hasn't heard anything from Alex for nearly seven weeks. The trouble is, whatever calming technique she uses, her feelings, like a jack-in-the-box, are liable to spring back, unbidden and uncontrolled, the very instant she stops.

For something to do, she snaps open the clasp of her handbag and draws out a folded piece of paper. Alex's last letter to her is worn and creased from having been opened and reread so many times, and Viv doesn't actually need to see the writing again to remember what it says. Nevertheless the simple sight of the words on the page invokes the sound of Alex's voice, the warm American drawl that made her stomach turn over that very first time he stopped her in the street to ask if she was a film star because he would never forgive himself if he walked straight on by without checking.

My Darling Girl, the letter begins.

> *This is so very hard for me to write but I have to tell you, sweetest one, that I'm being posted to some God-awful remote part of the country. Norfolk! Probably Norfolk isn't so very terrible but it's a million miles from you and that's quite enough to make it the worst place on earth in my eyes. Isn't it the cruellest thing? These last few months we've been dreading the time when I would be sent back to the good old US of A and couldn't believe our luck when they kept me over here. Now it turns out they had a plan all along and that plan is some dullard of a techno job at an airfield called Sculthorpe. Seems you Brits don't want all of us Yanks*

to leave just yet after all! But Sculthorpe is a long, long way
from you and realistically, my sweetest, I think we have to
face the fact we have come to the end of our time together. My
baby, believe me when I say my heart breaks at the thought
of never seeing your darling eyes again, touching that softest
skin, feeling you tremble in my arms…

Viv closes her eyes, holding the page flat against her stomach. She is well aware how the letter continues. How enormously hard it must have been for her to conceal the affair since Toby came home. How dreadful she must have felt. How he, Alex, loved her more than he had loved anyone before but would never ever forgive himself if he broke up her marriage. The posting to Sculthorpe, some back-of-beyond place near the Norfolk coast, was a sign the affair was over, though he would love her always. The always was written in capital letters and underlined with a flourish, as if this demonstration of emotion might compensate for the inescapable fact that he hadn't dared to tell her the news in person.

As soon as the page was back inside the envelope, Viv had thrown caution to the wind and gone directly to Alex's old base. Having paused by the perimeter fence to powder her streaked cheeks, she managed to control her voice long enough to ask in the office whether it would be possible to see Captain Alex Henderson on an urgent family matter. A heavily whiskered gentleman informed her that Captain Henderson had left the previous day. Nevertheless, the old soldier must have seen something of the anguish this response elicited because he motioned at the solitary straight-backed chair against the wall and suggested he might be able to find Captain Henderson's new address if she would care to wait. A few minutes later he returned with a slip of paper and a cup of tea in a blue cup balanced precariously on a white saucer.

For the next few days Viv couldn't even get Alice to school. Pressing a hand to unwashed hair, she complained of headaches or stomach pains and persuaded Toby to drop Alice off on his way to his job at the Dispersal Centre. Her requests made her realise she wasn't even certain what job he did there, other than some role processing the discharge of army soldiers, because he had said so little since returning from Germany. All his answers to her questions were perfunctory and at night he rolled away from her, careful, it seemed, to avoid touching any part of her body with his own. She hadn't minded, of course, not when she was seeing Alex. She assumed he was simply taking time to adjust to being home, relieved at the space his diffidence gave her to continue the affair. Yet even in the desperate aftermath of Alex's departure it began to strike her as odd how each evening Toby never appeared to notice she hadn't changed out of the housecoat she had been wearing that morning, let alone ask her why that might be.

Redemption came suddenly and unexpectedly, shortly after the very worst days had passed. One evening Toby put down his knife and fork and announced into the silence of the dinner table that he had some news. Viv was so taken aback to hear him say anything at all she simply stopped eating and waited. The following week, Toby said, he was being moved to a place called Salthouse. To run a new camp for German prisoners.

Despite herself, Viv was intrigued. 'Why are they opening new camps now?' she asked. 'The war's over.'

Toby picked up his cutlery, as if the question was too facile to need serious consideration. 'The fighting might be finished but it will be a long time before the country is back on its feet. We need men to work the fields and clear the beaches. Prisoners aren't good for much, but they're bloody useful for that kind of dirty work.'

Viv was perplexed. 'Is that allowed? Surely the prisoners want to go home?'

'You sound like the Red Cross. They're starting to make a fuss about it too.' Toby speared a lump of potato. The stew on their plates consisted of many more vegetables than the small, gristly pieces of meat Viv had spent thirty minutes queuing for at the butcher's.

'Well, we can't just keep them here indefinitely, surely?'

'We can bloody well hold onto them until they've cleaned up the mess they made. And if that takes a couple of years, so be it. The little bastards should have thought of that before they invaded Poland.'

'The prisoners didn't start it!' Viv is surprised at her own persistence. 'Most of them are probably just ordinary men. Boys, even.'

Toby stared at her. It was the first time, Viv thought, they had ever discussed anything political and it was certainly their longest conversation since Toby had come home. 'I don't imagine the camp will be operational for long,' he said slowly, 'but the beaches in Norfolk are littered with mines and somebody has to get rid of them.'

It took a few seconds for his words to sink in.

'The camp is in Norfolk?'

'The North Norfolk coast, apparently somewhere quite remote. There's a map in my bag if you want to look. I haven't yet checked the exact location.' He sounded relieved to be talking about geography.

Without replying, Viv pushed back her chair and poured herself a large sherry from the decanter on the sideboard. Later that evening, after Toby had gone to bed, she rummaged in his briefcase and dug out a rather modern-looking half-inch map of Norfolk. Spreading the paper over the dining-room table, she studied the unfamiliar names and landmarks. Sculthorpe was easy to locate. Salthouse, harder. Not least because she made herself start her search on the furthest section of coastline from Sculthorpe. As gradually she allowed her gaze to steal further and further north her heart began to gallop, and when she finally discovered the tiny dot the force of her luck felt like a physical blow. Head swimming, she walked slowly around the table before consulting the map again, but the proximity of the coastal village to the airbase – about twenty miles – was unmistakable. Her first thought was that she must write to Alex that very instant. Instead she made herself fold away the map, return it safely to the briefcase and join Toby in bed. Upstairs, she lay on her back, staring at the ceiling, unable to tell whether her motionless husband was sleeping or wide awake. The next morning, she informed him that she didn't want to stay in Oxfordshire. She and Alice would come to Salthouse too.

The bus is passing through a hamlet which looks drab and cheerless in the flat light of late October. Still, as Viv glimpses the village sign, her heart soars. According to the timetable, Sculthorpe is the very next stop. Returning the letter to her handbag, she draws out a powder compact and lipstick. In the mirror the wet-black gloss of her hair seems practically promiscuous against the pallor of her complexion, which, even to her, looks whiter, more translucent, than ever. Quickly she applies a touch of red to her mouth, presses her lips together and throws the make-up back into her bag.

Beyond the window, houses have given way to a plain board fence, the length and height of which suggest that what goes on behind the screen is not for public viewing. If this is the airfield, the bus will stop at the base any moment, and if Alex has received her recent letters he might – he should – be waiting at the side of the road.

When Viv gets up to press the bell her hand is shaking.

Alighting under the scrutiny of her fellow passengers, she opens her handbag again, for no reason other than to have somewhere to direct her gaze until the bus pulls away. Then she raises her head and looks up and down an empty road. Panic chokes her throat. She's pressing her hand to her mouth, eyes filling with tears, even as she sees him step out from behind the gnarly trunk of an oak tree further along the street.

'Alex!' Viv runs towards him. She is crying properly now, the sheer relief of his presence melting her like candle wax. 'I thought you weren't here! That you hadn't got my letters!'

As she approaches, he catches hold of her elbow and holds her a little way distant. 'Not here, darling. Anyone might see us.'

She glances over her shoulder, at the deserted road. 'There's no one about, Alex.' Pushing closer, she fingers the twill of his jacket. 'Just us.'

To her astonishment he steps backwards, though his hand still grips her arm. 'I said *not here*, Viv!' Steering her away from the airbase, he begins to walk quickly in the same direction the bus took moments earlier, twisting back every few steps to peer over his shoulder.

'Where are we going?' She is stumbling to keep up with him, the heels of her best shoes catching on loose stones and grit.

'Not far, somewhere private, that's all.'

Two minutes later he turns off the road and unlatches a five-bar gate where a barn stands at the edge of an empty cattle field. With his free arm, he pushes the heavy wooden door.

Viv blinks. The gloom is as thick as coaldust. Gradually shapes begin to emerge in the dregs of light trickling like water through the window high above the rafters. To her right, a heap of dirty-yellow straw bales climbs almost to the roof, while the remaining space is occupied with odd pieces of farm machinery: some kind of plough or hay baler, a small trailer with a missing wheel and one ridiculously big tractor tyre propped against the furthest wall. The air smells fusty, of earth and cobwebs and desiccated animal feed. The setting is hardly the ideal location for a romantic tryst, yet just as she is thinking it will have to do, she realises Alex is no longer holding her elbow. For a disconcerting moment he seems to have disappeared and then she spies him, leaning casually against the mountain of straw, the camouflage of his jacket bleeding into the shadowed hue of the dried grasses.

'Alex!' She takes the four paces necessary to bridge the distance between them and flings herself into his arms. Finding his lips, she pours the agony of the last few weeks into her kiss. At first, he doesn't respond and then he spins her round so that his mouth and hips are pressing her against the straw.

By the time they break apart both of them are breathing heavily. Gazing at her, Alex tilts his head. Viv is expecting him to kiss her again. Instead he tucks a lock of escaped hair behind her ear. 'Vivian Markham,' he says appraisingly, 'you sure are one beautiful woman.'

Viv catches his hand. 'I don't like it when you call me that.'

'What do you mean?'

'Vivian Markham.'

'That's your name!'

'My *married* name.'

'Well, last time I checked, honey, you are married. And' – even in the murky dimness she sees his brows furrow – 'not only are you married; your husband is back home again.'

Abruptly, the barn drops into silence. Viv turns over Alex's hand, traces the lines on his palm with the nail of her index finger. This might not be the lunch date she was hoping for, but at least they are together again. With decisiveness she drops his wrist and begins to unbutton her coat.

'I don't feel married,' she says quietly. 'Not to Toby anyway.'

'Viv…' The tone is cautionary.

'Toby has changed, Alex! We're like prisoners in that awful camp of his. People who have to live with each other whether they like it or not. Except we're the only two adults, stuck together in a great big house. He doesn't even talk any more, not to me anyway.' Her voice dips as she recalls how occasionally it seemed as if Toby *was* in conversation with someone, yet when she walked in the room, expecting to find him with one of his men, nobody else was there.

She steps into the lee of Alex's chest and starts to shrug off her coat.

Alex bends his head. Gently cupping her jaw, his lips graze hers before all at once he steps backwards. 'Viv, honey, I'm meant to be at work. If I don't get back to the camp soon, someone will miss me and start asking questions.'

She stares at him in bewilderment. 'Didn't you get my letters?'

'Sure, I got your letters.' Alex makes a noise as if he is swallowing something too big for his throat. 'I got all five of them.'

'Then couldn't you have asked for some time off? It's been so long since we've been together.'

Alex shakes his head. 'Sweetheart, it's not some little office job. I can't just help myself to an afternoon of holiday whenever I feel like it.' He pauses, and the hurt must show on her face because he adds in a softer tone. 'See, I have to be careful, that's all. And what about Alice? Don't you need to go home to pick her up from school?'

'It's not one o'clock yet! Besides, I've arranged for someone to mind Alice.' Daisy, the girl who works for Toby, had been willing to help, even if she hadn't seemed as pleased as Viv expected by the prospect of earning a little extra money. 'I thought we would have the rest of the day together.' The last sentence is no more than a whisper.

Alex takes hold of her upper arms so that the heat from his hands radiates through the apricot silk of her blouse. The coat has slipped awkwardly around her waist, and except where Alex is gripping her skin every part of her body feels suddenly cold. She's newly conscious, too, of the bitter wind gusting through the half-open door and the stink of cattle excrement lingering beneath the straw.

For a long moment Alex looks at her, rather as though he is admiring a painting, and then he tips his head to place his mouth on hers. The press of his lips and the taste of his tongue are as familiar as ever, yet somehow the kiss is not the same as when they first arrived. This time it's Viv who pulls away and drops her gaze. To her dismay her eyes are pooling. She can feel a thick, velvet tear teetering on her lower lashes.

Alex's finger settles under her chin and lifts it gently. 'When you come again, I'll have more time. I'll find somewhere better for us to go. All right?'

Viv doesn't trust herself to speak. At least, she tells herself, there will be another time. He does still want to see her again. She is still frozen, numb with disappointment, when she becomes aware of Alex taking hold of her elbow and guiding her towards the exit.

Outside, it is raining. The drizzle is a curtain, the raindrops hanging in the air as if no longer sure which way to fall. As they head towards the bus stop, beads of water appear on Viv's coat. She can feel them clinging to her hair and sliding between her neck and the collar of her coat. Alex makes some half-hearted joke about the weather, but she isn't really listening; she's thinking that, if anyone were to spot them, they would probably be mistaken for brother and sister. They may be walking arm-in-arm, his hip swinging inches from her own, but the contact feels deadened, almost chaste.

At the bus stop, Alex unlinks himself. 'I hope you don't have to wait long?'

'I don't know,' Viv mumbles, although she does. The next bus isn't for nearly two hours. It had never occurred to her this might be a problem; that she would be leaving so soon. She wonders if he will offer to stay with her for a while and knows immediately that he won't.

He bends to peck her on the cheek. 'I'll see you soon, sweetheart.'

Viv nods. Then, as he turns away, 'Alex?'

He pivots on his heel without moving closer.

'Shall I come next Tuesday too? At the same time? It will be Bonfire Night!' As if there's even the smallest chance of standing hand in hand with him beside the spit and crackle of flames.

He nods briefly. 'Next week, sweetheart! Same time, same place!' Despite his jovial tone of voice there's a sad, almost wistful, expression on his face that Viv can't read.

Chapter Six

1 November 1946

Fran is cycling home from work, the air blue with dusk and the smoke-filled start of November. She has been at the camp nearly a week now and can no longer pretend to June – or herself – that she doesn't intend to stay there. The day before, Major Markham had poked his head around the door to the corridor.

'Daisy looking after you all right?'

It was the first time Fran had seen him since she started, and she was too startled to respond immediately. Pushing back her chair, she began to stand up, unsure both of the required etiquette and whether she might actually grasp the nettle and ask to speak to him about the possible impermanence of her position. Major Markham, however, seemed to take her brief silence as a sufficient answer. Before Fran could say anything, he exhaled a lungful of smoke into the room and disappeared. A moment later they heard the opening and closing of another door.

Daisy sighed. 'He's in the meeting room again. Captain Holmes is away on leave. At least it means we can keep the window shut without suffocating from his tobacco.'

Fran hovered by her desk. She could, of course, go and knock on the door to Captain Holmes's office.

'What's the matter?' Daisy asked after a moment. 'Is there something you want to talk to the major about?'

For an instant Fran saw June's face, awash with hurt and anger. Then she glanced at her desk, at the open files and her half-drunk cup of tea. 'No… no, there isn't. I'd better get on with the orders.'

She sat down and picked up her pen. 'Goodness,' she said a minute later, 'it looks like we're about to run out of potatoes.'

A sharp-edged voice catches Fran's attention. Lowering her foot, she stops cycling. Ugly, aggressive insults are being hurled at someone whose replies fade before they reach her. Straining to hear, she pokes her boot into leaves now wet and heavy from the sleet that fell during the afternoon. In less than a week the weather has turned from autumn to winter, the cold descending with a hard, resolved grip that makes the grass crunch under the morning frosts and islands of ice float in the puddles.

More abuse cuts across the gloom.

Fran hesitates; she should probably leave the shouter to his quarrel, find another route, hurry to the warmth of supper and the waiting kitchen. Instead, after a moment, she finds herself dismounting and leading the bicycle along a flint wall towards the mouth of an alleyway.

At the far end of the passage a fair-haired man in a smart black overcoat is cowering by the brickwork. His spectacles are crooked as though recently dislodged, his hat askance. He appears not to notice Fran, probably because the alley is thick with twilight and his attention focused on the two scruffy-looking soldiers who are facing him.

'Did you get lost?' the first soldier is saying. 'Forget where you were going?' Although he's wearing khaki, his posture is slumped and a bottle dangles from his hand with the carelessness of an umbrella or a cricket bat.

The man gazes at him warily. 'I was just out for a walk. I walk every day.'

'It's a funny time of day to take a walk,' the other soldier says, 'when it's getting dark. But then' – he nudges his companion – 'I've heard you're a funny kind of chap.'

'I don't know what you mean.' The man attempts to shuffle backwards and collides with the wall.

'He means,' the soldier with the bottle says, and takes a step forwards, 'that you're not one of us. Someone who pulls his weight, if you get my drift. It's been pissing us off for a long while now – and we're not the only ones.' He glances sideways. 'Maybe now's the time to find out what you're really made of.'

'Jack…' The second soldier throws out an arm.

'Come on, Ken, he deserves a good roughing up. He's had it coming for a long while and now there's no one about to tell us differently.'

'There's me!' The words spring from Fran's mouth before she can stop herself.

Three pairs of eyes swivel around.

The soldier with the beer bottle does an exaggerated double-take that involves a little stagger and placing his free hand over his heart. Straightening up, he leers at her. 'Run along, darling. This is no place for pretty girls. Better go home before it gets dark or Mummy will be wondering where you are.'

'Let him go!' Anger is burning in Fran's throat, powering a determination she didn't know she was capable of. It's as much as she can do not to march across and smack the drunken soldier on the face. 'You're nothing but a couple of bullies, he's done nothing to you!'

Bottle-man turns the whole of his body around to face her with a deliberate, ominous slowness. Even in the half-light Fran can see the gleam in his eyes stoked by alcohol and opportunity. 'Now that's where you're wrong, little darlin'. Though, it's not so much what's he's done as what he's *not* done, if you get my drift.'

'Yes, do go home!' This time it's the man by the wall who speaks. His voice is so pleasant and clear that he almost succeeds in concealing his fear. 'There's no need to worry. I'll be fine. I expect these two lads only want a chat.'

'That's right,' growls bottle-man. 'We only want to *chat*. Now then,' he gathers himself like an animal before practically spitting at her, 'piss-off!'

Wrenching the bicycle about, Fran jumps on board and cycles away. Behind her she hears bottle-man say, 'Looks like Joan of Arc got cold feet after all!' and wonders what the trapped man is thinking, whether he assumes she has abandoned him, and how many minutes she has to fetch help before the soldier thugs start to get violent.

At the end of the flint wall she stops, heart banging against her ribs, but the rumble of a motor, the smattering of sound she thought she could hear from the alley, is now unmistakable. Headlights sweep into the street, illuming the black tarmac and the straggle of trees with a wash of yellow, quickly followed by the bulk of a lorry. The vehicle appears to be a truck from the camp, the benches on the back crowded with weary prisoners returning after a day working on the beaches or farms.

Leaving her bicycle by the wall, Fran leaps into the road waving her arms and shouting. At once the light-beams are blinding and the roar and smell of diesel overwhelming. All she can see is the engine grille bearing down on her like an approaching train. For a petrifying instant she's certain the driver hasn't seen her, that he won't stop, that she's about to disappear under the wheels of the truck. Then the brakes shriek with the sound of a thousand blackboard dusters and the lorry is shuddering to a halt in a whirlpool of fumes and noise.

A voice shouts down, 'Good God! What on earth are you doing?'

'Please!' cries Fran. 'There's a man in danger. He's being attacked! You need to help him.'

There's a pause before the motor is cut and a sudden and absolute quiet descends. The driver drops his voice to conversational volume. 'What's that you say? Who's in danger?'

'I don't know his name, but two other men are threatening to hurt him. To' – she remembers the horrible phrase they used – '*rough him up a bit.* You – someone – needs to come quickly.'

The driver blinks and gestures at the prisoners. 'Well, I can't leave this lot.' He looks at Fran again with disbelief. 'You nearly got yourself killed!'

'It doesn't matter now! We have to go and help.'

The driver must read something of the desperation on her face because after a moment he shakes his head and sighs. 'All right, this is what we'll do.' Turning in his seat, he points towards the back of the truck. 'Thomas, you speak English. Go with the young lady and see what the problem is. I'll wait here. But if you're not back in ten minutes sharp, no more privileges and you'll be headed for a spell in solitary. Understood?'

There's a murmur of assent, the clunk of the tailboard being released, and the thud of feet landing on tarmac, before a prisoner emerges from the side of the lorry.

Fran stares.

Thomas gazes back.

Brilliant blue eyes latch onto her own.

Fran swallows. 'Please,' she says. 'We need to hurry.'

Thomas nods. 'Show me.'

Fran spins on her heel and starts to run. Thomas lopes easily alongside. Together they race the length of the flint wall. At the corner of the alley Fran slows, scared all at once the passage will be empty, the men gone, that she will have stopped the army truck for nothing. The blood is pounding in her ears, her heart stammering, yet the moment their footsteps cease she hears a groan followed by a voice that is rancid with menace.

'Now don't you go all soft on me! That was just for starters. I've not got going properly yet. A real man should be able to take a punch or two, that's what I say!'

At the far end of the alley they see the fair-haired target. He is pressed against the wall, elbow shielding his face. The left arm of the bottle-man pins his quarry to the brickwork, while the right hangs loose, knuckles clenched and free now of the bottle that is rolling about his feet.

'See!' Fran whispers. She is horrified, and also – unforgivably – a tiny bit relieved not to have intervened in the truck's passage for nothing. Before she can say any more Thomas sprints away from her. The sink of bone into flesh carries over the cobbles, followed by a second, more anguished moan. As she watches, bottle-man swings back his arm again. This time, however, Thomas is close enough to grab his wrist, hauling the soldier backwards so that he reels away from the wall and staggers to keep his balance.

'I think that is enough. You must stop now.' Although Thomas has released his grip on bottle-man's arm, he maintains his ground so that barely the length of a broom handle separates the two men.

The soldier gapes at Thomas, digesting the black patches and the white letter P on the trousers. 'You're a fucking German!' His face ignites with fury. 'Fucking Hitler scum! And you dare to tell me what to do! We bloody beat you Krauts. I'll teach you to put your filthy fucking hands on me!' He dips towards the ground, hands scrabbling on the cobbles, but Thomas anticipates what is happening, locates the glinting bottle first and kicks the glass away.

As bottle-man rises, his features contort with rage. The fingers of his right hand curl into a fist. Fran waits helplessly, bracing herself for the impact, when the second soldier steps from the cloak of the shadows.

'Wait, Jack. You could be stirring up trouble. We don't know what's going on.' His eyes flit across the alley, as if checking for guards or a cavalcade of escaped prisoners. Then, roughly, to Thomas, 'Why aren't you locked up?'

'A whole truck of German prisoners and British guards is waiting over there.' Thomas indicates over his right shoulder, towards the solidity of the main road. 'Any minute they will come. And when they understand what you are doing to this man, they will call the police.'

'He's fucking lying.' Bottle-man looks to where Thomas is pointing. 'There's no one there.'

The second soldier shakes his head. 'Leave it, Jack. Not worth the risk. He can't be out on his own, can he? They don't just let the fucking Krauts wander about, do they? Besides' – he jerks his chin towards the fair-haired man who is cupping his nose, blood seeping between his fingers – 'you've already made your point. Let's go home.' He takes a few paces, before retracing his steps to yank his friend's forearm. 'I said, let's go, didn't I?'

Bottle-man nods slowly and makes as if to follow his mate. Suddenly he swivels round, heels grinding on the tarmac, and shoves Thomas in the small of his back. The German pitches forwards and sprawls onto the ground. 'That'll fucking teach you. Fucking Kraut.' With horror, Fran sees the soldier lift his boot, draw back his leg, but he must have second thoughts because after an unsteady second he lowers his foot and, swearing under his breath, lurches after his mate. Fran watches until she is certain they have exited the alley and are headed in the opposite direction to the main road.

When she turns back, Thomas is on his knees gathering a number of items – a notebook, a pencil, a small black wallet – that have fallen from his pocket. A long arc of dirt runs the length of his cheek while the skin underneath smarts sore and red. Instinctively Fran reaches out to help him up, only to retract her arm an instant later. She blushes as she sees him notice her confusion. She puts out her hand again. After a pause, Thomas takes it.

'Thank you.' As he gets to his feet, his eyes are smiling, blades of blue light slicing through the dusk. Fran looks down, uncertain if he is laughing at her. The grip of his fingers feels warm. She is aware of the cat's tongue texture of his skin and the curve of his thumb circling her wrist before she realises there is no longer any need to be holding his hand at all. Pulling away, she walks towards the fair-haired man who is leaning against the wall and pinching his nose with a red-stained handkerchief.

'Are you all right?' It is a relief to switch her attention away from Thomas.

'Absolutely.' The man nods emphatically through his handkerchief. 'Give me a moment and I'll be fine. I only need to clean up a bit.' As if to illustrate as much, he takes the cotton from his nose and spits onto the least soiled corner.

Fran watches as he starts to rub his face. Behind them, she can hear Thomas moving closer.

'They were such thugs,' she says, determined not to look around. 'Why would they set on you like that?'

'Oh, I don't know.' Oddly, the fair-haired man appears too preoccupied with the bloodstains on his face to want to give the matter much thought. 'I suppose they had their reasons. Anyway' – he makes a point of consulting a smart-looking, leather-strapped wristwatch – 'I really ought to be going. My family will be wondering where on earth I've got to.'

Briefly, Fran wonders if he means a wife and child, and immediately doubts that he does. Not because of his age – he appears to be only a few years older than her – but on account of a solitary sort of gaucheness. Somehow it's hard to imagine him going home to a partner, or a small, sick baby keeping him up all night with croup.

'Will you be all right,' he adds, 'getting home yourself?'

Fran nods, touched. After all that has happened, the question ought to be asked the other way around. The air seems to charge with static and without turning her head she knows that Thomas has come to stand beside her. The attention of the fair-haired man switches to Thomas too and a range of emotions pass over his features, far too quickly for her to track. 'Thank you,' he says, finally.

Then, dangling the bloody handkerchief, 'If you hadn't come along when you did, I fear the damage would have been a lot worse.'

'I helped very little. You should really thank…' Thomas looks pointedly at Fran.

Her mouth dries to ash. 'Frances. Fran.'

The fair-haired man alternates his gaze from one to the other, then clears his throat as if there's an awkwardness to the situation he can't quite identify. 'Thank you, both. I really am very grateful.' He pauses, 'Well, I'll wish you a very good evening.' There is a further beat or two of silence before he stuffs the handkerchief deep into the pocket of his trousers and with a final nod walks purposefully away.

Neither Fran nor Thomas speaks until the rap of departing footsteps has melted into the gloom. 'I must go back to the lorry,' Thomas says eventually, but he doesn't move. They are both standing exactly on the spot where the fair-haired man left them.

'You're not tempted to escape?' Fran says, and is immediately mortified she might have thought such a thing, let alone said it out loud.

His eyes flash with surprise. Or amusement. 'I would need a safe house and some English pounds. Prisoners are only paid in tokens. See…' Delving into his pocket, he opens his wallet to show a mauve slip of paper stamped *Bardhill Camp: 2s. 6d.* 'Without someone to help me, I have no chance to go anywhere.'

Fran has seen the tokens before, of course. She and Daisy spent several hours counting and allocating them at the end of the previous week, but naturally Thomas is not aware of that. He has no reason to know she works at the camp. She's wondering if – how – to tell him when a different, more troubling thought suddenly occurs. 'You're not suggesting I help you escape, are you?'

Thomas stops smiling. His expression becomes earnest. 'I would *never* ask you to do such a thing.' He puts the wallet away without looking at her.

For a while they both stand quietly. Somehow the silence softens, becomes more intimate. The hush feels like a blanket insulating her both from the cold and the rest of the world. Extraordinarily, she realises she wants to touch him. Her wrist is pulsing for the sandpaper touch of his thumb, while the mud on his face has acquired the pull of a magnet; she is itching to lift her hand to his cheek, to rub away the dirt. She can visualise standing on tiptoes to reach him, tucked against his chest, her fingers light on his skin. The image is so real that for a second she thinks it might even be happening.

Forcing her gaze downwards, she breathes a lungful of the bitter, sober air and makes herself take one, then two, steps further away. A little way beyond her right foot an object – small, shiny – is catching what remains of the light. It takes a moment to gather both her attention and focus and see that the item is a photograph. Crouching low, she picks up the glossed paper. The picture is of a child, a girl in a summer-ripe garden, aged about six years old. A blond, candyfloss cloud of hair surrounds a face that is rapt with happiness as she stares with adoration at whoever is holding the camera.

Fran holds out the image to Thomas. She can't quite manage to meet his eyes. 'Is this yours? Perhaps it fell out of your pocket when you fell.' He nods, takes the photograph from her and slides it inside his jacket without a word. A hundred questions buzz around Fran's head. Although she can't bring herself to ask him any of them, they hang in the air like a swarm of bees, shifting the atmosphere in a way that makes her suddenly able to say quite coolly, 'We really should be going. I'm expected at home and you will get into trouble for being late.' Without waiting for him to reply, she starts to head down the alley.

Late afternoon has solidified to evening. The plum-coloured curtain of the sky is broken only by a slice of moon and the thin black limbs of the tallest treetops. Fran trails a hand along the flint wall, fingertips bouncing over the egg-shaped stones, using the landmark to retrace her steps. Thomas follows, keeping, it seems, a deliberate half pace behind. Once or twice Fran senses the space between them crack open, as if he's going to speak, but before he says anything, they reach the junction of the main road where a torch beam is sweeping back and forth through the dusk.

'Thomas, is that you?' The driver's voice is tight with anxiety. 'Ten minutes, I said. You've been a bloody sight longer than that! I was beginning to think you'd bloody scarpered.'

'It wasn't his fault,' Fran says quickly. 'A man was being set upon. Thom—' she stops herself, sensing the familiarity would sound misplaced. 'This prisoner saved him.'

'Is that so?' The driver peers at her. His torch has dropped, pooling the ground and the underside of their faces with white-gold light. 'What about the police then? An incident like that should be reported.'

'I don't think so.'

The driver considers Thomas. Even in the dark his surprise is evident.

'The man who was attacked,' Thomas says. 'I don't think he would want that.'

As soon as he has spoken, Fran understands that he is right. The fair-haired man actually seemed to want to make as light of the matter as possible. And he certainly hadn't mentioned calling the police. She wondered if it was bravery or some other reason that had caused him to play down the assault with such nonchalance. At the time she hadn't given his reaction a second thought.

For a moment the driver seems undecided. Then, 'Right. Climb in, and let's get back to the camp.' There's relief in his voice, and sudden exhaustion too.

As Thomas moves away, Fran feels – *thinks* she feels – a slight brush against her arm. When she raises her eyes, he is looking at her, the blue of his eyes impaling her own. The same urge to lean forwards, to touch him, is so overwhelming she has to clasp her right hand with her left. She imagines her feelings must be as obvious as a scarlet cloak about her shoulders or a dog yapping at her heels, yet the driver seems oblivious, clambering into his seat and coughing the engine to life.

Thomas swallows. Fran watches the ripple in his throat, the tightening of his lips, as he turns away from her and vanishes behind the back of the truck. In less than thirty seconds she is standing on her own again. Slowly, she retrieves her bicycle from the wall and begins her ride home. The notion that jumped into her head the instant she saw the photograph – that Thomas must have a daughter, that he probably has a wife too, waiting for him somewhere in Germany – has at some point during the last few minutes taken root as a fully formed fact. Pedalling steadily into the night, she is shaken by the stone of unhappiness that accompanies this truth, the weight of sadness in her belly.

As she unlatches the gate, the lamps from the sitting room glow warm through the curtains. Opening the front door, her mother calls out, 'Why are you so late? Is everything all right?' Fran shouts back a reply and wheels the bicycle into the shed. For a while she lingers with the spiders, composing both herself and a plausible story about work at the camp. Providing the real explanation is unthinkable. The events of the evening are so infused with emotion that she doesn't trust herself to extract one from the other. To explain how a German prisoner helped her rescue an Englishman without revealing a lot more besides.

Chapter Seven

5 November 1946

Martin turns up his collar against the rain falling slantways from a weighty sky and keeps walking. In many respects he finds wet weather preferable to dry. He has a hat, which offers some protection against the elements. And he's far less likely to encounter trouble – at the first sign of drizzle, troublemakers, so he has discovered, tend to keep their drinking indoors. Nevertheless, the events of a few nights earlier have made him warier than ever. He starts like a fawn at the slightest noise, peers deep into side streets, and if his path is bordered by a hedgerow or other potential hiding place, hugs the middle of the road unless the appearance of a motor car compels him back to the pavement. He knows he had a lucky escape. If the young woman on the bicycle had been less insistent, less resourceful, the matter might have turned out very badly indeed.

An image of her comes to mind, as it has done repeatedly since their encounter. A slight yet strong-looking figure, hair the jumbled bronze of autumn leaves, and green-brown eyes that exposed every thought passing through her head as plainly as a clean glass window. As he's wondering if their paths might cross again, he leaps at the distant clatter of a fallen dustbin lid and immediately rebukes himself.

If he can't get a grip, stop behaving with less backbone than a teenager, perhaps he should cease these evening walks altogether? After the attack, pressing ice to his face in the half-lit kitchen, dreading the barrage of questions from his mother and sister, the notion of giving them up was very tempting indeed. Yet if he doesn't walk, how will he exercise? When every morning he drives to town and spends his working day in an office. When he can't play a game of football or cricket and is denied the breathy exhilaration of running, of holding his nerve in front of a goal or a determined bowler. And if he doesn't exercise, what will happen to his heart? A heart so appallingly, shamefully, weak, the British army found him to be incapable of so much as staggering onto a French beach and dying alongside the rest of his friends. No, he has to keep on walking. And perhaps even allow himself a small sense of achievement at writing in his daily diary *normal route to Salthouse and back, three minutes faster!* Or, *hard work today as strong headwind, but no obvious ill-effects.*

Slipping his palm between the folds of his raincoat and jacket, Martin feels the thud of his pulse. Beneath the layer of ribs and flesh the muscles are contracting and expanding, chugging dutifully away – for the time being at least. He has lain in bed like this for hours, trying in vain to detect the fatal anomaly. One day, he supposes, the flaw will make itself known. His heart will simply stop, not in the way a heart shuts down when anyone dies, a sign on a door flipping gently from open to closed, but more akin to a sudden break on the front wheel of a bicycle, a seizure that will send him spinning over the handlebars and crashing lifeless to the ground.

Returning his fist to his coat pocket, he moves forwards again and doesn't pause until he reaches the old cricket ground. At the memorial, he lingers to read the list of fallen men. The names are so familiar that he could almost recite them all without looking. Instead he makes himself read each one out loud while the usual fog of guilt, the same impossible question, descends. Why is he here, standing under the sting of the rain, when they are not? Feeling the ocean air raw inside his lungs, a chill in his toes and the stirrings of his empty stomach. Why did a random affliction spare him from the slaughter, but not them?

Eventually he sets off again. The final part of his ritual takes him up the hill that leads southwards out of the village and onto the heath. His destination is a wooden bench with vistas, on a fine day, over yellow-tipped gorse towards the shifting presence of the sea. The demands of the incline his best guess at an appropriate balance between effort and risk.

There is nobody else about, of course, no one else so foolish as to choose to soak themselves to the skin at the end of a working day in November, which is why it takes him a moment to register the figure hunkered low on the wooden bench. He or she is facing the shore, although by now it is surely too dark to appreciate the view, to see anything but a dismal slate-grey canvas falling away to the coastline with the lights of the village beckoning below.

As he approaches, Martin clears his throat, aware his sudden presence might cause alarm. 'Terrible weather,' he says, though in fact the rain seems to be easing. The silver threads still dripping from his hat appear to be from the earlier deluge.

The woman, for now he is close enough to tell she is a woman, flinches and swings around to look at him. Even in the sooty gloom he can see she is film-star beautiful. The rain has plastered long, dark hair to her face from which enormous eyes regard him with an unusual mixture of surprise and total disinterest.

'I say, is everything all right?' The woman's cheeks are damp with raindrops or, possibly, tears. Martin tries not to examine her too intensely, to keep his voice light.

The woman gets to her feet. 'I'm afraid I came for a walk and got rather caught out. I don't believe I could get any wetter!' She gestures at her coat, which is now so sodden the colour is unidentifiable, as if compelled by habit or good manners to pretend her behaviour is entirely normal.

Martin smiles politely. Yet, the notion she has been sitting alone in such a downpour is troubling, and it's beginning to dawn on him that he knows who she is – or at least, who her husband is. He takes a small step towards her. 'Will you come back to the village now? You would keep me company and it will soon be very dark.'

Extending his right arm, he makes a little play of crooking his elbow as though to escort her into a five-course dinner party with crystal glassware and candles rather than the rain-drenched dusk.

The woman hesitates. Martin assumes she's thinking how she might refuse his offer until he sees she's actually fiddling with a sheet of paper, folding the page surreptitiously as though hoping he won't notice. Once she's slipped the envelope into her pocket, she threads her arm through his but only part-way, as if to demonstrate that she's obliging him under sufferance.

As they descend the hill, he concentrates on navigating the swollen puddles. However, before they have covered more than a hundred yards, the quiet is broken by a yelp and the woman pitches heavily against him. As she regains her balance, he sees her shoes were not chosen with walking in mind; high-heeled and red, they appear more suited to a different type of evening altogether. She's shivering too, the vibrations from their interlocked arms scuttle through his torso. Slowing his pace, Martin wonders what on earth brought her to the heath on such a filthy night. He risks a sideways glance, but her focus on the road ahead makes asking such a question seem impossible.

The village is emerging below when all at once noise like anti-aircraft fire rips into the silence and the sky breaks into a shower of gold. Streamers flare and melt into the inky velvet, followed by an explosion of burning red. Martin and his companion come to a halt at precisely the same moment, tipping back their heads to watch the sparks dissolve and whirling comet tails surge into their place.

'The fifth of November,' Martin says. 'I'd quite forgotten. Had you?' Turning his eyes from the lights plunges him into absolute blackness, he can't even see the outline of the woman's face, let alone her expression.

'No,' she says in a clear voice. 'I remembered the date.' Her arm slides out from his, as if newly conscious of their physical contact.

'An event is happening on the green,' Martin says. 'I remember spotting the posters now. I believe there's a bonfire too. Quite a crowd will have turned out, I imagine. It's been a while since we've had a celebration like this.' As he speaks, fountains of yellow stars burst above them, followed by a crescendo of high-pitched wails that culminate in a torrent of gunshots and three deafening bangs. A ripple of what might well be applause floats from below.

'Oh!' The woman claps a hand to her mouth. 'My goodness, I have to go!' Bending down, she fiddles with the strap of her broken shoe, making little gasps of impatience.

Martin gazes at the top of her head. It's hard to imagine why the existence of a firework display should upset her further. 'Will you manage on your own?' he says.

'Of course.' She doesn't bother to lift her eyes.

He hesitates, uncertain what to do. Perhaps he should insist on accompanying her home? From the village there is another burst of staccato. His attention flickers back to the sky, to the umbrella of scattered colour that is beginning to disappear even as it blooms. When he looks down again, the woman is hurrying away. 'I say—'

She glances over her shoulder. 'Thank you! Thank you for your help.'

'That's quite all right.' He is speaking to her back. Under the spotlight of a rocket he sees her pick up speed and begin to run.

She has forgotten him already.

As soon as she's out of sight, Viv takes off her shoes and jogs in her stockings. The stitching on the shoe leather must have ripped when she turned her ankle because one of the straps has almost sheared off. How stupid of her to wear heels in this weather! It's hard now to remember what possessed her. Searching for an outfit that would make her irresistible seems like something she did last year, rather than this morning when a much younger version of herself was parading in front of the bedroom mirror.

Although the road is ice cold, she's far too preoccupied for the temperature of her feet to be anything but a mild distraction. Naturally she had been upset when Alex failed to show up. Within minutes, disbelief had curdled first to despair before igniting into a kind of helpless, angry panic. She was slumped against a tree, heart racing, struggling, it felt, even to breathe, when a boy of about ten appeared from nowhere and asked if she was supposed to be meeting an American soldier because, if so, he had been asked to give her a letter.

Tearing into the envelope, even while the child was still standing there, she scanned the sentences through a veil of furious tears that made her, she now sees, read them in the worst possible way. The more she has stewed over the words, the more she has come to understand their proper meaning – even if Alex might have explained himself a little more clearly. He is not, as she first thought, abandoning her. Rather he is asking her to make a decision. After all, didn't he make it plain from the very beginning that he wanted to take her back to America with him? Well, perhaps that time is coming. She has realised, sitting in the rain, that she will do anything to keep them together. What she can't do – really can't do – for very much longer is to stay here in Norfolk, living with Toby.

Her husband has become a stranger. A silent stranger. Some days she hardly speaks to anyone apart from Alice. It's like being less and less present in her own life, as if she's been reduced to a chalk drawing on a blackboard to which someone has taken a duster, and finger by finger, toe by toe, is slowly obliterating. The sensation is not dissimilar to the peculiar way she felt after Alice was born, when a kind of blue fog seemed frequently to make her tearful for no reason at all. With Toby away and the world preoccupied with war, she simply waited, hoping the clouds would pass, but they didn't, not completely, not for ages, not until Alex came along and blew clean away the last traces of that inexplicable sadness. And now, faced with the alternative of a lifetime of love or a life sentence of loneliness, who on earth – literally, who on earth – wouldn't choose love?

Viv touches the envelope in her pocket. Later this evening she will reread his letter and begin to craft her reply. Now she must focus on trying to get her daughter to the village green before the end of the firework display. Alice saw the poster a few days ago and pestered to be taken until Viv relented, telling herself she would be back from meeting Alex in time to keep her promise. Of course, as matters turned out, she could have been home early enough to claim a front-row place, had she not spent most of the afternoon distraught on the hillside. The display started at five thirty, she remembers, which means, incredibly, she must have been sitting on that bench for nearly two hours. Perhaps Alice has been able to watch the display from an upstairs window? It strikes her that missing the fireworks is nothing compared to the distress she might soon cause her daughter. Pushing the thought away, Viv quickens her pace.

By the time she nears the house her chest is heaving. She drops to a walk, slaps the grit from her heels and refastens her shoes as best she can. She probably resembles a rat half-drowned in the river, but Alice won't care, and Toby wouldn't notice if she came in naked. Tentative, all at once, she opens the door slowly, but before she even has a chance to call out Alice's name a golden-haired bundle flings herself at Viv.

'Mummy!'

Her daughter's face is distorted from crying. The sight of Viv provokes more tears that run unchecked down cheeks made mottled and red before she buries her head into the top of her mother's legs. Viv's gut cramps with guilt. 'Darling, I'm terribly sorry I'm so late. We'll leave right now. Quick, get your coat!'

Alice doesn't reply.

'Hurry up, darling! You still want to go out, don't you?'

Against her thighs, she feels Alice shake her head.

'Come on.' Viv crouches down. 'Don't be like that! We'll still be in time for the bonfire and you can have a toffee apple while we watch the Guy.'

Alice doesn't move. Instead her gaze stays fixed on the black-and-white check of the hall tiles. Gently, Viv places a finger under Alice's chin and lifts her face so that their eyes are level. Then she rocks back in surprise. Her daughter is not disappointed, she sees.

She is afraid.

'What is it, Alice? What's the matter?'

Alice opens her mouth, but all that comes out is a strangled sob before she attempts to burrow into Viv again.

A nub of dread swells inside Viv's chest. Holding her daughter at arm's length, she tries to keep calm. 'Alice, you must tell me what's happened. I can't help if I don't know what's wrong.'

She sees Alice struggling to speak, as if each word is a weight too heavy to lift. 'It's Daddy,' Alice manages at last. 'He won't come out.'

'What do you mean, *he won't come out*? Where is he? What's he doing?'

There's a fresh onslaught of tears.

Viv gapes at her daughter with panic and frustration. Then she grasps Alice's hand, 'Show me.'

Together they go to the back hall where a second staircase, narrower and more twisted than the grand one in the front hall, leads to the bedrooms on the upper floor. Wordlessly Alice points at the door to the cupboard tucked beneath the rising treads.

'Is Daddy in there?' Viv's voice sounds as incredulous as she feels.

Alice nods. She has stopped sobbing and is staring at Viv with enormous eyes in which a new chink of hope has lodged. 'Daddy was crying too,' she whispers.

Viv takes hold of the door handle, before pausing and instead rapping softly on the wood. 'Toby? What are you doing in there? Are you all right?'

Silence.

Viv waits. Knocks more loudly. 'Toby?'

Nothing.

After a moment Viv opens the door a couple of inches and peers around the edge. To begin with all she can make out is the ironing board, a couple of buckets, and the ropey grey mop used for cleaning the kitchen floor. Then, deep at the back, where the height of the cupboard is shorter even than Alice, she spies her husband curled on his knees, the whites of his eyes sudden and startling in the gloom.

'Toby?'

He doesn't reply.

As Viv's eyes adjust to the murkiness, she sees his hands are cupped to his ears and he is rocking back and forth.

'Mummy?' Alice's voice floats from behind her. 'What's the matter with Daddy? Why is he in the cupboard?'

Viv swallows, thankful she's blocking her daughter's view. 'I think Daddy must have lost something and is busy trying to find it. Why don't you' – she casts about for inspiration – 'go and fetch one of his jumpers. I think he might be feeling cold.' In fact, it is she who is cold, frozen to the marrow, she realises, in her drenched coat and soaked feet, but the task might at least occupy Alice while she tries to coax Toby from his hiding place.

'Toby...' Viv kicks off her shoes for the second time and slides into the instant dusk of the interior. 'It's time to come out now.'

Still no response.

'Toby,' she says more loudly, 'I said it's time—'

'Get down!' His eyes flash wide and terrified. 'For God's sake, get down! You're an easy target standing there!'

Viv hesitates before dropping to her knees. Manoeuvring past the ironing board, she crawls further into the cupboard until she's close to her husband. He nods at her approvingly. 'The explosions are coming from the West. It sounds like we're outnumbered, but they haven't yet broken over the top of the ridge. Keep your head low and movement to a minimum. It might be the only chance we've got. If they see us, we're done for.'

As he speaks, the crack and boom of a rocket penetrates the cupboard walls. Toby moans and presses his palms more tightly to his ears. Viv sees his lips moving, hears a low drone of words and realises with horror that she's listening to her husband recite the Lord's Prayer.

She runs a tongue over dry lips. What she really wants, she thinks with sudden and overwhelming clarity, is a drink. To be sitting in a bar with Alex, preferably in London or possibly New York. Sipping Gin & It. Watching him watching her. Music playing, a pianist, probably. Shared laughter and the smoky haze of cigarettes. Her blood on fire with alcohol and the anticipation of the next few hours.

Another bang provokes another whimper from Toby.

Viv shifts sideways to avoid a tack or piece of grit that's digging into her knee. She touches Toby's shoulder. 'The noise, those explosions, it's only fireworks because of Bonfire Night.'

He gapes at her.

'Today is the fifth of November. Don't you remember? They must have been talking about it at the camp.' She pauses. She has the sense that she might as well be speaking in Russian.

Outside the cupboard, footsteps. The door opens a tiny crack. 'I've got one of Daddy's jumpers. Do you want me to bring it to him?'

'No!' Then with forced gaiety, 'Wait there, darling. We'll both be out before you know it!' Viv considers the unfocused black of Toby's pupils, her own mind racing. Scooping her arm around

Toby's hunched back she lowers her mouth to his ear and says with as much authority as she can muster. 'We have to get somewhere safe. There's an abandoned farm on the far side of the valley. We can shelter there.'

Toby shakes his head wildly. 'That's madness, we'll get shot as soon as we move.'

'No,' Viv insists. 'Listen, it's quiet. The Germans are retreating. This is our opportunity. But we must go right now.'

Hesitantly, holding her gaze, Toby lifts his hands from his ears.

Viv daren't breathe. Surely, she prays, the village display will have finished by now. All that can be left are the last few locals letting off their own supply. Crouching in the darkness, waiting for the next blast, the blow that will scupper her plan, her own ears are raw with trepidation. She makes herself count slowly to ten, heart thumping in time with the numbers. Then, 'See, no guns.'

His chin dips slightly. A nod of acquiescence.

'Ready, then? Follow me.' Squeezing past the ironing board, she's relieved to hear Toby scrabbling in her wake, and as she stands up and pushes open the door, she's able to reach behind and yank him into the hallway with her.

'Daddy, are you cold? I've got your jumper!' Alice thrusts the sweater at Toby before he has even straightened up.

'Just give Daddy a moment...' Viv plucks her daughter's sleeve while she watches Toby gaze with disbelief at his surroundings. She wonders if he is seeing the slate floor, the wall lamp with the cracked glass shade and the heavy curtain that conceals the door to the cellar. Or some other scene entirely. A bomb-stricken bridge? Burned-out tanks? Or simply the stale emptiness of a deserted barn, perhaps, since she suggested that they were heading to one.

'Toby?'

He blinks and gives his head a little shake like a dog unclogging its ears of water. Three, four, five seconds pass, his expression clears, the wide dilation of his pupils shrinks, and his focus alights

on Alice and the garment she's brandishing. Leaning forwards, he
tentatively plucks the jumper from her grasp.

'Did you lose something, Daddy?'

'What?'

'In the cupboard? Mummy said you lost something and that's
why you wouldn't come out.'

Toby looks at Viv, twisting the wool through his fingers, over
and over, back and forth, as if the feel of the yarn is something
miraculous. She searches his face for a nameable reaction, embarrassment perhaps, or even gratitude, but his expression is unreadable
– not blank exactly, more overcrowded, as if his emotions are too
numerous and complicated to identify.

'Yes,' Toby says finally. 'That's right. I lost something.' For an
instant he clenches shut his eyes, then without another word heads
down the hallway. As he walks away from them his gait lurches as
if he has drunk too much at an army dinner or is navigating the
corridor of a moving train, while every few steps his hands grope
towards the solidity of the rose-papered wall.

Later, once Alice is in bed, Viv pulls off her ruined stockings
and damp dress and climbs into a deep bath. The heat of the water
is overwhelmingly blissful. One arm dangling over the rim, Viv
tips back her head so that her neck and shoulders slip below the
surface and the warmth begins to strip away the tension and the
cold. Downstairs, Toby is sitting in an armchair, swilling whisky
around his cut-glass tumbler in constant circulation. She knows
this, because ten minutes earlier she was with him, clutching her
own glass and waiting for the right moment to broach the subject
of the cupboard. Once or twice she cleared her throat, but each
time she did so Toby reached for the newspaper on his knee, only
to let it drop again the second he sensed the moment of interven-
tion had passed. She ought to have persisted, forced herself to ask
him if he had truly believed he was under attack, how often reality
slipped from his grasp, for how long his delusions – was there a

kinder word? – lasted. But eventually, overcome with exhaustion, she announced she was going upstairs.

Now she lifts her dry arm to eye level. Tucked in her palm is the letter from Alex. '*My Darling Girl,*' Viv begins to read; then, realising the writing is superfluous, closes her eyes and mouths from memory:

> *The time has come to tell you that I can't bear to share you any longer. The thought of you with Toby is simply more than I can take. We have both known, my baby, the day would come when our little paradise would have to end. It is the best and the cruellest stroke of luck that you are here in Norfolk. So close, and yet, my darling, still so far away. I shall love you always but agony though it is I must accept that you belong to another man and let you go…*

Opening her fingers, Viv allows the page to flutter to the floor and sinks slowly beneath the surface. As the bathwater closes over her head, she can feel her hair swirling long and black and the floating detachment of her limbs, but the rest of her sensations – the creaks of the old house, the sight of the pale pink wallpaper, the faint smells of supper – the hints and reminders of family life beyond the bathroom are obliterated. What if, she asks herself for the hundredth time, Alex didn't have to share her with Toby? What if he didn't have to worry about her being with Toby at all? Wasn't it up to her to choose the man to whom she wanted to belong? Surely, Alex, now she understood him properly, though he might be too much of a gentleman to say so explicitly, was really asking her to choose him?

Chapter Eight

21 November 1946

Fran's stomach is reminding her it must nearly be lunchtime, when the sound of rapid footsteps from the corridor makes her lift her head at the exact same moment as Daisy. Before either of them can speak, a soldier strides into the room, his face ashen and wide-eyed. 'Major Markham here?' Daisy nods and, without breaking his stride, the soldier opens the door to the adjoining office, then pulls it firmly shut behind him.

Over the top of the desk Daisy raises her eyebrows. 'What's all that about, I wonder?' For a minute or two they both sit motionless, the pile of letters beside the typewriters temporarily forgotten, even though the only audible aspect of the conversation taking place on the far side of the partition is its rather frantic tone.

'Perhaps a prisoner has escaped,' Daisy whispers eventually. 'It wouldn't be very difficult to give the British soldiers the slip on the beach.'

'Do you think so?' Fran remembers her conversation with Thomas. 'They don't have any money, so I don't know what—' She breaks off as the connecting door bursts open and the soldier hurries out of the office without so much as glancing at them.

A few seconds later Major Markham arrives by their desk. His face, Fran thinks, is even whiter than the soldier's complexion, while his right fist is clenched around the pen he must have been writing with when he was interrupted. He coughs as if to get their attention, although both she and Daisy are already staring at him intently.

'There's been an accident, I'm afraid. A mine has exploded. One prisoner is on the way to hospital and the local doctor is coming here to attend to another. I'm needed at the hospital, so one of you must escort the doctor. I want a note of everything the prisoner says. Just in case' – the major grimaces – 'just in case some awkward bugger starts to ask questions later on.'

There's a moment of silence. Fran imagines Daisy's horrified expression must match her own. *Some awkward bugger* probably means the Red Cross, or one of the people who writes to newspapers campaigning for all prisoners to be allowed home. She runs her tongue over lips that are unexpectedly dry. She can practically visualise the burst of flame in her mind's eye, hear the crack of explosives. 'How will the doctor understand the prisoner? Does he speak German? And how will we be able to take notes?'

'Another prisoner, one whom I'm told speaks excellent English, is acting as an interpreter.' Major Markham seems suddenly to notice that he is holding his pen. Uncurling his fingers, he ponders the item briefly before transferring the silver barrel to the top pocket of his jacket.

'I'll do it. I'll go to the sickbay.' Fran is on her feet before she has even formulated a conscious decision to stand up.

Major Markham and Daisy regard her with surprise.

'I mean, I don't mind helping. That is, if Daisy doesn't particularly want to go herself…' Fran can feel her cheeks heating up. Nevertheless, she reaches towards the desk for a notebook and a pencil. 'I happen to know the local doctor quite well. He's called Dr Lavender, and because my father isn't well he visits us regularly.'

'Well, in that case…' Major Markham glances at Daisy.

'I don't mind if Fran accompanies the doctor. I'll carry on with the typing here.' Daisy gives a small, dismissive shrug. 'To be honest, I'm not terribly good with blood anyway.'

*

Dr Lavender is waiting on the far side of the gate, holding his familiar black bag. The soldier standing alongside him is the same one that came to the office, and on seeing Fran and Major Markham his shoulders drop with relief. He turns to Major Markham, 'The doctor is very anxious to attend to the prisoner as soon as possible, sir.'

'I've been hanging about a good ten minutes,' the doctor interjects, 'when I could have been treating him by now. If the British army will insist on using prisoners of war to carry out such dreadful work as clearing mines, the least it can do is ensure that when things go wrong, medical assistance is provided quickly.'

Major Markham considers him coldly. 'I can't have someone coming into the camp without my permission. Besides,' his expression becomes positively glacial, 'it wasn't so long ago that the man you're so eager to treat would probably have thought nothing of blowing you, your good lady wife, and all of us standing here to smithereens.' He pauses before nodding at the soldier. 'Take Dr Lavender to the sickbay. Miss Taylor will go with you.'

The soldier sets off across the grass. Adjusting his grip on the bag, the doctor walks beside him with a grim set to his mouth. Fran follows a little way behind. Until now she has only ever been to the block containing the camp offices and the meeting room. Although the prisoners could be seen climbing aboard trucks at the beginning and end of the day, or collecting items from the storerooms, she and Daisy never ventured as far as their sleeping huts or the cookhouse. 'Best to keep to the office,' Daisy said firmly, when Fran asked if she was allowed to look around the camp, 'You don't want to get in trouble for going where we're not supposed to.'

Now, close up, the curved roofs of the Nissen huts appear stark in the feeble November light, while behind them she can spy a rectangle of turf marked in paint with a net-less goal at one end. A recreation area, she supposes, not that anybody is likely to be in the mood for playing games again for quite some time.

She shivers.

In her haste she forgot her coat, and it's too late to go back for it now because the soldier is already taking them through the doorway of the largest building on the camp.

Fran hesitates, surprised. 'I thought this was the cookhouse?'

The soldier replies without turning around. 'The sickbay is located here too. In a room at the back.'

As their footsteps slap against the concrete floor, the doctor stares dourly ahead. He hasn't spoken a word since the exchange with Major Markham, not even to acknowledge Fran. She is beginning to feel uneasy herself. The air inside the corridor is infused with the stink of cooking, something green and sour like cabbage or sprouts, and beneath the vegetables lingers the faintest but unmistakable trace of Dettol. Remembering Daisy's comment about blood, Fran hopes fervently her assumption that Thomas is the English-speaking prisoner, the one tasked with translating, is correct. Otherwise, she will wish she never volunteered for such an unpleasant task.

At the end of the passage, they turn left and come to a room with a barred window set high in the outside wall. Six metal-framed beds are arranged in two rows facing each other. All are empty except for the one nearest the entrance where a prisoner is sitting sideways on the mattress, bent almost double and clutching hold of his right arm. A second prisoner is crouched beside him speaking in a quiet voice with his back to the door, while another army soldier stands a little way apart.

Dropping his bag on the floor, the doctor steps towards the bed. 'I'm Doctor Lavender. I'm here to help you.'

The injured man doesn't respond. His overalls are charred along the entire right-hand side of his body, and on his forearm red, swollen flesh is visible, protruding between the tatters of fabric. Fran flinches. The stench of burned skin is much stronger than the smell of Dettol and she has to steel herself not to look away.

'Could you please tell the patient…' the doctor begins, but the second German is already translating, clambering to his feet as he does so.

All at once he seems to freeze in mid-air. 'The English girl!'

Fran catches her breath.

Thomas is gaping at her, visibly shocked.

Dr Lavender follows his gaze. His brows furrow in confusion. 'This is Miss Taylor. She works as an assistant to Major Markham. There's no need to be alarmed by her presence.'

Fran has time for the tiniest smile before Thomas wrenches his focus back to the doctor.

'Would you please ask the patient what happened,' the doctor says. 'How close was he to the mine when it exploded?'

Fran watches, spellbound, as Thomas interprets into hasty German, leaning near to the prisoner's face and placing, at one point, a hand on his shoulder. The prisoner mumbles a reply and shakes his head. Thomas turns to the doctor. 'He can't remember much. It happened very quickly. One moment he was using the prod to search for mines and the next there was noise, a white light, and then…' Thomas hesitates, 'and then pain.'

The patient murmurs something else.

'He thinks he was as close to the mine as the door is now.'

Doctor Lavender grimaces. 'Right. Well. I'd better have a look.' He takes a hold of the injured limb and begins to peel away the fragments of scorched cloth.

With a start, Fran realises she is supposed to be taking notes. Quickly she snaps the lid off her pen and starts to write.

Some time later the doctor clicks shut his bag and regards his handiwork with a look of satisfaction. The prisoner's arm is encased in white. The sleeve has been cut away and a bandage coils from wrist to shoulder while the right-hand side of his face gleams with a sticky, translucent cream. As Fran observed the doctor's deft fingers, she couldn't help but wonder about the other prisoner, the one taken to hospital, and how much worse his burns must have been. She was about to ask after him but then, above the doctor's busy hands, she caught hold of Thomas's gaze and immediately, shamefully, the room seemed to lift with sunshine and for a split second she forgot about the accident altogether.

'We need to get you into bed,' Dr Lavender says to the patient. He beckons forward the two army soldiers. 'One of you each side of the prisoner and on the count of three lift him carefully. He mustn't put any weight on that arm.'

As the soldiers approach, the prisoner leans forwards and mutters something to Thomas. 'He's very thirsty,' Thomas says. 'He would like a glass of water.'

'Of course. I should have thought of that before. Please fetch him one.' Reaching for his collar, the doctor unfastens the top button of his shirt. 'And while you're at it, you can bring me a glass too.'

While the soldiers link arms behind the injured man's back, an idea occurs to Fran with the swiftness of a slot machine. Tucking the notepad into her jacket pocket, she clears her throat. 'Actually, Dr Lavender, I haven't drunk anything since breakfast myself. I think I'll fetch some water as well.'

The instant they turn the corner outside the sickbay, Thomas plucks her sleeve. 'You work here?'

'Yes, in the office.'

'You are here, every day?'

'Every day during the week. Not on weekends.'

'You didn't tell me that before. When we met in the street.' He is staring at her, incredulous.

Because I didn't know, she thinks. I didn't know my whereabouts mattered to you. She swallows. 'There wasn't really enough time.'

They have come to a standstill. His gaze feels like the heat of a spotlight. Dipping her head, she looks beyond him to the wall where the paint on the plasterboard is grubby and peeling. She pulls off a flake and rubs the fragment into a powder. Without lifting her eyes, she knows he is still watching her. 'Don't you have to fetch the patient some water?'

He nods slowly.

They walk along the corridor in silence. Just before the exit, Thomas stops again. 'Wait here and I will bring you something to drink.'

'Thank you.'

There's a bubbling, churning sensation in her stomach as if she were about to sit her school certificate again, or speak to a crowded room. She's not sure she can actually drink anything at all, but Thomas has already vanished into a room on their right. Through the half-open door Fran has a glimpse of long trestle tables with benches underneath and cutlery in earthenware pots, knives, forks and spoons standing upright like bunches of silver celery.

He returns a minute later and hands her a glass beaker.

She takes the tiniest sip. 'Where is everyone? Isn't it lunchtime?'

'Everyone is at work. They eat in the evening.'

'No lunch? Golly, I'd starve!' She attempts a smile, although she doesn't feel in the least bit hungry, only a gnawing sensation of the seconds disappearing without being able to pause them or think how to use them best. She wonders whether to ask about the child in the photograph, the one that fell from his pocket, but the subject is too difficult to broach standing in a corridor, and does she, anyway, even want to know the truth? She gazes helplessly into the glass. By the time Thomas has fetched water for the patient and the doctor, she has still barely touched her own.

'Do you want to drink that now?' He gestures at her beaker.

'I'll bring it with me,' Fran says, but the moment they begin the journey back she regrets the decision. Uncontrollably, it seems, her wrist is shaking, and with every pace she leaves a steady trail of drips behind her on the concrete.

At the end of the passage, before they navigate the corner, Thomas touches her arm again.

'Fran.'

She halts, expecting him to say something. Instead, he simply gazes at her face. For a long moment, she feels the blue of his eyes ensnaring her like a net, until eventually she manages to gather herself and make herself walk into the sickbay as though nothing has happened.

Chapter Nine

1 December 1946

The cold is like a clamp, holding everything stiff and still and turning the ground to iron. Already the winter mood seems ominous, as if the bitter weather is merely a precursor, a steely overture, the flexing of a muscle or two, before the time comes for a show of real strength. In the church Fran can see her breath vaporise as clearly as if she were puffing on a cigarette, and when she tries to wiggle her toes, they respond with the dexterity of the sausages frozen inside her mother's icebox. She glances at June and the temperature dips still further. Not so very long ago, June would have been the one nudging Fran, making no attempt to disguise either her yawns or giggles at the vicar's interminable sermons. Now her back is rigid, her face grave, and when Fran's wriggling provokes an audible creak from the wooden pew, she swivels on the polished wood to shoot her sister a humourless stare.

Fran makes a renewed effort to focus on the vicar. He seems to be saying something terribly longwinded about compassion and forgiveness, and it's hard to concentrate. Apart from the arctic conditions, her head is full of thoughts which beat about like starlings; no sooner do they settle than the merest notion or recollection sets them flapping about again and the potential of calm is lost before it has even begun.

Since the encounter in the sickbay she has seen Thomas twice. The first time shouldn't count, not really, because they didn't even have the chance to speak to each other. Yet she revisits the occasion repeatedly like a favourite gramophone record, although unlike the gramophone she has learned to curb the speed of the memory to crawling pace and savour the encounter second by second.

She had just arrived at camp and was wheeling her bicycle towards the office. All at once she realised the prisoner walking straight towards her carrying a crate of turnips was Thomas and watched his face break into a smile. Slowing her steps, she saw him do the same, as if they were both timing their momentum to stop at the precise instant their paths would interlock. The meeting was both so unexpected and engrossing that she wasn't aware of Daisy's approach until a hand caught her shoulder. 'Fran! I've been calling and calling. Didn't you hear?' Linking her arm into Fran's, she chattered on happily and didn't appear to notice Fran's gaze lock on Thomas or the rush of heat as he passed.

The second occasion makes for an even richer source of reminiscence. It occurred only two days ago, on Friday afternoon. There was a rap on the office door and an instant later Thomas was standing in the entrance, explaining he had been sent to fetch the list of the new arrivals for the following week. The whole time Fran was locating the file her every movement felt weighted with significance, as if she were performing on stage in front of an audience of hundreds; and as she handed him the piece of paper the blueness of his eyes struck her so forcefully that she might have been seeing them for the first time. Unable either to look away or to speak, the seconds seemed initially to expand and then simply to stop altogether. It was Thomas who found his voice first.

'Hello, Fran, are you well?'

Fran nodded; her head too full of the sound of his voice to think of a reply. Although the air seemed static with possibility, she worried, for a moment, that the madness was unique to her. Perhaps the fact he had come to the office while she was on her own was simply a matter of chance? Searching for something to say, she started, 'How are you? Have you had any news from your…' when the word 'daughter' arrived and immediately died on her lips. She had tried to forget about the photograph, the possibility he had a child, and couldn't believe the thought had almost slipped out. 'Family,' she finished with emphasis.

There was time to notice the shift in his gaze, a slight intensifying of colour, that may have been surprise or even discomfort, before a crescendo of light, rapid footsteps signalled the return of Daisy from the lavatory. Fran felt the tug of paper through her fingers, before Thomas stepped smartly away from her just as the door to the office opened. 'Thank you, Fräulein.' He was holding the list aloft, as if to demonstrate the reason for his presence. 'I will take the information to Officer Williams.'

After he had gone and Daisy was back in her chair, she straightened a stack of files by rapping the short edge of them sharply against the desk, paused and glanced at Fran. 'He's good-looking that one, don't you think?'

Keeping her gaze focused downwards, Fran carried on writing out an order for medical supplies. 'I suppose so.' Then, with careful nonchalance, 'If you like that kind of thing.'

'*That kind of thing.* You mean a German man?'

Fran shrugged. She was aware that Daisy was now looking at her properly and, despite her efforts, a thin trickle of heat was seeping into her face.

'Well, I think he likes you.'

Fran swallowed hard, making sure to keep the pen moving. 'Why on earth would you say that?'

'I don't know…' Daisy sounded genuinely perplexed. 'I don't know *why* I think it, but I do.'

'Well, *I* think you're talking a load of old rubbish.'

Fran counted three breaths before Daisy picked up her pen and she could let out a long exhalation, releasing the air by degrees so as not to make a noise. Circles of sweat were pooling under her arms, and beneath the heading *Medical Supplies for the week beginning 2*

December 1946, she found she had written *plain absorbent gauze* three times over.

The memory is so consuming that Fran stops listening to the vicar entirely and only becomes aware he must have dropped in something unexpected about the familiar virtues of forgiveness on account of the sudden icy ripple that circumnavigates the church. Gazing around, she sees everyone sitting a little straighter in their pews and focusing on the vicar with unusual interest. Fran plucks at June's elbow. However, when her sister turns, such an expression of distaste is splashed across her face that Fran decides to forgo an explanation and simply shakes her head.

'I realise that some of you may find it harder to heed my words, than others,' the vicar continues, 'but I make this suggestion now that advent has begun, the time when we nurture our own Christmas spirit. As we do, let us not forget the message of our Lord Jesus Christ, who entreated his father to forgive his enemies even as he suffered on the cross. *Forgive them, Father, for they know not what they do.* How much easier should it be for us to take the first step in forgiving *our* enemies, and by so doing take the first step in healing ourselves?' Before anyone dares to suggest an answer to that question, the organ plunges into the final hymn and pulls the muttering congregation to their feet.

After the service, parishioners gather in knots outside the church. It doesn't take Fran long to understand what has happened. 'Can you believe it?' June storms, the moment they are through the door. 'Invite a German prisoner into our home for Christmas! The gall of the man! Tell me how we're supposed to eat Christmas dinner alongside the murderers of our husbands, sons and brothers? I would choke. We would *all* of us choke! It's bad enough seeing them strut about the village, now they're allowed to take walks, and having to hear their horrible language. But asking us to bring them into our own houses, and at Christmas too! It's impossible.'

'I don't think it's impossible, not now.' Fran speaks slowly, recalling a piece she heard on the news only days earlier. As well as allowing prisoners the freedom to roam up to five miles from their camps, the government had decided to relax the regulations preventing civilians from fraternising with them. The change wasn't enormous, but it meant that prisoners could now accept invitations into private homes over the festive period. They were also permitted to send and receive letters from the British public. For a while she had hovered by the wireless, unsure what to make of the announcement that had left her with a vague, rather prickly sensation of both trepidation and anticipation. According to the broadcast, the idea of Christmas visits had come from the clergy, so she supposed it was hardly surprising their vicar wanted to encourage the initiative. Besides, after the awful accident on the beach, some of the villagers might even be sympathetic to the idea.

'I mean impossible for us,' June continues. 'For any normal person. How can we welcome these beasts when they have caused such suffering? Especially at Christmas. Christmas is when, is when…' Without warning the anger evaporates and her voice collapses to a whisper. 'Is when the missing will be worst of all.' Twisting away, she draws a sleeve across her eyes.

Fran lays a hand on her sister's arm. The graveyard has the same icy dankness as the church, the sky the same grey as the arched stone roof, while under June's skin she can feel misery pulsing like a second heartbeat. As Fran gazes at the parishioners huddled among the tombstones, the air swollen with their muttered indignation, she's overwhelmed by the absurdity of her feeling for Thomas with the totality and suddenness of a bucket of water tipped over her head. She's shivering both with cold and a new sense of hopelessness when there's a crunch of gravel behind her.

'Fran!' Daisy's voice is an unexpected shot of colour. 'I thought it was you. Mother and I normally go to the church in our village but the vicar's away, so we came here. I'm rather glad we did! There's nothing like a bit of controversy to get everyone talking, is there?'

Fran smiles despite herself. 'This is my sister, June,' she offers, but June has disengaged from Fran's touch and is walking straight-backed towards a group of villagers.

'Oh dear,' Daisy says. 'Have I caused offence?'

'She was upset by the vicar's announcement. She's… we're all struggling to cope without our brother, so the idea of German prisoners sharing Christmas with us is unthinkable to her.'

'To her, but not to you?' Daisy's eyes are wide and curious.

'I don't know…' Fran drops her gaze to a nearby gravestone. *Albert Jones 1852–1924*. Already the lettering is worn by rain and crumbly yellow moss. She wonders what Albert would have to say about the vicar's speech, whether he would say that life was too short to waste with hatred and bitterness, or if he would consider it weak and unprincipled to befriend the very people with whom you were so recently at war. And what would his answers have been when he was alive, before he fully understood the truth of his mortality?

'I suppose,' Fran says slowly, 'that I don't consider the German prisoners are to blame for Robbie dying, or even the war, in the same way that June does.' Or perhaps, it occurs to her, she's deliberately choosing not to think that way because of Thomas.

To change the subject, she looks around the churchyard. 'Where's your mother? I should like to meet her.'

'Over there.' Daisy gestures towards a woman wearing a hand-some camel-coloured coat who is standing beside the gate that leads onto the lane. 'Come on, I'll introduce you. I've spoken so much about you and already told her you must come for afternoon tea soon. I must warn you though, she's recently fallen completely in love and hardly speaks about anything else!'

Fran stares.

Daisy laughs. 'It's perfectly all right. My father died so long ago I can barely remember him. I've been dying for Mother to meet someone else, and at long last she has. It's really quite wonderful to see her so happy.'

'And is she talking to him now?'

'What? Oh no, I don't think so.' Daisy peers towards the gate, where a man on the far side of it has just begun to stroll away. Her brow puckers. 'I've no idea who *he* is.' Then, raising her arm, 'Mother! Do come over here and meet my lovely friend Frances.'

Daisy's mother glances at the retreating figure before pulling the camel coat about her more tightly and walking towards them.

'Fran must come to tea, don't you think?' Daisy says the moment the introductions have been made.

'Why of course, that would be delightful.' The reply is distracted.

'What about this afternoon?'

'This afternoon?' Daisy's mother looks amazed. She gazes first at Fran and then at Daisy as if she must have missed something. Close up, Fran sees she has the same wide face as her daughter, with hair that must once have been the same ginger-gold but now is faded and flecked with grey threads.

'I'm sure you're very busy and today would be dreadfully inconvenient,' Fran says. The suddenness of the invitation has taken her aback and, despite Daisy's comment about her mother's new love, all Fran can see is a veil of anxiety.

'No, we're not busy at all.' Daisy is insistent. 'And my brother will be at home this afternoon. I'm certain he would like to make your acquaintance too. Mother' – she prods the camel coat to get her mother's attention – 'it would be all right for Fran to come to tea today, wouldn't it? About three o'clock?'

'Yes, of course.' Daisy's mother still sounds rather unfocused.

There's a short pause. Daisy frowns. She peeks at the lane beyond the church that is now beginning to fill with the departing congregation. 'Mother, who were you talking to at the gate? Who was that man?

'Nobody. Nobody you know. Just a doctor.'

'Was he in church?'

'No, apparently he was visiting a patient and happened to be passing.' *Apparently* is slightly weighted, laced with an emphasis that's almost, but not quite, unnoticeable. Fran is wondering whether Daisy heard the inflection too, when, as if to draw a line, Daisy's mother gathers herself and beams at Fran with a smile that seems to light up the whole churchyard. 'Do please come to tea this afternoon. We'd all be very pleased to see you.'

Chapter Ten

Daisy's house is big and square and full of tall sash windows with glossy green ivy curling between the frames. When Fran presses the doorbell, she hears it reverberate through the bowels of the building, and the slap of footsteps on tiles lasts for several seconds before the door swings open. To Fran's surprise, the person standing before her is neither Daisy nor Daisy's mother but a housekeeper, complete with a button-up black dress and full-length apron. She takes Fran's coat, which is damp with the snowflakes that have been falling ever since the church service finished, and gestures at a pair of double doors. 'Mrs Travis-Jones is waiting in the drawing room.' As if on cue, a grandfather clock rings in the hour.

Fran hesitates. Should she go in herself, or wait to be shown in? She's still hovering as Daisy appears behind her with the rapidity of a gust of wind.

'Poor you, did you get totally drenched? How awful the weather has turned out to be! If I had known before, I should never have suggested you come today.'

Fran reaches for her hair and touches a veil of ice. The walk from the bus stop was longer than she anticipated. She had been only too aware of the wind seeping between the folds of her coat, of the flakes oozing into her shoes, but until now she hadn't considered the effect the snow would have on her appearance. 'Heavens, I must be a frightful mess! Whatever will your mother think?'

'Not at all.' Daisy contemplates Fran in a way that is half amused and half something Fran can't quite identify. 'You look marvellous, all bright-eyed and bushy-tailed. And your cheeks have got a glow that I can only manage by spending hours in front of a mirror with the rouge. Come on!' Before Fran can respond, Daisy grabs Fran's wrist and sweeps her through the doors.

The drawing room is thick with curtains and rugs and the snap of logs burning behind a complicated wrought-iron guard. Fran perches on the edge of the sofa and accepts cucumber and crab-paste sandwiches. Daisy and her mother sustain the conversation by debating a recent talk at the Women's Institute on the virtues of growing onions, the dreariness of rationing, and Daisy and Fran's vital work at the camp. Although the discourse is pleasant enough, Fran can't help but sense there's a purpose to the occasion and either she has missed it or it has yet to materialise. A rather splendid gramophone is visible on a corner table. Daisy, she remembers, had at one time spoken of teaching her to jitterbug; however the idea of dancing seems to have been forgotten about entirely.

She's draining her second helping of tea when a light tapping on the door cuts through Daisy's account of how she almost muddled an order for semolina with one for powdered milk. At exactly the same instant that Daisy and her mother set down their cups, a young man with a stooped, apologetic frame enters the room.

Daisy bounces to her feet immediately. 'Frances, may I present my brother, Martin.'

Fran finds she is glued to the sofa cushion. Just as Daisy's smile is beginning to fade and Fran is finally able to move, Martin steps hurriedly forwards. 'Please don't get up. Absolutely no need at all.' Close up, Fran can see the faintest smudges of blue around the bone of his right eye socket and the bulge that spoils the line of his nose. His gaze locks with Fran's, the entreaty plain.

'It's a pleasure to meet you, Martin,' Fran says carefully. She's aware of Daisy's glance flicking back and forth between them as if trying to locate a station on the wireless.

'Martin had an accident a few weeks ago,' Daisy says, apparently having decided that Fran must be suspicious of Martin's appearance.

'He tripped and fell down a flight of steps when he was out walking after dark. You mustn't think he's the type to get into fights.'

'Of course not,' Fran says. Then to Martin, 'I'm very sorry to hear that. I do hope you weren't badly hurt?'

'Just a few cuts and bruises.' He finds her eyes again. 'I was lucky, all things considered. It could have been a lot worse.'

There's a pause.

'Well, then,' his mother's voice contains a trace of impatience, 'now that's all out of the way, please do eat something, Martin. It's nearly four o'clock and Irene will need to clear soon. In fact' – standing up, she glances sideways at her daughter – 'I may just go and see where Irene is.'

As soon as her mother has left the room, Daisy pours Fran yet more tea before embarking on a monologue that moves rapidly from Martin's work – *He's a solicitor, you know. Training practically finished and soon to qualify with the most wonderful firm* – toys briefly with the weather – *Quite alarming, the gardener insists we're in for a hellish few months* – before alighting on the subject of the cinema. *A Girl in a Million was terribly funny and just the thing to brighten up the cold climate.* At this point, Daisy leans slightly forwards. 'Have you seen it yet, Fran?'

Fran shakes her head.

All at once Daisy becomes preoccupied with a spot on her skirt, as if worried she might have spilled something. 'And what about you, Martin?' she says without looking at him. 'Joan Greenwood is quite hilarious, and I know how much you adore her!'

An in-breath of perfect quiet fills the room, a moment in which the aim of the conversation, of the whole invitation in fact, becomes as clear as the crystal rose bowl glinting at Fran from the sideboard. Fran drops her gaze and busies her own hands by dropping a sugar lump into her tea. She daren't even glance at Martin. It's bad enough to listen to the embarrassment in his voice as he murmurs that he has *been too busy recently to even think of going to the cinema.*

'Well fancy that!' A pause. Then, Daisy says, 'Please don't think me rude, Fran. I must disappear for a second or two to see if Mother needs any help.' A second later the smooth mahogany doors click behind her, leaving Fran and Martin in a pool of stillness.

Fran stirs her tea, focusing on the swirl of brown liquid that is now both too cold and too sweet to drink. Martin coughs gently. 'Sorry about that. Believe it or not, Daisy has no idea how dreadfully obvious she can be. I very much hope you'll take it as a compliment – the rather clumsy attempt at matchmaking, I mean. She's terribly protective about her older brother, although I'm certain that sort of thing is supposed to work the other way around!'

Fran lifts her head. Martin is propped against the mantelpiece, regarding her with a concerned sort of intensity. From where she's sitting, his bruising would be invisible to anyone who didn't know about the incident in the alley. 'Is that why you didn't tell her the real reason for your injuries?'

There's a beat of silence.

'She would only worry,' Martin says finally. 'And my mother would worry even more when I've already caused them quite enough heartache. I'm really very grateful you didn't say anything to give the game away.'

Abandoning the pretence of the tea, Fran deposits the cup and saucer on the tray. 'Daisy mentioned you have a problem with your heart. Is that why those men picked on you?'

This time the silence is longer. Martin gazes at his shoes until the memory of the accusations flung about the dark lane answers Fran's question. 'That's dreadful!' she bursts out.

Martin half-shrugs his shoulder.

'They attacked you for being a coward, when you were too ill to fight!'

'It's not so much an illness,' Martin murmurs, 'more of a defect with one of the valves, I believe. I suppose from their perspective it must seem rather convenient, rather *wet*, and I imagine they've seen some pretty awful things. It's only natural to want to take it out on someone. I can hardly bear to think how easy it's been for me.'

Fran stares at him. 'You sound like you think you deserved – what was it they said? *A punch or two!*'

'No, no, I wouldn't go that far.' Martin jabs the fire with a poker so that sparks cascade from a log. 'I only mean I understand how they feel. How pathetic I must seem. Look' – he clunks the fire iron back on its stand and straightens up – 'let's change the subject. I know how awfully tactless my sister is, but I haven't seen that film she mentioned, and a good laugh could be just the thing to raise the spirits. So, if you might be persuaded to take a chance on an evening with a bit of an odd crock like me...'

Fran blinks. It takes her a second to realise Martin really does want to go on a date with her and another to understand this is as close to asking her out as he dares to venture. She considers afresh the lanky frame that looks as if it must either be propped against a wall or ducking to avoid a beam, the fairish, floppy hair and the eyes, nose and mouth which all combine to convey a sort of hopeful kindness.

While she watches, his expression falters. 'Forgive me, I got carried away. There's absolutely no reason at all why a smashing girl like you would be remotely interested in going out with someone like me. Please forget I ever...'

'It's not that.'

She tries to gather herself, desperate both to end the conversation and not to crush his feelings. 'I don't mind that you... what you... I mean about your heart.' She takes a breath, her cheeks burning. 'But I hardly know you. This is the first time we've met, properly anyway, so stepping out together seems rather sudden, that's all.'

'Of course!' He nods eagerly. 'Of course. Perhaps once we... if we get to know each other a little better, you might feel—'

'Perhaps.' She dips her head again. What would she say if Thomas asked her out? If he wasn't German. Or if the war had never happened. If Robbie was settling into a job, about to marry a lovely girl who laughed at his awful jokes, instead of buried inside a French graveyard. She was certain beyond a shadow of a doubt that she wouldn't tell Thomas she didn't know him well enough to accept his invitation.

The double doors open to Daisy's gay voice. 'Not interrupting anything, I hope!'

Fran lifts her gaze in time to see Martin glare at his sister. Smoothing her skirt, she gets to her feet. 'I must be going. Thank you so much for inviting me.'

'Can I walk you to the bus stop? It's getting awfully dark out there.'

She throws him a smile, quick and perfunctory. 'It's quite all right, Martin. I'm sure I can manage.'

'Of course.' She doesn't have to look at his face to know that he is nodding again. 'Well, I very much hope we'll see other again before too long.'

Outside, the snow has stopped falling. Thick white fingers lie the length of the garden fence while the carpet of flakes swallows the creak and groan of Fran's footsteps. The Travis-Jones's gardener might be right, the next few months may well be hellish, but for now the world is a cake transformed by sugar icing.

At the bus stop she buries her hands deeply into her coat pockets and waits. The house was quite extraordinary. She never dreamed Daisy came from such an affluent home. The rugs, the gleaming wood, and the abundance of *things* seemed almost exotic. For a moment, she imagines telling her parents she is to marry Martin. She pictures their reaction, their astonishment, their *delight*, she could do so well for herself. And not only for herself; marrying Martin could give the whole of her family a sense of security that has been glaringly absent since their father fell ill.

Fran stamps her feet. The air is becoming raw. Merely breathing makes her lungs burn, as if the sensations of hot and cold have met at the same point and become indistinguishable. She recalls Martin's long-limbed frame, his kindness. She had meant to rebuff his invitation, gently of course, but also definitively. Instead she seems to have managed to do quite the opposite. To have left him hoping she will change her mind when, despite his many virtues, there really is no hope at all.

Chapter Eleven

For hours Martin has lain awake, staring into the dark until he has begun to imagine pinpricks of stars. The bedsheets are tangled from his tossing and twisting, and he has felt his feet turn to ice then all at once become too hot. He is certain there are voices in the drawing room, though he has no recollection of hearing footsteps on the path or the suddenness of the doorbell. Perhaps Daisy is talking to his mother. He glances at his bedside table and the clock winks back. Nearly one o'clock; unusually late for either his sister or his mother to be up, particularly on a Sunday.

Martin keeps still and listens properly. The drawing room is beneath his bedroom and the conversation is seeping through the floorboards in little gusts and eddies. The words are indistinct, but the timbre is intense and – he is certain – the speakers male and female. Deflated, he rolls onto his side. The answer to the mystery is obvious. Herbert. His mother's new friend. In fact, Martin is almost sure, his mother's lover. He wonders at the strangeness of the phrase, examines his reaction and finds he is adjusting to the idea, even if he cannot yet match the wholescale enthusiasm of his sister. At any rate, Herbert, with his silver-grey moustache, his solid grey suits, and his own substantial grey house, does not appear to be a risky prospect. No need for Martin – so his mother keeps telling him – to be quite so concerned. Hunching the blankets over his shoulder he watches as snowflakes begin to meander past the window, seemingly with only the haziest notion of gravity. It's a good thing the weather stayed dry long enough for Fran's journey home.

He recognised her the instant that he stepped into the drawing room. The girl from the alley. The feisty, determined angel who saved, if not his life, at least the symmetry of his features. He cannot remember ever having seen a face that holds his attention so completely, so raptly, as if his eyes have found an interlocking piece of puzzle that makes looking anywhere but at her impossible.

Fran.

Again.

How quickly his thoughts revert to her. To the same agitations that have occupied all of these last sleepless hours. He groans out loud. Why on earth did he ask her out to the pictures so soon? Make such a fool of himself and ruin whatever tiny chance he might have had?

An upsurge of voices penetrates the oak boards. At the sound of his own name, he sits up. 'Martin,' he hears his mother say, he *thinks* he hears his mother say, 'Martin must not know!' Which is odd, because he does know about Herbert; his mother has made no secret of her happiness, or indeed the evenings that turn into mornings with only the shared night in her bedroom to separate them.

The rumble of reply is unintelligible.

'... his heart,' Martin picks out, and rises a little straighter in the bed. Then, 'that blasted report!' Something indecipherable, followed by 'Serious.' Finally, louder and more highly pitched, 'Very serious indeed!'

There is sudden quiet, as if the occupants of the drawing room have realised their error. Gripping the blanket with one hand, Martin slips the other between the buttons of his pyjama top so that his palm rests on the skin shielding his left ribcage.

Very serious indeed.

Perhaps instead of revealing the extent of his disability to him, she has unburdened herself to Herbert? Beneath his fingertips, tucked under their bony roof, his coronary muscles are contracting and relaxing, his pulse is chugging gamely onwards. But for how much longer. Years? Months? Not weeks, surely? He would know if he was so ill that his heart was on the verge of expiring altogether. Wouldn't he?

'Don't touch me!'

Martin's eyes shoot wide open.

'I said, no!'

A gasped scream is alarmingly audible. In one continuous movement he is swinging out of bed, grabbing his dressing gown and diving towards the bedroom door. He is still too late. By the time he strides to the top of the staircase there is no sign of Herbert, or of anyone else. Only the sound of the front door slamming and bouncing in the woodwork.

Tightening the sash cord around his waist, he descends the staircase slowly. For all its flaws and frailties, his heart is certainly thundering now.

'Mother?'

The drawing room is dark, save for a single side lamp pooling yellow on the Chinese rug. His mother sits on the edge of the big armchair, the heels of her hands pressed into her eyes. From the doorway, Martin can see her shoulders are shaking. He is about to switch on the overhead light, then thinks better of it.

'Mother' – he clears his throat – 'was that Herbert who left just now?'

She lifts her head. For a split second she fixes him with a gaze that appears to be one of sorrow, almost pity.

Martin swallows. 'You're crying. Has Herbert upset you?'

'Herbert? Good heavens, no. I'm a little over-tired, that's all.'

'Someone was here. I heard them.'

Her focus sharpens. 'What did you hear?'

I heard you talking about me, Martin wants to tell her. *About my heart. I heard you say how serious it is. And then I heard an argument. You said, 'Don't touch me!'* The huge frame of the chair and the dim luminescence of the lamp make his mother seem both old and young, the always loved familiar figure and at the same time a stranger with a life woven from threads of a tapestry that have nothing to do with him at all. As he watches, she passes her right fingers slowly across her temple as if to erase whatever she might be thinking.

'Only raised voices,' Martin lies. 'The front door shutting.'

'He was an old friend,' his mother says. 'An unexpected visit.' She gets up and pokes the fire, the same diversion, Martin remembers, he employed earlier that afternoon with Fran, except that now the logs are grey and cold and prodding them only produces a cloud of dead embers and dust. 'It's very late. Time for bed.' As she turns, Martin sees she is wearing her long woollen housecoat over her nightdress.

'Mother, the report the doctor wrote about my heart…'

'What of it?' The tartness returns.

'Do we still have it?'

'Somewhere in my papers. I doubt we'll need it again, but I can find it if we ever do.' She snaps the switch on the lamp flex. 'Bedtime now.'

She waits for him to move into the hallway before shutting the drawing-room door and following him up the stairs. By the top step she dabs a kiss on his cheek – a brief, papery sensation that smells of rosewater. 'Goodnight, darling.'

Moonlight spills onto the counterpane while Martin lies rigid with sleeplessness. He wonders if self-preservation is in fact the cause of his insomnia, a fear deep in his subconscious that he might not wake up. Perhaps now that he has even more reason to suspect the true extent of his infirmity he will never sleep normally again. Eventually, he extracts his hand from under his pyjama top, pushes back the covers, and reaches for his dressing gown.

The house is heavy with the night. He creeps down the staircase, pausing on every creak, and when he finally reaches the hallway heads towards an alcove next to the kitchen. Not large enough to constitute an actual room, the space contains an old cane chair and mahogany desk on which a line of box-files is propped like books against the far wall. For as long as he can remember, this has been his mother's office, her engine room, her place where *she must not be disturbed*, although recently she no longer buries herself quite so often with her boxes of lists and papers.

There is a desk lamp with a green glass shade. Martin angles the light towards the files where it shines on peeling labels marked *Finance, House Maintenance, Garden Maintenance* and *Children* written in his mother's slanting print. The children's file is the largest, bulging with so much paper an elastic band has been employed to keep the sides closed. Inside he finds smallpox vaccination records for himself and Daisy, their school certificates and a jumbled stack of school reports: *Martin is thorough and careful in his work. His writing and arithmetic are neatly presented, and he always tries his best…* He flicks through the remaining pile. At the bottom he discovers a Mothering Sunday card from Daisy bearing pink tissue roses, one of which has been reattached with Sellotape. And beneath everything else an unmarked manila folder.

The medical documentation is merely one page. *Confidential,* the typeface warns. *Findings of the Medical Board held at City of London. Martin Travis-Jones was medically examined on 10 August 1941 and found to be…* Two options are given: *(A) Fit for military service,* or *(B) Unfit.* Dr Sands has ticked the box *Unfit* with a decisive blue stroke and given as the reason *dilated cardiomyopathy*.

Martin turns the page over. The reverse is blank. No details are provided. Maybe the gravity of his condition doesn't require further elaboration. Perhaps if he were to research the meaning of dilated cardiomyopathy, it would be all too obvious why his mother has chosen to use instead the vague terminology of *weak heart*. Maybe she specifically asked the doctor not to record the extent of the illness on the form.

Martin continues to stare at the paper. More confusing than his actual diagnosis is the reference to the City of London Medical Board. He doesn't remember travelling to London; indeed, he is certain the appointment was local. And the doctor is not familiar either. He has a vague recollection that he found the doctor's name amusing in some way, and it is hard to see what he might possibly have considered entertaining about *Dr Sands*.

Carefully Martin refolds the medical certificate. As he is returning the document to the file, he notices the manila folder was not the final item after all. A piece of paper is lying print side down, the blank white face giving the illusion of the bottom of the box. Martin picks up the page. Then he inhales sharply. Although he lifts the document closer to the green glass of the lampshade, there is no doubt about what he has found.

He is holding a death certificate.

The death certificate of his brother.

Frederick Travis-Jones died on 11 January 1925 from complications arising from measles when Martin was eighteen months, Daisy only just born, and little Frederick himself barely four years old.

Martin sits very still. The house seems to be holding its breath. He can hear the thick tick of the grandfather clock nudging the seconds forwards, but the sound feels artificial, as if time might instead have stopped altogether. Tributaries of the new reality soak into his brain like ink carrying a stain through blotting paper. For the very first part of his life it appears he had an older brother. Yet his earliest memories only feature Daisy: sand, squabbles, ball games and baths, with never any mention there could have been a third to lead the pack.

Martin shuts his eyes. Somewhere inaccessible is the vaguest sensation of closed doors, of blacked-out rooms, the sound of crying. A drifting, faraway notion that is as nebulous as a sea-fret and may be no more than the power of suggestion from the page in his hand. From the hall the clock strikes the half hour, but he has no sense of which particular hour that might be. The night has become its own landscape, alien and disorientating, in which he feels utterly lost.

Eventually, Martin extinguishes the green lamp and retraces his steps upstairs. Stilling his mind is now out of the question. He pads the length of the landing, eases Daisy's bedroom door just enough to spy the sleeping form of his sister, the soft slump and rise of the blankets. Already she thinks his health consumes him. He knows she worries about the length of time he spends on his own, his fixation with his daily walks, his seeming inability to find a girlfriend. What will she say if he wakes her now to discuss the oddities of his medical report, their mother's late-night visitor, and the death of another child before she was even born? That he has become obsessed, no doubt. That during the war it cannot have been unusual for forms printed for the City of London to have been used by other medical boards. That their mother is a grown woman who is entitled to receive as many late-night visitors as she wishes. That the loss of little Frederick is tragic but hardly urgent news.

That it is the middle of the night and they should both be sound asleep.

Martin returns to his bed and perches, shivering, on the edge of his mattress. A snowy chill is stealing through the cracks in the window frames and walls, but his trembling is more about the slivers of uncertainty residing in his gut than the temperature of the room. What would it have been like to have a brother? And how would they have all coped if Frederick had been sent to war, if Frederick had been killed, while Dr Sands declared his younger brother unfit to even raise a musket?

After a moment Martin pulls a shoebox from under the bed. Stacked inside are his diaries from when he first started keeping one at the age of fourteen. It takes no more than a minute to locate the volume for 1941 and less to find the entry for 10 August:

Unfit for medical service! Turns out I have a weak heart. Mother is delighted because she thinks it's a better option than me getting shot to bits by the Hun. Doesn't seem all that good news to me. Can't say I fancied going to the front, but a chap has got to play his part. King and country and all that. Not sure how I can serve the King with a dicky heart or even quite how crocked I am as doctor rather vague about it all. Time will tell I suppose. PS Doctor Dandy – like the comic, though not exactly a barrel of laughs today.

Martin climbs into bed still clutching the diary. If any of his questions have simple answers, at present they elude him; and for reasons he can't articulate, the prospect of asking his mother about them fills him with a strange and uncomfortable sense of foreboding.

Chapter Twelve

14 December 1946

Two weeks later and the inch of snow has multiplied to twelve. The salt marsh stretches clean and white into a colourless sky, while in the distance the sea is a cold grey line. Cycling is too dangerous, so Fran walks to work, the murky December dawn feeling like the dead of night. Often, she is passed by trucks from the camp, their headlights flooding the dark with a temporary burst of yellow. The prisoners bear shovels and pickaxes to throw sand on the road and dig out the snowdrifts before they start their real day's labour. All the forecasts are grim. Daisy's gardener is not the only one who seems to fear the weather predictions more than he ever feared the war, and amongst unease about fuel supplies and shortages Fran also worries about the seals, whose pups arriving on the spit are about to encounter the bleakest winter anyone can remember.

Now she blows hard on her hands before grasping the tree trunk that is jammed halfway through the open door of the kitchen.

'Push!'

'I am pushing. Pull harder!'

Fran yanks and heaves and finally the branches bend enough to allow the bushy bulk to slither through the gap. One final tug and she is able to rest the fir upright against the table. June comes in, thumps shut the back door and brushes a shower of snow from the shoulders of her coat. For a moment they gaze at the tree in silence. Fran is well aware of the thoughts crowding her sister's head, because she is thinking them too.

'Ready?' she says instead. 'Last part.'

Together they haul the fir into the sitting room and manoeuvre the trunk into the stand. By the time they are finished, pine needles and twigs gild June's hair while her blouse has pulled out of her waistband. Fran imagines her own appearance must be similarly dishevelled. This is their third Christmas without Robbie. The first December, they didn't bother with a tree at all, letting the solstice suck the light from the house without attempting to mitigate the gloom with baubles and coloured paper. For the second, Fran enlisted the assistance of a neighbour to place a small tree in the kitchen. Now the two of them have managed a much larger specimen on their own, although, she could, she is very well aware, have enlisted Martin's support.

A few days earlier, Daisy suggested they both join Martin for his evening walk. The night was unusually beautiful and still, with a low, fattish moon hanging silver over the frozen countryside. Immediately, Daisy looped her hand through Martin's right arm, so that when he also crooked his left elbow it seemed the only polite thing for Fran to do was slip her own arm through his. Although initially awkward, the brush of Martin's jacket, the proximity of his voice, soon took on a companionable warmth, as if the three of them were linked together like a trio of siblings or cousins. Like this, they climbed the hill and gazed across the snow-cloaked town. On one occasion, Martin twisted around and looked at Fran, opening his mouth as if to speak, but something in her face must have silenced him because he pressed his lips together again and fixed his eyes upon the view. Fran was certain, however, that if she were to ask for assistance with a Christmas tree he would agree to help before she had even finished posing the question.

'Well, look what my clever girls have done!'

Fran and June wheel around to see their father standing in the doorway, leaning heavily upon their mother.

'I'm quite all right.' He raises a flattened palm to stop his daughters darting forwards. 'Now...' Fran sees him nod at their mother before she helps him shuffle across the floor, and he sinks into an armchair. The effort leaves him gasping; the familiar, ominous rattle of his chest audible on every breath.

'He wanted to come downstairs to see the tree. The bedroom has become so boring.' If their mother sounds apologetic, it's because she's aware – as they all are – of the effort it will take to get him back up the stairs.

Fran fetches a blanket. Daisy more cushions. They wrap the blanket over their father's legs, position the cushions behind his back. As Fran tucks tartan wool under his knees, he catches her hand and squeezes her fingers. A gesture in place of the words for which he doesn't have the oxygen. Before the gassing that destroyed his lungs, her father used to have the same bronze hair as her own, the same hazel eyes sharp with energy and laughter – Fran has seen the photographs, faded and rucked yet still alive with the eagerness of youth. These days most people would mistake him for her grandfather. Hoping that sea air might be beneficial, they moved to the coast they loved shortly before Robbie joined up, and for a while the difficulty of taking on a new home in the middle of a war seemed to have paid off. Yet recently her father's chest problems have worsened again. When he inhales, the air sounds as heavy as water and on the exhale rough as sandpaper. She can hear the pain it inflicts to pump the breath through his body, the wretched graunch his lungs make, like an engine about to fall apart.

June places a whisky by his elbow. No doubt the alcohol will make him cough all night, but for now he is pleased to have it. He raises the glass towards the tree.

'Let's see' – a wheeze, a pause – 'the decorations then.'

After Fran and June have strewn tinsel, hung baubles and fixed the ancient fairy doll to the highest branch, their mother brings in dinner to balance on their laps. 'We'll eat in here and enjoy the tree,' she says, although they all know the real reason for avoiding another journey to the kitchen. As soon as she has finished, she puts her plate down on the carpet. Her own breathing suddenly sounds a little shallow. 'I have something to tell you.'

Fran stops eating. The 'you' she sees is herself and June. Not their father, who is continuing to chew and swallow tiny mouthfuls of corned beef fritters.

'I expect you remember what the vicar said, about inviting a German prisoner for Christmas Day?' Her pause leaves insufficient time for a reply. 'Well, your father and I have been giving it a lot of thought and we've started to come around to the idea.'

'*Started to come around to the idea.* What in heaven's name does that mean?' June's hand flies to the collar of her blouse.

Her mother looks down, then up again. 'I mean, we think it's a good idea.'

Fran's eyes dart to June and back to her mother.

'We have to remember these German boys probably have families just like us at home. Most of them didn't want to fight a war any more than Robbie did. And the best chance of there never being another war is if people, ordinary people like us, can bring ourselves to treat them the way we would want the German people to treat our boys, our sons, our *brothers*' – this last is directed at June – 'if they were the captured ones over there.'

'But the Germans started the war, Mother!' June has got to her feet and is pacing short, furious strides. 'They're beasts, animals. Worse than animals! Look what they did to the Jews! To British prisoners of war! Thousands of people either gassed to death or starved. How can you say the German prisoners of war are like our own soldiers? We fought the war to put a stop to their *evil*. And Robbie *died*, Mother. He *died*. Blown to pieces on a French beach to free a country that Germany had taken by force. How can you want to invite one of *them* to spend Christmas with us when Robbie will never, ever have another Christmas here or with anyone else.' She stops. Her face is wet and crimson.

'I know Robbie died, June. There's not a single minute, a second, goes by that I—'

'Then don't invite the people that killed him into our home! It's bad enough that she' – her gaze swings to Fran – 'works in that camp!'

'The boys in the camp, they didn't kill Robbie, June. They were probably made to fight by the Nazis.'

'How do you know? You don't know! You can't know! And if they didn't kill Robbie, they killed other people, whether they were made to fight or not. Other people's sons and brothers.'

There's a throbbing silence.

Fran can't speak. Her tongue is dry as grit. The argument is dragging her own dilemmas into the open and laying them bare as bone. Dare she allow herself to believe that Thomas was caught up in a war he wanted no part of simply because of where he was born?

'I killed Germans.' Their father's voice is barely audible.

He breathes in.

Pauses.

Breathes out.

'In 1916. I had no choice.' Another gap. Another jagged wave of air. 'War makes animals of us all.'

Another silence.

June stops pacing.

Fran gazes at her father, at his damaged body sunken in the armchair. She sees sadness in his eyes and deep, persistent grief, but, remarkably, no bitterness. An ache like hot ash stings in her throat. Eventually she says to her mother, 'Have you made up your mind?'

The seconds stretch until the answer is obvious.

June storms from the room, slamming the door behind her.

Neither her mother or father move a muscle, and all at once Fran understands they both anticipated, even expected, this reaction. That they have talked about the decision upstairs, quietly between themselves, and it is somehow strange to glimpse the workings of their relationship, to realise how much must pass between them of which she and June are utterly unaware.

'What do you think, Fran? Could you bear to have a German prisoner in our house at Christmas?' Her mother's voice is steady.

Fran imagines being with Thomas in their sitting room. Hours of delight. More than that – days of pleasure – given the weeks of anticipation beforehand and the memory to relish afterwards. But the question is a serious one and not to be confused with her feelings for Thomas. Could she welcome not Thomas but rather an unknown German, any prisoner of war, into their home?

The seconds tick.

Then, 'As long as he doesn't have a black armband.'

An armband would indicate a Nazi sympathiser. Although Fran has spied only one or two prisoners wearing them at the camp, the sight caused her such overwhelming revulsion that momentarily she even considered whether June might be right and she ought to resign her job. The other prisoners, though, she had told herself, were different. A German soldier was not, necessarily, a Nazi.

Her mother's mouth twists. 'I can't imagine *anyone* would welcome Nazi supporters. I don't suppose they would even be allowed out of the camp. I'll write to Major Markham telling him we would like to invite one German prisoner who has shown no sympathy whatsoever to the Hitler regime. You can take the letter with you in the morning. Perhaps a few other families will do the same, once they know what we've done. I can't stand' – all at once her voice frays high and brittle – 'I can't stand this suffering any longer. War after war! All these lives lost and ruined. And the politicians seem to make it worse. The only way to stop it is by people learning how to get along with each other. To understand that all these boys, German, English, French, are somebody's sons.'

Fran nods, but her thoughts are racing ahead. Should she suggest her mother make the invite specific, give her Thomas's name? But how to do so without arousing suspicion. *Good heavens, how do*

*you know him, Frances? How much time have you spent together? Do
you like him a lot?* Possible ways of broaching the matter are on the
tip of her tongue when the sitting-room door reopens. June hovers
in the entrance, gripping the handle as if the door were trying to
fly away from her. 'So, it's decided then?'

Three pairs of eyes turn in her direction.

'I was listening outside. You all sound ridiculous! Believing you
can tell the difference between a good German soldier and a bad
German soldier merely by an armband! Do you honestly believe
it's that simple? That *people* are that simple? You could say the ones
wearing the armbands have at least stuck to their guns, while the
others have just decided on the best way to play the system! What
you should be asking yourself is how many of these prisoners
would be loyal Nazis if Germany had *won* the war? The answer is
probably all of them, including whoever takes Robbie's place at our
Christmas table!' She pivots on her heel. A moment later they hear
footsteps on the staircase, the slam of her bedroom door.

Fran's mother looks at Fran's father then gets to her feet. 'I think
I'd better write that invitation now. Before I change my mind.'

Fran opens her mouth, and finds she has no words. Later, in
the kitchen, she is handed an unsealed envelope.

'You can read it if you like.'

Fran extracts the sheet. Pale blue Basildon Bond. Her mother's
best.

Dear Major Markham,

*After the church service the Sunday before last, it was
suggested that local families might be willing to invite a
prisoner from a local camp to spend Christmas Day with
them. Although I confess to having been initially surprised at
such an idea, my husband and I have come to the conviction
our greatest hope of future peace lies in reconciling with*

those German men and women who, like my own family, were forced into war by the evil ambitions of an evil man. We would therefore like to offer the hand of friendship and an invitation to our modest Christmas celebrations to any young German prisoner from your camp whom you are confident is without any Nazi sympathies.

Yours faithfully,
Miriam Taylor

Any young German prisoner. What are the chances that prisoner will be Thomas? One in twenty? One in fifty? Fran turns the page over, even though she knows nothing is written on the back. She should have spoken up more quickly, while she had the chance.

'Is it all right, do you think? Perhaps I shouldn't have said quite so much and kept to the essentials?' Her mother's brow creases, as if the phrasing is the thing that matters the most.

'It's perfect.' Fran says. 'And the vicar would be delighted to know his sermon has had such an effect.' Folding the paper, she slots the note back inside the delicately lined envelope. 'I'll keep hold of the letter, shall I? To make certain I don't forget to take it with me in the morning.'

As she is heading out of the kitchen, her mother's voice snags her from behind. 'I wonder who we'll get?'

Fran stops.

'Which prisoner, I mean. I wonder what he'll be like. Whether we'll take a shine to him or not?'

Fran doesn't turn around.

Her pulse jumps to her throat.

'I hope so.'

Once in her bedroom she extracts the invitation. On a separate sheet of paper, she experiments with replicating her mother's handwriting, copying the steady, round cursive, the small flourish on the tails of the *f*s and the *g*s, the slightly wayward dotting of the *i*s. Her idea is to insert a sentence at the end of the paragraph, *I have heard a prisoner by the name of Thomas might be suitable.* Or *my daughter, Frances, has suggested a prisoner named Thomas.* It is intolerable there should be an opportunity for Thomas to visit at Christmas that she cannot make happen. Yet as soon as her pen hovers above the page the flaws in the plan are evident. Although the forgery itself is not difficult, there is insufficient space to add a line before her mother's closing signature and her ink is darker in hue. More problematic still, she does not know Thomas's surname. There could well be several prisoners called Thomas living in the camp. How would Major Markham know which Thomas the writer had in mind, and what on earth would happen if he were to ask her mother?

For a moment she gazes at the letter before folding the paper away. Outside, night has fallen, but when she turns off the lamp beside the bed, the solid black beyond the window lifts to a softer mauve. The moon is visible, a silver bow tucked between the white-tipped roofs of the nearby cottages. She remembers the photograph of the little girl with silver hair. Thomas's reaction. His embarrassment. Why should she worry if he comes for Christmas or not? Any sort of future for the two of them is plainly impossible. She can't even be certain he has feelings for her. And yet some part of her *is* certain. Entirely certain. Somewhere deep and instinctive, she seems to know a good deal more than she can bring herself to properly contemplate.

Chapter Thirteen

18 December 1946

'Please, I only want to deliver a Christmas card.'

'And I've told you already, ma'am, access is forbidden to anyone without a security pass.'

Viv smiles her most dazzling smile. The one normally able to unlock doors and find favours – a slice of bacon added to her meat ration, a corner table in a jam-packed restaurant, a train held an extra minute so she can scramble aboard.

Hitching his gun holster a little higher, the American guard looks into the middle distance, the gesture emphasising the futility of her charms.

She's determined to have the final word, nonetheless. 'Do you really have to be quite so unhelpful? The war *is* over, you know.' Before he can reply, she walks quickly away. She has no plan of where she might go. The next bus to Fakenham will not arrive for several hours and of course she still has the card. Somehow, she *must* deliver the Christmas card to Alex. There can be no doubt about him having received it; he has to know as soon as possible that she has finally made up her mind.

She's heading, she realises, towards the barn to which he took her on the last occasion she was here. The road is longer than she remembers – and considerably more treacherous. Yesterday for the first time in weeks the temperature rose high enough to melt the top layers of snow, only for the surface to freeze again overnight. Picking her way across slush and panes of ice, she keeps her balance by grabbing at the overhanging bushes, some of which are holly and scattered with berries. The more berries, she recalls, the longer and harder the winter is supposed to be. And these holly trees are bright and heavy with blood-red fruit.

The gate into the field is jammed against frozen ruts but there is just enough room for Viv to wriggle through the gap and when she enters the barn the memory of being there with Alex is, for an instant, so intense she almost expects to see him waiting in the shadows. Instead there is a frantic burst of flapping as the wings of a pigeon beat bleakly into the rafters.

And then there is silence.

Perching on a straw bale, Viv's gaze sweeps over the machinery now rusting and dusty from lack of use. Not much farm work happens in December, she supposes, and there are few men to do it in any case. The last time she was here the air hummed with hay and cow manure, and while it was hardly the place for a romantic tryst, the barn at least seemed functional and alive. Now the freezing weather has petrified the smell and the space feels simply desolate and sterile.

Much like her marriage, in fact. The day before Christmas Eve, she notes drily, will be their seventh anniversary. The wedding had been a hasty affair, timed to coincide with the small amount of leave Toby had been given over the festive period. Alice was on the way already, and dancing after the celebration breakfast, a little giddy from champagne, Viv remembers feeling she had everything she could possibly want.

She pokes the toe of her shoe into the dusty ground. This year they are hardly likely to celebrate anything other than Christmas. She has tried to talk to Toby about the episode in the cupboard on several occasions, once broaching the subject when he was driving so that he wouldn't have to meet her eyes while he tried to explain what had happened. Instead of replying, however, he had pulled much too abruptly onto the verge, exited the car and smoked a cigarette while he leant against the bonnet. Afterwards he seemed to avoid her more completely than ever, as if angry she had dared even to bring up the subject. Then that dreadful explosion happened. Nobody had died – thankfully – but the incident had provoked an outraged letter to *The Times*, a visit from the War Office, and Toby had taken to starting on the whisky the moment he got through the door.

In many ways, his behaviour has made her actions easier.

Viv clasps her handbag to her chest as if hugging a baby. The stiff white envelope inside, addressed to Captain A. Henderson, contains a good deal more than a Christmas card with festive wishes. It conveys a decision she has been agonising over ever since the shock of Bonfire Night.

I want to leave Toby, she has written.

> *More than anything on this earth I want to leave Toby and go with you to America, just like you said we would do as soon as the war was over. I cannot bear to be married to a stranger for one moment longer. I feel as if I have loved you, and only you, for ever. The Toby I once knew never came home and I cannot even remember how it felt to love him. You are all I ever think about, my darling Alex, day and night, night and day, and once we are together you will never have to share me with anyone else ever again. Tell me when to come to you, and I shall be there!*

Toby is so remote, so untouchable, it's quite possible, Viv thinks, that once his pride has recovered from the blow of losing her to an American, he might actually be relieved to have her gone. She's horribly aware, however, that what she has written about Toby is much less troubling than what – or whom – she has failed to mention at all.

The card contains no reference to Alice.

While the prospect of leaving Toby, leaving England, feels like letting go of a trapeze – a moment of terrifying flight before she's caught in the loving grip of another – she cannot possibly abandon her daughter. Alice must come too. Surely Alex will understand, will assume this much, without Viv needing to spell it out? She could hardly put, *Of course I shall bring Alice with me*, as if her daughter were a pet dog or cumbersome travelling companion. More than that, as soon as she mentions Alice, sees the reality before her eyes in black and white, Viv knows she will also have to confront another matter. How Alice will react to being uprooted from her home and from her country. And from her father.

Shivering in the bitterly cold barn, Viv repeats what she has already told herself countless times, that until recently Toby has barely been present in the child's life. Merely for periods of leave, odd snapshots of time when Alice had to be reintroduced to him and often while she was squirming on one leg, seeking refuge behind Viv's skirt. Viv tries not to dwell on the photograph taken late in the summer of 1940, when Alice was only eight weeks old. Wrapped in a knitted blanket, she is lying in her mother's arms. Viv's hair makes a long, dark curtain as she stares at the precious bundle, while Toby gazes at them both, his young face etched with pride and adoration.

Viv shakes her head to jolt the image from her mind. Today is the last day before the Christmas holidays and she has arranged for Daisy to collect Alice from school. It's conceivable, perhaps even probable, that by the time term restarts she and Alice will be starting their new life in America. Surely, once Alex knows she's ending her marriage, he will understand they cannot possibly stay in Norfolk a second longer than necessary?

First, however, she has to find a way to deliver the card.

Viv consults her wristwatch. An hour has passed since her altercation with the soldier on the gate, but two more of them stretch ahead until the next bus. Perhaps there is another entrance to the camp, one with a less intransigent guard dog. Standing up, she brushes straw from her coat with renewed determination.

Outside, the temperature has dropped still further, solidifying all the moisture in the air and earth. When Viv inhales, it feels as though the oxygen is being carried to her lungs in sharp-edged chunks. She struggles back along the road and stops about fifty yards from the gate. The guard is no longer alone. Two tails of smoke are curling into the ether, two glints of orange burning through the gloom. As she watches, the intractable soldier takes the cigarette from his mouth and grinds the stub underfoot before striding away to leave his replacement in post. Viv can hardly believe her luck. She waits one more minute before approaching the new guard.

He looks at Viv appraisingly. 'Can I help you, ma'am?'

She explains her errand while his gaze slides the length of her legs.

'I'm not supposed to let anyone in without a pass.'

Viv pushes a lock of hair from her forehead and takes out the card to prove the purpose of her visit. 'Oh please. I've had a terrible journey, and in such dreadful weather. I'll only be a minute. *Less* than a minute – you can even count the seconds out loud, if you like!' She blinks slowly. 'You can't honestly believe that I'm a security risk!'

He grins. 'If you're very quick, I suppose there can't be any harm.' The sentry steps aside, making space for her to squeeze between the barrier and the hedge. He points across a large expanse of field towards a row of wooden huts. 'The office is the first on the right, that's where the mail is delivered. And, ma'am…'

'Yes?' She is already inside, close enough to see the flurry of pimples on his cheek, the attentiveness in his eyes.

'If you don't mind me saying so, ma'am' – he gestures at the card – 'he's a very lucky man.'

Viv drops her gaze, pauses long enough to acknowledge the compliment, before hastening away. Once free of the gate, she slows her pace. Since this is where Alex lives, it's possible they could run into each other at any moment. She casts around for any glimpse of him, heart racing at the possibility she might spy in the distance his tell-tale swagger, his resolute stride, before he veers towards her, arms widening, smile broadening.

'Viv, honey, what a sight for sore eyes! What a wonderful surprise!'

Yet the camp appears deserted.

Nobody is hurrying between the buildings, no conversation drifts across the snow-covered turf, no engine revs from trucks or lorries rupture the silence. Instead the grey of the December afternoon creates the impression of a ghost town. She taps on the door to the mailroom, half-expecting that hut to be abandoned too, but after a moment an invitation to enter is issued in a jaded-sounding drawl.

A counter at chest-height runs across the room and on the far side a soldier with hair as thick as shaving cream is sorting stacks of paper in a leisurely fashion. Before he can say anything, Viv thrusts the card over the counter. 'This is for Captain Alex Henderson. Please will you make sure he gets it by tomorrow?'

Heavy white brows plunge to a frown. The card is ignored. 'Now how the hell did *you* get in here, honey?'

'I was given permission at the gate' – Viv prays she isn't incriminating the pimpled soldier – 'to give this letter to Captain Henderson. It's really rather urgent.' Even as she waggles her hand, waving the clean, white envelope to emphasise the importance of her mission, she can sense her assertiveness nose-diving.

The mailroom manager removes a pair of wire-framed spectacles. His pupils impale Viv on two sharp spikes. 'Captain Henderson sure seems to get a lot of mail.'

Viv blinks. 'Does he?' When Alex moved to Norfolk, she sent him several letters – five, he had reminded her, which was possibly a little excessive in retrospect – but since his rather pointed comment, the only correspondence between them has come from him. Until now. She manages to smile. 'Like this, do you mean, by hand?'

'No honey, from overseas.'

'Well, he is American. I mean, you're all American. I imagine his family must write to him a lot…' She's stumbling.

The white-haired soldier regards her steadily. 'Well somebody does, honey. That's for sure.'

Something in his tone bites her, a scorn and condescension that makes her simultaneously understand the insinuation and want to slap his face. *You think you know about me*, she longs to snarl, *but you have no idea. No idea at all. Alex loves me. He really does.*

Carefully, she places the card on the counter, draws herself to her full height. 'Well, would you add this card to Captain Henderson's pile of fan mail? As I said, it's urgent and I'd like him to receive it as soon as possible.' Then – pointlessly – since she's already turning to leave, 'And please stop calling me honey.'

The bus arrives late before nearly bowling straight past the stop. When Viv realises the driver isn't slowing down, she steps into the road, gesturing wildly with both arms so that he careers to a halt thirty yards beyond where she is standing, back wheels skidding as he slams the brakes. Viv clambers aboard, too relieved to be angry, and before she has even taken her seat the bus leaps forwards again.

From the window the midwinter countryside looks bleak, the last of the light is draining from the sky, leaving the landscape drab and indistinct. It's easy to see why the driver failed to spot her, and now he seems anxious to make up for lost time – taking corners faster than is comfortable and pressing the engine to greater speeds as soon as the road straightens. Before they have travelled far, the tail of the bus swings suddenly sideways. Viv grabs the back of the seat in front to prevent herself from being thrown into the aisle. There's an audible gasp from her fellow passengers before the wheels find their grip and the chassis rights itself. Remembering the patches of ice on the road between the camp and the barn, a sliver of unease keeps her hand clutching her metal handle. She will be glad to get home. To light the fire and sit with Alice beside the dance of the flames. Perhaps she should tell Alice about Alex, that the three of them will be moving to America? Yet she mustn't risk speaking to Alice before she tells Toby. After she has done that, they will talk to Alice together and convince her this is the best course of action for everyone.

Viv closes her eyes.

She is being absurd.

Even if Toby recognises their marriage is over, there is no earthly chance of him allowing his daughter to move to another country. And what did that hateful old soldier mean about the letters? Does Alex have a sweetheart in America? Well, he has only had one lover since he came to England, and she's quite certain he has never looked at any American girl with the same infatuation, touched them with the same urgency, or made them the same smitten promises as he has done with her. The American woman, whoever she is, will simply have to step aside.

She's still lost in thought when the accident happens.

The bus shoots across the road as if shoved off course by a giant hand. There's a sickening crash, a tearing and crumpling of metal before the chassis begins to rotate. Viv is flung towards the gangway. Her grip on the seat frame loosens. She manages to stop herself from falling before abruptly she's hurled the other way. Her face smacks against the glass. She has a fleeting vision of trees crushing the window, their arm-like boughs stretching towards her until they whirl out of sight an instant later.

Everyone is screaming.

The bus spins faster and faster.

A child cries, 'Mummy! Mummy!'

'I'm here,' Viv thinks vaguely. 'I'm right here.'

The world disintegrates like a house of cards.

Now another lurch.

Now back towards the aisle.

Now her fingers are wrenched from the metal frame.

She has a sudden, startling vision of the bus floor, three cigarette butts, a small round tortoiseshell button, the pink studded cellophane wrapper of a packet of Parma Violets – Alice's favourite, she has time to register – before something seems to pick her up and throw her hard against the window.

Chapter Fourteen

The scrape of wood on concrete makes Fran lift her head. Daisy has pushed back her chair and is buttoning a second cardigan, one of the many extra layers they all wear these days to counter the arctic weather. 'I have to go and fetch Alice from school. Special request from Mrs Markham.' She pulls a face.

Fran glances at the clock. 'It's not yet three o'clock.'

'Last day of term, so no lessons this afternoon, just a Christmas party in the village hall.'

'Why can't Mrs Markham pick her up?'

Daisy shrugs, then sighs as she considers a small stack of letters on the side of her desk. 'I was supposed to deal with these today, but I've run out of time. Now tomorrow I'll have to explain to Major Markham that I left the office early. I'm awfully tired of being the Markhams' unofficial nanny, I've more important things to do and the extra hours put me behind with my proper job.'

'At least you're collecting Major Markham's daughter. He can't make a fuss about that!'

'Not if he knows what I'm doing.'

'What do you mean?'

'Well,' Daisy's lowers her voice, her fingers hovering over the last button. 'I'm quite certain Mrs Markham doesn't tell Major Markham when she asks me to help with Alice. She seems anxious for me to leave the house before he gets home and makes sure to pay me from her own purse.'

'That's odd!' Fran pulls a face. 'I wonder where she goes and what she does?' She recalls Vivien Markham's dreamy looks. Every time she pictures the major's wife, she sees fur wraps and cocktail bars, city lights and packed theatres, and there was none of that sort of thing around the village or anything remotely similar. 'They haven't been living here very long, so I don't suppose she has many friends.'

Daisy shrugs again, this time with one shoulder while directing a sly look over the top of the desk. 'Come on, Fran, *that's* not difficult to work out. The, *what she's doing* bit anyway!'

'Heavens!' Fran feels her cheeks bloom. 'Is that honestly what you think?'

'Of course.' Daisy walks towards a hat stand engulfed under a weight of winter coats and scarves. 'What else do you expect when someone who could double for Vivien Leigh discovers she's married to a barmy old soldier like Toby Markham!'

'Shush, Daisy!' Fran shoots a glance towards the hallway. 'For goodness' sake, remember where we are!'

'He's not here.' She shrugs herself into a navy overcoat. 'Haven't you noticed? Since that business with the mine, he comes in less than ever. Half the time when he claims to have an appointment outside the camp, I suspect he simply drives his car somewhere quiet and has forty winks. Not a bad life, if you ask me. He's got Captain Holmes running the place for him and us doing all the clerical work.'

'Daisy!' Then amused and exasperated, 'What was the other job you were meant to do today anyway?'

Daisy points at her papers. 'Remember the churches' appeal to forgive and forget? Those letters are each from a different family offering to have a prisoner from the camp spend Christmas Day with them. There's about ten altogether and I'm to select which lucky Germans get to go and match them with the invites.'

Daisy has slipped off her court shoes and is already pulling on lace-up boots, before Fran manages to speak. 'What are the criteria?' Fran says at last. 'I mean, for choosing the prisoners.' She's amazed how steady her voice sounds.

'Oh, well, let's see if I remember…' Daisy ties her left lace into a quick, efficient bow before sitting back and counting on her finger. 'No black armbands and no suspected Nazi sympathisers. No medical worries – obviously we can't have prisoners spreading nasty germs amongst the squeaky-clean locals – and the younger ones are to get priority, since they're more likely to be in a worse state, homesickness-wise. From that cohort, Major Markham wants me go through their papers and look for those who've made some kind of positive contribution to the camp.'

'What does *positive contribution* mean?'

'I've no idea. Major Markham gave me the files of the possible prisoners this morning, but I haven't begun to read them yet. I'll tell you tomorrow when I make a start. Now I really must go, or Alice will be standing abandoned outside the village hall. Or worse, beside a grumpy teacher who will give *me* horrible looks even though I'm not the child's mother and shouldn't need to be there at all!'

'Daisy?'

'Yes.' Her hand is closing on the door handle.

'I don't mind doing it for you. The allocation of prisoners, I mean. I would be happy to go through the files. I can always stay late to get it finished, and that way you won't have to mention anything to Major Markham about collecting Alice today.'

'Honestly?'

Fran nods.

Daisy says slowly, 'I suppose if it's really no trouble…'

'None at all.'

A quick glance from the doorway.

Fran clamps her lower lip. 'I know you'd do the same to help me out.'

'I imagine it's Vivien Markham whom you're really doing a favour, helping to guard her little secrets… But why not? Thank you. It's one less job on my list for tomorrow.' For an instant

Daisy's eyes harden, as if Fran is a piece of too-small print that she's trying to read. Then her shoulders drop. She smiles. 'See you tomorrow.'

The moment Fran is alone she scurries around to Daisy's side of the desk where a heap of prisoners' records is propped against a chair leg. Anxiously she begins to leaf through the pages. The seventeenth file is that of Thomas Meyer, aged twenty-four, who comes from Eisenach. The twenty-ninth is that of Thomas Fuchs, aged twenty-two from Berlin. Both have been assessed as having low Nazi sympathies. And in the fifty or so files that have not made the initial cut Fran estimates there must be at least three other prisoners named Thomas. She bites the top of her thumbnail, shearing a sliver of milky-white keratin.

The Fuchs file contains a note about woodworking skills. It seems that Thomas Fuchs crafts owl boxes from old grocery crates and hangs them in the cluster of elms beyond the Nissen huts. Apparently, he has obliged two British officers by making them each a bird box to give to their children. Is this a positive contribution to the camp? Fran supposes that it must be – everyone likes owls after all. But who is Thomas Fuchs? The Thomas with the blistering gaze who absorbs her every thought like sand does water. Or a complete stranger? She turns to the file of Thomas Meyer. No mention is made of carpentry skills or gifts to children, but there is an entry at the back of the file on A4 paper that has the appearance of having been scrawled in haste.

While returning to camp at approx. 17.00 hours we encountered a female cyclist who requested aid to help the victim of an assault. Since the truck could not be left unattended, I asked Thomas Meyer to provide assistance. I was subsequently informed by the female cyclist he did so successfully and that the involvement of the police was not required. In so acting, and displaying no inclination to *abscond, I am pleased to record that the prisoner justified the trust placed upon him.*

While the signature is indecipherable, the date is not: 1 November 1946. The shock of serendipity – the confirmation of both Thomas's identity (Thomas *Meyer*, she turns the name over in her mouth) and his entitlement to a Christmas invitation (surely this must be precisely the sort of thing Major Markham had in mind?) – ripples a shudder through Fran's spine like she has seen a ghost.

Or the future.

Quickly, she attaches her mother's letter to the outside of Thomas Meyer's file with a paperclip, then adds a second clip to be certain. For a while she stares at the coupled paper as if the hand holding it belongs to someone else. If mere minutes in his company feel incendiary, how much more electrifying, how much more perilous is the possibility of a whole day together? It's as reckless as lighting a thousand matches and throwing them into the woodshed one by one. She swallows and lets the seconds stop. Outside, the weather squalls. Whatever happens now, she thinks, she will probably remember sitting in Daisy's chair, the empty, watchful room and the wind, gusting at the windowpanes, for the rest of her life. After a minute she pushes the Meyer file to one side and lifts the others onto her lap.

By the time all the Christmas invitations have been secured to a pale brown folder, the ebony of evening has taken hold and Fran's head is heavy with facts and decisions. To avoid an inevitable flurry of questions from Daisy, she buries the Meyer file into the middle of the pile, immediately below the invite that will also be sent to prisoner Fuchs. Finally, she carries the entire heap of paperwork into the connecting office. Daisy is right, she notes in passing. The surface of Major Markham's desk is pristine. Devoid of clutter, of pens, of a diary, of any sign of industry whatsoever, and across the leather case of his magnifying glass lies a delicate film of dust.

From the door she casts one look backwards. Although none of the individual files are visible, Fran fancies she can see the glow of her mother's handwriting pulsing upwards through the paper, like the cautioning lamp of a beacon or lighthouse.

Chapter Fifteen

Christmas Day, 1946

From behind the screen of her book, Fran watches the mantelpiece clock. The minute hand is climbing towards the twelve and the prisoners, they have been told, will arrive before the hour. Prisoners. Plural. At the last minute the government forbade the issuing of individual invitations, so her parents are now hosting two of them. Perhaps, Fran supposes, a single prisoner cannot be trusted with an enemy family and a second, restraining influence is needed. Or does the protection flow the other way? Maybe it's the British families of whom the government can't be certain, who might be less interested in peace and reconciliation than they are in revenge.

Sitting in the loose-covered wingchair, her father is dressed in his only suit. Hands resting lightly on each knee, he makes no pretence at reading. Fran wonders what dilemmas are playing across his mind. The only clue is the speed of his breathing, the painful process of inhaling and exhaling that sounds both faster and a little more shallow than usual, together with the damp sheen of perspiration spread across his forehead.

There was a period after the accident when it seemed the Christmas visits might not happen at all. Toby Markham was not at the camp to approve the paperwork and nobody else appeared to have authority to do so. When Fran dared to raise the matter with Daisy, she was met with a rather shocked indifference, as if Fran was being callous beyond belief to be asking of anyone but the Markhams.

'You have no idea how awful it was when Mrs Markham didn't come home,' she told Fran for the third, or possibly fourth time. 'I thought she must have been delayed by the weather and so I put Alice to bed. Even after Major Markham came back, I didn't like to leave. I think I must have known deep down that something was wrong. And it was just as well I stayed because when the policeman arrived the major practically collapsed – he could barely string together a sentence. Luckily the policeman offered to take him to the hospital, because the major definitely wasn't up to driving himself.'

Daisy gazed into the middle distance, as if reliving the heavy rap of the policeman's knock all over again. 'She could have been killed, you know. The driver died at the scene and one of the passengers has broken his back and will never walk again. Reminds you of the war, doesn't it? When everything felt so fragile and someone you knew seemed to die or nearly die practically every week.' She sighed heavily. 'I thought those days were over for good.' Fran bit her lip, and each time someone in the camp mentioned Vivien Markham tried to quell her own selfish motives for hoping the woman's recovery would be quick enough for Major Markham to make an appearance before Christmas.

At the growl of an approaching truck, she meets her father's eyes.

'There's no need to get up,' Fran says. 'Why don't you wait in here?'

Her father lifts his hands from his knees, places them decisively on the arms of the wing chair. 'I'm not being introduced to any German soldier while I'm sitting down' – a ragged in-breath, a ragged out-breath – 'but you'll need to help me, Fran.'

Fran cups her hands under her father's armpits and tries not to notice the stringiness of his wasted muscles, the dank, cellar-like smell coming off his skin. While he pushes down on the chair, she makes an almighty effort to haul him upwards and loops his arm around her shoulders the instant she has dragged him upright.

She wonders how a body can be so withered and still so heavy; her father looks as though the merest breath of wind would blow him down, yet the weight around her neck is a sack of coal. They are inching across the sitting room when she hears the front door open. By the time they reach the hallway the door has closed again. Two German prisoners are standing on the threshold as if their boots have been nailed to the floor.

Fran tries not to look at Thomas but fails. She sees the surge of surprise that intensifies the blue of his irises, and the effort he makes to keep mute. Silent questions blaze from his face.

'Don, Fran, this is Thomas Meyer.' Her mother's tone is that of a rather nervous teacher bringing children together on their first day of nursery. 'Thomas, this is my husband, Donald, and my younger daughter, Frances.'

Fran feels her father's spine stiffen. He thrusts out his palm and opens his mouth, but the intended words stay trapped within his chest. Instead he swallows, his Adam's apple bobbing in his throat, and withdraws his arm the instant the Germans release their grip.

Fran holds out her own hand. 'Hello, Thomas.' She has to avert her gaze as the pressure of his fingers throbs through her arm.

'And Fran dear, this is Reiner Krause.'

Fran hauls her attention to the other prisoner, who is short and slight and staring intently at the floor through heavy-rimmed spectacles. His name is vaguely familiar from the files. When her parents agreed to have a second guest for Christmas, Major Markham must have chosen one of the youngest men because Reiner seems no older than a schoolboy, an impression exacerbated by the regular sniffing he makes no effort to stem. On hearing his name, he lifts his head. He looks, Fran thinks, on the verge of tears.

'Come this way,' her father manages. 'Come into our sitting room.'

Fran throws a glance up the staircase. At breakfast June asked what time the prisoners were due to arrive, and thirty minutes beforehand took herself upstairs, closing her bedroom door with a thump that was plainly intended to be heard throughout the house. While Fran is angry, she is also relieved. If any part of her feelings for Thomas were visible, June would be sure to notice. And even if they were not visible, June might still notice, in the way they each had the ability to discern buried vulnerabilities in the other that no one else could.

Thomas clears his throat. 'May I use the lavatory, please?'

'Of course.' Her mother appears a little flustered by the request. 'Fran, you show our guest where to go and I'll help your father take Reiner into the sitting room.'

Fran leads Thomas through the kitchen and into a covered passageway. When Fran was a child they lived in a house where the lavatory was in the back yard. Here, it is connected to the house by a corridor with brick walls and a roof which rattles with whatever weather happens to be thrown upon the corrugated tin.

The moment they are out of the kitchen, Thomas grasps Fran's upper arm. 'Wait!'

She swings around to face him.

'How is this possible?'

'What do you mean?'

'For me to be here. Did you arrange this?'

The urgency in his voice quickens Fran's pulse as if her heart is trying to run away.

She focuses on the bulk of his shoulder, which is no more than twelve inches from her own.

'No.'

'Look at me.'

She can't.

'Look at me.'

She is shivering, trembling. It might be the cold, but it might be something else. All at once she starts, as if touched by an electric wire. His thumb is on her cheekbone, caressing back and forth over a small patch of her skin. She tries to step backwards but there is nowhere to go, only the wall pressing into her back and the fact of Thomas before her, his shocking, unbelievable proximity.

'Fran' – his eyes are searchlights – 'I don't believe you.'

For a split second she has forgotten what he is talking about.

'I think you did arrange for me to come here.'

This time she says nothing, abandons the pretence.

His mouth widens to a smile. She is close enough to see the strongly angled planes of his face, a chipped front tooth, the small, puckered whorl of a scar on his forehead, and the extraordinary eyes which wash her away in their flood of blue light.

'Fran!' From another world her mother's voice slices through the moment. 'Where are you? What's taking so long?'

Fran lowers her lashes. Opens them again. Thomas is still there.

'My mother is calling.'

'Yes.' He drops his hand. Moves further away.

'The lavatory…' Fran gestures vaguely along the passageway. She feels entirely cold now, as if she has just removed her overcoat or thrown off a blanket.

'I don't need…' He stops. 'You go back. I will come in a minute.'

Fran's mother and father are waiting in the sitting room together with Reiner, who is balanced on the very edge of the sofa cushion. Every so often he pushes his spectacles up his nose to counteract the downward tilt of his gaze which is still focused on the floor.

Her mother gets up. 'There you are,' she says, her relief evident. 'I need to go and see to the dinner or else we'll be eating at midnight. I don't think' – she lowers her voice – 'I don't think Reiner speaks any English.'

It seems her mother is right. Fran starts by asking Reiner where he lives, if he has a family, speaking as slowly and clearly as she can, but she elicits no response until Thomas returns and begins to translate her questions. From working at the camp, Fran has become used to the sound of German. Even so it is strange to listen to the language being spoken in her own home, incomprehensible and foreign, the tongue of war, of the enemy. She glances at her father, sunk within the wing chair beside a stack of her mother's dressmaking patterns. He is watching the German men with the appearance of impassiveness, yet Fran sees his arms are crossed as if he is holding himself together, his fists tucked into his upper arms, his chest labouring like a bicycle pump.

Reiner provides his answers in short, quiet sentences. There's a small delay between each question and the response that gives the impression of something awkward being hauled by a clinking chain from the bottom of an ocean. Little by little, they learn that Reiner comes from Frankfurt. That he is nineteen years old. That his father is a mechanic. That he has a younger brother. That he has an older brother. Then Reiner stops. Pushes the spectacles up his nose. Corrects himself. No older sibling. A younger brother now.

The room falls into silence, broken only by the rasp of breathing from the wing chair.

A minute passes. Eventually, Thomas clears his throat. 'I have a gift,' he says, 'a Christmas present.' He reaches into his overalls, where a cigar-shaped wedge protrudes from the top right pocket. Unfurling a piece of paper, he walks over to Fran's father and crouches beside the chair. 'I like to draw,' he says. 'Although it is hard, when something is beautiful, to show in a picture what makes it that way.' He throws a glance at Fran before turning back to her father. 'This is the view from a hill close to here, I think—'

'Yes.' Fran's father interrupts. Inhales. Exhales. 'I see exactly where it is.'

Fran gets up and comes to the empty side of the chair. Observed from the highpoint of the heath, Thomas has sketched the coastline. Sparsely shaded in tones of blue, grey and green, his strokes capture the washed-clean light, the peppering of flint and brick, a windmill with its spinning arms. The unity of sea, sky and salt marsh. And a possibility, beneath the loveliness, of emptiness and desolation.

Fran's father gently runs a yellowed fingernail along the shoreline. 'It's good. Very good indeed.' A pause. A breath. 'Do you like it, Fran?'

She keeps her eyes on the artwork. 'I think it's wonderful.'

He holds the drawing out to Fran. His eyes are brighter than she has seen them for some time. 'Yes, it is. We must put it on the mantelpiece.'

'The mantelpiece?'

He nods. 'Where we can all see such fine talent.'

Fran crosses the room slowly. The mantelpiece is bare apart from the clock and a brass-framed photograph of Robbie in his army uniform. Her brother's eyes seem to be watching while she props the sketch against the wall. Does he mind? Will her mother mind? She knows without asking that June will cause merry hell. Once June understands who drew the picture, she is more likely to tear the paper into pieces and throw them into the fire than let the gift occupy the same location as Robbie. Before Fran can decide what, if anything, to say, her mother calls that lunch is ready.

The kitchen smells of roasting meat, and cinnamon and spiced fruit from the pudding warming on the hob. Vegetables steam gold and green beside a tall jug of gravy while a crisp brown turkey occupies the space by her father's seat. Fran shows Thomas and Reiner to the table, where they stand behind their chairs and gape as her mother bustles forwards with one further dish of stuffing, gesturing at the Germans to sit, *please sit*. June, who is draining carrots from a saucepan, doesn't take her eyes from the sink.

Eventually they are all seated, apart from her father who remains on his feet, bearing the silver scythe of the carving knife. Fran is next to Reiner, whom she has placed opposite June in Robbie's old place, and Thomas is beside June. The table appears to have shrunk in size. Every so often Fran's knee or elbow brushes against the bony promontory of Reiner and whenever she raises her head Thomas seems to intercept her gaze.

Her father pierces the turkey with the carving fork. Juice runs over the blade. Propped against the lip of table, he is managing to dissect the bird without assistance. Beside Fran, Reiner chews his lip impatiently.

'Are you hungry?' she says, before remembering Reiner doesn't speak English.

This time, however, he seems to understand. 'Yes.' He holds out his plate for the first slices of meat. Like a child, Fran thinks, at a Sunday lunch.

Her father has just served himself, when there is a nudge against Fran's thigh. About to jerk her arm away she spots that Reiner has taken her mother's hand, that his head is bowed, his eyes closed. Hesitantly, Fran encloses Reiner's fingers with her own and one by one the rest of them link hands until the only missing connection is between June and Thomas. Fran sees her sister's face fill with rage at the ambush, her back lift and tighten as she pushes back her chair.

As Reiner begins to mutter soft words of German, Thomas holds out his left hand to June, rotating his wrist so that his palm faces upwards. 'Please.' June shuffles her chair forwards again, but then with a glance at Fran places her right hand very deliberately on top of the cloth.

After the grace, they eat. Soon, stoked by food, the warmth of the kitchen, and some small glasses of apple wine, Reiner's spirits appear to lift, and he begins to offer animated snatches of conversation in broken English. Eventually, after what she judges to be a respectable amount of time, Fran takes a sip of wine and turns to their other guest.

'What about you, Thomas? Tell us something about your life in Germany. Whereabouts do you come from?' When she tries to look at him, it's like being dazzled by the headlights of an army truck. She concentrates instead on the mechanics of eating and drinking. Positioning her glass back on the table, cutting with her knife, loading her fork. It feels as if each action is something she has learned to do only recently.

'A small village, I don't think you know the name. It is close to the town of Eisenach.'

'Near Berlin?'

'It is south-west of Berlin. Not so close.'

'And your family,' Fran's mother interjects, 'are they still there?'

There's a pause.

Fran risks a glimpse across the table.

Thomas is staring into the depths of his wineglass. 'I have had no contact with my parents for almost two years. Towards the end of the war Eisenach was bombed very heavily. There were many fires in the town. Too many to stop. A lot of homes were destroyed, and a lot of people killed.' His tone is neutral, as if he is delivering a news bulletin. Fran wonders how much effort this takes and, suddenly, if after all it is wrong for them to be sitting here together, when the suffering is so recent. Whether the meal is tantamount to sharing a picnic over the rubble of a burned-out home without daring to acknowledge the ruins underneath.

Her mother leans forwards. 'If your parents live in a village, they may have escaped the bombing. Do they know where you are, where to write?' She seems oblivious to the fact her sleeve is trailing into her plate.

'I sent a lot of letters as soon as I arrived, to my family and our neighbours. I wrote also to the German Red Cross.' He hesitates, 'No one has replied.'

There is silence. They have all stopped eating, apart from Reiner, who is working steadily through his dinner. Fran can see her mother hunting for something positive to say but the seconds fall away from her. Eventually, she touches her napkin to her lips. 'Perhaps there is someone else, apart from your parents?'

'Do you mean a girl, a sweetheart?' There's a sudden weight to Thomas's voice.

Fran's heart leaps as if from a starter's pistol.

Her mother dabs the napkin again. She looks a little perplexed. 'I suppose so, yes.'

Fran raises her eyes to Thomas and finds he is gazing back at her.

He shakes his head. 'No. I have a sister, that is all. A younger sister who lives with my parents.' He pauses, before saying more quietly. 'My sister's name is Gisela. I have heard nothing from her either.'

Fran's mother smiles. 'That's a pretty name.'

'And is she the girl in the photograph?'

There's another pause, fractional but long enough for Fran to wonder how she could have been so thoughtless, so reckless. It was the relief, she decides, uselessly, still slightly giddy from the rush of it.

Inevitably, June lifts her head. 'What photograph?'

'I carry a picture of Gisela in my pocket. Here—' Thomas extracts the creased snapshot from his pocket, placing it on the table in front of June. Though the image is upside down, Fran can discern the small figure beside the garden bush, the cloud of white-blond hair.

June ignores the photograph. Her gaze flies back and forth like the carriage of a typewriter. 'I mean, how did Fran know about it?'

'She saw it before. I dropped the photograph and she picked it up.'

'I didn't see you drop any photograph.'

Thomas's face creases with confusion. 'Not here. Another time.'

Fran closes her eyes. Opens them. Waits for the string to start unravelling.

'So, you have met before then?'

June sounds like a lawyer, Fran realises. Cold, curious and logical. If her sister was less bored, her mind more occupied, might Robbie's death consume her less? Perhaps June does not merely disapprove of her job at the camp, maybe she is jealous too?

'Yes, we have met before.'

There's no reason, of course, why Thomas should understand the suspicion this will inflame, or know that Fran has never mentioned the incident in the alley. She steels herself for the inevitable. 'One evening,' she begins, 'as I was coming home from work…'

'We saw each other in the camp. I was showing the photograph to another prisoner and it fell from my hand as Frances was passing. She picked it up for me. Very kindly.' Thomas smiles at June. Lifts and drops his shoulders. 'That is all.'

June glares with disbelief. Fran begins to eat, clearing her plate in a business-like fashion although the food is now almost cold.

After a moment June says to Thomas, 'Your sister is much younger than you.'

'Gisela is only three years less than me. The picture was taken when she was a child.'

'Isn't it rather odd, that you carry a picture of her when she was small. I mean, rather than—'

'For heaven's sake!' Her mother's cheeks are splashed pink. 'That's quite enough! Thomas and Reiner have come for Christmas dinner, not to be interrogated.'

'It's all right, I don't mind.' Thomas looks directly at June. 'Gisela was in an accident. A tram collided with another tram and came off the rails. My mother was not badly hurt, but Gisela had many injuries and has to walk with sticks now. Afterwards she did not like to have her photograph taken, and besides…' He falters. 'Besides, I like to remember how she used to be.'

There's an uncomfortable pause.

Fran glowers at June, who stares straight back at her.

After a moment, Thomas says, 'For many years we had a nurse, an English nurse, who helped to take care of Gisela. She lived with us until the war meant it was not safe for her to stay in Germany. That is how I learned to speak your language.'

'And you've learned to speak it very well indeed. Now' – their mother prods June's arm – 'will you please collect the plates while I fetch the plum pudding. And if I can find a tot of brandy, I'll make it flame so we can all have a wish.'

June begins to stack the china. Her hand hovers over Fran's dish. 'What will you wish for, Fran?' The question sounds innocuous but the tone is enough to reveal her sister hasn't been fooled. She's well aware something is up, even if she might be struggling to identify precisely what it is.

Fran gets to her feet. 'If you tell someone your wish it won't come true. We both know that. I'm going to help Mother.'

The rest of the meal is without incident until Reiner discovers a sixpence in his pudding. Spitting the coin into his hand, he gazes at the silver with disgust, and when Fran's mother attempts to explain the tradition appears so bemused that the rest of them burst out laughing. Even June's expression lightens briefly. Fran's mother gets up and fetches another bottle of the apple wine. Circulating the table, she tips two inches into each person's tumbler. Once back in her place she remains standing and lifts her glass.

Slowly, raggedly, the rest of them rise to their feet.

A hush descends.

Fran looks around the table.

The air seems to be quivering like the string of a violin.

'To peace,' her mother says. 'And friendship.'

'To peace,' is the echo. 'And friendship.'

And everyone drinks their wine.

As the glasses clink back on the table, the spell is broken.

Fran's mother says, 'No need to help me clear up, girls, you must entertain our guests.'

June says, 'Nonsense, you can't do all of that on your own.' She appears slightly winded, as if shocked by her participation in the previous few minutes. 'Besides, once we've finished in the kitchen, I have another letter to write upstairs.'

Fran's mother sighs. 'Well then, Fran' – she touches the sleeve of her younger daughter – 'why don't you show Thomas and Reiner the garden? I expect they could do with a breath of fresh air after such a big meal.'

'The garden?'

Although the first wave of snow has waned, the prospect of the sodden lawn, of creating a show from the dormant vegetable patch and the bare-stemmed roses, is not enticing. Yet there is no obvious alternative to occupy the remainder of the visit. Once Fran has helped her father to the sitting room, she searches out suitable garden attire for Thomas and Reiner, something warmer than their insubstantial prison dress. She intends for Thomas to wear her father's coat, and smaller, slighter Reiner to have Robbie's navy school one. Yet when she comes to distribute them, she finds herself passing Robbie's coat to Thomas.

Outside, the temperature is even colder than she anticipated. The path that leads towards the greenhouse glistens with frost, and the tangled stems of the shrubs and bushes are black with the impending dark. Reiner hunches against the wall, delves into his trousers and pulls out a tobacco pouch. When Fran gestures at the garden, he continues to gaze at the bruise-coloured sky with the same sad, closed-off expression as when he first arrived.

'Leave him.' Thomas's voice is next to her ear. 'Show me instead.'

Thrusting her hands into her coat pockets, she braves the icy paving stones. While her fingers toy with a coin and crumbles of grit, she's aware only of the space between herself and Thomas, which seems to connect them like rope or an electric current. Every time she takes a step, she feels the tug of him beside her.

Dutifully, she points out the dark-green viburnum etched with rime, the red-edged hebe, and the holly trees. On each occasion she pauses, waits, but he says nothing, and she starts to doubt if his English is even good enough to understand plant names. Finally, they reach the end of the path where she halts next to the greenhouse. More snow begins to drift from the heavens, and she has to blink droplets away from her lashes. 'This is where we grow tomatoes and cucumbers. Peppers too, sometimes. My mother once planted a grapevine, but the grapes were too small and bitter to eat.' Given the interest either of them has in the potential of the greenhouse, she might as well be reciting nursery rhymes or the contents of the telephone directory.

Thomas nods. 'Is this the end of your land?'

'No.' Fran gestures at a small wooden gate in the wall. 'On the other side is our vegetable garden. The people who lived here before used to keep a swing and slide, but we dug it over to produce food.'

'Shall we see?'

'There's nothing to show you at this time of year. Just a lot of brown earth and maybe a few onions and some garlic.'

'I'd like to look anyway.' Thomas has stepped ahead and is already unlatching the gate. Fran follows. Her pulse is jumping in her throat. They are moving further from the house, out of sight of the downstairs windows. It's possible that Thomas is anxious to view the winter yield of an English vegetable patch. Possible, but not likely. Not remotely likely.

Carefully they circumvent the growing area, keeping to the narrow strip of grass surrounding the chocolate soil. When they reach the corner furthest from the gate, Thomas spins around. Fran almost walks into him, stopping just before she collides with his chest.

'Fran, I think you like me?'

Flakes are tumbling from the sky, as if a feather pillow has been emptied. She watches the crystals of ice settle on his nose and forehead, before dropping her gaze.

'Yes.'

'I like you too.' He grasps her forearms so that the gap between them drops to practically nothing.

Fran shuts her eyes. She feels the cold, wet swirl of snow on her cheeks, her fingers balled and frozen, then his mouth on hers hot and sudden. It is both astounding and a relief, as if an inevitable journey, both feared and longed for, has begun at last. Before she can respond, he draws away.

'Fran?'

She says nothing, eyelids pressed tight. Lips naked.

'Fran, talk to me. Do you mind? Do you mind that I kiss you?'

Blindly, she reaches forwards, cups her hands around his face and tugs him towards her.

Eventually it is Fran who breaks the connection. Thomas is staring as though she is an apparition about to disappear. He brushes a snowflake from her left eye socket with the underside of his thumb.

She catches hold of his wrist. 'I shouldn't… We shouldn't.'

'But we did.'

She swallows. The taste of him is still on her tongue, melting her from within. All she wants to do is press her mouth to his again. She must have hoped for this to happen from the minute she watched him arrive at Salthouse, from the second she arranged the Christmas visit, from the first click of the latch on the little wooden gate. Yet how can she be this certain of what is so plainly wrong? She feels her eyes prick with tears.

'Thomas! Wo bist du?' From the top of the garden, Reiner's voice. 'Was machst du?'

'Warte, ich komme sofort!'

Gently, Thomas lifts her chin. 'Reiner is wondering where I am. We must go.'

She knows this is true, even though the turn from this moment to the next, where they must exist again in separate worlds feels unbearable. She buries her face into the navy wool of his coat. Only of course the coat doesn't belong to Thomas, but to Robbie. Used to belong to Robbie. Until he was killed by a soldier, a soldier very much like the one she has just kissed and is longing to kiss again. A sob churns her ribcage. Arms encircle her back.

'Thomas! Wo bist du?' Closer, this time.

She feels Thomas's lips graze her hair.

'Ich komme!'

Fran steps back. She drags the back of her hand over her face, rubs away the snow and tears.

'Are you ready, Fran?'

Reiner is waiting for them on the other side of the gate, cowering miserably by the greenhouse. On seeing Thomas, he stands up. There is a sharp exchange of German which Thomas translates for Fran.

'Reiner wonders what we were doing. While he was freezing his balls off.'

'What did you tell him?'

'That you were explaining how to grow the different vegetables.' He must catch her look of unease because he adds in a steady voice. 'Reiner only asked questions because he is cold. He wants to go indoors.'

As they pick their way back up the path, the upstairs curtains twitch and when they come inside Fran's mother is drawing the downstairs drapes as well. Against the light of the living room, the windows are blank, black rectangles. Fran thinks of the invisible garden cloaked by the night. It seems as if a part of her is still out there, standing with Thomas in the falling snow.

Her mother says, 'Goodness, you were a long time. You must all be perishing by now. Anyway, they'll be here soon. The transport from the camp, I mean.' And right on cue the rumble of an engine swells and then cuts outside the house.

Fran's father stays in his armchair while Fran and her mother escort the German prisoners to the door. All the while Fran keeps her gaze on Reiner, on her mother, on the floor, anywhere but Thomas. The pitch and toss of her emotions feel like a freight train passing through her body. Yet when she glimpses herself in the hall mirror, she is astonished to see she looks perfectly normal.

The doorbell rings. Fran's mother shouts into the stairwell. 'June! Our guests are about to leave, come and say goodbye.'

There is no movement from above.

'I expect June is busy,' Fran says. All at once she is desperate for her sister to stay away. A mirror is one thing, but her sister is likely to observe a good deal more than Fran's reflection.

'Goodbye, Fran.'

Thomas is halfway over the threshold.

For a fleeting moment their eyes lock.

'Goodbye.'

The door shuts.

Shakily Fran climbs the stairs and sits in the dark on the edge of her bed. Why does she feel as if someone has taken a hammer to her heart? They will see each other again at the camp. Surely, they can find a way to do that. She thinks of Daisy, the soldiers in the camp, June, her parents. All the people from whom she will have to hide everything she does, everything she feels. Suddenly she doubles over with her head in her hands, her forearms pressed together and her ribcage shaking with sobs.

Some time later the grunts and shuffles of her mother helping her father climb the staircase become audible. A door opens. There are footsteps on the landing. June says, 'I'll take the left side.' Fran knows she ought to be helping too. Instead she waits, listening, until she is certain the trio are in her parents' bedroom – hoisting her father onto the mattress, untying his shoes, plumping pillows – before slipping downstairs and into the sitting room.

From the mantelpiece she plucks the drawing. She couldn't possibly stand for Thomas's present to be lost or destroyed by her sister in a fit of temper. Besides, her father will not venture from his bed again for days, and it is doubtful either June or her mother were even aware of the gift. Upstairs she studies the sketch for a long while, imagining his fingers curled around the coloured pencils, his frown of concentration, the quick scan of the horizon before the focus upon the page. Closing her eyes, she presses the paper against her cheek. The silk of the crayons feels like a balm, a comfort, and at the same time the most beautiful piece of artwork that she has ever seen.

Chapter Sixteen

3 January 1947

'Is that the operator? Good. I want a City of London number, please. The name is Sands. *Dr* Sands.'

Martin is standing in the drawing room beside the Christmas tree, which has shed most of its needles onto the Chinese rug and is ready to be carted outside and converted into firewood. Although he has offered to perform the task several times, his mother has insisted on waiting until the gardener returns. Probably, Martin thinks bitterly, because she's worried that lugging the nine-foot monstrosity into the garden, not to say chopping the gnarly old trunk into logs, might finish off his heart completely. And since the snow has barely stopped plummeting in each of the ten days since Christmas, there's no telling when the gardener might be back. Nor, for that matter, when his own firm might re-open. Even the camp office is closed. Daisy and Fran have been told to stay at home until Monday so that an electric heater can be found.

'Hello? I'm still here... No, I'm afraid I don't have either an initial or an address, but I'd be happy to take both of those numbers... Indeed. Thank you.'

Martin replaces the receiver and paces a circuit of the Chinese rug with the page he has just torn from the notepad clasped between his thumb and forefinger. Both his mother and Daisy are out, braving the polar drifts with hats and galoshes to buy milk and eggs from the local shop. This opportunity may not come again for quite a while.

He returns to the telephone and dials the operator.

'City of London 419.'

When the connection is made the voice on the line is young and brisk. And entirely unfamiliar. Martin ploughs on.

'I'd very much like to ask you some questions,' he says. 'About an examination you may have conducted in August 1941 for the army medical board.'

'I'm afraid I can't help you.'

'I understand the difficulty,' Martin says, 'with patient confidentiality. Only in this case I'm the patient who you may have examined, so you see it really doesn't—'

'No, you don't understand.' There's an exasperated sigh. 'I'm a doctor of medieval literature. A professor. You've got the wrong person.' Before Martin can apologise, the call is terminated.

A female voice answers the second number. 'Old Street Practice.'

Martin says. 'I'd like to speak to Dr Sands, if I may?'

'Dr Sands?'

'Yes.'

There's a tiny pause. 'Dr Sands is no longer in practice. Would you like an appointment with one of the other doctors?'

'I don't want an appointment.' Through the front window Martin spots his mother and sister turn the corner and begin to navigate the ravaged road towards the house. 'I simply need to speak to Dr Sands. Perhaps you have his home telephone number, or an address where I can write to him?'

'Unfortunately, that isn't possible.'

'I wouldn't ask,' says Martin, 'but I'm concerned about—'

'Dr Sands passed away,' the receptionist says quickly. 'Such a lovely man. He died several years ago, so obviously I can't give you a telephone number for *him*. Though if it's a personal matter, perhaps his wife…?'

'No.' A wild goose-chase to precisely nothing. 'It's a medical matter.'

The front door clatters open.

Voices and footsteps from the hall.

'Am I cold? I'm *so* bloody cold I need a long hot bath and tea with a shot of rum to warm me up. I can't believe I shall have to go back to work on Monday. They better have found me and Fran a heater, or we'll freeze solid! Martin, are you there?'

'One last thing,' he tucks the telephone closer to his face. 'When did Dr Sands die? Do you happen to know?'

'Not off the top of my head, but it won't take me a minute to find out when he stopped working. I'll check the old appointment diaries.'

'Martin, where are you?' Daisy's voice is practically a wail. 'Mother and I are utterly exhausted and completely drenched. In places the snow must be five foot deep. There's barely anything on the roads. If this weather keeps up for much longer, we'll be using the German prisoners to distribute food parcels. Be a darling and make us a cup of tea. Or something stronger!'

'July,' the receptionist is saying above the rustle of a turning page. 'July 1941 is when Dr Sands left the practice, and I remember the cancer already being quite advanced. I believe he died within a matter of weeks.'

'Do you think,' Martin lowers his voice, 'that Dr Sands might have conducted a medical assessment for the army in August 1941?'

'I'm quite certain that he wouldn't have done. By July Dr Sands was only seeing his regular patients on days he felt well enough, and he most definitely didn't sit on any medical evaluations for the armed forces as late as August.'

'Martin?' Daisy bursts into the drawing room as he is laying the receiver back in the cradle. She stops in her tracks. 'Who was that?'

For a split second he almost tells her. Perhaps she would fathom an explanation for why his medical report is signed by a doctor who probably died before the examination took place. He considers her bright, uncomplicated face. Then again, perhaps he should find out a little more information before involving his sister in God knows what. He slips an arm around Daisy's shoulder. 'Just an old school friend. Nobody you know. Let's go and make that pot of tea.' He glances back at the telephone as if the helpful receptionist might still be there, and with an answer to his questions. 'Afterwards, I might brave the elements and go for my walk.'

*

A little further along the coast June is washing dishes. Fran drying. Their mother has accompanied their father to the hospital. Seeing him on the passenger seat swamped in blankets, his face pinched by the pain of movement, it seemed incomprehensible to Fran how anyone might think a bitterly cold journey followed by an hour of tests and assessments could possibly improve his health. Nevertheless, despite the awful conditions on the roads, their mother refused to miss the appointment to which an old friend had offered to take them before Christmas. Fran had wanted to go as well, but her mother insisted that she stay with June and *hold the fort*, as if the threat of an invading army appearing at the bottom of the garden had not entirely gone away.

Fran continues to rub the same plate with the tea-towel, carefully wiping every inch of the blue-and-white china. Any distraction to stop herself from glancing at the kitchen clock. She tells herself that Vivian Markham's accident has made her over-anxious, too quick to assume the worst. A second later she lifts her head again. Nearly three o'clock.

'They've been a long time. They left before ten.'

June shrugs.

'Perhaps they didn't get seen at the hospital on time? Maybe the snow has kept some of the staff away, so they've had a long wait?'

June washes another plate, rinsing off the soapsuds under the cold tap without looking at her sister.

Fran sighs. June has barely said a word to her since Christmas. At first Fran was too absorbed by her own emotions to notice her sister's curtailed sentences, a one-word reply where before a river of easy conversation might have flowed. Then she assumed the empty landmark of the New Year – the new start that was never new, or the start of anything at all except the calendar – and the miserably short days of early January had pushed June's mood even lower than usual. Yesterday, however, she returned from work chilled to the bone to find June and her mother laughing in the kitchen. 'What's so funny?' Fran pleaded, unbuttoning her sodden coat. 'Do tell?' By way of answer, June exited the room and the atmosphere deflated as though Fran had taken the toasting fork to a balloon.

She places the dry plate on the table and reaches towards the draining board. Instead of a plate, her hand touches June's elbow.

'What's going on? Why won't you speak to me?'

June moves her arm away. 'Nothing.'

'Yes, there is! You've been acting queerly ever since Christmas. As if I've done something awful to you and I'm supposed to know about it.'

June holds a saucepan clear of the water and examines the efficacy of her cleaning. 'I imagine that you do know about it. I'm quite certain you don't need me to spell it out for you.'

As Fran stares, the silence begins to jangle with awful premonition, like church bells ringing chaotically and all at once somewhere in the distance.

Placing the saucepan next to the sink, June swings around. 'If you really can't think, you could always ask your German friends.'

'So, it's the Christmas visit,' Fran says cautiously. 'You're still angry about that?'

June doesn't reply.

'The invitation was Mother's idea, not mine! You know very well it was the church that suggested asking German prisoners to come for Christmas, and that Mother wanted us to be one of the families to extend the hand of friendship.'

June breathes one beat, two beats. Then, 'Well, you certainly did that. I would say the hand of friendship was well and truly extended!'

The room grows very still.

Heat is spreading through Fran's chest. 'What do you mean?' she says, although she's horribly afraid she already understands.

'I saw you.' June swivels back to the washing-up bowl, as if she can't bear even to set eyes on her sister, grabs another dirty plate and shoves it under the water. 'I saw you in the vegetable garden. I saw you and Thomas. And not just' – she chokes on a sob – 'not just kissing. You were *engrossed* in each other. Like you might not stop! Like you couldn't stop!' She throws a quick glance at Fran with eyes that are wide and incredulous and full of tears. 'What were you *thinking*?'

'Where?' Fran whispers. 'Where were you?' The garden had felt alone and private. A secret world, belonging to her and Thomas. The notion of being watched by June stains like ink or chip-fat the purity of the falling snow, the precious, giddy memory of ice and fire.

'Mother asked me to draw the upstairs curtains. I was standing by your bedroom window… Fran, how *could* you? How could you do *that* with a German soldier?'

Fran swallows. It feels as if a pine cone has lodged in her throat. 'I think I love him.'

'*What?*'

'I love him.

'No, Fran.' June wipes her cheek with the back of her hand. 'Don't say that. Please don't say that. You can't mean it.'

'I do mean it.' Then, with wonder. 'And Thomas loves me too, I'm sure of it.'

'He's a German soldier!'

'He's *not* a soldier. Not anymore. The war is over! Why shouldn't we love each other? The church asked families to befriend the prisoners. Even Mother and Father believe it's the best way to stop a war from ever happening again.'

'You don't want to be friends, though, do you? From what I could see it looked like you both want a good deal more than that!'

'So what if we do?' Fran finds she is practically shouting.

The words ring through the kitchen and die away, as if they have reached an unexpected dead end.

Eventually June says, 'It's not possible, Fran.' Her voice has become low and grim.

'Why not?'

'Think about it, Fran, for just one moment.'

'I've thought about nothing else since Christmas! Just because Thomas is German doesn't make him a wicked person.'

'How can you say that? You hardly know him!'

'I do know him. I feel like' – she takes a juddering breath – 'I feel like I know him better than anyone else I've ever met. I've felt that way since the moment I laid eyes on him. It's like recognising somebody from long ago, yet thrilling in a way I can't explain. Like sunshine through a stained-glass window, lighting up colours I've never even seen before!'

June steps forwards and grabs Fran's wrists. 'You have to stop this! This… this *nonsense*!'

'I don't think I can!'

'You have no choice!'

Fran gapes at her.

The space between them opens, a fissure splitting the earth.

June takes a breath, drops the dishcloth into the bowl. 'Come and sit down.' She steers Fran to the kitchen table, pulls out two chairs. 'Listen' – the voice of a schoolteacher, a businesswoman – 'the Germans are brutes—'

'Not all of them! Only the Nazis!'

'Fran, look what they did! The death camps, the Jews they slaughtered. Millions of lives destroyed by fighting and bombs. The horror—' June stops, continues more steadily. 'Even if you're right, even if it was only the fascists, most of the families in this village have suffered dreadfully in the war. We lost… We lost Robbie. But we're not the only ones. Every family is grieving for somebody. Nearly the whole of the cricket team was killed on D-Day. The Blunketts lost *two* sons. Imagine how awful, how unbearable, it would be for them to see a local girl stepping out with a German prisoner. Imagine how Mother and Father would feel. The shame of it.'

Fran says, quietly, desperately, 'Mother made a toast at Christmas. To peace and friendship.'

'Peace, yes. Everyone wants peace now. Friendship? Well, maybe one day that might happen. But not romance, Fran. Not *marrying* a German. Not *love*. Living here would be impossible. You must see that. Thomas would never be given a job, and nobody would accept you – or your children.'

'I could go to Germany!'

'Why would things be different there? We won the war, so they probably hate the British even more than we hate them. And besides, what about us? Your family, your own flesh and blood?' She takes both of Fran's hands in her own so that Fran can feel the warmth of her sister's flesh, the blood pounding beneath the wet residue of the soapsuds. 'Could you really leave *us*, Fran?'

Fran's whole body starts to shake. Once at school she fainted, her class presentation floating out of reach as the world turned black, one piece at a time. Now it seems like the room is disintegrating around her, as if any object she touches must instantly crumble to nothing in her fingers.

'It would be the final straw for Father, Fran. We've already lost Robbie; he simply isn't strong enough to stand losing you too.'

For two, perhaps three seconds the sentence hangs like the blade of a guillotine, before June gets to her feet and says in a normal voice. 'I'll finish clearing up. Why don't you go for a walk? Clear your head before they get back from the hospital.'

*

Outside, Fran picks her way over the snow and ice, barely conscious of which road or direction she is taking. It's as if her sister has stood her in front of a mirror and pointed to a dozen scars blighting her face. Although she might close her eyes for a moment and ignore the ugliness, eventually she has to open them and confront the awful blemishes with June's voice jabbing in her ear: *How could you, Fran? The shame of it! It would be the final straw for Father.* She wonders exactly how much June has told their mother and whether the reason she wasn't required on the hospital trip was so June could hold the conversation her mother couldn't bring herself to start.

Fran stops, clenches her eyes for real. She sees Thomas's face, the flood of light just before they kissed. Already the image has a fantastical quality, like a film she once watched, or a scene imagined from a book. *How could you, Fran?* Easily, is the answer. Willingly. Longingly. What would Robbie say, if he had survived the war, if he were alive today? Probably, Fran, supposes miserably, something very similar to June. She remembers the crowd who gathered to watch the prisoners arrive, the raised fists, the baying, the deliberate choice of location in front of the cricket team memorial. The tide of fury dragging the whole village along. Until the rules changed at Christmas, she could have been prosecuted for so much as talking to Thomas outside the camp, let alone pressing her mouth to his, flinging wide her heart, forgetting every inhibition. It is she who is out of kilter, out of step, out of *spirit*, with the rest of the world. She and Thomas. And June is right, a relationship between them is utterly unthinkable.

She is walking again, west now, along the coast road where tyres have flattened the snow into dimpled trenches that are easier to follow than the buried pavement. On the horizon the sun hangs low, gilding the grey bowl of sky and casting yellow fire across the pockets of ice between the marsh and the shingle spit. She tries to distract herself with the landscape, makes herself notice the fingers of light, the white emptiness and the calling birds. In her haste she forgot to bring gloves. Pulling the sleeves of her sweater over her wrists, Fran realises the wool is still damp from the grip of June's fingers. *How could you, Fran?* She quickens her step. A little later she is shaking her head, as if her ears are full of water, as if to forget Thomas she must physically dislodge every memory of him, every trace.

'Hello, Fran.'

For an absurd instant she believes she has conjured him up.

'Is everything all right? You seem rather distressed.'

But it is not Thomas.

She blinks. Touches her hair. Tries to still the whirling chaos. Her mouth opens instinctively. 'A headache coming on, I think. The cold wind, perhaps. I should have worn a hat.'

Martin's features crease with concern. His head tips slightly to one side. 'We must get you indoors. Somewhere to warm up.'

She lifts her gaze, expecting bare fields, icy mudflats, wanting to acknowledge both the charity of the suggestion and its impracticability, and sees to her astonishment that she has nearly reached the village where Martin and Daisy live. A hundred yards ahead is the first cluster of cottages and on the next corner the welcoming lamp of the local hotel. A second later Martin has her arm. A minute or so later he is pulling on the heavy wooden door and a rush of warmth is billowing around her ankles.

All at once there is a bar, a log fire spitting in an iron casket, and a wide selection of empty tables. Martin ushers Fran towards a chair upholstered in faded velvet and helps to remove her coat.

'I'll fetch you a brandy.'

Unlit lamps and the greenish light of late afternoon give the room a brackish feel that is far removed from the kitchen with June, or even the turning world. In a dreamlike haze she watches Martin approach the counter and raise his palm to get attention. She can't remember if she has ever drunk brandy before.

When he returns he sits down carefully and positions his chair a respectable distance away. He gestures at their drinks. 'I thought I'd join you.' There's a grimness to his tone and with surprise Fran notices that his mouth is a straight, humourless line. He raises his glass without waiting for her. 'Cheers.'

She reaches for her own glass. The kite tail of fire from throat to stomach makes her choke in surprise. She wants to gag. Instead she takes a second gulp and feels the heat flare rapidly through her blood, and with it a certain kind of bravado, a steeliness, a fatalism. With a final slug, she empties the tumbler.

Martin stares at her. 'Looks like you needed that. Another one?'

Fran nods, although once Martin has fetched two more brandies she makes a point of drinking the tiniest drop and putting the glass straight down. When she lifts her head, she sees his attention has been caught by a painting. Dappled hounds are descending on a fox, surrounded by the blood red coats of the huntsmen and prancing horses with docked tails and manes.

'Poor little blighter.' His eyes are downcast.

'Is there anything wrong, Martin?'

He leans forwards. 'I should be asking you that. Or at least how you're feeling.'

'I'm feeling much better. I think the brandy helped. And getting out of the cold.'

'Good.' He appears riveted by his glass, as if the drink itself is cause for sombre reflection. She notes the crisp profile of his chin and nose, the flop of hair over his forehead. He lifts his gaze, smiles. She sees the effort it takes, his instinct to be kind. 'No need to worry about me. Bit of an odd day, that's all.'

'Something you want to talk about?'

'I'm not sure I'd know where to start.' His gaze flicks briefly against her own.

'Martin?'

'Anyway' – his tone is determinedly jovial – 'I'm certain we can find a more interesting topic of conversation than me.'

A vision of Thomas, the blaze of his face. She rams the thought aside.

'Martin?'

His focus sharpens.

Fran takes a mouthful of brandy. 'Before Christmas, when I came to visit at your house, you mentioned… you asked… whether… if I might like to go and see a film with you. Was it called *Girl in a Million*?' She recalls the name perfectly well, but Martin has acquired such a fixed, deadpan expression she wonders whether she might have made a terrible misjudgement, if he has quite gone off the idea of stepping out with her. 'Well' – she resists the temptation to close her eyes – 'I was wondering if you would still like to take me. That is, if you haven't seen it already, or they haven't stopped showing it, or—'

'There's nothing I would like more.' He is beaming at her now, his whole face radiating incredulity. It's as though the barman has just switched on the fringed lamp hanging above their table. 'When would you like to go? Tomorrow? Or Monday? I'll need to check where it's on. What time would suit you best? If we see an evening show, we might possibly want to get a bite to eat first?'

'Perhaps not Monday. I have to go to work the following day. Next weekend would be better, if you…'

'Of course.' Martin nods vigorously. 'Of course. I'll make enquiries about Friday. And if I might call you…?'

She nods slowly. She feels like she has stepped on a slide.

'Wonderful!' His voice drops, suddenly serious. 'You never know, do you? I mean, here I was, having had, well, not the easiest of days. To be honest, I was feeling a little low. And then I happened to run into you, and now the world seems an entirely different place.'

Fran smiles. At first out of politeness, and then because she realises that she likes Martin. She likes him a great deal.

A clock chimes from somewhere beyond the bar. Hastily, Fran lowers her glass. Her parents probably returned from the hospital ages ago and she has hardly spared them a moment's thought. 'I really must go home. My family will be wondering where on earth I am.'

'You can't possibly walk. It's practically dark and far too cold. You must wait here, and I'll fetch my car.'

Before Fran can object, Martin is standing up. For a second he hesitates, his face folded inward with concentration. All at once he leans forwards and pecks her on the cheek before sweeping up his coat and hurrying away. Fran lifts her hand to the site of his kiss. Her skin feels very slightly chafed, as though she has just brushed away an insect, while her insides are churning with the brandy and a raft of emotions that she's quite unable to name.

Chapter Seventeen

'I've told you before,' Vivien says with a sigh, 'I don't remember how I came to be on the Sculthorpe bus. I must have taken the wrong one from Fakenham and been making my way back.'

On the other end of the telephone, her mother seems unable to drop the subject.

'Yes, I *am* a lot better now, but it doesn't make any difference. The afternoon of the accident remains a complete blank. I can barely recall going out in the first place. I suppose I must have been doing some Christmas shopping…' She leans back against the hall table. 'Well, maybe I didn't find anything to buy, or perhaps the bags were lost in the wreckage of the crash!' Viv's hand goes to the left side of her scalp and her fingers brush the soft stubble that is newly visible and itching in the place where the surgeon shaved her head. Although she examines the horrid bald patch every morning in the bathroom, it's still too early to tell whether the hairs will retain their chocolate lustre or, as the doctor has warned, the trauma will turn them grey. 'Alice is a little better… Yes, beginning to get over the shock… No, not this evening. It's nearly nine o'clock and she's fast asleep in bed. You can speak to her in a few days' time. Anyway, I really must go and see what Toby is up to… Of course, that would be…'

The front door opens.

Viv's voice suddenly hardens. 'Actually, Mother, I have to hang up right now… No, there isn't a problem exactly. Only that Toby needs help with something rather urgently.'

The receiver clatters into the cradle.

Viv gapes at her husband. 'What on earth are you doing?'
Framed by the lintel of the porch, he is standing with a rifle slung
casually over his right shoulder.

'We've got intruders. There's somebody outside, I'm certain of it.'

Reluctantly, Viv comes forwards and peers into the inky depths
of the garden. For all she can see, she might as well have her eyes
closed. 'Did you actually spot anyone?'

Toby shakes his head.

She reaches behind him for the brass handle, waits for him
to step into the hallway before shutting the door quickly. 'Why
would we have intruders? We're almost in the middle of nowhere.
I'm sure it was nothing.'

'I heard noises. I think someone's after us, coming for us tonight.'

Viv swallows. The intensity of his gaze is disconcerting and, if she
doesn't concentrate, make an effort to stay sane, almost believable.
She has to remind herself that her husband is plainly not himself
these days and there is no conceivable reason why anyone should
be prowling around the exterior of their house.

'I expect you heard the neighbour's dog. He probably got the
scent of a rabbit or a fox and found a hole in the hedge. He's not
much older than a puppy and doesn't understand that he's supposed
to stay in his own garden. It wouldn't be the first time!' She takes
Toby's elbow, ushers him a little way forwards. 'Put the gun down.
You don't need that now.'

As if in response to a hypnotist's command, Toby eases the
leather strap from his shoulder and lays the barrel across the
mahogany mirror of the hall table. He looks at Viv for approval.

'Why don't you put it away in a cupboard?'

He considers the rifle again and his mouth jerks, making his
whole face twitch. 'They might come back.' His conviction, his
anxiety, pulses like an electric current. Aware she is being ridiculous,
Viv can feel herself tensing, straining into the silence for any sound
from the winter's night outside. She walks back to the front door

and pulls across the heavy velvet drape, glad for the distraction of the snap of her heels and the grate of the iron curtain rings along the pole.

'I think we should have an early night. It will do us both good. My head is beginning to ache again, and you, you seem…' She doesn't finish the sentence, unable either to articulate her fear for Toby or find a suitable form of words to disguise her disquiet. Instead she switches off the chandelier and begins to climb the stairs. After a moment, to her immense relief, she hears the treads behind her creak and Toby muttering something indecipherable under his breath.

Two hours later Viv is more awake than when she first lay down. Lately, every night has become an ocean, with morning, the shell-grey cracks of breaking light, the shore to which she has to navigate without even the guidance of a star or compass. Only the knowledge that she has managed to cross the deep before stops her from venturing downstairs in search of water, or a book – or the gin bottle.

It's more than two weeks since the accident, yet each time she closes her eyes, the possibility of sleep is hijacked by the piercing scream of brakes, the crunch of metal on metal. The very next instant the mattress begins to lurch and sway, and she has to grab the bedstead to stop herself from falling onto the floor with her pulse jumping nineteen to the dozen. It's a lie, of course, that she can't remember why she was taking a bus from Sculthorpe. All of that afternoon, from the awful American officer in the post room to the infinitely long seconds of the crash, is so garishly and dreadfully clear the scenes might be drawn in the same thick wax crayons Alice likes to use. Nobody, however, seems to suspect her secret. Except, Viv muses, possibly her mother, who at least has the good sense to keep her doubts to herself.

And she has still heard nothing from Alex.

Viv rolls onto her side, away from Toby, who is lying on his back and snoring slightly with his mouth open. A hard, white channel of moonshine spills between the curtains onto her pillow, revealing her rosebud housecoat discarded on the carpet, the mess of hairpins and make-up strewn across the dressing table, and the milky translucent skin of her own forearms.

Alex must have heard about the accident.

For several days afterwards the local papers talked of little else, the story even made a brief appearance on the national news. Assuming Alex received her letter, he must have wondered, must surely have *worried*, if Viv might have been on the fated bus. She has told herself he couldn't have known which hospital she was in, didn't dare make contact with her at home because of Toby. Yet in the spotlight of the unforgiving moon, a little voice reminds her there are only two local hospitals, that it isn't difficult to call a switchboard, that a card – flowers even – could have been sent from a concerned anonymous friend.

Viv swings her legs out of bed slowly, as if experimenting with the idea of standing up. For a second she waits stock-still, focused on Toby as his chest continues to rise and fall with peaceful oblivion under the covers. Then she threads her arms through the sleeves of the housecoat, tiptoes towards the dressing-table stool and lifts its pink padded lid. Inside the seat, a store of clean nightdresses is folded between perfumed sachets that smell of lavender and violets, of pristine laundry, home-making and domestic order.

Viv delves deep beneath the cotton and pulls out a stack of envelopes secured with a rubber band. There must be a dozen of them at least. Letters from Alex during the first months of their affair, sent to the old house when Toby was fighting in France and there was no one but her to pluck them from the doormat as if they were nectar from the gods themselves. She raises the bundle to her face. The paper smells of Alex's aftershave. Of musk and sandalwood. Of longing and anticipation. Of recklessness. Of guilt. Of sex. She imagines Alex spraying each sheet, fully intending the scent to transport her straight back to the helpless inevitability of their liaisons. And the contents of the writing too couldn't have made the depth of his feelings plainer. *You mean the whole damn world to me, Viv. Life without your beautiful face, your beautiful body, would be empty as hell, and one heck of a lot colder, if you know what I mean!*

She should read the letters again now. To quell the doubts and remind herself how very much he loves her while she waits for him to get in touch. He is probably worried sick but understands that Toby will have spent more time at home since she left the hospital. No doubt he doesn't want to risk revealing their relationship until she is well enough to tell Toby herself their marriage is over.

A creak of mattress springs makes her jump, then freeze. As she watches, Toby shifts and levers upwards onto both elbows. Sleep-drunk eyes stare unblinkingly at the bedroom door. Viv follows his gaze, pulse quickening. She's starting to imagine she can see the handle turning, sense shadows lurking on the landing, when her husband carefully lowers himself down again and almost instantaneously the gentle snoring resumes. Viv exhales a steady breath. Hugging the envelopes close, she begins to slink from the room.

A moment later she stops again. From outside the window creeps a muffled knocking, like the sound of branches rubbing rhythmically against a fence. Her heart leaps into her mouth again. Silently, she repeats her earlier rebuke to Toby: *Why on earth would we have intruders here?* The noise probably *is* the wind brushing the fir tree against the wooden fence at the end of the garden. Just as she convinces herself, the faintest, lightest tinkling of breaking glass floats through the window. Viv tweaks the curtains. A shiny shilling of a moon sprinkles the lawn in silver light, but she can see nothing untoward, certainly no black-figured intruders slinking about with swag bags, or new trails of footprints in the snow. Besides, why would any burglar loiter *outside* rather than trying to break into the house?

The neighbours' dog.

She must have been right all along. The Labrador next door has escaped again and broken the cold frame beside the tool shed. Immediately, relief transitions to frustration. If the wretched dog *has* stepped on the glass, he is bound to have some nasty splinters lodged in his paws. Viv considers the bundle of letters. The prospect of curling up in an armchair and rereading them is infinitely more attractive than braving the frozen night to search for a limping, bleeding dog whose name she can't now remember. Even climbing back into bed beside her husband is more appealing than that. She glances at the window. The coal-coloured, silk-purse feel of the Labrador's coat, his panting exuberance, press into her thoughts and tug at her conscience. Besides, she's already wide awake. With a sigh, Viv capitulates to the inescapable. Dropping the letters back inside the dressing-table stool, she adjusts the belt of her gown and slips quietly out of the bedroom.

The garden is like a foreign country or a scene from a fairy tale made wicked with cold. Familiar contours of lawn and shrubs have become ghostlike in the pearly wash of the winter moon, while the ice-stricken landscape feels tense with apprehension, as if Viv's arrival is both unexpected and unwelcome. Although she has thrown Toby's overcoat over her housecoat and pulled on a pair of fur-lined boots, the chilled density of the air is shocking. Her feet sink through the crusted snow with the creak of an unoiled door and somewhere overhead a tawny owl hoots, low and lingering. Shivering, Viv lifts up her torch towards the reach of the trees, but the glow diffuses to nothing in the strange grey light.

As quickly as she can, she hurries towards the distant landmark of the tool shed. Behind the shed is the border of the neighbour's fence, while the empty cold frame sits nearby. On her second sweep of the boundary the torch beam hooks upon a broken plank. Like the final moments of a baby tooth the wood is dangling at an angle, creating a gap from which a trail of paw prints makes neat, deep indents in the snow. With a sense of vindication, Viv straightens up and peers into the gauzy night. Something small and furry scuttles with sudden energy into the shelter of a bush, but there is no sign of the Labrador. From the fence she follows the line of prints to the shed and from there to the cold frame itself where the roof has collapsed leaving translucent chunks scattered on the grass.

Crouching down, Viv picks up one of the shards. A bead of blood crawls across the surface. For some reason the dog must have bounded on top of the frame and has now limped further into the garden. She gazes into the darkness, trying and failing to remember the animal's name, and when she attempts to whistle her lips are too numb to draw together. As she wonders what to do next, the shine of the torch seems all at once to bounce back at her and she sees the light has struck the blade of a spade propped against the far side of the shed. Raising the beam exposes other items too – a hoe, a rake, a pitchfork, a wheelbarrow – as if the gardener has emptied the entirety of his work tools from the shed and forgotten to put them away. Viv blinks in confusion.

And then she screams.

A face, white and disembodied, is staring at her from the blackened shadows of wood and metal. Before she can move a muscle a man steps forwards, left arm raised to shoulder height.

'It's a'right. I'm not gonna hurt you.' The words slur into each other as if colliding on a downward stair.

Viv steps back and her foot twists sideways over something hard. The pain, sharp and unexpected, is like a switch that flicks her fear to anger. 'Who are you? And what are you doing in our garden?' The object that made her trip, she sees with added fury, is a beer bottle. She badly wants to rub her ankle yet dares not bend down and look away.

'Nothing. I'm doing nothing.'

Her focus flits rapidly between the face and the shed. 'The tools! You're taking our tools, aren't you?' She imagines him emptying the shed, cracking open a beer and waiting for the cover of the night or the help of a friend to carry the bounty home. Probably the Labrador was drawn to the noise, curious to investigate, before being shooed, or most likely booted, away and running straight into the cold frame. Her foot brushes against the bottle again and this time she kicks out hard, making the glass rattle across the frozen ground and smack into the fence.

For a moment, the racket stuns them both into silence. Then the man says, 'I was just borrowing them. For a job I need to do.'

Viv stares at him hotly. 'I don't believe you! You were trying to steal them! I'm going to call the police.' The moment the words leave her mouth she's aware of her distance from the house, the long yards to the black telephone sitting on the table in the hallway. High above, the treetops rustle, as if the emptiness of her threat is palpable even to them. Suddenly Viv wishes that Toby was with her.

The man steps forwards. 'Call the police, will you?'

'Why shouldn't I? You're stealing our things! I'll go straight to the house and telephone them now.' Viv half-swings away from him, desperate to run, to sprint towards the sanctuary of a lockable door and an electric light, yet terrified to turn her back.

'It's always the same with people like you.'

The bitterness in his voice surprises her. Slowly, she turns around. 'People like us?'

'Rich people. With your big fancy house and big fancy garden. I bet that husband of yours didn't see any real action. I'd bet my last shilling he spent his war moving toy soldiers over maps instead of burning to death in a desert with nothing but sand and flies and the stench of dead men rotting in the sun. And a girl, whose brother is a fucking *draft dodger*' – the words burn through the moonlight – 'gets a nice little office job while proper soldiers like me come back to nothing!'

Viv glares at him incensed. 'My husband did *not* spend the war in a command room! My husband fought like you did. He must have been just as frightened as his men, but he had to lead them, he had to stay strong even when his friends were dying all around him. Despite the terrible, terrible things he saw, he had to keep going every single day!' To her astonishment she realises that she's shouting. She tries to swallow, but the ache in her throat is like a fire in a stubble field. Too late she realises she's on the verge of tears and before she can stop, her voice cracks completely. 'It's ruined him, the war!' Then abruptly, 'It's ruined us.' She swallows and gazes at the man sadly, 'Like… like it's ruined you too.'

For a long moment they stare at each other. Viv shuts her eyes. Opens them again.

Eventually she says with an attempt at normality, 'What do you mean about Daisy?'

The man is gazing at her mutely.

'That her brother was a draft dodger?' Viv prompts. 'What did you mean about that?'

'Don't you know? Everyone else around here does.'

Viv shakes her head.

'He never fucking signed up. Got a bit of paper to say he has a dodgy heart and couldn't fight. Why d'you think he has to work in town? Because nobody round here would give him a job, that's why!'

'But if he has a weak heart…?'

'Weak heart, my arse! The only thing wrong with him is his lily-coloured liver—'

'Shh!' Abruptly, Viv turns away. 'The dog, I think I heard the dog!' She peers deep into the gloom. 'Yes, I'm sure that was a whine. He's been injured by the glass. I need to find him before—'

The blistering crack of a rifle cleaves the sentence in two.

Shockwaves reverberate around them like the wash of an ocean liner.

'What the fuck was that?'

Viv says, 'I don't know.' However, she does know, they both must surely know. They have both heard gunfire before and her best guess as to why she might be hearing it now makes her heart gallop with fear. She ought to move, but her feet are heavy as clay. Motionless, she watches as the bottle-man retreats into the shadows of the tool shed before slipping silently towards the broken fence panelling. An instant later she's on her own again.

'Toby?' The word comes out as a whisper. 'Toby?' Louder this time. Wrenching her feet free of the earth, Viv makes herself face towards the house. The ice-capped lawn stretches before her, the bulked house brooding in the distance. Her eyes sweep the scene, back and forth, back and forth. Then all at once her gaze locks, a terror she has never known before grabs her heart and she is racing, stumbling in her clumsy boots towards a small heap of clothing that is lying motionless near the edge of the patio.

'Alice! Oh my God, Alice!' She is screaming now. A cry of anguish from so deep inside she is choking on her own voice. 'Toby? Toby, where are you? What have you done? What in God's name have you *done*?'

She sees the blood first. A scarlet river streaming through the snow, a deep sluice of red turning pink at the edges where the warmth of the fluid is melting the flakes. Breathing hard, she slithers to a halt and claps her hand over her mouth. Revulsion and relief are thundering through her ribcage simultaneously making her shake uncontrollably.

She gapes at what she believed to be a bundle of clothes but is in fact the tousled whorls of an animal's fur dusted in white crystals. Winston, she remembers now. The dog's name is Winston. How could she have forgotten that? The empty eyes of the Labrador stare back at her. His chest is an open well of flesh, an indistinguishable red mess of ripped muscle and bone where the bullet felled him in his tracks.

'Oh my God.' Crouching down, Viv places her palm on the dog's tranquil ribcage. His coat is still warm, a perfect black, gleaming in the moonshine.

Footsteps crunch behind her shoulder. 'I got him! He was coming for us and I got him with one shot!'

Viv twists a piece of ebony hair between her fingers, unable even to glance upwards. 'This is Winston, Toby. The neighbours' dog.'

'I told you we had intruders. You didn't believe me, but I was right, wasn't I? I was *right*!'

'This isn't an intruder, Toby! This was a *dog*, a friendly dog. He wasn't coming for you. He probably just wanted to say hello. He was just a puppy. He came through a hole in the fence. He... he must have heard something in our garden.' It strikes her like a slap in the face that if Toby had seen the bottle-man first he probably would have shot him instead. That if the Labrador hadn't startled Toby, she could be kneeling beside the corpse of a human being. That her husband would be guilty of murder. And what if Alice *had* been in the garden? Her first paralysing, petrified instinct when she saw the mound on the snow might have been right. Bile rises in her throat. Still, she can't lift her eyes.

'He was attacking us. All of us. You and me and Alice.' Toby's voice is higher, tighter. Viv can't tell if he is being defensive or is genuinely confused.

'No, Toby...'

'I had to protect us. That's my job. To keep everyone safe.'

'Not from a puppy. We don't need protecting from a *puppy*.' Although her head feels heavy as a cannonball, she manages at last to look up. To her surprise, Toby is focused neither on her nor the dog, but somewhere far into the middle distance. As Viv gets up, he snaps around to face her.

'They're coming! There'll be more of them any second now!'

'Nobody's coming, Toby.'

'I can hear them, Viv. Listen!'

There's a moment of quiet, of pearly blue silence, when the night softens around them before Toby throws the rifle onto his shoulder and fires into the distance.

Viv grabs his arm. 'Dear God, Toby, stop! STOP!' She is weeping, the tears oddly hot against her face.

'We must take up positions. There's not much time to lose.'

'Toby!'

The gun is flat against his cheek, his finger ready on the trigger.

'TOBY!'

His empty black glance almost makes her crumble to her knees. Words desert her. She thinks, *I have never been this tired. Or this alone.* Then, steadily with determination. 'If they're coming and you need to protect me, I think you should take me inside. That way you can look after Alice as well.'

She holds his gaze. The cliff edge feels just inches away. From the darkness above, the owl calls again, homeward bound over the trees, announcing his return.

Slowly, very slowly, Toby lowers the rifle. 'I suppose you could be right.' He motions with the butt, as though the weapon is merely an extension of his arm. 'Walk ahead of me and I'll provide cover from the rear.'

Viv starts to move before he can change his mind. As she heads towards the open doors of the dining room, she's aware of Toby barely a pace behind, his breath grazing her ear, the clunk of the gun as he settles and resettles the casing on his collarbone. Instinct – or fear – tells her not to look back at him.

Eventually her hand is reaching for the door frame, her foot stepping over the threshold. Once inside, she stands for a moment absorbing the warmth, the contained silence, the smell of furniture polish, before she flicks on a lamp and the outside night turns the colour of a raven's wing as if a theatre curtain has dropped and the lights have gone up in the auditorium.

Cautiously, she turns around. Toby is staring at the garden, the rifle hanging at his side. Eventually he steps away from the window and lays the gun across the mahogany stretch of the dining table.

'Toby?'

'Sorry…' He shakes his head.

'For a moment,' Viv says quietly, 'I thought you'd shot Alice.'

He shakes his head again more violently. 'That dog… I believed…' He stops. For the briefest instant only, his eyes meet hers. 'I don't know what I believed.' He steps past her to pour a whisky from the decanter on the sideboard. She watches the quiver of his wrist, the amber puddle that gathers on the wood and then begins to drip down the front panel of the cupboard. Without a word, he picks up the glass and leaves the room.

Viv touches her hair. She is newly aware that the rough furrow of stiches is throbbing, but the sensation has a dull, familiar quality as though she has been experiencing the pain for some time without really noticing. She will have to ask Toby to move the Labrador's body first thing in the morning, before Alice wakes up and sees the carnage on the lawn. And then, of course, she will have to inform the neighbours that their dog is dead.

What can she possibly say to them? What reason can she give to explain the fact that her husband has shot their puppy? Viv shuts her eyes. Tadpole tails of half-light swim before her lids. The truth is stark and unavoidable. She will have to tell them that her husband is ill. Very ill. That he needs medical attention and she, his wife, is going to find someone to help him. Her gaze moves to the rifle, left casually beside the silver candelabra. The echo of her terror when she first spied the slaughter makes her whimper out loud. And straight away her conscience brings the next ghastly thought: if Toby is fragile, so vulnerable, how can she possibly leave him and take Alice to America? The dog, poor Winston, was tragic enough, but how much worse might the outcome have been – could things become – if Toby is left alone?

Yet how can she possibly stay?

As she heads to bed, a sliver of light is seeping from the drawing room. Viv leans against the door and peeps through the opening. Toby is sitting with his hands over his face, the whisky untouched at his side. He is silent, but Viv can see all too plainly the shudder of his shoulders, the ragged heaving of his chest. She prepares herself to go to him, then stops. Although only feet away from her, the blue pile of the carpet might as well be the North Sea and Toby on the other side of it. For a moment or two Viv watches her husband, her bones aching with sadness, before she turns away and climbs slowly up the stairs.

Chapter Eighteen

4 January 1947

'Martin, for heaven's sake! That's the third time I've tripped over you this morning!'

'Sorry! Sorry!' Backing away, he draws out a chair from under the kitchen table and sinks down heavily.

His mother disappears into the larder and returns a moment later bearing a large terrine. 'Irene made oxtail soup yesterday because she won't be coming in again until Monday. I'll heat us some up for lunch and Daisy can join us when she gets back.' She glances at him. 'Are you quite sure you're all right? Did you want to speak to me about anything?'

'No… I mean, yes. Everything is fine.' He pulls a packet of Swan Vesta matches from his trouser pocket and taps them lightly against the table. The snug, square fit of the box in his palm is a comfort and at least keeps his hands busy. It's tempting to light up, but his mother would never tolerate smoking in the kitchen.

'Where is Daisy?'

'Visiting Barbara. She said she would be back by half past twelve, but you know what those two are like once they start chatting. And with Daisy working, the weekends are their only chance to see each other.'

Martin glances at the clock. Five past twelve. With Daisy out of the house all morning, this has been the perfect opportunity to ask his mother about the discoveries he made yesterday. How the wrong doctor's signature could have ended up on his medical report, and why he and Daisy have never been told about the existence of little

Frederick. Yet the morning is almost over, and still he hasn't been able to broach the subject. Swivelling the matchbox between his fingers he watches his mother ladle an unappetising brown liquid from the tureen into a saucepan. From the back she still appears youthful – slim waist and styled crop of gingery curls flecked by the mere occasional silver thread.

Martin grimaces and his grip on the Swan Vestas tightens. He has no desire to have this conversation, to talk about Frederick or cross-examine his mother about the medical report, for which, he assures himself, there must surely be a straightforward explanation. Nor, however, can he spend another sleepless night wrestling with the impossible until he finds himself doubting everything and anything he has ever been told.

'Martin! That tapping, it's driving me quite mad! Do stop fiddling with the matchbox, dear. Are you very hungry? I could heat up your soup now, if you like. You don't have to wait for Daisy.'

Martin's palm collapses around the packet as if he is entrapping a small animal. 'Don't bother with any soup for me. I'm not particularly hungry.'

'What on earth is it then?' His mother swings round, wiping her hands on an apron. She examines him appraisingly, head on one side. 'You seem to be all at sixes and sevens.'

Without thinking he begins to rap the matchbox on the table before dropping the box abruptly and folding his arms. 'Actually, there *is* something I want to talk to you about. A couple of things, in fact.'

'Right.'

'Maybe you should sit down.'

'Goodness, that does sound rather serious!' She smiles, but when he doesn't respond he thinks he sees her colour dip, or a dart of fear, perhaps, flicker across her face.

Getting up, he pulls out another chair from under the table and watches as she wipes her hands on her apron and lowers herself onto the seat. She throws him a quick glance before her attention is caught by a mark on the oilcloth.

'I want to ask you about my medical report. The conclusion of the medical board that I was unfit for military service.' He stops, considers for a moment the wretched matchbox. Then, 'Dr Sands found that I couldn't fight because I suffer from dilated cardiomyopathy, didn't he?'

His mother lifts her gaze from the blue-and-yellow check. 'You know about this already, Martin. You've always known about this.' She sounds perplexed, and also a trifle relieved. Frowning, she licks her forefinger and rubs at the stain.

'I haven't—'

'Dilated cardiomyopathy means you have a weak heart. That's what the doctor told you at the time.'

'*The* doctor, yes. But not Dr Sands.'

'What on earth do you mean?'

'I wasn't examined by Dr Sands. I never even met him. The doctor who conducted my medical board was called Dr Dandy.'

The rubbing stops. Both of her hands fly to her lap.

'You must be mistaken, Martin. It was such a stressful time for us all. I expect you've misremembered the doctor's name. It's very easily done—'

'No—'

'It was years ago and in the middle of the war. So much has happened since then—'

'I haven't misremembered the doctor's name!' The voice, his voice, is shockingly loud. He lowers his eyelids, presses his fingers to his forehead. The last thing he should want is to drag his mother's secrets into the daylight and dissect them as if he were conducting an autopsy, and yet the last thing he finds he can bear is to suffer these dreadful, cancerous, destabilising doubts a second longer. He takes a breath. 'I checked my old diary for the day of the examination, the tenth of August 1941, and the entry says I was seen by Dr Dandy. The name must have struck me as a little odd, humorous even, I suppose, and so I wrote it down.'

'Well, perhaps you got the name wrong at the time. Perhaps you misheard. Sands and Dandy do sound alike. Very similar, I would say.'

'*Sands* isn't a bit like *Dandy*. Besides' – Martin feels his torso drawing upright, as if he is about to hurdle a fence – 'there's another reason, an extremely good reason, why I couldn't have seen Dr Sands…' A pause. A breath. 'Dr Sands had most probably died by the tenth of August 1941 and if he wasn't dead, he certainly wasn't well enough to see any patients!'

Martin's mother stares at the floral print of her apron. For a while the silence vibrates around them, lapping at the table as if they are victims of a shipwreck stranded upon an island, until eventually she says quietly, 'How did you find out?'

'It wasn't terribly hard. I obtained the number for Dr Sands' surgery and spoke to the receptionist.'

Her head snaps upwards. 'But why, Martin? What on earth made you do that?'

'The night you had a visitor, when I came downstairs because I thought you were upset, I overheard part of a conversation, someone talking about my heart condition and describing the situation as *very serious*. You've always been so vague about the diagnosis, so I decided to find the medical report and see for myself exactly what it said. When I didn't recognise the name of Dr Sands, I hunted for the record in my diary.'

'You went through my private papers?' His mother's face is a mask of alarm and fury – and something else too, an emotion he can't quite identify.

'Only in search of a document about me. That belongs to me in actual fact!'

He squints at the clock again, steadies his breath and gently encloses his mother's hands within his own. 'Look, never mind about that now. Please. I need to know what happened. Tell me before Daisy comes home, while it's just the two of us and we can talk by ourselves.'

'I can't.'

To his amazement, she pulls away.

'I'm sorry, Martin. All you need to know is the army medical board diagnosed you with a weak heart.'

'I have a right to know everything!'

'It's not just about you!'

He gapes in disbelief. 'It's more about me than anyone else!' He sees her lips twitch, her mouth open, very slightly, yet the seconds pass and still she says nothing.

He picks up the matches, tosses them aside and strides across to the sink. Outside the window, somewhere on the other side of the world, a bullfinch is perched on the bird table drinking from a saucer. His mother must have put fresh water out that morning, like she always thinks to do when the ponds and puddles are frozen. The notion of her reliably tending to the birds makes him hate himself even more for what he is about to say. Taking hold of the sink, he leans forwards and addresses the bird through the glass. 'If you don't explain what happened, I'll tell Daisy your other big secret.' The clumsiness of it – his bluntness, his brutality – appals him.

'What other big secret?'

His knuckles are a row of bony white peaks. The hands of a stranger. 'That Daisy and I had a brother. An older brother, Frederick, who died when he was four years old.'

'Oh.'

The anguish conveyed by the single syllable spins Martin on the spot. His mother is crumpled over as if he has kicked her hard and quite deliberately in the stomach, and in a manner of speaking he has done exactly that. 'I'm sorry. I'm so sorry…' He hurries towards her chair, then halts and rakes his fingers through his hair. Takes another step forwards.

She is staring in bewilderment, tears falling unchecked, 'How did you find out about my Frederick? You *did* go through my things?'

'I found the death certificate. It was underneath the medical report. I chanced upon the paper, that's all... Please, Mother, I didn't want to upset you like this, but I must understand what happened. I can't bear to be kept in the dark. There's so much it seems I don't know. If you won't enlighten me, I shall find out somehow. I simply must, or else...' The sentence tails away. He draws the back of his palm across his face. His cheeks are wet too.

The silence stretches to such a length, he is beginning to think she will never reply. Finally, she says in a voice no more than a whisper. 'I only did it because of Frederick.'

'Did *what*?'

'You can't possibly understand, Martin. I pray you *never* understand what it's like to lose a child. The despair, the unending pain of it, the *helplessness* when you would give anything, anything at all, to hold them in your arms again, to feel their breath, warm against your face, instead of watching their little life slipping away from you. I could *never* go through that wretchedness again.'

'Is that why you didn't tell us – because we wouldn't understand?'

'You were less than two years old when he died, far too young to make sense of it, and Daisy a tiny baby. After your father passed away, I didn't want to burden you with more loss, more sadness, and I needed to protect myself. Explaining to you about Frederick would have meant me grieving for him all over again when for a long while I could barely cope as it was. Before I found the right time to tell you, the war came along and everyone was suffering so badly it hardly seemed possible to talk about a different tragedy, one from so long ago. And then of course the medical happened, and I couldn't say anything to make you think, that might have made you suspect...' Her voice disappears.

'Suspect what?'

She doesn't reply.

'Suspect *what*, Mother?' The question comes from the pit of his stomach.

The kitchen has become unnaturally still, the seconds hang like icicles, frozen and suspended. All at once he understands what she is going to say. And a part of him feels as if he has known about the lie from the very beginning. That somehow, he must always have been aware of it, have been complicit in the deception, in his own cowardice.

'You don't have a weak heart, Martin.'

For an instant the world stops spinning. He is aware only of the muscle beating behind his ribcage. The steady thud so reliably sound, so obviously regular. Of course, he has always known.

'As far as I'm aware you don't have dilated cardiomyopathy or any other medical problem that would make you unfit for service.'

'But the report...'

'The report isn't true. I asked Dr Dandy to find you medically unfit and...' – her voice snags – 'and after some persuasion he agreed. Apparently, Dr Sands was a colleague in a London practice; because Dr Dandy knew that Dr Sands was dying, he signed the report in Dr Sands' name to protect himself if the report should ever be challenged.'

Martin takes a large pace backwards. 'How could you do that?'

'Martin—'

'How could you turn my life into a lie? When everyone we know sacrificed so much, suffered so much.'

'I did it to protect you!'

'No' – he is reversing towards the sink at speed, as if he might turn the years back too – 'you did it to protect yourself! I may not have wanted to fight, but I didn't want to be an invalid either, to consider myself useless, unable to play a part in defending my country in our darkest hours. You prevented me from seeing and doing terrible things, you may even have spared me from being killed, but you also stopped me from being brave, from having the chance to feel proud, to look back at the war with honour and dignity and…' He closes his eyes. All those ridiculous daily walks to keep his heart healthy. He is even more laughable, even more pathetic, than he believed.

He opens them again to find his mother fixing him with a dry-eyed stare. 'War isn't about honour and bravery, Martin. It's about people having to survive the most inhuman conditions you can imagine, commit unspeakable crimes. It's about young, wonderful lives being thrown away, torpedoed at sea or bombed or machine-gunned, or jumping into oblivion with parachutes on their backs. It's about agony and destruction. And death. Over and over again. I couldn't bear for your life to be wasted. I simply couldn't bear to lose you as well.'

Outside on the bird table the bullfinch has been joined by a mate. Both are dipping their wings into the saucer of water, bathing companions amidst the chill. The chirruping and beat of feathers are audible even within the kitchen. Martin remembers his continual sense of exclusion, the pointed remarks he tries to ignore – the attack in the alley. He wonders if Dr Dandy has remained as discreet as his mother thinks, what the price of his silence has been. And for how long his mother has had to bear the cost. Presumably, he supposes, the night visitor he heard was actually Dr Dandy demanding his next instalment.

'I don't suppose this Dr Dandy falsified his medical report for nothing, did he? I imagine he charges a good deal of money for his services. How long do you have to keep paying him until he finally lets you off the hook?'

'That's not your business, Martin.' Her tone is low and steely. 'I don't regret what I've done for a moment and I won't apologise to you for it either. Here you are, standing in front of me with years stretching ahead of you, instead of a name etched upon a memorial and all those days of living, feeling, breathing, loving, thrown away—'

The front door clunks shut.

'I'm home! I do hope lunch is ready, I'm absolutely starving. I would have come back sooner, only Barbara has developed the most idiotic crush on her piano tutor and wanted to… Oh!' Daisy stops in the entrance. 'Have I interrupted something?'

'Not at all. We're quite finished.' Their mother gets to her feet. 'Martin and I were having a little reminisce, and I completely lost track of the time. The soup will only take a few minutes to warm through.'

As his sister pulls off her gloves, she searches Martin out with her gaze. He can see a whole host of questions practically printed in black ink across the middle of her forehead. Dipping his head, he hurries towards the door before she can ask him any of them.

'Martin!' Daisy's voice, light and quizzical, floats across the kitchen and lassoes him in the hallway.

He pauses, but he doesn't turn around.

'Don't you want your matches? You've left them in the middle of the table.'

Chapter Nineteen

10 January 1947

'Fran!'

Stumbling against her bicycle frame, she squints into the coal-dust gloom of the camp. Pockets of light from windows of the Nissen huts reveal only the white-tipped field and husky outline of two parked lorries. Yesterday, as the sky began again to empty of feathers, the respite of the last few days from fresh snowfall seemed merely an illusion. They were back in the full grip of winter, the roar of the cold louder and angrier than ever.

'Over here. Behind the lorry.'

A figure fleetingly emerges from the cover of the nearest cab. The powerful shape of the silhouette is familiar and so, all at once, is the voice. She breaks into a jog, yanking at the bicycle so that the pedals bang and scrape against her leg. There is the smell of escaped diesel and then the blue of his eyes searing through the dark. She stops. Recalls, aghast, the promise she has made to herself.

'Shouldn't you be inside? Won't they be doing the roll call soon?'

'Someone is covering for me. He will say I have a special job to do. And I do have a special job to do – meeting you.' Hunching slightly, he tucks his hands under his armpits and stamps his feet.

How long has he been waiting for her? She delayed leaving for at least an hour, hoping the snow would stop, and only gave up when she realised if she dawdled any longer she would never be ready for Martin in time. Now, seeing Thomas and thinking of the evening ahead, her body starts to vibrate as if the pieces might fly apart.

'Come here. Nobody will find us.'

Looking around, she sees he is right. A half-hearted attempt at security has led to search lights being strung around the perimeter fence, but they are angled towards the lane, designed to catch absconders and visitors, not a rendezvous within the camp itself. Tucked into the lee of the truck's black shadow, they are entirely lost to the glare of the beams. She moves closer, hauling the bicycle after her like a dog.

'I so much wanted to see you, Fran. Since Christmas I can think of nothing else.' He stretches out a hand, pulls off a glove and his frozen fingertips graze the outline of her face.

She tilts her chin away. Clenches her jaw. 'Christmas was a long time ago, almost three weeks.'

'I wrote a letter to you. Maybe you didn't receive it?'

She shakes her head decisively, and untruthfully. The note had been contained in the kind of envelope used for a card. Anyone who happened to spot it on Fran's desk would have thought nothing of her receiving belated Christmas greetings. Now the piece of pale blue paper is held between the pages of a bedside book, the words read, and reread so many times that the message – *I love you, Fran* – barely seems to matter anymore, only the connection between the writer and the recipient, between Thomas and herself, made tangible and tactile by the indent of his pen, the smell of paper embedded with his breath as he inked the sentence she already knew to be true.

His brow furrows, 'I left an envelope—'

'I made a mistake! What happened at Christmas was wrong, I should never—'

'No!' He grabs her elbow. A heartbeat of silence. Then, more quietly, 'There was no mistake. How we feel about each other is not a mistake.' His gaze is fervent. Fervent and entirely certain.

'I am English, and you are German. Our countries have been at war for six years. Even if we wanted to, we couldn't be together. Nobody would accept us, our families, our friends, our communities would never understand.'

'*Even* if we wanted to…? Of course, we want to! It is all we want!'

His fingers seem to burn through the sleeve of her coat, melting her resolve. She shakes free her arm. Although she can't meet his eyes, she forces herself to look at his cheek, his left ear, a lock of hair curled and darkened by melting ice. 'That's not true, Thomas. You might want to be with me, but' – a breath, ragged and shaky – 'I don't want to be with you. The garden, the kiss. It was all a mistake.'

He stares at her.

She feels a stain seeping upwards through her stomach. A horrible black treacle rotting away her core. And when she opens her mouth, more poison, more lies, will spill out of her. A sob pounds her throat, the ache pushing for release.

'I don't believe you.' The light of his eyes intensifies. 'This is not you. Someone else is making you do this.'

Fran remembers June's outburst in the kitchen, her anger and contempt. *It would be the final straw for Father.* She swallows hard, 'My sister saw us together in the garden. She was standing by a bedroom window.'

'So, I am correct. It is your sister who is making you say these things!'

'She's right, Thomas! My sister is right! We have no future together.'

'We can make a future. We will find a way. We love each other.'

The pull of him is extraordinary, like gravity, like quicksand, a rope around her waist dragging her inexorably towards him. She hauls away her gaze. In the distance glimmer the metal bars of the exit gate and the rifle butt of the guard. The barriers are there to restrict the prisoners, but she feels no less trapped than they are.

'I don't love you.'

'What?'

'I became carried away at Christmas, swept up in the romance. That's all. There's *no* special connection between us.' She watches the snowflakes slip between his neck and the collar of his coat.

'Perhaps I needed my sister to make me realise it. I don't love you, I'm sorry. I'm sorry if you believed my feelings were different.'

'You can't mean it.'

But she can hear he is starting to believe that she might.

'I do mean it. And I must leave now. I have to get ready to go to the cinema with someone. Another man.'

She manages not to cry until she has wheeled her bicycle to the gate, bid goodnight to the guard and is so far from the camp that she can no longer sense the incredulous blue-eyed gaze beating upon her back. When she's certain the darkness is empty, that she's entirely alone, she slides off the seat and lets the frame crash to the ground. Crouching on her heels she buries her head in her arms. Her body feels in shock. She imagines Thomas returning to the hut, frozen not with cold but with stunned disbelief. If he doesn't hate her now, he will by morning, once he has spent the night reliving her rejection. And already her words seem so alien, so ridiculous, she can only believe that somebody else must have spoken them for her.

A radio is playing in Martin's car. Frank Sinatra is crooning a gentle sort of jazzy number and the volume is perfect. Fran hadn't noticed the radio the last time she was in the Crossley or anticipated such luxury. She imagines Martin fiddling to get the sound exactly right before he picked her up. Not so loud they can't talk over the top of the record but not so low that when Martin picks up the lyrics, as he does every chorus, he can't slip easily into the song. *Five minutes more, five minutes more…* as if the words reflect his own contentment with the present moment.

Fran glances sideways. The singing is steady and melodious and appears to be entirely natural, as if something Martin always does when he is in the car and is barely aware of his own habit. Whatever the reason, the music is making it hard for Fran to act as she planned. She had intended to tell Martin before they got to the cinema that, while she was happy to step out with him as a friend, she wasn't, after all, ready for a closer relationship *because she was in love with another person and couldn't imagine ever loving anyone else* – not, of course, that she could possibly say the last part out loud. Now, she would have to switch off the radio and make such a serious announcement into a tense and startled silence.

She stares in desperation out of the windscreen. They are driving into a curtain of white, the wipers beating back the snow in steady, heroic sweeps, but the inside of the car is comfortable, the tune catchy, and when Martin breaks off from humming the refrain to murmur how pleased he is to be with her, how happy he would be to think they might, perhaps, go regularly to the pictures together, she hesitates one moment too long and before she knows it the comment has slipped away unchallenged.

When they get to the cinema, he drops her at the door, telling her to wait somewhere warm while he parks the car and queues for tickets. She is doing exactly that, standing beneath a poster of James Stewart with her hands on a radiator when a voice drags her away from her anguished thoughts.

'They say we'll have to make do without electricity.' An older woman wearing a felt hat is regarding her through prominent, rather orb-like eyes.

Fran takes a small step sideways. 'I beg your pardon?'

'If this weather keeps on, it won't be long before the coal won't be able to get through and then the government will have to cut the electricity.'

Fran gapes at the woman in alarm. 'Gosh, I do hope not.' No electricity would mean searching out every last candle stub, dinner cooked on the camping stove, no coal for her father's bedroom, or any fireplace come to that, and a permanent veil of ice on the inside of the windows. And the lovely new heater in the office would be useless.

There's the tiniest of pauses. Then, 'I just love him, don't you?'

It takes Fran a second or two to move from the threat of power cuts to James Stewart.

'Every picture he's in, I make my hubby take me the moment it comes out. I shall count down the days to *It's a Wonderful Life*, cross them out on my calendar. Is your hubby buying tickets too? Which one is he, or shall I take a guess? I can always tell these things. It's a knack I have, practically a sixth sense. Now let me…'

Fran gestures at Martin quickly. 'My…' she hesitates, reaching for an appropriate word, '*escort* is over there.' Wishing the woman would disappear in a puff of smoke she watches as Martin slides three shillings across the booth.

'Just stepping out, are you?' The felt hat tilts sideways. 'Well, that's definitely the one I would have picked if you'd let me, no question at all! As I say, I'm quite an expert in this department. Those wedding bells are just around the corner, you mark my words. And I do like a tall man…' She breaks off as Martin arrives and turns her owl's gaze on him. 'I was just saying to this pretty young lady of yours, what a lovely couple you make.'

'Thank you.' Although he throws Fran a bemused glance, she can tell he's pleased.

'A sight for sore eyes.'

'That's very kind…'

'I get such pleasure from seeing young couples out and about, having fun. After all we've been through these last years. And the pair of you look so fine, so *unscathed* by the war, if you know what I mean. Particularly you, young man!' Plucking Martin's sleeve, she adds conspiratorially, 'This is what you fought for, isn't it? I'll bet the thought of this beautiful girl waiting at home was what kept you going against those Huns! Well, you enjoy yourself, my dear. You deserve it.'

There's a second of frozen silence before Fran snaps to attention. She gives the woman a glacial stare. 'Do please excuse us.' She drags Martin away and as soon as they are out of earshot squeezes his arm. 'What a ridiculous creature! How dare she be so familiar.' She glances over her shoulder, not caring how abrupt she seemed or even whether the woman can hear her.

Martin's mouth is set in a grimace.

'She didn't know about your heart,' Fran persists. 'I mean, how could she? Otherwise she would never have been so tactless.'

To her surprise he doesn't reply. Instead he takes her arm and heads towards the auditorium with his gaze fixed ahead. Eventually, at the entrance he stops. 'It doesn't matter. We mustn't let something silly like that spoil our evening.' She has a brief glimpse of his face, a resolute smile that fails to mask a simmering, sad kind of anger before they are plunged into the gloom of the cinema and the glow of the usherette's torch is directing them to the back of the stalls.

The newsreel begins as soon as they sit down, making further conversation impossible. At first Fran is relieved – what could she possibly say to raise Martin's spirits? – but soon her thoughts are tumbling over each other in a horrible kind of soup. The heartbreak of the encounter with Thomas churns miserably with the absurd premonition of the woman in the felt hat and the wretched business of Martin's weak heart, which seems, she now sees, to haunt him everywhere he goes. She feels terrible for him, as if the pain were her own, or at least the hurt of a very close friend – which, she supposes, in many ways he is. Confused, she peeks sideways. His focus is directed squarely ahead, but Fran would bet her life that he isn't concentrating on the black-and-white news clips either.

In the interval before the main picture Martin insists on going to buy them both ice creams. On his return he holds aloft two pots triumphantly. 'Glad I was near the front of the queue, they're about to run out!' Although the notion of eating anything makes her feel quite sick, Fran takes one of the tubs with murmurs of appreciation and watches Martin open his own with enthusiasm. Settling down, he crosses his legs and turns to her with determined cheeriness.

'Now, you must tell me what it's like, being in the camp. I bet you have some tales to tell, but I can't imagine how anyone manages to do a stroke of work sitting in the same room as my sister!'

Somehow the time passes. Eventually the lights lower, and Fran sinks into the darkness as if it were a mattress, using a moment when Martin is searching for his handkerchief to slide the untouched ice cream under her seat. He appears more relaxed now and she realises with a lurch of guilt just how much he is enjoying himself. When Joan Greenwood appears on screen, he briefly touches Fran's knee, as if to register the moment, and as the best jokes happen, he laughs loudly and happily before glancing sideways to check she is amused too. Although she manages to smile back, her mind is so agitated that she can barely follow the plot.

Towards the end of the film she becomes aware of a weight in her lap. In a slow, almost dreamlike kind of way, she feels Martin's hand enclose her own and then his thumb press against her palm, encouraging her to open her fingers. He has shifted position and is now leaning slightly towards her seat so that if she should lean back, if she should turn her head, they would be close enough to kiss.

She stays stiller than ever. Although she longs to pull away her arm, she cannot bring herself to wound Martin again, not when he has only just recovered from the business in the foyer. Instead she focuses on not moving her fingers, on not giving him the slightest encouragement to make any further advance. As her hand grows clammy and hot she stares straight ahead until her arm seems to detach itself from the rest of her body altogether.

'Are you ready to go?'

To her amazement the credits are rolling.

Most of the row the far side of Martin are on their feet and he is half-standing too. He smiles, 'You seem in a bit of a daze.' If he feels let down by her response, her chilliness, he is hiding his disappointment well.

On the journey home there is no Frank Sinatra. Martin fiddles with the radio with increasing impatience, but in the end they have to settle for a gardening programme and an earnest discussion about the relative merits of different spring flowers. As they leave the town the snow becomes heavier. A laborious squeak accompanies every sweep of the wipers and Martin perches forwards on the seat, peering into the swirling vortex with a frown of concern. By the time he finally draws up outside her house, Fran feels emptied out, as if she must have lived the day several times over. She releases the passenger door with a sense of relief just as Martin appears by the window to open the door for her. When she gets out, he barely shuffles backwards so that she can't move without squeezing rather obviously between him and the car.

'I've had a wonderful evening, Fran…' He pauses. 'I hope you enjoyed it too?'

'Of course, I've had a lovely time.' She is blinking back the flakes, desperate to get inside.

'Good. Good. That's marvellous.' Oblivious to the weather, he is obviously plucking up courage to kiss her, and avoiding his embrace is impossible unless she pushes straight past him and makes her rejection crystal clear. An instant later he places his arms around her waist. She is fleetingly aware of the bulk of his approaching body, the yearning adoration splayed across his face, before his lips press against hers. She tastes the sweet trace of vanilla ice cream and the salty, cushiony swell of his tongue as his grip around her back tightens.

Within moments he straightens up again, loosens his hold and draws his wrist across his forehead. 'I shouldn't have done that. It was very forward of me. Please forgive me for letting my emotions get the better of me, I've had rather a difficult time of it recently. Of course that's no excuse, if you didn't want… don't want.' His voice tails away and he considers her anxiously. 'I do like you so very much, Frances. Very, very much indeed. You really are quite the best thing in my life. To be honest, if it wasn't for you, I think I might start to wonder why I was even bothering to get up in the mornings.'

Fran makes herself meet the desperate shine in his eyes.

It is impossible, utterly impossible, to say what she intended to say, what she ought to say.

Immediately, she drops her gaze. 'I really must go inside now, Martin. If my mother heard your car, she'll be wondering what's going on. Besides, it's absolutely perishing out here!' She is only just managing not to rub the back of her hand across her mouth.

'Of course, of course you must go inside. How selfish of me!' He takes a large step sideways. 'Do get into the warm quickly before I make you freeze to death! Perhaps next week, another film or even dinner…?'

She hurries past, pretending not to hear, and when she calls over shoulder, 'Goodnight, Martin,' his answering farewell ripples uncertainly behind her.

Once through the door she heads straight to her room and collapses onto the edge of her bed. If only her affections for Martin mirrored his feelings for her, the solution would be beautifully, wonderfully simple. She thinks of the woman in the felt hat. Her stupid premonition: *Wedding bells just around the corner.* Both her parents and June would be delighted to see her marry so well, and to such a nice man. *What a fortunate girl, to have fallen on her feet like that.* And she *would* be lucky, she knows it. Both she and her whole family would be showered with kindness, want for nothing.

Fran touches her mouth. The skin feels numb.

She remembers the heady, helpless sense of falling as she kissed Thomas. That overwhelming sugary heat. Closing her eyes evokes the electric gaze she could follow to the ends of the earth, the startling sense of authenticity whenever she sees him, as if the rest of her life is merely the backstage preparation for those precious few moments.

All at once she gets to her feet and hurries downstairs. When she returns, she is holding a piece of paper and an envelope from her mother's stationery drawer. Didn't she hear on the radio that prisoners of war were now allowed to receive letters from members of the public? Well, she knows exactly where to send one to reach Thomas. Sweeping the bottles and jars on her dressing table to one side, she finds she is trembling even before the pen makes contact with the page. Thomas, she writes, as if calling out to him, and then, I'm sorry, and then, I love you. Over and over again, the same two phrases – *I'm sorry* and *I love you* – until the sheet is full of words and her sobs have swelled and spread the ink into a watery black howl of longing.

Chapter Twenty

Viv stares out of the window. Snow has engulfed the country, drowning the land in a frozen canvas that obliterates everything but treetops, telegraph poles and church towers. The news is all about the weather. Animals are starving to death in the fields, the Thames is as solid as a skating rink, and yesterday *The Times* carried a photograph of two women in Northampton delivering milk by sledge with ropes tied around their waists. Having endured the war, it hardly seems fair. All at once, winter has become the new enemy, the alien invader, grounding the delivery vans and coal trucks so that the shops are nearly empty and the country can barely generate heat. Viv carries their one electric fire with her from room to room, despite the fact the two small bars seem to make little impression on the dampness of the air. Besides, even electricity is rationed now and for five miserable hours a day all the power is turned off completely.

Shivering, she pulls her coat tighter. These days everyone wears their outdoor clothes inside, and since the accident she feels the cold like a poker, prodding and poking her with sharp aches of pain. Why *can't* the fuel trucks get through? Great big lorries like that ought to be able to cope with a snowdrift or two. Sighing with frustration, she peers over the front hedge for any sign of traffic on the street beyond.

Her worry about the roads is not only because of the coal. She has convinced Toby the highways are still passable for the simple reason that they have to be. There is no other option. His appointment today with the doctor feels like a lifeline, something she's gripped with increasing intensity as his behaviour has deteriorated. After the awful business with Winston she hid his gun at the back of her closet, tucking the deadly metal behind dresses of emerald silk and pink chiffon. She can hardly believe she ever wore them; the woman who floated on the arm of the handsome army captain is as ethereal and elusive to her as a figure from a dream. Now she listens to the same man turning the house upside down – hunting, she knows, for the rifle. Every so often, when she's certain Toby is downstairs, Viv opens her wardrobe door and reaches behind the soft folds of fabric to check the weapon is still there. And when Toby isn't searching the outhouses or ransacking cupboards, she finds him sitting with a whisky at his side, his body hunched, rocking gently, backwards forwards, backwards forwards…

On the other side of the glass nothing is moving. All the while Viv has stood by the drawing-room window nobody has ventured past their front gate, either by car or foot. The grey sky seems to bulge with the weight of the elements while glass-like daggers hang from the bird table. The city might as well be the North Pole rather than thirty miles away.

Viv scans the deserted street. She could, of course, arrange an appointment with the local doctor. However, she has finally found someone who professes to have an expertise in mental disorders. Besides, seeing a local doctor would be even riskier than braving the ravaged roads. How long would it be before news of Toby's illness became common knowledge, a source of whispers in the street, the theme of jokes in the public house? A day? Two days? A week at tops, and only if they were lucky. Soon after that would follow his dismissal from the camp.

And he cannot lose that too.

Not when he's about to lose Viv and Alice.

When Alex takes them to America.

Viv's train of thought trips as if over a paving stone, before she pushes quickly onwards. No, the roads to the city must be driveable. And Dr Dandy must be in his surgery, because she simply can't bear to think what might happen otherwise.

Mechanically she raises her hand to the scar on the side of her scalp. The gesture is frequent and automatic, her fingers feeling for the rough rope of skin to assess how much her hair has grown. Although the stubble has blossomed into the downy softness of a baby's pelt, the colour is turning silver and will, she fears, make a badger's stripe through the centre of the black as soon as the strands are long enough.

'What are you doing, Mummy?'

Viv swings on her heels. Alice has come through the door trailing a dolly with a single button eye and stuffing oozing from the seam at the back. 'I was looking out for Daisy,' Viv says truthfully. Since the classrooms are unbearably cold and most lavatory pipes have frozen, the government shut the schools two days ago. Viv has had to ask Daisy to mind Alice while she takes Toby to the doctor. Not that she has given Daisy any hint of the purpose of the outing. Even when Daisy seemed reluctant to oblige, Viv only tried to impress how badly she needed help, assuring her that Major Markham really wouldn't mind her not attending camp for one day.

'How long will you be gone?' Alice tugs Viv's skirt. Her eyes are big and round and anxious. Ever since the accident, Viv's comings and goings have to be carefully managed. Alice needs to know exactly when Viv is leaving and when she will be coming back – there's no room at all for spontaneity or poor timekeeping. Once, when Viv was half an hour late after a hospital appointment of her own, she found Alice curled up by the front door like a kitten, refusing Toby's attempts to prise her away.

Viv squats down and takes hold of both her daughter's tiny wrists. 'I've told you already, darling. Mummy and Daddy have something very important to do today. We might be away until teatime, but Daisy will stay here until we get back and I shall be home in time to put you to bed. 'Now' – she considers her daughter's pinafore dress and jumper – 'where are your cardigan and mittens? You must be so chilly!'

'They were scratching me. I took them off.' Pulling from Viv's grasp, Alice points through the window. 'Someone's coming. Is it Daisy?'

The top of a woollen hat is visible over the garden fence. A second later the wearer unlatches the gate and turns into the driveway. The postman, who has swapped his peaked cap for a thick balaclava and submerged his uniform beneath an overcoat, is picking a route up the front path.

Viv's chest tightens. The taste of anticipation rises in her throat. She has the same reaction each time she sees the postman approach or an envelope lying pale and promising on the hall floor. Yet the subsequent disappointment has become so habitual that even as she hears the clunk of the letter box and the gentle rush of falling paper, she's already steeling herself for the let-down. She tells herself there's no point in looking straight away, because Alex won't have written. That is, not unless she waits. If she can make herself last at least half an hour before checking, there will be a chance, a small possibility, that today might be the day her future lands golden and bright on the door mat.

Less than ten minutes later she interrupts a game of snap with Alice and the one-eyed dolly, placing her cards face down on the rug. 'Mummy just needs to fetch the post, darling.'

Alice frowns through wisps of white-blond hair. 'Why?'

'I'm expecting something important. And I ought to see if it has arrived before I go out with Daddy.' She gets up before Alice can voice an objection. 'I'll only be a moment.'

The envelope is conspicuous even from the doorway of the drawing room. Despite being brown, the colour of correspondence from the bank or a utility bill, the document is plainly not official because their address is scrawled in large black lettering across the entirety of the surface. Hurrying to the door, Viv grabs the letter from the pile and sees straight away the handwriting does not belong to Alex. The disappointment is a physical blow, a punch to the stomach that knocks the air clean away. An instant later she spots with another jolt the postmark is stamped Sculthorpe. About to rip the paper, her fingers suddenly freeze. The only explanation for why someone other than Alex would send her a letter is because Alex can't write one himself, and the only reason for that is because he is ill – or worse. Viv's heart falls off the edge of a cliff. There must have been another dreadful accident. Much more slowly, she slides a trembling thumb under the pasted flap and eases the envelope open.

Inside rests a single sheet, thin with inked lines of pale blue that appears to have been torn from a notebook. As she unfolds the page, a snapshot flutters to the ground. Viv is too transfixed, too numb, to pay any attention to the photograph. The letter is only three lines long and composed by the same unruly black pen. She can read the words almost instantaneously, but their implication seems to penetrate in stages, each surge of understanding bringing a fresh wave of anguish.

Dear Mrs Markham,

Captain Alex Henderson has returned home. He left the camp last week and by the time you receive this he will be back in America. He was looking forward to the weather in Kentucky, but mainly to seeing his wife and two children again (a girl and a boy).

Sincerely,
First Lieutenant W. Drummond

PS The enclosed Kodak was found under Captain Henderson's bed after he vacated his room.

'Mummy! Where are you? Hurry up, it's your turn and dolly's bored of waiting!' Alice's impatience floats to the hallway from a different continent. America, perhaps.

Viv opens her mouth, but her lips and tongue seem to be locked in place and make no sound at all. Wordlessly, she bends down to pick up the photograph lying on the black-and-white tiles. At the sight of Alex her heart contracts. The image has captured his profile as he gazes at a woman with pretty blond curls. The baby in the woman's lap wears a dress with ruffles spread like a dinner plate, while beside them stands a shy-looking boy in a miniature cowboy hat.

The most shocking thing of all is that Viv is not shocked. A dreadful, slicing kind of hurt is exploding from her core, but the pain is tinged with something else.

Humiliation.

And anger. Not just at Alex. Not even mostly at Alex. With herself. She gazes at the little family, the picture of happiness. Of course Alex was not interested in marrying her. He never had any intention for her to set even one foot in America. She has closed her eyes and ears, refused to know the truth, when the truth has been hammering on the door, processing the streets with placards, for months. What a fool she has been. Turning over the photograph she sees written on the back, *Louisville, February 1942. Come home to us soon, sweetheart! S xx*

The white-haired soldier in the mailroom, the one who treated her with such scorn when she delivered her final message to Alex, knew all about *S*, Viv thinks bitterly. He probably never even gave Alex her letter, which would explain how he came to have Viv's address. When she looks again at the spidery writing, she hears every word being articulated in that condescending drawl, and her flesh burns with loathing.

'Mummy! Why are you being such a long time? And where's Daddy?'

'I'm coming.' Her voice has the volume of a whisper. She tries again, but this time the words splinter into fragments, torn apart by the sob she flings a hand over her mouth to contain. Hauling herself together, she says more steadily, 'Alice, darling, I have to do something, just for a minute or two. Daddy is sitting in his study. Why don't you and dolly keep a lookout for Daisy? I'm sure she'll be here any minute.'

Before Alice can reply, Viv runs up the stairs and into her bedroom where she shuts the door and leans back against the wood. To her surprise, the swell of emotion that downstairs threatened to overwhelm her doesn't materialise. Her tears seem to have frozen solid, maybe because of the ice-cold temperature – the electric heater has been moved to the drawing room and there is now a definite frost on the inside of the window.

After a moment Viv walks to the dressing table. The sight of her reflection in the unforgiving light makes her moan with horror. Somehow, she always manages to forget the brutality of the haircut forced upon her by the accident, her gleaming locks replaced by a dull brown helmet through which the badger's streak of grey is becoming undeniable. And in the harsh, colourless morning she can see how age will steal away the rest of her looks. Fine lines spread from her eyes and mouth like cracked pottery over a face that is pale and gaunt with unhappiness.

He didn't love her. Alex never loved her. He desired her, that was all. While to her he had been like a knight from a fairy tale, a hero who banished those horrible, paralysing bouts of despondency, her body, her appearance, was the only part of her he wanted. The glittering romance, her justification for leaving her husband and turning her daughter's world upside down was, for Alex, merely a quick fuck and fumble while his wife was on the other side of the Atlantic. And maybe Viv wasn't his only lover. Although she could never know for sure, she wouldn't be unique among women to be charmed by a chat-up line asking if she was a film star. Well, now her beauty was gone, and so was he. The bitter symmetry of the timing was almost laughable.

She peers at her reflection. Smeared mascara from the earlier bout of weeping has blackened her eye sockets as convincingly as a fist. Reaching for her jar of cotton wool, Viv realises she is still clutching the note from First Lieutenant Drummond – and also that the dressing-table stool contains all of Alex's letters. Wrenching open the lid, she rummages beneath her rosebud housecoat for the stack of envelopes and pulls a letter from the pile at random: *My darling sweetheart, since we met I can't ever stop thinking about* you… She flings down the page. Pulls out another: *Gee, Viv, what have you done to me? You've turned this American soldier soft as Jell-O…* A third: *Fighting my feelings for you, sweetheart, is harder than fighting all of the lousy Hun at once.* And finally, the most painful one of all, the one she should have seen straight through from the very beginning. Envelopes are strewn about her feet like confetti, but the letter she most wants, yet can hardly bear, to read is conspicuous from the rest because on this occasion Alex wrote in green ink…

> *I can't ever stand to be parted from you, Viv. As soon as this lousy war is over, I'm taking you straight home with me, sweetheart, whether you like it or not. I can already see you standing in the sun on the deck of some big old steamer. You'll be the sexiest damn import the good old US of A has ever had…*

'Mummy?'

The plea barely glances the surface of her thoughts.

'MUMMY!'

Alice is hovering on the threshold of the bedroom, twisting on one leg. 'Daisy is here. She arrived a few minutes ago.'

Viv touches her forehead, tries to find some focus in her pounding skull. 'Tell her to wait. I'll be down in a moment, and that—'

She breaks off at the sound of the stairs creaking and Daisy's voice calling upwards.

'Don't worry, Alice. Mummy might be busy.'

Alice's gaze darts anxiously between Viv and the mess of scattered paper.

'It's all right, I'm coming now.' Viv scoops the pages higgledy-piggledy into the top of the stool.

'What were you doing?'

Chucking the housecoat on top of the letters, she hastens across the room. 'Just reading some letters, that's all.'

'You look funny. Your eyes are all black.'

Viv remembers the sooty clouds of make-up. 'I'll sort myself out in a minute, darling. Why don't you go downstairs?'

Alice doesn't move. She peers around her mother's hips towards the dressing-table stool.

Steering Alice onto the landing, Viv closes the door behind them. She tweaks her daughter's hair. 'Hurry up, you don't want to keep Daisy waiting.'

'No need to worry about that.'

Viv starts in surprise. Daisy is at the top of the staircase and staring with curiosity at Viv's face. Viv feels heat creeping into her cheeks. She swallows quickly. 'Wait in the hall, Daisy. I didn't invite you upstairs.' The rebuke sounds rather severe, harsher, in fact, than she intended.

There's a pause, before Daisy clamps shut her mouth and begins to descend the stairs in an ostensibly slow and precise fashion. As Viv watches, she feels her own pulse accelerate and only once Daisy has reached the very bottom does she pull Alice forwards. 'Come on, darling.'

'What about your dirty face?'

'I'm not going to bother about that now.' She almost wants Daisy to remark on her appearance so that she can snap something back. Possibly something rude.

At the foot of the stairs Daisy is standing in front of a picture frame, examining from unnecessarily close quarters an oil painting that used to belong to Toby's mother. Her back is very rigid, and she doesn't move until Viv clears her throat.

'Major Markham and I will be leaving soon. Since the weather is so bad, I can't be certain what time we'll be home, but there's a cottage pie in the larder to heat up when you and Alice get hungry. The drawing room is the warmest place to sit because that's where the electric fire is at the moment. Please make sure Alice keeps on her cardigan and mittens, otherwise she gets very cold.'

Daisy seems to have to drag her attention away from the painting. 'You will be back this afternoon? I can't be too late.'

Viv blinks. 'I hope to be home fairly soon after lunch, but as I just said' – her voice rises slightly – 'I can't make any promises because of the snow.'

'I shall need to leave by four o'clock. Otherwise I'll be walking some of the way in the dark. The buses aren't running and the journey this morning was bad enough in the light.' As if to emphasise the point, Daisy glances down at the hem of her overcoat, which is dripping slowly onto the tiles.

'You didn't mention that before. When I asked you to take care of Alice, you didn't say you needed to be back by a particular time.' Viv can feel her nerves fraying further, beginning to unravel like a bad run in a stocking, one that can't be stopped with either soap or nail varnish.

'I hadn't realised you might want me to stay the whole afternoon. You didn't say anything about being gone all day, you simply asked me to look after Alice while you went out with Major Markham.'

Viv swallows. She can't tell if the throbbing in her head is because of the awfulness of the letter, her annoyance with Daisy or another of her accident headaches. Nor can she remember precisely what she did tell Daisy, but they can't possibly miss the appointment because of the girl, this sudden contrariness. Her voice sharpens again. '*You* work for Major Markham. Perhaps you should have consulted his diary. If you had, you would have seen he has booked the entire day away from the camp and would have known what to expect!'

For a moment Daisy simply scowls at her. Then, 'There's nothing new about that.'

'What did you say?'

'I said' – Daisy's chin tilts upwards and her voice is bolder – 'there's nothing new about that. Major Markham is often away from camp for the whole day. In fact, the truth of the matter is that he's hardly ever there! These days the camp is run by Captain Holmes, with Frances and I doing our best to manage the paperwork.'

Viv gapes at her. What on earth does she mean? If Toby hasn't been at the camp, where can he go every day? The vision of him hunched in his armchair comes to her, and all at once she sees as clearly as if she has witnessed the scene herself, Toby sitting in his parked car, staring for hour upon hour at the surly grey sea as the sky lifts from winter morning dark and sinks back to plum again. Her blood seethes with a fresh tide of emotions, all probing for a crack, an outlet.

She draws a breath. 'At least he was there when it mattered. During the war, I mean. He didn't avoid his duty then.'

There's a terrible silence.

She sees Daisy step backwards, as if Viv had actually walked over and shoved her in the chest. 'Who told you…?'

'Nobody. Nobody important.' Viv thinks of the encounter at the tool shed. Until that moment she hadn't even realised the comment about Daisy's brother had registered. She says quickly, 'I expect the person in question didn't know what he was talking about. I really shouldn't have said anything.' But Daisy continues to glare at her so dreadfully that Viv is suddenly afraid the girl might walk straight out of the front door.

Footsteps on the tiles come to her rescue.

'I thought I heard voices.' Toby nods an acknowledgement to Daisy, before turning to his wife. 'Have you seen the weather?

Surely it can't be sensible to travel today, not with all that snow. There's no traffic on the roads. I think we ought to postpone. I'll telephone Doctor—'

'No! Don't do that!' Viv cuts him off. The last thing they need is for Daisy to understand the reason for the trip is medical. And besides, cancelling is not an option, particularly after what Daisy has told her about Toby's absence from the camp. 'Listen, darling, the local lanes are bound to be quieter than the main roads. We'll be fine once we get going. And, after all, we don't know when we'll next be able to meet our *friend*. Conditions might get worse before they get better, and you know how anxious he is to see us.' She finds his eyes and tries to inject a sense of purpose, of common purpose, but his focus has the same vague, absent quality she's noticed of late. The gaze of a dreamer desperate to cling to sleep rather than wake and confront reality.

Stepping smartly forwards, Viv takes his elbow. 'Look at the time! Practically eleven! We really must leave. Daisy had a horrible walk to get here, and she doesn't want us back late.' She throws a beaming smile to Daisy over her shoulder, part apology, part an attempt to undo the damage of the last few minutes, but the expression that greets her is as cold as the leftovers of last night's dinner. As she ushers Toby away, collects his leather gloves, overcoat and car keys, Viv can't tell whether she's the one who is holding everything together, constructing some semblance of normality, of married life, or the culprit who is responsible for ripping everything apart.

The view through the windscreen is relentless. Where there should be sky, meadows and road, a vista expands before them that is so bleached and uniform the lack of colour seems to affect Viv's balance. Every time she closes her eyes the world lurches sideways and seasickness rocks her stomach. Thank heavens Toby insisted on driving; she would never have been able to navigate, to peer relentlessly into that white frozen space the way he is doing now, bent low over the wheel, his haggard face grim.

The streets close to home were bad enough. As the tyres struggled to find purchase, the wheels spun and slipped. Several times the thorny fingers of a hedge scraped like nails against the paintwork and more than once they took a corner on the right-hand side of the bend. Further from the coast, the difficulties are of a different scale altogether. The long, straight stretches of road are bordered by treeless fields which the winter gusts have exploited to heap snow into unpredictable traps. One moment Viv is briefly reassured by a glimpse of tarmac and the next the way is obstructed by a drift so large it seems a dumper truck has spilled a year's supply of laundry at their feet.

She glances at the speedometer and then at her watch. They are travelling between five and ten miles an hour, have covered less than half the distance and the time is nearly one thirty. The appointment is at two, and at this rate they will not get to the city until much later than that. It is possible Dr Dandy will wait, that he will see his other patients first and fit Toby in when they arrive. It's also possible nobody else will be foolish enough to relinquish the security of their four walls in this dreadful weather, that the surgery is deserted, and that Dr Dandy will leave at the earliest opportunity. And even if they see the doctor, they will have to face the drive back, probably in the dusk when the temperatures will be even lower and the ice more copious. Viv can't bear to think about that. Nor about Daisy's reaction when they do finally get home. The only thing worse is the worry of not going at all.

The Ford Anglia slews sideways again, and Viv grabs the armrest of the passenger door. Every time the vehicle loses traction, she's returned to the ill-fated bus, the squeals of brakes and passengers ringing in her ears, being flung against the window, the floor, and the crack of bone on glass… She hadn't anticipated this aspect of the journey, the ordeal of reliving the trauma of the accident every few minutes. As the rubber bites the ice, she feels the chassis steady, the wheels find a forward direction, and her heart starts beating once more.

A second later Toby stops the car. He stares at the wipers, not turning his head. 'We have to go back.'

Her first reaction is relief. Still she cannot quite bear to give up. 'The worse might be behind us.'

Toby gestures through the windscreen. A little way ahead, a boulder of white taller than the bonnet extends almost the width of both carriageways. 'I'll never get around that, and even if I do, there'll be another one in a hundred yards and another after that. Enough is enough, Viv. There's a bloody good reason why nobody else is out on the roads today.'

Viv opens her mouth to argue and finds she can't. Snow is starting to come down again. A fog of flakes enveloping the car so that in a matter of seconds even the drift ahead is barely visible. All at once she wants nothing more than the drawing room, the comfort of the electric fire. And Alice. 'Yes,' she says, and her voice sounds small and frightened. 'Let's go home.'

Slithery inch by slithery inch, Toby manoeuvres the car to face the other way. 'If there's anything coming…' he mutters at one point, but of course there's nothing travelling in either direction and eventually they begin to battle back along the route they have just crawled. For a long while neither of them speaks. Progress is so slow that Viv sometimes doubts they are moving at all, driving into the hypnotic flakes is like walking through a beaded curtain. They part barely enough to let the car pass and immediately close behind them again, obliterating all sense of direction and progress.

Eventually, somewhere between the city and the coast, Toby clears his throat. 'I'm sorry,' he says, 'for bringing you out in this weather. And for making you behave so uncharacteristically.'

Viv turns in surprise. 'It was me who insisted we came. I—'

'It was my fault, Viv, not yours.' He takes his eyes from the road to engage with hers. 'You had no choice, not in the circumstances. You mustn't blame yourself.' Immediately, he looks away again.

'Toby?'

Although he doesn't respond, the silence feels expectant, bursting with possibilities. Viv's head is spinning. Was he talking about the snow, or something else entirely? Something that perhaps might only be acknowledged in a situation as alien yet strangely intimate as the one in which they find themselves. Tentatively she places her hand on his sleeve and tries again. 'Toby?'

Before he can respond, the tyres begin to slide. Slowly, the car glides through the middle of the carriageway and across the opposite lane like a skater balanced on one leg. Viv sees Toby wrench the steering wheel to no avail, hears a muttered curse under his breath, before the front wheels lose contact with the surface and there is a softly definitive thump as the chassis lurches downwards and the glass fills with snow.

Viv peels herself off the dashboard, shaking but unharmed. 'Toby! You're bleeding!' As he draws his palm across his forehead, crimson streaks his leather glove. 'Are you hurt? Let me see.'

He twists out of her reach. 'It's nothing. Only a scratch.'

Viv hesitates, then leans back again.

The engine purrs into a pocket of silence.

'What do we do now?' A crystal dam has filled the windscreen and both of the front windows. Smashed stars press the glass, blocking the light as if a drape has been pulled. The road can only be seen through the back windows, the surface tilted at an angle and plainly higher than the boot. Viv has to quell the bubble of panic in her voice. 'How do we get out?' When Toby doesn't answer straight away, she yanks on the passenger handle. The lever swivels uselessly on its hinge.

'I have to turn off the motor.'

Viv gapes at him. Her hand is still on the door. 'We'll freeze to death!' The efficiency of the Ford Anglia's heater was one of the reasons she risked the journey and, so far, the temperature of the car has been no less pleasant than that of the drawing room. Once the engine stops turning, they both know the position will change very quickly.

'If I keep the motor on and the exhaust pipe is blocked, we'll be suffocated by fumes. Besides, if I don't switch it off, we'll use up all the petrol.'

'How long do you think we'll be here?'

He meets her gaze. There's a graze on his forehead, a red, angry smudge. 'It could be quite a while.' Whatever he reads on her face makes him hold the contact and his tone softens. 'When the cold becomes unbearable, we'll switch on the engine for a few minutes to warm ourselves up.'

'What about the exhaust, the fumes?'

'We'll just have to hope the pipe isn't clogged, but if the air seems to change then I'll have to shut the motor down again.'

He reaches for the ignition.

'Suppose the car doesn't start again, once you turn it off?'

'I don't know. We have to hope it will.'

Viv swallows and nods.

Within seconds the warmth in the car begins to dissipate. Viv can visualise a bead of mercury shrinking before her eyes, the silver thread collapsing as if the liquid were being sucked out of the tube. Balling her woollen-clad fingers into fists, she jams them into her pockets and stares at the blank wall of the windscreen. With no traffic on the road, who, exactly, is going to find them? And when? And what happens when the petrol is finished, the feeble winter sun has sunk beneath the horizon, and there is nothing to prevent the temperature shrivelling and solidifying into a death chamber of ice.

Viv glances at Toby. His expression has become vacant, like someone lost within himself. 'What are you thinking about?'

He blinks in surprise. The query was plainly not one he was expecting. In fact, he seems surprised to see her sitting beside him. 'Not a great deal.'

'I'd like to know.' She hesitates, then. 'You spend a lot of time on your own, but you never say why, or tell me what's on your mind.'

His pupils dart between the passenger and driver's door, as if his instinct is to escape from her questions. 'It's better you don't know.'

'It isn't better, Toby.' She leans across the gear stick and puts her hand on his arm. 'Not better for us. We never talk anymore. You've become a stranger. A silent stranger. And Daisy said…' she stops.

'What did she say?'

'That…' – she gives him a squeeze through the pelt of his sleeve – 'that you're hardly ever at the camp. But you leave for work every morning. So where do you go? What are you doing all day?'

He doesn't reply.

Viv waits.

The silence stretches like a piece of elastic, the import gathering until unexpectedly the moment passes, the tension dissolves and Viv removes her hand. Miserably, she gazes at the blue folds of her coat. Daisy and Alice must have eaten the cottage pie by now. Daisy must be checking the time, no doubt becoming even more annoyed than she was when Viv left. Perhaps when she and Toby don't come home, Daisy will raise the alarm and telephone the police or the fire service. Unless, of course, she is so angry she simply abandons Alice and…

'I drive to the cliffs and watch the waves.'

Viv lifts her head.

Toby seems to be addressing the steering wheel, the wipers or the acres of snow outside the car – anywhere except the seat next to him. 'I don't really think, not as such, not that I'm aware of. I just see things. I can't stop them. The pictures, the scenes, they keep coming at me. Even when I close my eyes. Often, shutting my eyes makes them worse.' He lowers his lids now, jamming the thumb and forefinger of his right hand into the corners of his eye sockets. 'It's like I'm trapped in the past, forced to live the same hours, the same minutes over and over again. But those images don't feel like the past, they seem real, as if the war is happening right this minute and all around me, yet I still can't do anything different to change the result.'

'What things do you see?' Viv says gently.

Toby shakes his head. 'You don't want me to tell you. You really don't want that.'

He falls quiet and for a while they sit in silence.

Eventually, Viv takes his left hand and draws it into her lap. 'The doctor will find a way to make it stop. He'll know what to do, the medicines that can help.' She pauses. 'Once we finally manage to see him.'

The car is becoming darker. A slice of sky is visible through the back windscreen, the thin, grey sliver is turning a sullen shade of purple, and the chill inside the Ford Anglia has the sting of a slap or winter seawater. The time is nearly four o'clock, dusk is pressing on the heels of the afternoon, and after evening, Viv thinks, comes nightfall.

All at once Toby shivers, the vibration reverberating from his hips, through to his torso and shoulders.

'Should we switch the engine on again?'

'Not yet.' There's a tremor to his voice. 'We should hold out a little longer if we can.'

A spark of inspiration makes Viv suddenly reach around the seatback and into the well of the floor behind. She pulls out a green tartan rug braided with woollen tassels which she put in the car at the start of the awful weather, before Christmas, before the accident – a lifetime ago. She should have remembered the rug earlier; and also thought to have brought another one with them.

'Here.' She tucks the blanket behind Toby's shoulders, draping the other end over his knees.

'You should have it, not me.'

'I don't need it.' Viv is being truthful. As cold as she feels, it seems a perfectly normal state of affairs, natural even. Perhaps she's adjusted to the arctic conditions. Or maybe she's stopped feeling anything much at all.

She sits still for a minute, deliberating. Then, 'Toby, is the shovel in the boot?'

Over the top of the tartan, his eyelids flicker. 'I don't remember. Normally, I put it in the car every winter, but it may still be in the tool shed. It doesn't make a great deal of difference, since we can't reach the boot.'

'I might be able to reach it.' She twists in her seat and points. 'The back windows are barely obstructed at all. I should be able to wriggle out of one of them. And' – an image of the garden tools, lined up like metal soldiers in the moonlight comes to mind – 'I'm fairly certain the shovel was not in the shed a few weeks ago, which means you must have taken it away.'

'You would never be able to dig us out. Not on your own.' Now his eyes are wide open, watching Viv who is already clambering into the back seat.

'I don't have to dig out the whole car by myself.' She peeks back over her shoulder. 'I only have to dig enough so that you can open your door.'

Close up, the idea that a moment ago seemed wonderful is less convincing. The placement of the hinge does not allow the window to fully open, so the space through which she must wriggle is narrower than she anticipated. But what alternative does she have? Viv hesitates, then unbuttons and peels off the blue bulk of her coat and before she can change her mind pivots the window lever. A rush of flakes falls over the lip and onto her dress. Beyond the glass she can just make out flat white fields and mould-coloured sky.

Her head fits through first. Next her shoulders, which stick and chafe against the frame. Twisting and wrenching, she squirms her torso through the gap while her fingers scrabble for purchase in the ice until, all at once, the resistance dissolves and she tumbles face down into a basin of frozen white fluff.

When she flounders to her feet the snow is thigh deep. Her woollen stockings, her dress and heavy Aran cardigan are all soaked, while the flakes cling to the fabric like spilled icing sugar. For a long moment she can't even catch her breath. A terrible chill has carved its way beneath her skin, cutting into her flesh with the sharpness of a paring knife. It is as if she has fallen from a ship and, submerged and overwhelmed, her body has petrified with shock.

Eventually, her chest judders. She bangs her palms against each other and stamps her feet. Her boots feel like bricks tied to her ankles, her toes completely numb. Light is draining from the landscape; the sky is a hood of a mauve-grey with a thinning band of yellow at the western edge. The silence, the emptiness and the impending dark all seem to roll together into one combined sensation, as if the world is shutting down.

Nose-down in the drift, the Ford Anglia's boot is some way above her head and by the time she has scrabbled up the side of the ditch to reach the back of the car, her teeth and lungs are aching from the freezing air. She turns the handle as soon as the knob is within reach, making one swift movement that doesn't allow for the possibility the space might be empty. Even before the lid is fully open, she sees the metal face of the shovel glinting back at her, together with a pair of Toby's wellington boots. Grabbing both, she howls into the dusk in triumph.

With the relief comes awareness of another desire, the need to pee. The possibility of waiting, of more hours in the car without visiting a lavatory, is impossible. First an instinctive, pointless, sweep of the deserted road, then she hitches her dress, pulls down her knickers, and squats. A hot jet of urine spurts between her calves. As the dirty gold stream drills into the snow, the heat, even the smell, of her own piss is strangely comforting. An act of survival in the wilderness. The second that she's finished, she hauls up her underwear, picks up the shovel and drives the blade deep into the drift on the right-hand side of the car.

'We're back!' Viv exclaims into the empty hall. Apart from a single light shining from the landing the house appears to be in total darkness. Nevertheless, she has never been so utterly and purely thankful to be home. She waits a couple of seconds, calls again, 'Hello! Daisy?'

The front door clicks shut, and Toby comes to stand beside her. 'Where is the girl? Do you think she's gone, left Alice alone?'

Viv shrugs. She has the impression that she and Toby are leaning towards each other. They are both so exhausted they can barely stand up.

'I'm here.' With the suddenness of an apparition or ghost, Daisy appears on the landing. Even from below, even in the shadows, Viv can see the ice-white fury on her face. 'Do you have any idea how late you are?' With impeccable timing, the grandfather clock begins to chime; ten loud, long strikes that resonate against the floor tiles, swirl around the chandelier and linger accusingly in the air.

'We had a problem,' Viv begins. 'We never got as far as the city because the roads were too bad. Then when we turned around the car skidded into—'

'I have to go. I telephoned my mother earlier, but she will be quite frantic by now.'

'It will be quicker to walk than take the car,' Toby says. 'Otherwise I'd give you a lift.'

'Why don't you stay here for the night? We can telephone your mother again.'

'I'd rather go home.'

'But it's awful out there. I can make up the spare bed in no time.'

'No. Thank you.' Daisy kicks the offer aside as she walks down the stairs. At the bottom she glowers at Viv. Her expression of disdain doesn't entirely mask an earlier stamp of anxiety, lurking like a stain that refuses to wash out. 'You're six hours later than you said. *Six hours!*

'I'm so sorry. There was nothing we could do. At one stage I thought we might not...' Viv bites her lip, looks down. On the inside of her stockings she can spot splash marks and mud. She lifts her head. 'What about Alice? Did she worry terribly?'

'She wouldn't go to sleep. Not for a long while.' Daisy breaks off and fetches her coat from the hat stand. For somebody impatient to be leaving, she seems to spend a good deal of time adjusting and fastening the buttons and avoiding Viv's gaze.

'So, what did you do?' Viv asks finally.

'I put her in your bed and...' Daisy reaches past Toby, opens the door. There's rush of cold air just before she closes it again. 'Well, you'll see for yourself soon enough.'

The moment she has gone, Viv races upstairs. The Tiffany lamp is burning on her bedside table, casting small squares of red and aqua onto the cream of the counterpane. Alice is lying on her side, lashes curled against her cheek, hair fanned across Viv's pillow. Viv listens to her daughter's breathing, watching the bedclothes rise and fall. She can see nothing untoward, no discernible reason for Daisy's parting comment. Hooking her finger over the blanket edging, she draws the cover back. Conspicuous against the plain cotton sheets, is Viv's housecoat. The panels of silk have been tucked around Alice's small body to make a private cocoon. Viv stares at the rosebud print, the delicate pink petals entwined with the pale green thorny stems, and a warning bell rings within her stomach as clearly as the peals of the grandfather clock.

Chapter Twenty-One

26 February 1947

'Are you cold?'

'I'm too happy to be cold.' Fran is leaning against Thomas's chest. They are sitting behind the stage curtains of the village hall on chairs they have pushed close together. His right arm is pinning her close while his left caresses her cheek, the flat of his nails running across her skin and leaving a trail of sparks in their wake. The curtains, Fran sees, are filthy. Ropes of dust make stripes in the velvet folds from years of hanging bunched at the side of the stage. A far as she knows, nothing has been performed on stage for years, but when they were new to the area, in the middle of the war, she used to come here with June and her mother to help knit blankets for the bombed-out and the bereaved. Now she is hiding away with a German prisoner of war.

They find opportunities to be together so frequently that she can't remember, not properly, how she filled her spare time beforehand. Although she recalls the hours reading in her bedroom, bickering with June or peeling vegetables for dinner, the memories are a sputtering, silent film, devoid of colour and emotion, and trivial to the point of irrelevance. She feels alive only at the end of her working day, when she finds Thomas hiding in the shadows of the military trucks, or at the weekend when they see each other outside the camp and risk an hour – or longer – together.

The first time they met in daylight was on the third Sunday in January. They went straight to the marsh, thinking the solitude and desolation of the place would protect them. Yet as soon as

Fran saw Thomas's outline, dark and loud against the pale lustre of the fen sky, she realised how the starkness only made them more conspicuous, the absence of any other person less safe than ever from a lone walker's gaze. Hurrying inland they roamed the heath instead, but the weather was so brutal that, on returning to her family, frozen to the core, Fran struggled to come up with a reason as to why she might have gone out at all.

The next day the snow meant she had to walk to work again, which gave her time to ponder. Instead of turning into the camp, she continued on towards the church and, glancing over her shoulder, picked a path over the grass that led to the adjacent village hall. The entrance was locked, but when she tried the side access, the knob shifted and the door swung open with a gentle, oozing groan. Although the room was grimy and unheated, at least it was out of sight of prying eyes and a refuge from the relentless winter that everyone said was harder to cope with than the war had ever been.

Thomas pauses the motion of his wrist. 'I had an interview yesterday.' His voice is low. They whisper, both of them, all of the time, and keep behind the screen of the curtains in case anyone should happen to peer through the windows.

'An interview?' She twists in his lap. 'What for?'

He takes a breath.

'To test what kind of German I am. Very bad, or maybe not so bad.' He must sense her bewilderment. 'I mean, to make certain I am not a Nazi.'

The word, its ugliness, makes her stiffen. 'What did they ask you?'

'About my family, where I grew up, when I joined the army. The last question was, did I think it was a good thing that Germany had lost the war?'

She shakes her head, confused. 'A good thing? For Germany?'

'A good thing because it stopped Hitler. They wanted me to say it was more important to defeat fascism than that my country should win.'

'What did you say?'

'What do you think I said?'

Fran grows still. Her heart is pounding against the confines of her ribs. She badly needs his answer to be the same one his interrogators required. Yet surely that is an impossible thing to ask of a man whose blood is German, who must have lost friends and comrades to the guns of the Allies, and who believes his family to have been killed in a bombing raid?

'I don't know.'

'You don't know!'

She locks onto the smooth, black buttons of his coat.

'Fran? Please…' He tugs her hair, gently at first then harder until she lifts her gaze. 'Tell me what you think I said!'

Conviction burns from his eyes. It's true, she thinks, with wonder. I don't feel cold when I'm with you, I don't feel anything but joy. She touches his face and says slowly, 'I don't believe even the tiniest part of you to be a Nazi, or that you hoped Hitler would win the war.'

For a long moment he holds her gaze. Then he says, 'For the first six months of the war a Jewish man, a friend of my father, lived in our basement. He stayed with us until my father found enough people who were willing also to take the risk of hiding his friend as he travelled across Germany to escape. I fought in the war because I had to, because there was no choice, because if I had refused, my parents and my sister would have been shot as well as myself. And at the interview I told them that history will say it is a good thing that Germany lost the war and our country will be scarred by shame for many years. But I also said that you cannot ask me to celebrate that defeat when my home is in ruins, when I have heard nothing from my family for so long, and when I and my fellow men are still kept prisoner although the war has been over for many, many months.'

He stops as if to gauge her reaction.

But Fran is already struggling upright. Cupping her palm around his head she draws his mouth towards hers. Then all at once she breaks away. 'You know what this means, don't you?' He nods, but she says it anyway. 'You'll be repatriated. Now you've passed their test, they'll send you home. That was the purpose of the interview, wasn't it? To help them decide which prisoners at the camp will go back to Germany first.'

'I should have pretended to be a Nazi, to stay longer with you.' His tone is serious.

Fran doesn't reply.

They are so close she can see the brush of stubble beginning on his jawline, the comma of a scar just above his left brow, the pucker of determination on his chin that deepens even while she looks at him.

'I want to marry you.' He says the words at normal volume, so that the loudness seems to have an energy all of its own and ricochets around the painted walls. 'I love you, Fran. I want you to be my wife.'

She opens her mouth. What he has said feels both as normal and obvious as saying it will snow again tomorrow or be dark by five o'clock, and at the same time as impossible and ridiculous as saying that he wants to sail to China or have breakfast with the king. She buries her fingers into his hair. She can feel his skull, and beneath the bone the blood and soul of him that slot together with her like a jigsaw puzzle.

'We can't. It's not allowed.' Her voice is thick with emotion. 'Just being here together is against the law.' A copy of the local newspaper had been left on the kitchen table that morning, open to a photograph of a woman who had been fined twenty pounds for fraternising with a German prisoner. Although the article didn't specify the nature of the fraternisation, Fran suspected the woman's actions were a lot less culpable than her own. The temporary respite over the festive season was over. And fraternisation could simply mean talking with a German or offering gifts of food or cigarettes. It barely began to describe the raw intensity of her meetings with Thomas.

She was still standing, glued to the kitchen floor, when she heard June's voice in her ear. 'The magistrate was far too lenient, if you ask me. That woman should have gone to prison.' All day, Fran has been wondering why the paper happened to be turned to that particular story, if June had arranged the pages deliberately. And if her sister was responsible, was that because of what she had seen at Christmas or – more worryingly – because she had guessed what Fran was doing now?'

'Are you scared, Fran?'

She swallows. She imagines her own face blazing from the front of a newspaper. 'Sometimes.'

'We could stop meeting?'

'No!'

She is already kissing him. The fold-out chairs shift and creak.

'Stand up.' His breath is hot on her face.

His arms circle her waist and his mouth finds hers. As she opens her lips, a rush of sweetness floods her throat. She feels his hand reach between the folds of her coat and burrow through the layers of wool until he is stroking the cotton of her bra. Her own hands pluck at his clothes, searching for his skin, while her tongue presses deeper. She is aware of fabric falling, the brush of something soft around her calves and realises their coats are on the floor. As he reaches inside her dress, she feels his fingers tug gently at a button, then hesitate. Catching hold of his wrist, Fran stares into his eyes. Her pulse is beating so fast her blood is singing in her ears. *I don't want anyone but him*, she thinks. *Even if June were to walk in, I wouldn't care.* Slowly and deliberately she unfastens the front of her dress until the opening is wide enough for the material to slide over her shoulders and fall free to her waist.

'Fran!' He drops to his knees and buries his head on her stomach. Against the texture of her vest, his breath is heaving.

She is about to pull the garment off, when he sits back abruptly. 'I must stop. We must both stop. Before it is too difficult.' His gaze is a kaleidoscope of blue.

Her belly feels cold where an instant earlier there was heat and flames. The words, *I don't want to stop*, are on the edge of her tongue, teetering like a high-board diver. She closes her eyes, opens them again and gazes over the top of his head. Outside, a piece of panelling or tarpaulin is slapping steadily against a wall and the light inside the hall has become mercurial. She wonders if it is snowing again. She can't remember the last time she saw the sun, not properly without a gauze of cloud. The winter seems endless, the previous summer a dreamlike memory, or something imagined from a book, and next July and August as remote and invisible as another century or becoming old like her parents.

Shivering, she slips her dress back over her shoulders and does up the buttons. She feels shy, suddenly, almost ashamed, and at the same time a defiant sort of regret for what didn't happen. Thomas gets shakily to his feet and passes over her coat. Neither of them looks at the other. Eventually he says, 'Did you know a band is going to play here? In one week from now.'

'A band? What kind of band?' Although Daisy mentioned something about it the other day, she asks, glad of the distraction.

'German prisoners are going to make a concert for the village.'

She stops threading her belt. 'Is that allowed? Will they sell tickets?'

'Yes, it is a new thing, but there can be no tickets and we must be careful not to have private conversations with anyone. The concert is free for anyone who would like to listen.' He frowns. 'I hope people will come. It is supposed to be a gesture of friendship. Of new beginnings.'

'Will you play?'

'A little. I do not play well. I will also help to set out the chairs and welcome our guests.'

'You'd better not seem too familiar with the hall, or people may start to wonder why that is!' She flicks him half a smile, before looking away.

'Fran…' He grabs her wrist, lifts her palm to his lips. 'I stopped because I want you. I want you so badly I can't trust myself.'

She feels herself dissolving, thinks, *It's going to happen all over again. Every time he touches me, I turn into someone else. Or rather, I become myself, whole and fully alive.* She wrenches the thought aside. 'I'd like to hear the concert. My mother won't leave my father at home on his own, but I'll try to persuade June to come with me. It would do her good to go out somewhere.' And to see the prisoners entertaining the village. Perhaps she should also mention the concert to Martin? She rejects the idea the instant it presents itself, and a surge of guilt makes her swallow a sigh.

As she puts on her gloves, she realises Thomas is watching her. 'We must go.' She tries to keep her voice bright.

'Yes. But first…' He pulls her close.

His lips graze her mouth.

Already she's counting the seconds to the next time, like holding her breath underwater.

Eventually he lets her go.

And they both turn towards the door.

Chapter Twenty-Two

5 March 1947

Martin kills the ignition and leans back in his seat. The sudden hush is disconcerting because it means there's nothing now to stop him from getting out of the car. He peers again through the window. The number on the gatepost is most definitely 83 and, he chides himself, is likely to stay that way for whatever length of time he continues to stare at the ironwork.

Dr Dandy's practice was not difficult to find, located, it seems, within a large residential house. The army board assessment must have been conducted somewhere else, however, because he has no recollection of this busy road on the outskirts of the city, the elm trees stationed at intervals along the pavement, or the wide front door with its white plaster portico. As far as he can recall, the examination happened on a back street, similar to the grubby type of place he imagines a woman might in desperation go to terminate a pregnancy. He remembers an unheated anteroom, blue linoleum peeling from the floor, a row of wooden benches – and a handful of other young men who refused to make eye contact with him or anyone else. Because *they* already knew the score, Martin thinks bitterly – why they were there, the choice they were making, the bartering of self-respect in exchange for safety.

Unlike him, they were not being duped by their own mothers.

Sweeping his fedora from the passenger seat, he exits the car and strides through a veil of slush up the gravel path.

The woman behind the reception desk lifts her head as he enters, revealing a small, weary face with a deflated quality. Her surprise on seeing Martin solidifies as she consults the register in front of her. 'Dr Dandy isn't expecting any more patients today.'

'I don't have an appointment.'

'Oh. Is it urgent? Have you injured yourself?' Her gaze skates the length of Martin's torso as if counting limbs or checking for bandages or blood.

'I'm not ill. I need to discuss a personal matter. And yes, you could say it's urgent. In fact, I consider it to be very urgent indeed.'

'I see.' She doesn't sound particularly interested.

Martin wonders if perhaps this is a regular occurrence, unhappy patients presenting themselves for unexplained reasons. Perhaps they are usually more considerate than to do so late in the afternoon. He realises he is spinning his hat, passing the rim through his fingers like a steering wheel.

Grudgingly, the woman stands up. 'Wait here. I'll go and see if Dr Dandy is available. What is your name, please?'

He stills his hands. 'Travis-Jones. Martin Travis-Jones.'

'And will Cyril… the doctor, know what it's about?'

'There's a very good chance that he will. Yes.'

He perches on the edge of a chaise longue that is covered in fading velvet and affixed to the frame with brass studding. The piece seems more suitable for a bedroom or drawing room. Seats of varying types are set around three walls papered with a red-and-gold stripe. The fourth is occupied by the reception desk, together with an imposing painting of a warship and smoking guns. The area, Martin surmises, must once have been a morning room, while another part of the house has been converted into a surgery for Dr Dandy's consultations.

The woman pads across the hallway and taps on a door. An inaudible sputter of conversation floats across chequered tiles. When she returns, her expression appears more sunken, more set than ever. Martin supposes she is anxious to get back to the peace of her book or knitting, or whatever else she was doing when he arrived. 'The doctor says he's busy at the moment. You'll need to make an appointment.'

He lets the fact of the empty waiting room swirl around them both for a moment, before placing the fedora carefully on his knees. 'I intend to wait here until the doctor has time to see me. This is the first day for weeks the roads into the city have been passable. Even if the worst weather is over, there might be flooding when more of the snow melts, and my village could be cut off again. I'm sure the doctor can spare a few minutes.'

There's an uncertain silence. He tries to meet the woman's gaze, but she turns towards the passageway as if expecting Dr Dandy to appear at any moment and berate her for Martin's stubbornness. He has the sudden insight that she's Dr Dandy's wife. And that she's not terribly happy.

'Kindly inform the doctor I'm here to discuss a medical assessment conducted for the army in 1941. That might jog his memory. And if it doesn't, then' – he presses his lips together – 'well in that case tell him Dr Sands sent me.'

He sees the woman jump, as if stepping on a tack or an electric wire, before scuttling back across the hall. He hears her knock, followed by a flare of rising voices before the clunk of shutting wood mutes the crescendo and Martin is alone again.

A minute passes. Two minutes. Five minutes. He consults his watch. Daisy told him the concert in the village hall would start at five thirty and already the time is quarter to four. Since she hadn't wanted to go herself, Martin almost invited Fran to join him. He didn't in the end for the very reason he couldn't be certain how long this wretched business would take. And – he peeks into the deserted passageway – it appears his caution was well placed.

The hat slides to the ground and he retrieves it with a sigh.

The unpredictability of his timekeeping wasn't the only reason he didn't ask Fran. There was bound to have been some pretext or other – her job at the camp, the weather, being tired, needing to help her mother – why she couldn't say yes. Since their outing to the cinema he has managed to see her only once. Throughout a brief lunch the Saturday before last, she seemed to glow with energy, burn with an inner fire as if a spotlight were trained upon her, yet she ate practically nothing and every so often appeared on the verge of making an announcement, only to cast him an unhappy glance and close her mouth an instant later.

A cloak of disappointment settles with a rustle around Martin's shoulders. The nature of that unmade declaration, her relentless busyness and parade of excuses are, of course, perfectly clear. She doesn't care for him after all.

From somewhere in the house a clock peals the hour. Martin rises to his feet and heads into the hallway. A little further along the corridor he finds another door. Pressing his ear to the panelling, he hesitates for no more than a second before rotating the brass knob and walking inside.

Immediately, the countenance of Dr Dandy, lifting in astonishment from the papers on his desk, is familiar. Two minutes earlier Martin couldn't have begun to describe the man's appearance, yet now he is confronted with a pair of close-set eyes and glassy domed forehead, he is transported back four and half years, to that same face inches from his own as an ice-cold stethoscope was pressed first against his chest and then his back.

'I thought my wife told you to make an appointment.' The sentence is an admonishment, not a question.

'This will only take a minute.' Martin closes the door behind him. 'I've travelled a long way today and don't intend to have made the journey for nothing.' He sees another, smaller doorway beside the doctor's desk, which is presumably how his wife escaped in order to avoid further dealings with the difficult man in reception. 'My name is Martin Travis-Jones.'

The doctor blinks. 'And?'

'In August 1941 you examined me and found that I was unfit for service.'

'I'm afraid that's quite impossible.'

'I can assure you it's not. I remember the occasion… I remember you, very well indeed.' He fancies the doctor's face flickers briefly.

'It's impossible because I was not authorised to conduct medical assessments for the army. My specialisation is mental disorders.' The man gestures towards the wall where a gilt-framed certificate displays a diploma in psychological medicine. 'Are you suggesting you have a report signed by me?'

'The report is signed by Dr Sands.'

'Then I don't understand why you might think—'

'Dr Sands didn't write the report.'

'I've heard enough of this rubbish!' The doctor calls through the smaller door. 'Mary? Where are you? I need you to see this gentleman out.'

Martin steps forwards. 'We both know I wasn't seen by Dr Sands! We both know I was examined by you! And we both know the report is false!'

The doctor stands up. He is a short man with a short, thick neck and Martin can see his Adam's apple bobbing furiously in this throat. 'Now listen to me, what you are saying is slanderous. I've every mind to call my solicitor. I'm afraid I must ask you to leave immediately.'

'A statement is only slanderous,' Martin says quietly, 'if it is untrue.'

The doctor doesn't reply. He glances over his shoulder, but there's no sign of his wife. After a while the silence seems to burrow into the noise and bluster of the previous minutes like a knife prising open a tin and laying bare the inside.

Eventually Martin says, 'It so happens I am familiar with the law of slander because I'm a solicitor.'

There's a pause.

I shouldn't have said that, Martin thinks. The law won't help me now.

The doctor gives him a slow, thin-lipped smile. 'In that case I wonder why you are here at all. I don't suppose your profession would look kindly upon one of its own *dodging the draft*. I'm sure you're well aware that refusing to serve His Majesty's Government is a criminal offence?'

'I didn't refuse to serve! Nobody told me the report was false!' Martin recalls the nights with his fingers pressed upon his upturned wrist, timing his pulse with the second hand of his watch. The long and lonely walks on the heath to keep his heart beating, his health strong. 'I only discovered what happened recently.'

'How convenient.' The doctor stops. Then, steadily, 'You'd better hope that other people believe you.'

There's another, flatter silence before Dr Dandy places his hands palms down on the desk and rocks forwards. 'Now, what exactly do you want with me?' All at once his tone is chummier, conciliatory. 'I'm sure we've both got better things to do than rake up the past. Let's say – for argument's sake – that I did assist Dr Sands with one or two medical boards when he was too ill to conduct them himself; what's done is done. You're hale and hearty and the war is over. Good news all round. No point at all in either of us getting worked up about it now.'

Martin swallows. What did he want? To confront Dr Dandy and be certain of the truth? And after that, what then? Whatever he expected from the encounter – an apology, a sense of reckoning, of closure – has not materialised in the slightest. If anything, he feels worse than he did previously, for having been duped so easily. Yet, the doctor is right, neither the police nor the Law Society would believe for one moment he could have been so naive, that he wasn't complicit in saving his own skin. And if the fraud were to come to light, the consequences would be very serious indeed.

The doctor is regarding him closely. Despite his confident little speech, Martin can tell he is anxious for the encounter to be over. Yet the sense of unfinished business lingers in his nostrils like the stench of garlic or week-old fish.

Very serious indeed.

He recalls the argument in the sitting room, the man's voice shouting at his mother, rising through the floorboards of his bedroom. A low-backed leather chair is positioned in front of the doctor's desk. With exaggerated care, Martin pulls out the frame and sits down. 'The question is not what *I* want, but what *you* want from my mother? Some weeks before Christmas, you came to our house one night. I overheard you both talking.'

The doctor sinks back into his own seat.

'Do you deny it?'

'Why should I deny it? Your mother has remained an acquaintance.'

'Whom you visit late in the evening?'

'That is your mother's affair and has nothing to do with you.'

'I assume,' Martin says bitterly, 'that you asked her for money? I imagine she paid you very well for the report at the time, but you go back and demand more when it suits you. Or your funds are running low. I suppose you threaten her with the consequences of the lie being discovered.'

'As I said, my business with your mother is nothing to do with you.'

The doctor drops his gaze and picks up a paperweight. The glass contains a picture of a riverbank, an antique picture with a rowing boat and trailing willow. As the doctor passes the dome from one hand to the other, Martin can feel the solidity of the item, the blemish-free surface gliding over his skin as vividly as if he were holding the object himself.

'From now on I'm *making* the arrangement my business.' He stops, waiting until the doctor raises his head. 'Whatever she's paid you, that's enough. If you ask for any more…'

'You'll do what?'

'I'll go to the police.'

The doctor's eyes glitter. 'And show them what? Dr Sands' report? You'll only implicate yourself. And your mother, of course. I can't imagine you want that outcome.'

All at once Martin longs to reach across the desk, grab the paperweight and bury the glass into the shiny bulge of the doctor's forehead. Instead he says in a level voice, 'I keep a diary. I've done so for a number of years. The entry I wrote for the tenth of August 1941 records that I was seen by a Dr Dandy. I can also establish that Dr Sands had stopped practising by then and I will tell the police the false diagnosis was my idea, the product of my own cowardice, and my mother had nothing whatsoever to do with it. As you said yourself' – he finishes sourly – 'who would believe that I didn't know?'

He watches Dr Dandy watching him. I mean every word, Martin thinks, I don't care about the consequences for myself, only for this vile man to be out of our lives for ever.

It's the doctor who drops his gaze first. 'I think you need to leave now.'

'If—'

'I heard you the first time.'

Martin gets to his feet, a flame of triumph hot in his chest. His hand is on the door when the doctor speaks again.

'Money, is that what she told you?'

Martin turns around.

The doctor's expression is smug. Vindictive and smug. 'Why do you assume I wanted money? When it was clear your mother would do anything at all to save her boy from the horrors of the front.'

As Martin stares, the penny drops, and all at once he understands the real purpose of the doctor's late-night visit. His mother's reticence, her caginess to expand on what had happened, and the reason why her recent relationship should have provoked such turmoil fall into place with horrible completeness. He thinks of his mother, her kind, handsome face, and his fury at the exploitation is unbearable.

I am not a violent man, he reminds himself, yet the vinegar of hatred is ballooning on his tongue, the strength of his loathing is swelling in his chest, and already he is walking, striding towards the desk, his fist is coiling into a ball, and before he can hesitate or think or reason his way to stopping, he is plunging his knuckles deep and hard into the doctor's bloody face.

Halfway home Martin pulls over to the side of the road. He has no memory at all of the first part of his journey. Presumably he must have left the surgery, retraced his steps along the gravel driveway and unlocked the car. At some point he must also have put on his hat and driving gloves, for he is wearing them now. Yet he has no recollection of doing so, nor of how he took his leave from Dr Dandy. He can hear the man's groan of surprise and picture him doubled over, cupping his nose, while a sticky crimson stream dripped down his chin and puddled onto the desk. After that, nothing – until a few moments ago when he noticed his own hands were shaking and that the unencumbered sky of the countryside had opened out in front of him like the start of a whole new day.

Reaching into the glovebox he extracts a packet of Churchman's and a box of matches. Not that he's a smoker, not really. Or a fighter, come to that. He gets out of the car and takes off his gloves to strike a flame. The knuckles of his right hand are still red and smarting. He must have given the doctor a pretty good whack, yet the only emotion he can sense somewhere beneath the shock is grim and total satisfaction. Drawing on the cigarette, he gazes over the fields. For the first time in weeks the colour green is visible, flickering into view like a piece of jewellery bedazzling a tired old dress. Neon blades of grass crest ripples of retreating snow and mud, while in the late-afternoon sunlight a sparrowhawk dips and dives over the hedges.

His mother slept with Dr Dandy. That was the unforgettable, unmistakable insinuation of the doctor. Martin makes himself focus on the smoke-tipped wings of the bird to block the possibility of other, far more troubling, images filling his head, and finds his fingers are trembling again. Not, then, shock at himself for striking the vile little man, shock at what his mother was prepared to do to keep him from the front line. The price exacted for his safety could hardly have been higher. He thinks of all the death and suffering: his mother's grief – Frederick, his father – the loss of the cricket team, the heartbreak of a village, while he was tucked up in his bed each night with only himself to worry about.

I'd better bloody hope I'm worth it.

Taking a final drag, he feels the nicotine punch his lungs before pulverising the butt under his heel.

If that man ever shows his face again, I'll bloody kill him.

The sparrowhawk flies closer, circling, once, twice… Martin waits for the sudden plunge, the sight of something small between its claws. Instead, unexpectedly, the bird banks, lifting away and upwards into a liquid sky. Martin stares until his eyes water, until he can decipher nothing except the canvas of cloud and sinking sun, and then he climbs into the motor and starts the ignition with a sudden burst of enthusiasm. If he gets a good run back, he might still make the second half of the concert.

By the time he reaches the village hall the day has all but disappeared, leaving only a glow of yellowish pink in the western sky. Parking on the edge of the field, Martin exits the car quickly. If Fran is here, then he will try one last time to ask her for another date. Perhaps she really has been too busy to see him? He may have read too much into her demeanour at their lunch; his preoccupation with the wretched army medical might have made him take an unnecessarily bleak view of the situation. He flexes his right hand experimentally. His knuckles are sore, yet the ache feels somehow agreeable, much like a badge of honour from a playground scrap or rugby match. He wonders what Dr Dandy will tell his wife. Presumably the bastard is sufficiently adept at spinning lies that he won't find it too hard to invent a reason why the man in reception punched him on the nose. Perhaps he will suggest Martin was suffering from a mental disorder. And in a manner of speaking, he would be right.

As he hurries from the car, music drifts across the grass. A rather melancholic number, by the sound of it, the notes carried with precision by the still night air. Martin slows his pace. It occurs to him he would do better to use the side door, which would allow him to slip into a seat discreetly. Changing direction mid-stride, he heads towards the far side of the building.

The instant he steps around the corner, he comes to a halt. Through an uncurtained window, the inside of the hall is shining back at him like his own private theatre. Fran is sitting next to June and so close to the wall she would be within touching distance. Her dress is one Martin has never seen before, red with white polka dots, the fabric is fitted over her bust and falls to a skirt that brushes the floorboards. Even if I wasn't in love with her, he thinks, I would find her the most beautiful girl in the room. Altogether about a dozen rows of chairs are facing the stage, where a drummer, a pianist and a saxophonist are gathered in a semicircle. German prisoners, of course – though, for a split second, it strikes him, they were simply musicians.

He raises his hand to tap the glass, then hesitates. While most of the audience are twitching fingers or feet in time with the rhythm, Fran is sitting utterly motionless. Exposed by the glare of the ceiling lights, the gleam in her eyes, the flush on her skin, and the upturned arc of her lips radiate complete happiness. Beside her, June's face is a stony mask. Martin is still pondering the comparison when a flourish of drumsticks brings the music to a finish and a woman wearing a matching twinset stands up to say something about a ten-minute break and cups of tea.

Martin doesn't move. He finds his gaze being drawn to the saxophonist, and after a second or two he realises the man is familiar, and shortly after that it dawns on him that this is the prisoner who came to his rescue in the lane. Even while Martin is speculating whether Fran will recognise him too, the German hops down from the stage and begins to walk directly towards her.

At first, Martin is merely surprised. A moment later his heart is disintegrating. The glow of Fran's anticipation, the brilliance of her smile, and her utter enthralment as the German approaches are unmistakable, and his scattered thoughts slot together with the suddenness and clarity of the answer to a crossword clue. As a hollow sort of numbness fills his legs, he grasps hold of the window frame. *She's in love with the German,* he realises with incredulity. *It's plain for everyone to see.* All at once the truth of that conclusion strikes him afresh – and with alarm. An instant later he is hurrying through the side door.

By the time he reaches them, Thomas is standing a little way distant, as if an invisible line has been drawn across the floor. June is scowling, while Fran's gaze darts between her sister and the German. As soon as she sees Martin, her face blossoms into a kind of agitated relief. 'This is Thomas,' she says quickly. 'My family invited him to our house at Christmas.'

Martin can't tell whether she's forgotten he has already met the man or the omission is deliberate. In any case he hardly wants to be reminded of the previous encounter himself. Keeping his expression blank, he nods at Thomas. 'How do you do.'

As their eyes engage there is a flash of blue.

He is better looking than me, Martin notes heavily. And a soldier. Whereas I am a man who spent the war behind a desk nursing a heart problem that never existed. The familiarity of his shame is exhausting. Miserable and exhausting. Instinctively, his fist clenches and the prick of bruised skin over his knuckles conjures the image of Dr Dandy holding his nose, the red rain spattering onto the surgery carpet. He breathes out slowly, uncurls his fingers.

Before he can speak, words bubble from Fran like a shaken bottle of soda. 'You play the saxophone wonderfully!' She's talking to the German, of course. She seems incapable of focusing anywhere else.

Thomas smiles and inclines his head. 'Thank you, but I do not play so well. The man who plays the piano, he learned music at Leipzig.'

'Well, I think you're marvellous—'

June cuts across her. 'What's going on?'

'What do you mean?'

June's gaze swivels from her sister to the German. And back again.

'The way you stare at him! You're shameless!'

Panic arrives on Fran's face.

'You've been seeing him, haven't you? All your recent excuses about going for walks or collecting something from the camp were just that, excuses. Really you were meeting him! You've made it quite obvious tonight. You can't take your eyes off him!'

Fran gapes at her helplessly.

'It's called *fraternising*, Fran. Fraternising with the enemy. And in case you've forgotten the war, about the fathers and sons and husbands and brothers who are dead because of it, *in case you've forgotten about Robbie*, let me remind you: the Germans were our enemies and you're breaking the law!'

The hall has fallen very quiet. While nobody is being so obvious as to gawp, there is a hushed attentiveness to the posture of the couples and family groups. Martin wonders what they are thinking. How many of them would agree with June and whether they might have a different opinion if they had seen Thomas defend him in the alley or knew that when the weather was at its worst the coal trains only ran because of the Germans who cleared the snow from the railways. Meanwhile, Fran appears so stricken he can hardly stand to look at her. He gropes for something, anything, to say, and to his surprise the solution presents itself quite easily.

'I'm afraid there's been a misunderstanding.'

Around them, interest sharpens.

Martin clears his throat to speak a little louder. 'On the occasions you mention, I expect Fran was with me. Perhaps she felt too shy to tell you, but since our trip to the cinema we've been stepping out together.' He adopts a slightly harder tone, the one he sometimes takes with over-bullish clients. 'I imagine you *are* aware that Fran and I went to the cinema together a few weeks ago?'

June doesn't reply. She seems a little dazed.

Martin turns away from her and takes a step towards Fran. In a smoother, gentler voice he says, 'I'm sorry I was late this evening, dear. My appointment in town lasted longer than I was expecting. Shall we go and fetch ourselves some refreshments before the interval finishes?' Before she can respond, he takes her elbow and steers her towards the trestle table where tea is being poured from an enormous urn into white china cups. For a fleeting moment, he fancies he is outside the hall again, watching someone else escort the woman in the dazzling dress across the room, an impartial observer, a bystander or passer-by, and not someone whose own heart hasn't just been shattered into fragments.

'How could I be so careless in front of June?'

'It's easily done.' When you're in love, he wants to add. The exuberance, the happiness is like being drunk, at least the buoyant stage of the first few drinks when you feel invincible and the centre of the world. They are standing on their own now, at the back of the hall. Fran is stirring her tea, her mouth a wretched line, her complexion the same colour as the porcelain. 'I suppose June was right, that you have been meeting Thomas in secret?' Despite his effort to sound casual, the desperation in his voice is plain, even to himself.

Fran glances over her shoulder, but June disappeared in the direction of the lavatory some minutes ago and has not yet returned. 'He told me he didn't play very well,' she whispers, as if she either didn't hear Martin's question or the query is too obvious to require an answer. 'I suppose he wanted to surprise me. He's very artistic. At Christmas he gave my family the most wonderful picture of the coastline. He drew it himself. I think he must…' She stops, lays the spoon in the saucer with a clatter and touches his arm. 'I'm so sorry, Martin. I should have told you. I should have tried to explain. You've always been so kind. And just now, when June was being so awful…' She smiles up at him. 'You were like a knight in shining armour!'

The pressure of her hand is both exquisite and unbearable. He swallows. 'In the fairy tales I used to read, the princess wants to marry the knight. Not run off with somebody else.'

Her gaze plummets. For a long while she stares at her shoes.

'I do like you, Martin. I like you very much indeed. But…' The sentence dissolves.

'You love him.' His mouth, his tongue, seem to taste as if he hasn't brushed his teeth for days.

'I am dreadfully sorry.'

Martin gazes into the tea he has no wish to drink.

She lifts her head. 'It's like… it's like I'm staring at the sun. I can't see anything but him.'

'Right.'

'I hope you understand? That we can be friends?'

'Of course.' He sounds, he thinks, as if she has merely ruled out the possibility of a trip into town the following weekend.

'If I hadn't met Thomas, I don't know, perhaps…'

He realises that she's trying to make him feel better, but his reaction is the same hollow sensation he experienced outside the hall. To be second choice, is to lose. What if she had never met the German? If he had never been attacked in the street that night, *if he had never been declared unfit for service*, she may not have done. In that case, could he have married Fran, knowing his feelings for her would always utterly and completely eclipse her feelings for him? His answer, without a doubt, is yes. A thousand times yes.

'The musicians are back. We'd better take our seats.' As he speaks, the call of the saxophone permeates the room and Fran's eyes leap to the stage. Taking her cup, he slips his free arm around her waist so he can murmur more easily in her ear. 'June is right about one thing. You must be careful. Fraternising with a German is a criminal offence. Nobody can help you very much, should you get caught.'

While the jazz plays, Martin sinks inside himself, hearing instead Fran's words, earnest and sweet: *it's like I'm staring at the sun. I can't see anything but him.* Although he knows nothing about astronomy, he recalls, suddenly, the image of a moon in a blue summer sky. He was walking on the beach some time before the war, before mines were buried into the sand, before the dunes were dotted with concrete bunkers and the coast roads barricaded with coils of barbed wire. There was a picnic. A basket swinging from eager hands. Laughter, singing, the smack of sunshine on bare skin and, above the pines, the moon. Pale and ghostlike, a crest of silver light was hanging like a pennant, like a sentry, like a talisman of the unassuming, over the treetops.

Martin closes his eyes. Even if Fran is lost to him for now, he won't give up hope, not entirely, not yet.

Chapter Twenty-Three

7 March 1947

'Well, *that* was a complete waste of time.'

The sound of Mrs Markham's voice takes Fran by surprise. Alice too, who scrambles to her feet, knocking the wooden jigsaw and shooting the pieces over the drawing room rug. She beams at Fran. 'Mummy's back!'

'Shall we go and say hello?' Fran holds out her hand.

Vivien Markham is in the hallway, taking off the blue coat Fran so terribly admires. There's no sign of Major Markham. Fran assumes he must be putting away the car, or perhaps he has driven straight to the camp. It rather implies that Mrs Markham was talking to herself and there's something very precise, very *coiled*, about the way she is hanging up the coat and brushing flecks of rain from the blue tweed that makes Fran hang onto Alice and stop her from running across the black-and-white tiles.

'You're back early.' Fran ventures. 'I haven't given Alice her supper yet.'

'Yes.' Vivien's features are tight and closed. Fran is thinking that is all the explanation she will get when Vivien groans unexpectedly and her face cracks open. 'We drove all that way and he said he couldn't help! Not even one session! The man is retiring soon, apparently. Moving to a different part of the country. I don't know why he couldn't have told us that on the telephone instead of making us waste a whole day! And now... now I don't know what we'll do.' She sinks onto a small leather chair as if she has only that second become aware of its existence.

Fran stares blankly. She has no idea what Mrs Markham is talking about or who the man in question might be. The whole episode, in fact, has been something of a mystery.

Yesterday Daisy had stopped her as she was leaving. 'I've been asked to look after Alice Markham tomorrow.' She paused, as though hoping Fran might work out on her own why this was relevant.

'I don't mind if you need to be away.' Fran was threading a scarlet scarf around her neck, anxious to go in case Thomas was by the trucks and waiting to intercept her for a stolen five minutes.

'The thing is,' Daisy said, 'this time I can't do it.' She was holding a fountain pen, clutching the barrel tightly as if someone might try to snatch it away from her.

'Well, tell Major Markham you're busy. I'm sure he won't mind.'

'I'm not busy. Rather, I *am* working of course, but Major Markham is happy to give me Friday off.'

'Then what's the problem?'

'I can't do it because I don't want to do it. I will never babysit for the Markhams again! Ever!'

Staring, Fran stopped winding the scarf.

'We had a bit of a falling out. The last occasion I was there Mrs Markham was frightfully rude. She said something horrid, something about Martin.'

'Martin? What did she say?'

Daisy opens her mouth, stops. Colour seeps into her cheeks. 'I… It doesn't matter…' She regathers her momentum. 'Anyway, they were dreadfully late back. I had the most awful time of it getting home myself. Apparently, their car had gone off the road, which I suppose they couldn't help. But they never should have gone in the first place. Not in that weather.'

'Where *did* they go?'

'Only to visit a friend! Even though it meant driving a long way and asking me to come out in the worst conditions imaginable.

The thing is' – Daisy closed her eyes and her blush deepened – 'I really can't go back. Not now.'

'What do you mean, not now?'

'It's rather complicated. When I was putting Alice to bed…'

Fran glanced at the clock. How long would Thomas wait? 'You'd like me to look after Alice instead of you. Is that it?'

Daisy looked surprised. 'Yes.'

Fran turned to the door.

'Fran? I know it's none of my business, but might you step out with Martin again? He came home from the concert yesterday ever so blue. I can't help wondering if Vivien Markham may have something to do with it. Perhaps it wasn't just me she spoke to. Perhaps she's been spreading awful rumours about Martin to other people as well—' She broke off. 'Are you in a terrible hurry again?'

'Sorry, Daisy, Mother wants me home early.' And without looking back, Fran rushed out of the office.

Now Viv beckons to Alice. 'Come here, darling. Let me give you a cuddle.' Although she holds out her arms, there's a slump to her shoulders and the badger's streak of grey is starkly conspicuous under the lamplight. She looks quite desperate, Fran thinks. At the end of her tether. Whoever the Markhams were supposed to have seen, they must have been counting on him terribly.

Alice twists on one leg and grips Fran's fingers. 'Where's Daddy?'

'I don't know.' Viv gazes around the hallway as if the fact of Toby's absence has only just registered. 'He was ahead of me. I wonder where he went. I expect he'll be here any moment.'

'I want to see—' Alice breaks off. 'There he is!'

The front door opens, and Toby appears looking more like an apparition than a husband, father, or the commander in charge of a prisoner-of-war camp. The grey of his coat, hat and face seems hazy and insubstantial, and the expression in his eyes vacant yet at the same time deeply intense, as though the real Major Markham were somewhere else entirely and the person in the doorway a hastily put together imitation.

In silence he gazes at the three of them before swivelling abruptly on his heel. Something in the unexpectedness of his movements, the brittleness of his back, makes Fran suddenly shiver. For some reason she can't look at either Vivien or Alice.

'Daddy! Where are you going?'

With his hand on the front door, Major Markham pauses. 'I'm going to the camp, Alice. There's some work I have to do.' Then to Viv, 'Don't wait up, I won't be back until late.'

The door opens and shuts and none of them say a word.

Eventually Viv gets up and comes across the hall. Bending down, she tucks a lock of white-blond hair behind Alice's left ear. 'There's nothing to worry about. Daddy is very tired, and he's had a disappointing day, but he'll be back to his normal self in no time.' Although said for Alice's benefit, Fran supposes she is meant to listen too. Presumably, Mrs Markham is concerned she might gossip about her husband at camp. She could tell her that his behaviour is already a cause for concern. Or at least it would be, if he were ever there long enough for anyone to see him.

Instead she says, 'Would you like me to cook Alice some supper? You might want to rest for a while in your bedroom.' When Viv nods gratefully, she tugs Alice gently towards the kitchen. Over her shoulder the creak and release of the treads on the staircase sound heavy and measured, as if a mountain were being scaled.

Upstairs, Viv can't decide whether or not to take a bath. She stands for a while at her dressing table and slowly unclips her earrings. They are one of her favourite pairs, tiny crystals shaped like a leaf with a flesh-coloured pearl in the centre – for some reason she had felt the need to dress up for the doctor, make a good impression, as if that would encourage him to take Toby on as a patient. Now she can't imagine why she bothered. He was such a sleazy little man, with a great big forehead and a nasty-looking bruise over his nose. Not that she would have minded his appearance if he could have helped Toby, but the man didn't seem at all interested. Did he say he was moving or retiring, or both of those things? He hadn't even seemed too sure himself.

Carefully, she puts away the earrings and loosens the collar of her blouse. The luxury, the stupor, of a bath would be wonderful. To immerse herself in the steam and forget the awfulness of the day, but there probably wouldn't be enough hot water to fill the tub more than a few inches and she would only have to get out again in ten minutes' time to put Alice to bed. And where is Toby? She can hardly relax when he could be anywhere and, it hits her, doing absolutely anything. Covering her face with her hands, she slumps onto the bed. She badly wants to cry, the release and comfort of tears, but she is too exhausted. And she is also too exhausted to take a bath.

Afterwards, when she's unpacking those minutes second by second, Viv realises she must have fallen asleep, sitting bolt upright on the counterpane, because the very next thing that seems to happen is Fran calling up the stairs.

'Mrs Markham? Are you there?'

It takes Viv a moment to collect herself, and when she stands up she feels light-headed. Stifling a yawn, she hurries to the door. Outside the window the arrival of evening is plainly imminent, although she could have sworn that when she came upstairs the sky was still blue.

'I should be leaving now, Mrs Markham. Alice has had her supper. I made her corned beef fritters and have settled her in the drawing room with the puzzle.'

Already? Viv wants to say. *Alice has eaten, already?* Instead she shouts, 'Thank you, Fran. Do go home before it gets dark. I'll be down soon.' Her hand reaches again to her blouse, where the tie-bow collar of the crêpe de Chine seems intent on strangling her. All at once she cannot bear the bows and buttons and tight-fitting seams of these ridiculous clothes an instant longer. Unzipping her skirt, she lets it drop to her ankles, next she rolls down her stockings, followed by the bliss of unhooking her girdle. Once the wretched blouse has come off as well, she's left with nothing but her slip and puddles of fabric lying at her feet. In the bedroom mirror a wraith appears: a thin, white body of a ghost with an older woman's head and silver-striped hair. She barely recognises herself.

Mechanically she collects the discarded garments and hangs them up. Oddly, the wardrobe door is open already, but before she can ponder why this might be, she hears from downstairs Fran say something to Alice, followed by the crunch of the front door. Hurrying to the dressing-table stool, she pulls out her housecoat and slips the gown on top of her underwear. From the depths of the stool, Alex's letters glower at her accusingly. I must throw them out, Viv resolves. *Perhaps I should even get rid of them now, before Toby comes home.* The notion of doing so, the finality of the gesture and all of its implications, is like a blade turning slowly in her stomach.

Suddenly she stretches into the stool and extracts the compact bundle. On the face of it there is nothing amiss: the envelopes have been neatly stacked and secured with an elastic band, and yet there is something wrong, she's sure of it. Something badly wrong.

Thumbing through the wedge of paper, Viv casts back her mind. The last time she held these pages was just after she learned Alex had returned to America and shortly before she had that awful argument with Daisy. Viv colours, remembering the glare and hostility of the girl and her own dreadful mood. Alice arrived unexpectedly in the doorway of the bedroom while she was still reading, so didn't she simply throw all the letters into the stool? She has no memory of organising them into a bundle or using an elastic band. Nor of tidying up the mess afterwards. And in the days since then she hasn't been able to think of Alex, let alone want to reread all his lies and tinpot endearments.

Panic grips her.

Viv removes the band. She begins to sift through the envelopes slowly, pausing to study each one. When she has finished, she does the same thing again, this time more quickly. A confused sort of sickness is rising in her throat. In desperation she makes a fan of the letters and holds them under the bedroom light. However, there is no mistaking what she can see. Or rather what she can't. There is no green ink. The worst of the letters, the one that nearly caused her to lose her mind, to leave Toby, the one in which Alex said he would take her back to America, is missing. Kneeling on the carpet, she gropes wildly under the bed, but all she retrieves are two hairpins and a sugared almond coated with fluff.

Viv stands up, shaking. Has Toby taken the letter? After their conversation in the car, she suspected, almost believed, he knew about Alex. Or if not Alex himself, the existence of someone like Alex. Yet he gave no hint he feared Viv might actually leave him, leave the country in fact. Is that what he thinks now? If he has seen the green-inked letter, he might very well make that assumption. Once he gets back, she will have to talk to him candidly and try to explain the madness that overpowered her for a while. The notion of such a conversation is horrifying. Yet there no longer appears to be an alternative. If she wants to save her marriage, she has to find out what Toby knows – and what he might be prepared to forgive.

For now, however, Alice. Twenty minutes must have passed since Fran went home. Knotting the sash of her housecoat, Viv hastens onto the landing. 'Alice? Are you waiting for me? I'm coming, darling. Have you finished that jigsaw puzzle yet?'

There's no reply.

From somewhere a draught is blowing. As Viv descends the stairs, cold air is curling around her bare ankles, while in the hall the curtains are rippling as if hanging out to dry on a washing line. Yet when she checks the front door, she finds it closed, the panelling snug against the frame.

She heads towards the drawing room. 'Alice?'

At the threshold she stops. The room is unoccupied. Beside the fire, pieces of the jigsaw lie abandoned on the rug.

'Alice? Alice, where are you?'

Viv rushes to the kitchen.

And from there to the larder.

It seems like she's going mad. As if from the moment Fran left the house, from those lost minutes sitting on the bed, she has been plunged into the irrational, confused terror of a nightmare. Could Alice have gone upstairs? If Alice used the back staircase, she might not have heard her. She calls into the stairwell. 'Darling, why are you hiding from me? This isn't a very nice game, is it? I'm beginning to get quite worried!'

Silence.

Viv shivers.

She cinches the housecoat more tightly. The temperature is freezing, she realises. Somewhere close the night is blowing unchecked straight through walls. With sudden and alarming knowledge, she runs to the dining room. The door that is generally shut, clicked into place by an upward tweak of the handle, is slightly agape, while light spills through the gap like a path to a forbidden land.

Tentatively, Viv pushes the door and over the creak of the hinge hears herself gasp. On the far side of the dining table, across from the expanse of polished wood and the bowl of apples, the amber glint of the whisky decanter and Toby's best crystal, both of the French windows are standing ajar.

She rushes to the threshold.

The garden, darkening and empty, stretches before her.

'Alice? Alice? Are you there?' Viv stares into the dusk. Alice would never have managed these heavy doors herself, she is sure of it. Not unless, it suddenly strikes her, they had been opened already. Earlier she wondered if Alice had slipped unheard up the back staircase, but perhaps, instead, Toby had done so. Perhaps he came inside through the French windows while she was talking to Fran?

Swivelling on her heel, she races to the main stairs and climbs them two at a time. In the bedroom, she takes a breath to steady herself before wrenching open the wardrobe door. Blindly, she gropes behind the rows of coloured silks and heavy velvets, beyond the memories of champagne and dancing, of parties and cigarette smoke, yet all she can feel is an unfilled void and the hard, hollow knock of the panelling.

Chapter Twenty-Four

Fran cycles behind Thomas with her eyes fixed to his back wheel and the ruby pull of the reflector. On her right the marsh stretches towards the pocket of sea trapped by the spit while the last smudges of light flare in the sky ahead. She doesn't know where they are going. Only that when she left the Markhams' house she was supposed to be going home, and now she most definitely is not.

She was squatting on her heels, attaching the dynamo to the rim of the wheel, when she saw him step from the hedge a little beyond the Markhams' gate. His shape was so familiar she didn't even jump, merely dragged the bike over the gravel until his solid presence was wrapped against her and breathing in her ear.

'How did you find me?'

'Daisy told me you were here.'

Fran stiffened. 'You went to the office?'

'Don't worry, she didn't suspect anything. I had a meeting.'

'With Major Markham?' Fran was confused. 'But he was away all day.'

'With Captain Holmes.' He tugged her hand. 'Come with me.'

'*Come with you?* Where?'

'You'll see!' He reached into the hedge.

Fran blinked. 'You have a bicycle, but how?'

'From one of the soldiers. I borrowed it.' Leaning forwards, he kissed her lips. 'It's not so surprising. We have lived together for many months, now some are like friends. Perhaps, being soldiers, they realise most of us only fought a war because the guns were forced into our hands. While other people' – she knew he was thinking of June – 'cannot understand the difference between a German and a Nazi.'

He swung his leg over the saddle. 'Ready?'

The tarmac is wet with slush. Often Fran has to swerve to avoid puddles or blink away spray from the tyres. A mist of dampness settles on her hair while her chest burns from the effort of keeping up. He's worried someone will see us, she supposes, that's why he's going so fast, and glancing over her shoulder to check for other cyclists, she almost loses her balance. They race beside the mauve haze of field and fen until they reach the next village, where some time last century she drank brandy with Martin. Then, just in front of a windmill, Thomas veers onto a track that heads towards the sea.

'Wait!' Fran stands on the pedals. 'Thomas, wait!' Stones squeal under his tyres as she cycles up to him, breathing hard. 'We can't go this way. The lane is blocked because of the mines on the beach.' She points ahead to where coils of barbed wire and two upended pallets make a barricade across the mud.

'Don't you want to see the ocean?'

'I would love to, but I don't want to get us killed!'

He touches her arm. 'Most of the beach is safe now. And I know where to go.' Lifting his foot off the ground, he propels himself forwards. 'Trust me.'

She watches him approach the barrier, slide off the seat and lever the frame between a pallet and the fence. An instant later he has vanished. Alone in the fading light, the spirals of wire with their ugly little knots appear almost menacing. Will he not wait for her? She opens her mouth but before she can call him, he reappears, clambering around the pallets without his bicycle, and beckons her forwards.

On the far side of the blockade they ride side by side. She had forgotten the twists in the lane, how it turns one way and then the other as if in no hurry to arrive anywhere at all. They are cycling more slowly too. With high hedges either side, it feels like their own private world. For miles there is nobody and nothing, except the beach somewhere ahead and the sky, which, when she tips back her head, is deepening in hue with the first pinpricks of stars starting to show.

At the end of the track they dismount and leave the bikes on the ground. Thomas takes her hand and together they clamber up the shingle bank that runs west until the dune diverts from the mainland to become the ocean edge of the spit. Fran inhales deeply. The air is thick with the smell of salt, and the crash and drag of the waves seems to be coming from all directions and filling her head like a familiar, favourite piece of music. At the top of the ridge, she cries out in delight. She had almost forgotten the joy of the sea, rising and falling over itself in foam-tipped swells that blaze against the dark expanse like strings of white lights.

'Can we go down to the edge?'

There are stakes with tape strung between them dividing the beach into segments while a long metal rod lies abandoned only a few feet away.

'We must stay to the right of that line.' He points to the closest line of stakes. 'The land is safe here. Further west, towards the spit, I am not certain if all the mines have been cleared.'

Fran nods. Her heart is thumping with gratitude and love and the thrill of being alone with him in such a marvellous place. She wonders what June would say if she could see her now, and to her surprise feels a jolt of pity. She imagines her sister writing yet another letter or helping her mother to clear the supper dishes. The dullness of the evening as inevitable as the onset of dark.

Jogging to the water, she crouches at the foot of the waves. The tide is retreating, each surge reaching a little less further up the shore than the previous one and depositing a trace of spittle on the gleaming stones. When she dips her fingers into the water, the cold makes her gasp.

'Fran?'

She looks up as the wave pulls back, sucking away the sand from her hand. He is standing right behind her.

'They are sending me home to Germany. Me, and thirty other prisoners from the camp.'

'What?'

She scrambles to her feet.

'I am being repatriated. Captain Holmes told me today. As long as Major Markham signs the papers that are necessary. Apparently, he has not been at the camp very often.'

Fran stares at him. 'How can they have decided already? I didn't know anything about it and' – desperately she tries to remember her recent conversations with Daisy but the only one she can recall of any substance was about Alice – 'I don't believe Daisy did either.'

'Maybe the camp was told only recently. Maybe they had to pick quickly.'

The world seems to be rocking, wobbling on its axis. She tries to gather her wits, but a single thought is filling her head.

'I don't want you to go.'

'Then I won't.'

He takes hold of both of her wrists, circles them with his thumbs and forefingers.

'But you don't have any choice!'

'I could escape, run away from the camp.'

She can feel the strength of his grip, the heat of his skin. It seems that if he were to let go of her, she might simply collapse onto the shingle.

'The weather is a little warmer. There are barns to sleep in and farmers who so badly need labour they may feed me in return for work.'

'You could be shot!'

'Only if they find me. They may not search for very long.'

Her eyes fill. Much as she wants to believe him, she knows the situation is hopeless. It has always been hopeless. How foolish she was to feel so happy only moments ago. Turning her head, she fixes her gaze on the sea. She is determined not to cry. Not now. Not in front of him. 'Perhaps,' she manages, 'you could write to the Home Office and ask to stay? Captain Holmes might send a letter on your behalf, since you're such a good worker.'

'They would demand to know why I want to remain here, why I am not anxious to return to my own country.'

'Then tell them you love me! That I love you, and we want to be together!' Pulling free her hand to swipe away a tear, she adds fiercely. 'What's so wrong about that?'

The horizon is a blur, the vaguest shift from green-grey to grey. She can't tell if it's because of the falling light or the wetness pooling on her lashes.

Thomas says quietly, 'You know I can't say that. You could be sent to prison. Your parents, your family, they could not support such a thing.' He pauses. 'I could not support such a thing. Not when it is certain they would refuse my request.'

She glances sideways. He is staring at the sea too, his features tense and unreadable. She touches his cheek. 'In that case, I'll wait for you. Go back home. Go to Germany. It doesn't matter. The rules are changing, attitudes are changing. Little by little. One day we will be able to marry. Being apart will be unbearable, but it won't be for very long.'

To her surprise his gaze doesn't waver.

'Thomas?'

Still, he doesn't move.

'You *do* want me to wait for you, don't you?'

With disbelief she watches him close his eyes then open them again before finally wrapping an arm about her shoulder and guiding her away from the shoreline. At the foot of the shingle bank, he undoes the buttons of his coat and holds out the flap. 'Sit with me, Fran.'

She sinks onto the stones, heart scudding with alarm while his arm enfolds her within the woollen cape. The smell of him; the trace of sweat and soap and animal musk are like a drug. In her ears the rock of the waves seems timeless, as if it might be possible to stay in the present, remain in that precise moment, by keeping motionless, by not speaking, by doing nothing except simply breathing.

'You cannot wait for me.'

For a second she thinks she hasn't heard him right. Then, 'You don't believe I can wait for you? You don't trust me?'

'If I go, you *must* not wait for me. *If* I go, I won't come back.'

She jerks away and gapes at him in horror. Her tears have gone, blown away by shock, but a chill is spreading through her chest, worse than the cold of a winter sea or the snow of the last few months. She is certain he is telling the truth and at the same time utterly and wretchedly confused.

'Two days ago, I had a letter. It was from neighbours in my village. Remember I told you I live near Eisenach?'

She nods stupidly.

'After the war the town was controlled by the Americans, now it is controlled by Russia. Until I received that letter, I wasn't certain which side of the border my home would be, but now I know. The village is within the Russian occupation area. It is the reason why I have heard nothing for so long. Nobody can get out and because of the restrictions letters are only now beginning to come through.'

'You couldn't come back? Not ever?'

He shakes his head.

'Then I'll come with you!'

'Nobody is allowed to leave the Russian part of Germany, Fran. Not the Germans, not the British, not anyone. If you go with me, you may never see your home or family again.'

Her body stiffens. She imagines saying goodbye to her parents, to June, to the house with its memories of Robbie, leaving forever the cries of the birds and the upturned bowl of sky over the marsh. For a split second, it's merely a checklist in her head, and then the enormity of the hole hits her. She gasps and her hand flies to her mouth. She feels him tighten the coat around her shoulders and realises her whole body is shaking.

He looks at her steadily. 'So, now you understand why my best chance, *our* only chance, is that I escape.'

For a moment she can't speak.

Eventually she whispers, 'And *your* family? What about them?'

Dropping his head, he scoops up a handful of shingle. 'The neighbours say the house was badly damaged when Eisenach was bombed. Nobody has seen my parents or my sister since that time.'

'That's dreadful! Is that all the neighbours said?'

'The message was very short. They were probably afraid if they wrote more the letter would be thrown away.'

She gazes at him, perplexed.

'They – the authorities – open letters and remove the dangerous ones.'

'*Dangerous* ones?'

'The ones that say anything the Russians don't like.' Flinging the stones down, he stands up suddenly and peers along the beach. 'I thought I heard something…'

They freeze. Fran strains her ears, listening for a voice, or the grind of footsteps on the stones, but the only sound she can detect is the constant beat of the sea.

After a few seconds he sinks down again.

Fran leans against his ribcage. His tunic, stiff with age and dirt, is rough against her cheek yet there is no place on earth she would rather be. This is why he came to find her at the Markhams' house, she realises. Why he took the risk of borrowing a bicycle and bringing her to the beach. So that he could break the news to her here, where the heartbreak might be a tiny bit more bearable.

Quietly she says, 'I'm so sorry about your family, Thomas.'

She feels a hiccup in his breathing, a shudder in his chest.

He squeezes her close. 'You are my family now.'

He buries his hand into her hair.

She tips back her face.

'Kiss me.'

He throws a quick glance along the beach. Then he shrugs off his coat, spreads the fabric out on the ground and lowers her on top of it.

Fran gazes up at him.

There are stones under her back, under her skull. As their mouths press together the pebbles shift beneath their weight. His fingers are inside her jumper, then her shirt, searching for her flesh through the layers of fabric.

Fran traps his hand. 'Wait!'

He pulls back. 'I'm sorry, I—'

She shakes her head. *That's not what I mean.* Holding his gaze, she sits up, lifts her jumper over her head and drops it to the ground. Next the buttons of her blouse, her movements steady and deliberate. A brief sensation of ice-cold air, before he is easing her backwards again, his lips are on hers, and they are both tugging and pulling at the rest of their clothes.

There is a moment when he hesitates. A question without words. Then there is nothing but his hips hard against her own, his hand in the crevice of her thighs, and a wondrous sort of heat flooding through every fibre of her body. As the stones melt away, she hears her own breath, gasping and loud, and she guides his face onto the chalk-soft skin of her breasts and closes her eyes.

By the time they leave, the shoreline is dark. Hundreds, thousands, millions of stars are shining. Tiny diamonds of hope and the milky shift of faraway galaxies pepper the swathe of sea-sky. Thomas's arm curls around Fran's waist. Their footsteps match, crunching the shingle, their breath like lace in the chilling air.

'When are the prisoners going?' she asks. 'The ones being repatriated.'

'The day after tomorrow. Trucks will take them to a camp close to London, where the government will give them the rest of their papers.'

'What! So soon? On a Sunday?' She halts, horrified. She imagined it would be weeks away.

'I think they do it like this deliberately. That way the other prisoners have no time to argue it should be them instead.'

Fran gapes at him.

'I told you, I won't be with them. I will escape before then.'

'That means tomorrow.' She can barely keep the panic at bay. 'You'll have to escape tomorrow!'

'I know.'

'But what will you do? How will I find you?'

'I will meet you at the village hall. Not the day they leave, but on Monday in the evening. You might know something by then from the camp, how hard they are looking for me. Whether I need to make a very clever disguise!'

He is trying to make her smile, but her blood is churning like the sea, frothing and foaming with fear. It feels as if a whole lifetime of living has been crammed into the last two hours. They reach the bicycles and clamber aboard. Thomas leads the way back along the lane towards the coast road. Fran follows in his tracks. She tells herself to trust him, somehow his plan will work out, that it's only because he loves her so much that he's risking everything.

At the junction they turn left towards the camp and stop a little way from the gate.

'I should accompany you home.'

Fran shakes her head. 'I'm used to doing this part on my own. And the road could be busier. Someone might see us.' The words are no sooner out of her mouth than the clink and swish of tyres are suddenly audible and out of the dusk a dynamo lamp appears. She retreats into trees just as the cyclist draws level.

'Thomas! What are you doing with a bicycle? Did someone lend it to you?' The voice belongs to Daisy. Leaving work, slightly later than usual.

'Yes.'

There's a pause.

'Well, I suppose it doesn't matter. You're nearly back now anyway.'

The bicycle moves forwards, then halts a little way distant. 'By the way, a letter arrived for you. In the second post.'

'From Germany?'

'I can't remember. No, from England, I think.'

'Perhaps it is about the repatriation?'

'Perhaps.'

Daisy's tone sounds odd, Fran thinks. Distracted and not at all like herself. Maybe Martin is weighing on her mind again. She watches until the light from Daisy's back wheel has completely melted away before emerging from the trees, For a moment she and Thomas simply stand together, as if testing the stillness.

Eventually, he glances towards the gate. 'So, now I must go…'

Her throat fills with rocks. She wants to say something. Something normal and reassuring but all at once she can't say anything at all.

He tilts her chin.

A kiss, butterfly soft.

'This isn't goodbye, Fran. I will see you on Monday.'

Chapter Twenty-Five

'Where have you been?'

Fran shuts the kitchen door and unwinds her scarf.

'I said, where have you been? With Martin?'

'I was out, yes. Meeting Martin.' Her mind is swirling. Although she might be looking at her sister, she's hearing Thomas's voice, seeing the flicker of stars over the sea, his face above her own. She ought, she supposes, to be ashamed of what happened on the beach, but instead the remembering, the reliving, provokes a hot wash of pleasure. It feels as though a torch has been lit, burning deep inside of her, something precious and vital to lessen the darkness of whatever lies ahead.

'Fran!' June grabs her arm.

She blinks. The nip of June's fingers, the alarm in June's voice, drags her into the present, to the solitary lamp burning over the Aga and in the shadows at the back of the room, her mother standing with her hands clasped, as if she's trying to stop them from flying away.

'What is it? What's happened?' She's thinking they've found out about Thomas, that he's going to escape, even as she realises the panic can't possibly be true and recalls that June asked about Martin and not Thomas at all.

'It's Alice.'

Fran looks blankly at her sister.

Their mother steps forwards. 'Mrs Markham was here about an hour ago. Alice is missing. She hoped you might be able to help.'

'Missing? How can Alice be missing?'

'Apparently, she disappeared shortly after you left. Mrs Markham was upstairs changing her clothes and when she came downstairs Alice was nowhere to be seen. Mrs Markham was quite beside herself. I actually think the poor woman ought not to have been on her own.'

'How would I know where Alice is?'

'You were looking after her today.' June's tone is accusatory.

'Until her parents got home! I left her with her mother!' Fran stops, suddenly, remembering that in fact she left Alice alone in the drawing room.

'Did she say anything odd? Anything to suggest she might run away?'

'Of course not! I would have—'

'What about games? Perhaps hide-and-seek might have given her the idea for a secret hiding place.' Her mother this time, more placatory.

'We didn't play hide-and-seek. She doesn't like it. We did jigsaws and dressed up some of her dolls… It's an awfully large house.' Fran swallows. 'She must be there somewhere!'

'Mrs Markham said she had looked everywhere. And spoken to the neighbours. For some reason their French windows were left open, so she thinks the child might have ventured outside. Coming here was a last resort, just in case you could shed any light.' Her mother throws a glance at June. They have obviously been talking about what Fran might know. Where she might have been all this time.

'I can't help! I have no idea where Alice is.' An ache is swelling in her throat. Alice roaming around the garden, searching for a place to disappear is unimaginable. The child hated to be alone for even five minutes. Why did she leave before Mrs Markham was ready? It now seems inexplicable, although at the time it had felt perfectly natural. She can even picture Alice on the rug, busy with the puzzle, her blond hair a halo in the firelight.

There was not the slightest inkling the world might implode two minutes later.

She turns to her mother anxiously. 'What on earth can have happened?'

The question hovers. Her mother and June exchange another look. Their mother's hair is swan-white, her complexion ashen and etched with fine lines that suddenly appear deeper and more plentiful than usual.

'What is it?' Fran demands. 'What aren't you telling me?'

There's a pause.

Her mother opens her mouth, but June speaks first. 'Earlier this evening that German prisoner was seen near the Markhams' house.'

Fran's heart seems to stop. 'Which German prisoner?'

'The one who came here at Christmas. The one you liked.' The barb is unmistakable.

'What are you suggesting? That he abducted Alice? But that's impossible!'

'Impossible? Why is it *impossible*?'

Fran can't answer. Her pulse now is racing, the blood pounding in her ears with an awful, private thunder.

Her mother says, 'One of the Markhams' neighbours said he was lingering near the gate shortly before Alice went missing, and nobody has seen him or Alice since. We mustn't jump to conclusions but—'

'He didn't take her!'

June is watching her carefully. 'How can you be so certain?'

'Because he wouldn't!' Because he was with me, she wants to say. Kissing me, loving me on the beach. Telling me that our only chance to be together is for him to run away. Instead she says, 'You've met him yourself! How could you possibly believe he would snatch a seven-year-old child?'

'The police must be dreadfully stupid, don't you think? If everyone else can tell who the criminals are by simply looking at them!'

Fran glares at her.

Their mother interjects. 'Stop it! Arguing won't help anyone. A soldier from the camp called round, Fran. Just before you got back. There's a meeting at the public house to organise a search party. I'd better stay with your father, but you should both go and see if you can lend a hand.'

'I'm ready.' Fran begins to button up her coat again. Her heart feels sick and heavy, like something ill or wounded that she can barely carry. Why hadn't she waited for Mrs Markham? It would only have been another ten minutes. Now Alice is missing, and Thomas might take the blame. Another thought stops her breath. If Alice isn't found and Thomas disappears, June won't be the only person in the village to connect the two events.

She jumps. Her mother has stepped forwards to do up her last button. 'Try not to worry, dear. Alice may have fallen asleep under a bush or locked herself in an outhouse. The sooner she's found the better, of course, but children do all sorts of odd things.'

Fran turns to leave. She ought, she supposes, to linger while her sister fetches an overcoat. Then she hears June say from behind, 'Not that odd. Children don't just disappear.' And Fran decides not to wait for her after all.

The public house is a mixture of familiar and unfamiliar faces. Only those closest to the bar are supping pints, the rest are standing with their hands in their pockets looking about anxiously. Villagers are pressed alongside soldiers while in the furthest corner a knot of German prisoners are whispering, heads bent, amongst themselves. Although there is no sign of Major or Mrs Markham, the sense of urgency is palpable from the shuffling feet and agitated nature of the conversations. A coldness on the back of her hand makes Fran jump. Someone appears to have brought a Labrador. Is he to take part in the search as well? She recalls how sniffer dogs are used to hunt for missing persons, and a horrible taste spreads through the back of her throat.

'Can I have your attention?'

The words make little impression on the gathering.

'Can I have your attention!' Not a question this time and accompanied by the scrape of chair legs. A second later the bespectacled face of Captain Holmes appears above the vantage point of a table, the faces in the room tilt upwards and very gradually a hush descends. Captain Holmes holds out his arms. 'Now as I'm sure you are all aware, a little girl called Alice Markham disappeared this evening—'

'Poor little mite!' The murmur in Fran's ear comes from a woman with a headscarf tied under her chin whom Fran recognises from the church.

'She's been missing for nearly three hours and the weather is deteriorating, so speed is of the essence. Please pay attention, I'm going to divide everyone into groups of six. Half of the groups should focus their efforts on the area between here and the Markhams' home, and the others on the area further west. We need to check very thoroughly all the places a little girl might hide: sheds, stables, that sort of thing. Knock on people's doors and ask if they've seen her, or anyone' – he snags awkwardly – 'anyone they don't know, particularly someone acting suspiciously.'

The temperature in the pub dips slightly, and into the silence rain begins to patter, brittle gusts rapping on the roof tiles, as if the downpour has been timed deliberately to coincide with Captain Holmes's address.

'What's she wearing?' Someone shouts.

'I… I don't know.' The captain casts around the room.

'A pinafore dress,' Fran says, her voice quavering. 'Alice is wearing a red pinafore dress and a knitted Fair Isle cardigan.'

'Nobody can hear you.' The woman in the scarf yanks a chair from under a table. 'Stand on this, dear. Try again.'

Fran hesitates, then clambers upwards. Suddenly, the whole room is visible and also reduced in size. From her new height it's evident there are fewer villagers than she previously thought, while the squares of night pressing at the windows seem blacker, more intimidating, the oasis of the pub more fragile. In the corner she catches sight of Thomas with the other prisoners. His eyes meet hers like the strike of a match.

'A pinafore dress!' she yells. 'Alice is wearing a red dress and a patterned cardigan!'

There's a murmuring accord. Captain Holmes begins to count, sorting men and women into groups as he does so, 'One, two, three, four, five, six – you together over there. One, two, three…'

'Not so fast!' A voice sounding rough and rather pleased with itself cuts through the commotion. 'No point in search parties. The answer's in this room already. All you need to know is who to ask.'

The bustling stops.

The man who has spoken pivots on his bar stool.

Fran shivers as if an outside door has been opened. Although his features are familiar, it's the set of his shoulders and the pint glass in his hand that immediately conjure up the darkened alley, the beer bottle rattling on the stones, the swinging fist and Martin pressed, helpless, against the wall.

Thick black eyebrows pinch to a frown. 'You won't find the girl hiding in a shed. Someone's taken her. And that someone is a German! A bloody Kraut who should never have been allowed out. Who should be locked up like the Hitler dog he is. Alice Markham isn't lost. Either she's been locked up herself or…' – he swigs his beer, swipes a hand across his lips – 'she's dead already.'

All of the room gasps.

Fran watches incredulity and anger ripple across the villagers' faces. Mr Graveling, the publican, leans over the beer taps and murmurs something to the village smithy. In the corner the prisoners cluster together more tightly. Thomas is translating for the smaller, slight man beside him. It is Reiner, she realises, as she sees his face fill with astonished horror, and he gapes in bewilderment towards the bar.

Captain Holmes bangs together his hands. 'What nonsense! What dangerous nonsense! There's no reason to believe anyone has taken Alice.' He gestures towards the huddled figures. 'These prisoners aren't brutes or dogs, but men who have volunteered to search for the missing girl!'

The man at the bar levers himself off his stool. 'Dangerous nonsense? Is that so? I'll tell you what's dangerous. In fact, I'll do better than that. I'll show you *who's* dangerous, because he's here. Standing among us. Hiding in plain sight.'

A pause.

An inhale.

'Right there!' As he flings out an arm, a surge of beer cascades over the glass and splashes onto the floor. 'That piece of scum was seen hanging about the Markhams' house. Hiding in the trees. What business could he possibly have there on a Friday night? None – except the cravings of an evil Kraut!'

Scrabbling and jostling break out as the villagers attempt to follow the pointed finger, but Fran can see without needing to move or whisper to her neighbour how the arc of hate rises and falls on Thomas with the certainty of a spotlight. He must sense the accusation because his eyes widen in shock. Fran tries to find his gaze, but he avoids the contact and looks away. He wants to protect me, she guesses, and as she thinks it, the crowd seems to close in and take one step nearer the prisoners' corner.

Near the door, June has slipped into the throng. And behind June is Martin. A late arrival, he is holding his hat in front of him, casting his attention left, then right, as if trying to make sense of the scene. The sight of him, tall and steadfast, gives Fran courage. 'It's not true!' she cries. 'The prisoner didn't take Alice. I know it's not true!'

Heads swing in her direction. Mrs Reynolds, the owner of the village shop, smiles encouragingly. Fran heaves a breath. The room swims. What can she say? The only explanation she can give is like a badly built bridge, an old and crumbling bridge, that will collapse the moment she steps on the planks.

She's still frozen with indecision when June interjects. 'Have you found the photograph yet?' she says loudly. 'The one the prisoner carries in his pocket. It's a picture of a little girl. I've seen it myself.'

A buzz, a static, seems to suck the oxygen from the air.

'What's this about a photograph?' Captain Holmes sounds flabbergasted.

Fran gapes at June. 'The picture is of his sister. You *know* that. Thomas told us at Christmas…'

'That's what he *told* us…'

Captain Holmes interrupts them. '*Do* you have a photograph?' he says to Thomas.

'Yes, but only of my sister…'

'I think we'd better have a look.'

Slowly, Thomas reaches inside his coat. The crowd appears to be holding its breath. He extracts his hand. 'This is my sister. Her name is Gisela.'

As Captain Holmes studies the image a curtain seems to fall across his face. Reluctantly, he holds the photograph aloft.

There's a stunned hush.

Fran is rooted to the chair.

The picture is the one that fell from his pocket in the alley. The one he showed her family at Christmas. Yet from a distance there's no denying the likeness with Alice: the white-blond hair, the tentative smile, the combination of innocent self-possession and shyness. Fran is amazed she never saw the similarity between the two girls before.

A man close by says in a shocked tone, 'It's Major Markham's daughter herself!'

Fran shakes her head fiercely. 'That picture is *not* Alice,' she shouts. 'It's the prisoner's sister!'

'How do you know?' A voice asks.

'He told me!'

Someone sniggers.

Somebody else says, 'If she's the prisoner's sister, why is she so much younger than him?'

There's a muttering of accord. As the photograph is passed around, questions are grabbed and tossed from one person to the next.

'The child is only seven or eight!'

'The same age as Alice Markham!'

'She *is* Alice Markham, I'm sure of it!'

Anger wheels about Fran's head, thickening and multiplying and impossible to catch.

Bottle-man's voice rises above the crowd. The photograph has made its way to him and he sweeps the image around the room. 'The Kraut was seen outside the Markhams' house minutes before the child went missing. And he was carrying her picture! You surely can't believe this is a coincidence? We don't need to send out search parties to look for Alice Markham, do we? We know who took her. And since he's standing right here, he can tell us where she is!'

A growl of assent rears up on itself, like a wave about to break. Fran turns to Captain Holmes, but his eyes are full of doubt. As if in slow motion, he looks towards the waiting volunteers, then back to the prisoners. The command to bar the door, to detain, to arrest, is visible, hovering, on his lips.

And still, Thomas won't look at her. His gaze is everywhere and nowhere, his mouth clamped shut. He will risk prison, she realises suddenly. Or worse. He will let them accuse him of taking Alice Markham simply to keep me safe. The insight is both a gift, the truest declaration of his love, and the heaviest of responsibilities because the decision what to do, what will happen next, rests with her alone.

A hand plucks her skirt. 'You can come down now, dear.'

Fran sways with indecision.

The rain is falling harder, beating against the pub's old walls, pressing the building into submission. She imagines the deluge filling the rivers, the marsh, the sea, in an unstoppable cycle. Slowly, she grasps the back of the chair, bends her knees and begins to drop towards the floor.

Captain Holmes clears his throat.

As her fingers encircle the wooden chairback, Fran spots sand under her fingernails, tiny flecks of black and gold, the glittering dust of that other world, dance in front of her eyes. *I was with him* are all the words she has to utter. *When Alice went missing, we were together at the beach.*

Straightening her legs, she lifts her chin. The faces of Thomas, Martin and June float before her. The man at the bar and the villagers are watching her too. *Captain Holmes doesn't really believe Thomas is guilty*, Fran guesses, *he wants me to tell him something different.* Well, in that case she will oblige. Loudly, she says, 'I have something to say!'

The door to the pub flies open. Rain, wind and cold snatch everyone's attention and in the entrance stands Vivian Markham, her cheeks wet and pinched, her hair in clumps. 'Please, I need your help! Alice is with my husband. I think he's taken her onto the beach.'

There's a collective blink.

The room quivers with confusion.

A second, two seconds, pass, as though to test the major's wife really is standing on the threshold. She's dazzling, Fran thinks with wonder. Dishevelled, damp and clearly in distress, Vivian Markham nevertheless possesses an undefinable air. No longer a romantic one, perhaps, rather a tougher type of beauty altogether.

Martin is the first to step forward. 'If Alice is with Major Markham, I don't understand the urgency.' He glances through the doorway into the lightless void beyond. 'Of course, it's turned into a filthy night, but I imagine…'

'You don't understand.' Viv touches her forehead, as if the effort of making anyone understand her is physically painful. 'My husband, Major Markham, is not well…'

There's an interruption from the bar, 'How can you be sure the child is with her father? A prisoner was seen—'

'I'm quite certain. A girl from the camp telephoned. She told me that Toby came into the office to sign some papers. As he was leaving, Alice appeared.'

'Then surely…' Martin murmurs.

'Apparently he said something about the beach. The girl, Daisy, reminded him the beach was shut off, but my husband took no notice. She said, he seemed' – Viv swallows – 'he seemed upset.'

Fran lowers herself into a sitting position. The relief for Thomas, for herself, is so sudden and acute she feels faint. Yet at the same time there's something about Mrs Markham's panicky appearance she doesn't quite understand.

Martin sounds perplexed too. 'Then they may be home again already. Or back at the camp, perhaps?'

'I've just been to the camp. His office is empty.'

'Well, presumably they will go for a walk, get a little wet and come home later?'

'No! At least, he may… he might…'

'What? Stay out too long?'

Viv stares at Martin. Her eyes held wide. Then she snaps. Her lids drop. Her shoulders shake. 'His gun is missing.'

Martin swallows, coughs. 'But you surely can't think he would use it on himself or Alice?'

'He's been very upset,' Viv says again. 'Not himself at all.' She stops. After a moment, she says very slowly, 'Sometimes… some-times he seems to think he's actually on the battlefield. Or under attack. Or being shot at or captured. Other times he stays alone in the dark for hours. As if he has locked himself out of the world and can't get in again. Or doesn't' – her voice chokes – 'doesn't want to come back in.'

Fran thinks, *I know this already. Daisy and I, we've known this for a long time.* The time spent away from the office, the disconcerting emptiness to Toby Markham's face on the rare occasions when he is sitting at his desk. Vivien's revelations make perfect, horrible sense. Come to think of it, Fran wonders, where is Daisy? Why isn't she here? She obviously knows that Alice is missing.

Martin says, 'We'll find them, Mrs Markham. Don't worry. We'll form a search party. Take torches, blankets, and get them both back home to you in no time.'

'A search party may not be a simple thing.' The crowd turns and parts in surprise as Thomas comes forwards. 'If they walked east there is no problem, but to the west, towards the end of the spit, all of the mines have not been cleared.'

'The beach is still mined!' Viv begins to tremble. Her eyes rove the room for reassurance. 'Toby will go east, won't he? He wouldn't risk the mines.'

Nobody replies. Fran imagines that everyone is thinking the same awful thoughts as her. That Major Markham might not be thinking rationally about the mines, or anything else.

Thomas says, 'I will go. I know the beach better than anyone else – the parts that are cleared, the parts where to be more careful. I can bring Alice back. I can bring them both back.'

Viv steps forward. 'I'm coming with you!'

'No, ma'am, the beach is too dangerous.'

'I'm coming with you! It's *my* husband and *my* daughter who are out there!'

'I'll go with him, Mrs Markham.' Martin looks from Thomas to Viv. 'It won't help anyone to endanger yourself.'

Thomas shakes his head. 'I must go alone. That way there is less chance someone will get hurt.'

Viv fastens the top of her coat, turning up its blue collar. 'I don't care about being hurt!'

There's a short silence. Slipping his hand under Viv's elbow, Martin murmurs to Thomas, 'We'll both come with you as far as the beach. And if you insist that we wait there, I can at least keep Mrs Markham company.'

All at once the room comes to life. Someone hands Thomas a blanket. Somebody else, two lanterns. As if to make amends for their earlier accusations.

Scrambling off the table, Fran pushes past the woman with the headscarf. She walks up to the man at the bar and whips the picture still dangling from his fingers. 'This belongs to the prisoner. That piece of Hitler scum who's about to risk his own life to save Alice. And I'm sure he'll be very glad to have his photograph back again.'

She turns to Thomas, 'I'm coming too.' She has no right, no reason, to join him, of course. Other than their private, unspeakable connection, which all at once feels as loud and as obvious and as shameless as a song sung at full volume. And taking one of the lanterns she slides her free hand into his.

Chapter Twenty-Six

They take Martin's car, passing briefly by the camp where Thomas collects a mine prod from one of the trucks. At the sight of the stake, Fran's heart contracts. She remembers the explosion before Christmas, the burned flesh of the prisoner in the sickbay throbbing through the remains of his overalls. The reaction must show on her face because Thomas murmurs, 'Don't worry. I'll be careful,' and lays the metal prod casually at his feet as if it were a bag of shopping or a walking stick.

They stop again at the barricade, dismantling enough of the barbed wire to allow the vehicle to pass, before Martin parks as close to the shore as he can and kills the ignition. Viv gets out immediately and begins to climb the shingle bank. Within moments she's melting into the night, blurring out of focus, so that Fran has the fleeting sensation of watching an echo or a memory and not a living, breathing person at all.

'Wait!' Martin calls, and the shadowy figure slows.

When they catch up, Thomas passes Viv one of the lanterns. 'You keep this one, so I can see where I, where *we*' – the correction is swift – 'need to come back to.' The other lantern he takes in his left hand, with the blanket over his forearm. His right hand is holding the mine prod.

'Which direction did Toby take?' Viv twists from side to side, scanning the blackness.

Fran follows her gaze. Although the rain has stopped, the sky is still heavy with cloud. Yet a faint luminosity rises from the water, enough to shape the coast in a charcoal outline that reaches long and straight towards the east and curves gently west to the tip of the point five miles away. Both directions are bleak and empty.

'I don't know.'

And then, and then...

Fran screws up her eyes, points a finger. 'Look! Over there, can you see something?' In the distance, some way short of the point, might be a tiny, bobbing candle of light. The more she stares and tries to focus, the less confident she feels that anything is there at all.

Viv peers into the dark, teetering on tiptoes. A second later she grabs Fran's shoulder. 'That must be them! Who else could it be at this time of night?' Cupping her fingers around her mouth, she hollers, 'Toby! Alice! Stay there! Stay, right where you are!'

'They won't be able to hear you.' Martin peers anxiously into the gloom.

'And it is better perhaps, not to shout. Not to tell them you are here, if' – Thomas hesitates – 'if your husband is very upset.'

'Oh my God!' Viv drops her arm. 'But they need to stop. If the beach has mines, the further they go the more dangerous it will become.'

'I think they may have stopped already.' The flicker of flame is deceptive, dancing and dipping as if on the waves, yet the arc of land beyond the light appears to be getting no shorter.

'Then why don't they come back?'

'Maybe, they can't.' Fran says. 'Perhaps Major Markham doesn't dare risk the mines again.' There are other reasons too, of course, ones she won't articulate to Mrs Markham. That taking himself to the loneliest, most beautiful brink of habitation she knows, may mean he has only the haziest notion of making the return journey.

Thomas hunches his shoulders. 'I must go.' His eyes linger on Fran.

'Be careful. Please be careful.' She bites her lip so hard the taste of salt pricks her tongue.

He nods.

The gravel grinds under his weight.

'Just a moment!' Viv dips into her coat and pulls out the one-eyed dolly. 'I forgot to give you this.' She stuffs the toy in Thomas's pocket. 'For Alice,' she adds unnecessarily, 'when you find them.' He turns to leave, but Viv keeps hold of his sleeve. 'Tell Toby that we'll find another doctor. A good one. And tell him' – her voice waivers, her fingers pluck the wool of his coat – 'tell him, I'm sorry. That I'm staying here. Always.'

Thomas nods, his expression impassive. Fran glances at Martin, who responds with the merest shake of his head.

Before long, Thomas is lost to the dusk and all Fran can see is the golden orb of the lantern moving gradually further away. Every so often the light stops. She imagines him prodding the ground with the probe, the spike slicing the sand, the explosives skulking inches beneath, and shivers.

'Should I shout again, do you think? In case Alice can hear me. They say sound travels over water. At least if I call them, Alice will know that I'm here.' Viv has been crouching on the stones. She gets up now, paces a little towards the sea before spinning round and facing them.

'I would try to be patient,' Martin says. 'I know it must be hard—'

Suddenly Viv's face cracks open. 'This is all my fault!' She flings her arm over her mouth as if about to vomit.

Martin takes a step forward. 'Mrs Markham, this isn't your fault.'

'Yes, it is.'

'You mustn't blame—'

'It *is* my fault.' Her voice is bursting with emotion. 'This is *all* my fault. What my husband saw, when he got to the office… It was my fault, I tell you! My fault!'

'Why? What did he see?' Martin sounds dazed.

Viv seems to choke on air. Helplessly she shakes her head, as if to sweep away the memory. Eventually, she whispers. 'He saw a letter to me he should never have seen. A letter that should never have been written. A letter that' – she hesitates – 'that had been put on his desk amongst the papers he had to sign. It was still lying there for anyone to read when I got to his office.' Then, she says in a louder, flatter voice, 'Toby thinks I'm leaving him for someone else and going to America. He's bound to assume that Alice will go with me. That he'll have no one left!'

Daisy was right, Fran thinks with astonishment. Vivien Markham *was* having an affair. Yet for some reason it's hard to imagine. She seems too resilient to need transient admirers or succumb to the charms of an American. Then another, more horrible, possibility strikes her. Might Daisy have stolen one of Vivien Markham's letters? If she did, she had the perfect opportunity to slip it into the repatriation papers while Fran was out of the office.

'You must think I'm a terrible wife. And a terrible mother,' Viv continues. 'A terrible person, in fact! I had an affair with an American soldier while my husband was away fighting, risking his life and being terrified out of his mind. It hardly gets worse, does it? But I loved the American. I was so dreadfully in love with him that every second I wasn't with him hurt. As if I was starving, and he could stop me from dying of hunger.'

The air is raw and clean from the earlier rain. The blast of the lantern makes a ghost of Viv's face while behind her head the sky swirls purple and black over the water. Fran swallows. The confession resonates so deeply she is almost seduced into getting up herself and declaring her own love for Thomas. Except, Fran realises, she doesn't feel contrite. Or apologetic. Or actually want forgiveness from anyone.

'He didn't love me, of course,' Viv continues. 'The American. Although his letters were full of fancy words and promises, it turns out he had a wife and children waiting for him in Kentucky. A boy and a child about the same age as Alice. What a fool I was! And now... now I'm going to pay with the lives of my husband and daughter!' Her chest judders.

'Don't say that!' Martin shifts awkwardly on the stones. 'Thomas will bring them back safely, I'm sure of it.' He takes another step towards Viv, then seems to think better of it. Instead he adds quietly, 'The war made liars out of a lot of people, but we have our whole lives ahead to put things right.'

Viv's mouth twists. 'It's rather ironic, don't you think, that the fate of my family depends on the bravery of a German prisoner?'

After a moment she drifts back towards them. Putting down the lamp, she sinks onto the pebbles with her knees drawn up to her chin. Fran squats the other side of the light. She's still wondering what Martin meant by his last remark as he comes to sit beside her. Silently they all stare at the hulking crescent of the coastline, the stuttering twinkle just short of the point and the flag-like flame inching in tiny increments towards it. Their own lantern hisses. Eventually, Fran drops her head onto her knees and closes her eyes. The shingle shifts and Martin moves a little closer. She guesses he is deliberating whether to put his arm around her shoulders, and part of her wishes that he would. The solidity of his chest would be a wall to lean against.

Seconds pass, minutes, before time slips free of any kind of measure. The soft spit and sputter of the lamp is hypnotic. Fran drifts in and out of dreams that skim her consciousness, pulling her beneath the surface one moment and jolting her awake the next with images of fire and explosions and bloody gunshot wounds. Even the temperature seems to fluctuate. One moment the cold is seeping through her bones like water in sand. The next, she feels almost hot from churning panic and alarm.

'No!'

Viv's gasp rouses Fran in an instant. 'What is it? What's happened?'

'The light, Toby's light has disappeared!'

Fran screws up her eyes. A hazy dance of one, not two, stars, glimmers in the west. Her throat constricts. 'How do you know

Toby's lamp has gone out? It might be the one that Thomas is carrying.'

'It's Toby's lamp. I'm sure of it. Something awful has happened!'

'Most likely the gas has run out. I expect it's nothing more than that.' Martin's tone is reassuring. 'And Thomas looked to be so close to him it was impossible to tell whose light was whose, anyway. It's nothing to worry about, Mrs Markham—'

The crack of a rifle rips across the water.

Viv screams.

'Oh my God.' Scrabbling to her feet, she stumbles to the edge of the sea. 'Alice! Alice, my darling! Toby!'

Fran looks at Martin. His horrified expression mirrors her terror. Together they hurry to Viv, who is bent double at the water's edge, arms wrapped around her waist as if she's breaking in two. 'He's shot himself, hasn't he? Toby has shot himself!' Her voice is directed to the waves that are almost lapping the toe of her boots.

'You mustn't jump to conclusions.'

'Or Alice! Perhaps he shot Alice to stop me taking her away!'

'Surely he wouldn't do that. Not her own father.' The words are sticky and slow in Fran's mouth. She can still hear the boom of the gun echoing in her ears. And with it fear so acute the sensation feels like she already knows Thomas is the one who was shot. When Toby saw someone approach, wouldn't he have believed he was on the battlefield again, being attacked? The conclusion seems so obvious the force of the logic shakes the whole of her body.

'I think we should sit down and try to keep warm. There's nothing else we can do.' Fran can tell Martin is trying to sound calm as he steers Viv back up the beach, but his complexion gleams deathly white.

All at once Viv digs in her heels and flings out a hand. 'Look, it's moving! The lamp is moving closer!' Fran follows Viv's finger. To begin with she can't tell one way or the other. Eventually, as her eyes begin to smart, the glow seems to shift a little.

'I think you're right,' she says. And for a while they all stare mesmerised until the progress of the solitary light is undeniable.

'Let's sit down,' Martin says again, but none of them do. Instead, after a while Viv fetches their own lamp and bears it aloft, as high as she can reach. When her arm begins to tire, Martin takes over, and after him Fran. All of them taking turns to illuminate the way home to whoever is picking their path so slowly around the headland.

Nobody mentions the gunshot. As her muscles ache with the effort of holding up the lantern, Fran finds herself praying. Please, she begs silently, let Thomas come back with Alice. It comes as a shock she's able to barter away the life of Major Markham so willingly. They must all be making their private pacts of some kind, she supposes, and wonders with a lurch what Martin is hoping for. Would a part of him like Thomas to be lying dead or hideously injured? She has as good as told him that, if not for Thomas, she would marry him. She glances sideways, but Martin seems entirely focused on the sweep of the spit, his face contorted with concentration.

Viv sees the figure first. A drag on her coat tails makes Fran look down. Vivien's fingers are clutching at the fabric as if she were hanging to a life raft. Wordlessly, she tugs and points. Peering into the gloom, Fran sees that a person is materialising some way in front of them. Almost imperceptibly the outline of a head and torso are beginning to form behind the bobbing glow of yellow.

'Who is it? Can you see who it is?' Viv bursts out.

Martin says carefully, 'I can't tell, not from this distance.'

Although Fran says nothing, she lets out a quiet breath. She can recognise the posture of Thomas already, the strong square shoulders hunched very slightly, and the steady, even gait, even though there's something unusual about his stance, the bulk and shape of his silhouette. Relief, sweet like rainwater, soaks into her soul. She waits until she's so certain it's him that she fancies the blue of his eyes are piercing her through the dark.

She turns to Viv. 'I think…' she starts.

Viv interrupts. 'It's Thomas! It's definitely Thomas! He's carrying Alice. Is she hurt? And where's Toby? I can't see Toby! Oh my God, where's Toby?' She plunges forwards.

Martin grabs her upper arm. 'Just a few minutes more. The mines…'

Viv waits no more than a couple of seconds before wrenching free of Martin's grip and racing up the beach.

When Fran and Martin catch up, Thomas is already lowering the blanket-wrapped bundle of Alice onto the sand. 'I think she is fine,' he is saying. 'A little frightened, a little cold and a little tired, that is all.' He is worn out too, Fran sees. As he steps away from Alice his legs almost buckle. Fran is desperate to ask about Toby but doesn't know how she can in front of Alice. Besides, the question must belong to Viv, who is kneeling on the wet shingle hugging Alice tight against her chest.

'Darling, it's all right. Everything is all right.' Viv murmurs repeatedly into the silver cloud of Alice's hair. Eventually she lifts her gaze and looks at Thomas, her face filled with torment. 'Toby?' she mouths. The sight of Vivien hunched on the ground, the sound of Toby's name makes Fran hear the terrible blast all over again as if there might have been a second shot, a new bullet.

Before Thomas can reply, Fran watches Viv's expression freeze. Over the top of Alice's head her attention is fixed on the middle distance, while the palm that was rubbing her daughter's back falls still. Fran follows the path of her eyes.

Another figure, stooped and stumbling, is making his way along the shoreline. Despite his painfully slow progress, it's clear he is aiming for the pool of torchlight on the beach, the small, huddled knot of people that contains his wife and daughter.

'Toby.' This time it's not a question. Slowly, Viv stands up. One hand touches her forehead, the other presses Alice to her thigh.

Then she starts to wave. 'We're over here, darling! We're right here.'

*

Thomas and Fran are lingering by the edge of the water. Since they arrived, the tide has turned, releasing the beach in tiny increments. There are stars again too, and a slice of moon sliding between ship-like clouds.

'You're a hero. You saved them both.'

'It wasn't so hard.' His focus lingers on the invisible horizon. 'Major Markham wanted to be found, I think.'

'Why did he take Alice?'

Thomas shrugs. 'I don't know, perhaps he started with bad intentions. Or perhaps he meant only to go for a walk. He was very upset, very angry. And also, very confused. He needs a doctor, I think. Maybe a hospital.'

'And the gun?' Fran is beginning to wonder if she dreamed the rifle shot, if they all invented hearing the blast through some horrible collective feat of imagination.

'When I got close, Major Markham panicked. Luckily for me, it was dark. Luckily for me, he missed.'

'He aimed at you?'

'He didn't know who I was. And after he fired the gun, Alice began to cry. I think it helped to make him see some sense again.'

Thomas sighs.

'You must be so tired,' Fran says. Not just tired, she thinks. Under the dim moonlight he looks utterly spent. And older too, as if the pale and silvered man beside her has stepped back from a future decade. She longs to kiss him, touch the fine lines suddenly visible in his face. Instead she squeezes his arm. 'You need to sleep.'

'Yes.'

'Thomas?'

He jumps at the change in her tone.

'You realise this could change everything? When Captain Holmes finds out about this, you really will be a hero. There's a good chance he would write to the government and ask if you can become a civilian. At the very least the camp might let you stay while a request is made.'

'Fran…'

'You must ask him! You will ask him, won't you?'

'Suppose they find out about you?'

'I don't care. It doesn't matter, not anymore.' She beams at him. 'Don't you see? You haven't only saved Alice; you've saved us too. How could anyone think badly of you now?'

He puts his arm around her shoulder, presses her close. 'Fran…'

'Fran, we need to leave!' Martin's voice calls from the shingle bank.

'We're coming!' Then to Thomas, hushed and urgent. 'Promise me, you'll go straight to Captain Holmes first thing tomorrow.'

He doesn't reply.

He's exhausted, Fran thinks. Utterly exhausted.

On the far side of the shingle bank Martin is standing beside the door of his car. Alice is already squeezed between her parents on the back seat. 'I'll take them home first,' Martin says. 'There's not enough room for everyone. I'll come back for you both as soon as I can.' Then to Thomas, 'You must have had quite enough walking for one day.'

'You can come back for me,' Thomas says. 'There is space for Fran on the front seat.'

She smiles at him, 'I don't mind waiting with you.'

'It's very late. I expect your parents will be worried.'

'It doesn't—' Fran starts, then stops. She's happier than she has felt all winter. Happier, in fact, than she can remember ever feeling. The events of the evening seem almost to be a gift. She will see Thomas soon, she can be certain of that. It's unthinkable he will be forced to leave the country now. Major Markham or Captain

Holmes must be able to stop the repatriation. He only has to ask them, surely? If I had to, she thinks, I would wait a thousand winters for him. Yet I only have to wait until Monday.

From inside the car, Alice coughs.

'Fran? We need to go.'

Thomas is right, her parents will be anxious to hear everyone is safe. And June too. After tonight her sister is bound to accept that Fran was right about him all along.

Alice coughs again. A thin, raking sound that makes her mother tighten the blanket around her shoulders.

'I'll come now, Martin.'

And kissing Thomas on the lips, she hurries towards the passenger seat.

Chapter Twenty-Seven

10 March 1947

Fran sits on the edge of the stage, a sheet of music dangling from her hand. After the concert the chairs were stacked away, the china washed, and the hall swept, yet the evening has left its mark nevertheless: a solitary teacup on the windowsill, a crumpled handkerchief by the main door, and the stray piece of music, a map of grids and squiggles which might make perfect sense to Thomas, but not to her.

She has been waiting for over an hour, racing to the village hall the instant the hands of the clock crawled to the five. Not that anyone would have stopped her from leaving work early today. With more than half of the prisoners gone, the place had a sad, deserted air. She had little contact with anyone all day. Daisy had sent a message to say she wasn't well and didn't know when she might be back. Fran was relieved to receive the note since she didn't feel ready to talk to Daisy quite yet.

As for Captain Holmes, he seemed to be permanently engaged on the telephone in the meeting room. Fran could monitor his strident conversations through the wall and heard enough to understand he had officially taken over from Major Markham – for as long as the camp continued, at least. It sounded as if the remaining prisoners would soon be repatriated too, which presumably means her job will come to an end as well.

At least she will be able to spend longer with Thomas.

Her heels thwack against the boards. Did she arrange to meet him at a particular time? She's certain he only said after work and already the clock on the wall is approaching half past six. Perhaps he was sent to clear mines again and didn't return until late? Surely, she frets for the hundredth time, he would have asked Captain Holmes to cancel or delay the repatriation order and surely, Captain Holmes would have agreed?

Once, during the day, she very nearly approached the captain herself. As her knuckles were poised over his door, she heard him say into the telephone, 'An affair, apparently… Yes, the far end of the point, and with his daughter. God only knows what he was thinking.' Then, 'One of the prisoners, a plucky fellow…' It seemed the perfect opportunity, until Captain Holmes's voice took on a clipped, more sombre tone, and the direction of the call changed. 'We'll have to see,' he said. 'He won't come back for a while. It's rather obvious the chap is in a bad way… A spell in hospital, I suppose, then home to his wife. As long as she doesn't bugger off with another bloody American.'

In the end Fran accosted a prisoner near the sluice hut. But it was hopeless, the German hardly spoke English and didn't appear to know who Thomas was, let alone where he might be. After that, she lost confidence. Suppose, her doubts whispered, Captain Holmes had refused to write to the Home Office? Suppose he didn't have the authority to change the repatriation order? Perhaps Thomas found he had no option but to abscond from the camp and hide. The more people she alerted to his absence, the less opportunity he would have to find somewhere safe and the greater his chance of being found and arrested. After two circuits of the whole site, when she was still no closer to knowing what had happened, she decided to be patient.

Now the light is dimming fast. Colour has seeped from the room and the hall is a palette of browns and greys, a faded photograph of the present. She stops drumming her feet and after a moment slides off the stage. From the side door she can look both ways up the street, but there is nothing to see except the lengthening shadows and a team of pink-footed geese banking high above the marsh.

A nub of panic tightens her throat.

Maybe she has misremembered.

Perhaps Thomas told her to meet him at the beach? Or he has gone to the beach mistakenly, where this very moment he is wondering, worrying, where she might be. She dithers, undecided. Trying to quell her alarm, she counts out loud. *One, two, three, four...* forcing herself to retrace and repeat the counting whenever the numbers gather momentum and race away. The instant she reaches one hundred, she shuts the hall door and hurries towards her bicycle.

On the coast road, the sea air feels thick as treacle. She focuses on pumping her pedals, on breathing deeply, but she has the sense of making no progress, getting no closer to her destination, like the kind of nightmare where her legs won't work, or nobody can hear her, or everything happens in slow motion. When she gets to the blockade, she finds the wire reinstated, the pallets in place, and the struggle to haul the bicycle around the barrier makes her weep with frustration.

At the edge of the shingle she drops the frame and scrambles quickly up the ridge. Ahead the beach opens out on both sides, the reach of pebbles hazy in the weak light, the water darkly luminous.

Nobody is there.

She calls anyway.

Any second he will appear, she tells herself. Where *were* you, he will say. What took you so long? I've been waiting.

The wind rips his name from her mouth.

Shouting is futile.

She blinks, rubs the heels of her hands into her eyes, looks again. The beach is still empty.

Numb with terror she scrabbles down the bank, back to the lane. She should never have left the village hall. He probably arrived the second she left, and is this very moment pacing the room, checking the clock, watching the door. Too nervous to light a lamp in case he is discovered.

At least the wind is behind her now. Head down, she pedals furiously, cursing the impatience, the doubt, that made her so quick to abandon their meeting place. Yet when the village hall finally comes into view, the energy seems to flood suddenly from her legs and her speed drops away so that she covers the last hundred yards practically at walking pace.

Slowly she dismounts and props the frame against a tree trunk. In her absence the building appears to have acquired a newly forlorn and abandoned air. The afterglow of the sun has drained from the sky, leaving the evening bleak and grey as if all the sadness of the last six years is somehow leaking through the dusk. Fran swallows. She hardly dares peek in the window.

If he is not inside, what then?

A pedal has holed her stocking and grazed her leg. For a long moment she watches as a bead of blood trickles sluggishly down her calf. Then she licks the palm of her hand, rubs the broken skin and approaches the glass.

'Fran!'

His voice fells her like a bullet.

'Thomas!'

She stops, spins and sprints towards the side door.

To the figure waiting in the shadows.

Chapter Twenty-Eight

Deciding what to do kept Martin awake all night and made him delay so long leaving the house that when he arrived and found the hall empty, he thought he had messed everything up anyway. For a while he paced inside, clutching Thomas's letter, wondering, as the light dipped and the room stilled, whether he was brave enough – selfish enough? – to capitalise on his enormous stroke of fortune. A piece of luck that could spin his entire life on a sixpence. After a past of loneliness and failure, a future of all he could ever want was literally within touching distance.

A stray sheet of music lay abandoned on the stage. The excerpt was from one of the compositions played at the jazz evening, the saxophone's part, he guessed, and immediately the thought struck him he had to sit down. The memory of watching Fran, that moment of revelation when he realised that she loved the German, filled his soul with a deep, cold ache. Martin folded the paper up and shoved it away in his pocket. He was only too aware he was not her first choice. She would never feel for him the overwhelming desire he felt for her. Yet she would grow to care for him, surely? Now that Thomas was out of reach. Particularly, he brooded, if the German should turn out not to be quite the hero she thought. If she had reason to doubt the man loved her as much as she believed him to have done.

If Martin kept the letter, the explanation meant for Fran, to himself.

He was outside the hall, about to give up and leave, when her bicycle came into view. Overcome with uncertainty, he hurried to the back of the building where the church loomed over him, sombre and huge. He was about to break her heart, he knew that. But afterwards, what he did next, that was the thing he couldn't resolve. He hated for her to suffer, and yet, and yet… If he couldn't avert her pain, why not give himself, give them *both* – for in the long run wasn't a sense of finality, of stability, in her interests too? – the greatest chance of happiness. How, he agonised, was he supposed to know whether it was nobler to tell the truth, or better, more sensible to keep quiet? He needed to see into the future, their future, to be able to judge that.

Returning the letter to his trouser pocket, he inhaled a lungful of dank air and stepped around the corner.

'Fran!'

'Thomas!'

She runs towards him, her face alight. For an instant the sun returns, the dreariness demolished by the blitz of her smile, before her face freezes and she comes to a halt.

'Martin! I thought you were Thomas.' She peers around him into the gloom. 'I was meant to meet him earlier, but I'm late. I wondered if I ought to be at the beach instead. I expect he came while I was there. So stupid of me, I can't think why—'

'Thomas has gone.'

'I knew I should never…' She closes her eyes in frustration. 'How long ago? Did he say where I can find him?'

'Thomas has gone to Germany.'

She shakes her head. 'No, Martin. That's not right. He was supposed to go back to Germany, but he asked to stay longer. After the awful business of Friday night, he thought Captain Holmes would be able to pull some strings; and if the captain couldn't, or he refused, well' – although they are alone, she lowers her voice – 'actually Thomas planned to abscond. To hide and find some work on the farms until we can get married. He's a hero now, saving Alice and Major Markham like that. I don't think anyone could possibly—'

'Fran,' Martin places his hands on her shoulders, tipping her slightly towards him. 'Thomas left yesterday evening. He went on board the trucks with the other prisoners who were being repatriated.'

She stares at him. 'That can't be right. He wouldn't leave without telling me. He wouldn't leave at all. You're lying! You just want me to believe he's gone.' Wrenching free, she runs a little way into the dark. 'Thomas? Are you there? It's me, Fran!'

When she reappears, her face is white. 'Where is he? What's happened?'

'He's gone, Fran,' Martin says quietly. 'He's gone home.'

She shakes her head again, more slowly this time. 'No.'

'I'm sorry, Fran. I'm so sorry.'

'No.'

Martin steps forward and wraps her in his arms. To begin with she seems as rigid as a mannequin, then all at once she crumbles and he has to hold her upright. As she shakes against his chest, he tightens his grip. He inhales the smell of her hair, feels the press of her against him and knows that part of him, most of him in fact, is not sorry at all.

'Fran?'

Eventually, she lifts her head.

With his heart sinking, Martin reaches into his coat. She must, he has concluded, have the chance to read the letter, to know whatever explanation the German has come up with for abandoning her like this, even if seeing that letter means she might never let the man go. Might never give up. Might never stop hoping. Might never love Martin nearly as much as he loves her.

He proffers the crumpled paper. 'Thomas told me to give you this.'

'You already knew he was leaving? He *asked* you to come here tonight?'

'He spoke to me on Friday, while we were in my car together. I agreed to meet him yesterday before the trucks left. That was when he said he was going home, and I should come here this evening – for you.'

'But why didn't he tell me himself?' She stares in disbelief. 'We had enough time at the beach, plenty of time!'

'Maybe he hadn't decided.' Martin recalls how in the car the man's voice had wavered. How the German seemed to be staring blankly out of the window for the entire journey. At the time, Martin had put his behaviour down to fatigue. After all, who wouldn't be exhausted after carrying a little girl all the way back from the point? It was probably not something he could have managed, even with his new healthy heart. He says carefully, 'I suppose Thomas might not have made up his mind until the very last minute. Or...' he pauses, 'or if he did, perhaps he just couldn't bring himself to tell you.'

For a moment Fran seems to sink deep within herself.

Then she fumbles with the folded paper.

She stops. 'Do you know what this says?'

'No.'

He closes his eyes.

Waits. Already, he wishes he had kept hold of the letter.

'What *is* this?'

She's gazing at the item in her fist with incredulity.

'I think...' Martin stops. He blinks. His amazement matches her own. He has pulled out the sheet of music, the saxophone score, from his pocket instead of the envelope. How could he have been so idiotic? As he delves into his coat again, he watches her face fill with fury. Fury, and a horrified sort of comprehension. I love her, he thinks desperately, every tiny, every flawed piece of me loves her. And I am here, right now, wanting to spend the rest of my life with her.

If she will have me.

If she can forget the other.

Slowly he retrieves his hand.

His empty, letter-less hand.

He clears his throat. 'I believe the music is for the saxophone. The piece Thomas played at the concert.'

For a long second she stands utterly still.

His pocket feels on fire.

'Perhaps he thought it might be something to remember him by?'

Still she doesn't move.

Martin's fingers twitch. He can feel his resolve stretching, breaking. Then all at once she crumples the sheet and flings the paper onto the ground. Her eyes clutch hold of him. 'I thought he loved me!'

'I expect he did—'

'But he left me. Without even saying goodbye. Without so much as a note or a promise even to write! And after what I… what we…' She stops. Then, more quietly, 'He said he wanted to marry me.' Her eyes are wide and shocked.

He places his lips on her forehead.

He knows exactly what she is saying.

'I want to marry you, Fran.'

She gazes at him.

'I want to marry you more than I can say.'

She takes a step backwards. 'I don't know, Martin.' She draws a sleeve across her face, trailing a snakeskin of tears on the wool. 'I can't think about anything like that right now…'

'There's no hurry,' Martin says quickly. 'I'll wait as long it takes.'

I will wait, he thinks. I'll wait for years if I have to. I shall want to marry her as much ten years from now as I do today. I don't care about the German, what they might have done together, or even whether she will ever forget him completely. All I know is that marrying Fran will make me the happiest man alive. And I'll do everything in my power to make her happy too.

She gives him a long, penetrating look so that for one disorientating moment he fancies she can see into his thoughts, his failings, and even into the unopened envelope lying deep within his pocket.

'I know you will, Martin. But for now,' she touches his arm, 'please just take me home.'

Chapter Twenty-Nine

East Berlin, The German Democratic Republic

10 November 1989

Day is dawning over the city. Thin grey light illuminates a view of grey streets and grey buildings, together with a beer bottle clinking haphazardly along the pavement. Tiffany steps away from the window, checks for the second time the buckles on her rucksack and shrugs on her coat.

Room 14 was better than she feared. Modest, but clean. A hard, single bed and wallpaper patterned with psychedelic brown and cream circles. Although there was no bathroom, further along the corridor she found a door bearing the sign *Toilette* and behind that all she needed.

Even so, she remained unable to sleep.

From the wall a photograph of a thin-lipped, silver-haired man watched her toss and turn through the night and is now observing her departure. Herr Erich Honecker, she supposes.

'What are you doing in East Berlin?' his expression seems to say. 'Why are you meddling in the past?'

He might well ask, Tiffany thinks. Except this is no longer East Berlin, not really. Not since last night. And part of the reason she remained awake was that more than once she wished she were still outside celebrating, partying with thousands of ecstatic Germans.

Downstairs the reception desk is empty, so she leaves the billiard-ball key behind the counter. Halfway to the exit she sees that one of the men from the previous night is still there, sleeping on the sofa with his jacket pulled over his chin. As she walks past he sits up and the coat slides on the floor.

Her eyes widen. 'Ralp?'

He struggles to his feet, rubbing a hand across his face and swaying slightly. Without his glasses his eyes look almost naked. There are stains on the knees of his trousers and something sticky attached to the front of his jumper.

'What are you doing here?'

'They told me an English girl checked in last night. A girl from London.'

She blinks at him.

'We danced all the night. We sang songs. We drank a lot of champagne…'

'I can tell.'

'Wait…' He fumbles in his trouser pocket before producing his spectacles. The instant he puts them on, his face acquires its familiar, likably serious, appearance. 'I wanted to know if you were safe. And' – he shuffles rather awkwardly – 'to ask if you want someone to show you Berlin.'

'You're offering to show me around Berlin?'

'I think so, yes.' He nods.

'That's very kind' – she's speaking slowly, regretfully even – 'but I haven't come to see Berlin. I'm here to find someone living in East Germany.'

'You have a friend living in East Germany?'

'Not exactly. I have an address for someone, a friend of my grandmother.' She pauses. 'An old address.'

'Your grandmother?' He adjusts his glasses. 'How old is the address?'

There's a longer pause.

'Very old.'

'So, you are here to locate a person who you don't know, and you have only a very old address?'

'Yes.'

'And you are trying to find this person without speaking any German?'

'I can say *Die Mauer ist weg!* And *Trink nach Berlin!*

His expression doesn't flicker. 'That perhaps is not enough.'

Tiffany unbuckles the strap around her waist and lowers the rucksack onto the floor of the lobby. An idea is forming. Leaning on the pack, she regards him steadily. 'It will have to be enough.'

'You are crazy. I think it is better you have a nice time and see Berlin.'

She shakes her head. 'I would like that. But not today. Today I have a job to do.' She hesitates, bites her lower lip. Waits. Then, 'You could come with me.'

'To find an address in East Germany, for a person you have never met?'

She doesn't reply.

'That would make us both crazy.'

She gestures at his dishevelled clothes, at the sofa where he spent the last few hours. 'You came back to find me. That's pretty crazy already.'

He stares at her.

Bending down, Tiffany picks up his coat and lobs it towards him. 'Come on, help me catch the next train to Eisenach. Please.'

The journey to Eisenach will take three and a half hours. At least this is what Ralp told her, before falling asleep again with his head wedged against the rim of the train window. His spectacles have slipped halfway down his nose, and after a second's hesitation Tiffany removes them and holds the delicate wire frame loosely in her lap. Gazing out of the glass at trees and fields that seem to be exactly the same as the ones in England, she wonders what on earth she will say to this man, to Thomas, when they get there.

He may have moved house, of course, since he returned home from the war all those years ago. Ralp pointed this out several times on the way to the station, as soon as she explained where they were going. Yet somehow she doesn't think so. If this man loved her grandmother as much as her grandmother seemed to have loved him, as much as his letter suggested, wouldn't he have stayed at the same address, never quite losing hope, never entirely giving up, that one day her grandmother might contact him?

Or perhaps she's being ridiculous.

She found out about the letter during the summer. When she was struggling in London after Paul left – some days even to wash her hair or go to the supermarket – her father suggested a visit to her grandmother, who would appreciate the company now that she was on her own. The dose of salt air and clean sheets was working right up until the moment Tiffany dissolved into tears during the washing-up over something so trivial she has now forgotten what it was.

Her grandmother took her out for a walk. Up over a heath aflame with flowers and humming with bees. And there on a bench she said when she was Tiffany's age, she lost someone too. She spoke about Thomas. That when Thomas went back to East Germany, when there was no hope she would see him again, she couldn't imagine how she might live through the following week, let alone the years that stretched into the future like a wasteland.

Tiffany was aghast. 'But you married Grandpa. You loved him!'

'Yes.' Her grandmother fell quiet. She was staring at the view.

In a silence broken only by the bees and the song of a woodlark, Tiffany felt the two truths come and settle together, side by side. At last she said, quietly, 'Why did he leave? Did he tell you?'

'He had a reason. A very good reason and he wrote me a letter to explain. Though at the time' – there was a slight clicking sound – 'at the time I didn't understand, and I was even more unhappy than you are now.'

Tiffany swivelled on the bench. 'Then, why don't you contact him? If you have an address. Perhaps it isn't too late?'

Her grandmother kept her eyes fixed firmly on the sweep of green, yellow and blue. 'I'm not sure how your grandfather would feel about that.'

'But he's…' she stopped. Gathered herself and thought more clearly. Then she said slowly and deliberately. 'Grandpa would want you to be happy. That's all he ever wanted.'

That evening when they were in the kitchen cooking dinner, over the steady chop of onions she said as casually as she could manage, 'Would you show me the letter? The one that Thomas wrote to you?'

Her grandmother looked taken aback. 'Nobody else knows about that letter.'

'I won't tell a soul, Granny, I promise.'

Her grandmother wiped her hands several times on her apron. 'Well, I suppose so,' she said. 'I don't see why not.' Later, after they had eaten, she went upstairs and appeared again after a few moments, clasping an ancient-looking envelope. Tiffany read the letter in silence. The contents were heartbreaking, the position in which the writer had found himself impossible, but the part that interested her the most, the part she was determined to remember, was his address.

Beyond the train the land has become undulating and heavily wooded. In the distance rounded mountain peaks jut against a pale-blue sky while the space between is filled with a dense lake of trees. Much less like England now, much more like pictures in a book of children's fairy tales.

Ralp stirs and lifts his head away from the glass.

'You're dribbling.'

He stares at her groggily for a moment before swiping his hand across his mouth. As he peers out of the window, Tiffany passes him his glasses.

'I think we are there nearly.'

'Good,' she says. Even though her stomach feels queasy at the prospect.

A short bus-ride and a longer walk later, they are standing in front of the address that matches the one on the piece of paper torn from Tiffany's Filofax. The farmhouse is built mainly from brick, apart from one wing that appears much older than the rest of the building with whitewashed walls criss-crossed by a lattice of dark wooden beams. To one side of the property there are stables, a cart-shed, and a paddock in which a man is forking hay beside a grey horse. As he straightens up, he lays a hand on the neck of the horse, who begins to eat, the grind of his big jaws carrying across the driveway. Tiffany remains rooted to the spot. It requires Ralp to nudge her side and make her wave her arm.

'Hello!'

The man lifts his gaze. 'Wie kann ich Ihnen helfen?'

She looks at Ralp in panic. 'What did he say?'

'He said, how can I help you? I am going to ask if he will speak with us.' Ralp raises his voice. 'Guten Tag! Haben Sie eine Minute, bitte?'

The man props the pitchfork against the paddock fence and ducks under the rail. He seems, Tiffany thinks, considerably older than her grandmother, with a stooped back and a slight limp. A few feet away from them he halts, cleaning his hands on his trousers. Tiffany turns to Ralp. She feels an odd, rather unaccountable sense of disappointment. 'Could you ask him if he speaks English?'

But the man is shaking his head already. 'Nein. Ich spreche kein Englisch.'

'In that case, could you ask him if he knows…' She stops.

The man is pointing further along the yard where a younger man with strong, square shoulders and grey-blond hair is coming purposely towards them. He's carrying a metal bucket in each hand and despite the biting wind is wearing only a green pullover. As he smiles, Tiffany spots a small scar just above his left eyebrow.

'I speak English. Can I help you?'

Her weight shifts on the gritty ground. 'Is your name... are you by chance Thomas Meyer?'

'Yes.' He puts the buckets down. 'Why do you ask?'

'Well,' she glances sideways at Ralp, but he is no help to her now, 'I think you may have known my grandmother. Shortly after the war ended. You see, her name is Frances—' She stops abruptly. The man looks to have had the breath knocked out of him. He stares at Tiffany with alarming intensity. For a moment the decades fall away.

'Your grandmother?'

'Yes.'

'You are her granddaughter? You are Fran's granddaughter?'

'Yes, I—'

He gathers himself with evident effort. 'I think perhaps we should all go inside.'

Tiffany cups her hands around a mug of tea. Her fingers are stiff from the cold. Thomas and Ralp both have a whisky, though as Ralp has barely touched his drink Tiffany suspects he's still feeling the effects of the previous night.

Thomas leans across the table. 'Tell me about your grandmother. Is she well?'

'She's very well.' Under his gaze she can hardly move. He has barely taken his focus from her since they came into the kitchen, his eyes like searchlights pinning her to the chair. Slowly she adds, 'Although the last year has been difficult, since my grandfather died.'

'Your grandfather is dead?'

She nods.

After a moment he says, 'And who was your grandfather?'

'His name was Martin. Martin Travis-Jones.'

With a sudden scraping of wood, Thomas stands up and moves to the sink, an enormous china basin that is practically big enough to bathe in. Dirty crockery, Tiffany sees, is stacked upon the draining board, while the room itself is trailed with muddy coats and boots. The only concessions to homeliness are two watercolour paintings, one hung above a woodburning stove and the other stood on the dresser against a pile of books. She imagines Thomas must live alone.

'I am sorry to hear that news.' He is staring out of the window towards the paddock. 'Your grandfather was a nice man. May I ask what happened?'

'He died of a heart attack.' Tiffany says. She feels a little dazed. How did this man even know her grandfather? 'It turns out he didn't fight in the war because of his heart, so perhaps it wasn't as unexpected as it seemed. Anyway' – she puts down her mug – 'I'm not here because of my grandfather. The reason I came to find you is because I thought you might like to see my grandmother again.'

Thomas spins around. 'To see Fran?'

Tiffany doesn't reply.

After a while he says slowly, 'There is nothing on this earth I would like more than to see your grandmother again. But I do not believe she wants to see me. I do not think she forgave me for leaving England when I may have been able to stay. If she had, I think she would have told me. She would have written me a letter.'

'I don't know why she didn't write. But I think she would like to see you again.' Tiffany holds his gaze. 'In fact, I'm certain of it.'

'How do you know that?'

Because of her voice when she spoke about you, Tiffany wants to say. Because even saying your name after all this time seemed to create such a mixture of pain and pleasure. Because there was something about what happened, that Tiffany felt she didn't understand or hadn't yet been told.

'I just do,' she says simply.

They both fall silent.

Eventually, from outside the horse neighs. 'He wants food,' Thomas says. 'When you arrived, I was about to bring his oats. He is telling me that he is hungry.'

Pushing back her chair, Tiffany gets to her feet. 'We should go.'

'So quickly? Do you want to eat something first?'

She shakes her head. 'We need to catch the train back to Berlin this afternoon.' Besides, food is the last thing she wants right now.

Thomas walks across the kitchen. On reaching the kitchen table, he hesitates before coming up close to her. Placing his hand against her cheek, he considers her intently as if trying to work something out or memorise her face. 'Thank you, Tiffany, for coming here. For telling me about your grandmother. You must love her very much.'

'I do.'

Extracting the page of her Filofax from her pocket, she puts the paper down on top of the table. 'My grandmother still lives in the same village. I've written down the name of the road and the house.' For some reason her eyes are smarting.

Thomas picks up the page. 'I will think about what you said. I will think about it very carefully.'

Ralp is waiting by the door. He seems to be preoccupied by something, his gaze switching back and forth between her and Thomas as if he is watching a tennis match.

'What is it?' Tiffany whispers. 'What are you looking at?'

'Nothing,' Ralp says, but after they have said goodbye, he turns back to Thomas and says suddenly, 'Die Mauer ist weg Es wird Zeit für einen Neuanfang, Wer weiß, was Sie finden könnten?'

She catches his sleeve. 'What does that mean?'

He bundles her along the driveway. 'I will tell you later.'

*

Since the train is more crowded on the way back to Berlin, they sit side by side.

'Are you going to fall asleep again?'

'I do not think so.'

There's a pause before Tiffany says, 'I'm so glad you went with me. I don't know how I would have managed. I should have learned German before I came here.'

He gives her an inscrutable look. 'Perhaps you should learn German anyway. Perhaps you will come here again.'

There's another pause.

'You have beautiful eyes. They are very blue. When I was dancing, enjoying the party by the wall, I could not forget them.'

She smiles at him, then looks away. 'Thank you.'

Leaning back against the seat, the rhythm of the train, the clatter and pulse of the track is hypnotic. She can feel herself relaxing, becoming drowsy. Perhaps on this journey she will be the one who falls asleep rather than Ralp. She wonders what Thomas will do. Is he still studying her grandmother's address or is he tending his horse, their visit receding into the past, already partially forgotten? She sits upright again, 'What did you say to Thomas? As we were leaving.'

'I said it is a time for new beginnings. And maybe for finding out more than we expect.'

Chapter Thirty

Norfolk, England

23 December 1989

Alice has done a wonderful job with the village hall, Fran thinks. The Christmas tree already gave the place a festive air, but the gold balloons and streamers adorning the walls are a talking point amongst the guests. Along one side a noticeboard is pinned with photographs while a rather beautiful banner has been strung the whole way across the stage. The message reads, *Happy 50th Wedding Anniversary Granny and Grandpa!* and is clearly the work of Alice's daughters, both of whom are looking disconcertingly grown-up in lipstick and tight-fitting jeans.

Fran sips her champagne. Viv and Toby are still not here. Alice insisted everyone arrive by twelve noon sharp so her parents can make something of an entrance when they appear a little later. Fran hopes they won't be very long. She glances hungrily at the table laid with fancy sandwiches, pastries and a very large cake coated in dark-yellow icing. Drinking on an empty stomach is apt to make her light-headed and this is already her second glass.

The trouble is that she misses Martin most of all when she's at a party. Being in a crowd of people without him feels lonelier, somehow, than the evenings spent on her own. She yearns for the exchanged look when they were both ready to go home, and the sense of anchor which meant she never felt adrift, or trapped, and could always say to a bore or a gossip, 'I'm so sorry, I've just remembered something I *must* tell my husband.'

Even though it's been over a year since he died, she still can't believe he has left her. And sometimes she thinks he hasn't. Not completely. Occasionally, when she's reading by the quiet of the fire or watching television, she could swear he's right beside her. In any case, most evenings one of the children phones, which occupies a good half an hour. Longer in fact, by the time she has settled again afterwards and allowed the not-quite solitude of evening to seep back. Diana tends to call around 7 p.m., Robert a little later, the habit formed when Martin was alive and able to enjoy the conversation with an after-dinner whisky in his hand. Robert misses Martin dreadfully, she knows that. Both of the children do, of course, but Martin made such an effort with Robert when he was small, creating a wonderful bond, as if to prove to Fran, to all of them perhaps, that fatherhood is a matter of time and love more than anything else.

Fran glances at the window. Rain is smacking against the glass like handfuls of grit and there's a steel-grey, hood-like quality to the sky. She hopes Alice's husband had the sense to collect Toby and Viv by car. Her own umbrella could barely cope and is now dripping on the cloakroom floor with one of the spokes bent out of shape.

Not that the weather or the broken umbrella is her real concern. Fran draws her wrap a little more tightly about her shoulders. She hasn't yet shown Robert the letter.

She will soon. Now that Tiffany has seen it, Robert should too. But she can't tell Robert about the letter without letting him read Martin's note as well, and while she has come to terms with what happened, she wouldn't want to do anything that might spoil her son's memories. After all, he could never begin to understand the complexities of that awful time or realise how grateful she was, in the end, for Martin's devotion, his unquestioning devotion, when they didn't know, and could never know for certain, the answer to the most natural, most obvious, question of all.

Despite the wrap, she shivers suddenly.

The village hall always reminds her of that terrible evening, the frantic cycle to the beach and back, the increasing panic as she tried to deny what she already knew in her soul, that Thomas was gone. Gone for good. It doesn't help either that recently the weather has been so awful. For the last few days there has been one downpour after the other, just like that dreadful winter all those years ago. Except then, of course, the rain soon changed to snow and didn't stop falling for weeks.

Fran drifts towards the display of photographs. Although she's friendly with several of the other guests, it's much easier to look at pictures than to make conversation. Nobody knows whether to mention her dead husband or act as if everything – herself included – is miraculously back to normal again. Only the children and June can be relied upon to say the right thing. Alice had in fact invited June, but it was too much to expect her sister to travel halfway across the country and abandon her own family so close to Christmas.

The photographs, she sees, are arranged on the board in a haphazard sort of collage. There's one of Viv and Toby dancing on their wedding day, utterly radiant and glorious, of course. Another of Alice as a baby in Viv's arms, a whole array that feature Alice growing up, followed by Alice and Ben's wedding, and finally Toby and Viv each holding one of Alice's twin girls and looking as though they might explode with pride.

Peering more closely, Fran's gaze fixes on a small black-and-white snap. The picture must have been taken shortly after Toby took command of the camp because he's standing right beside the whitewashed building that became his office. Gazing at his starched, wary gaze is like dropping straight into the pond of the past. She almost expects Daisy to walk across the frame and wave. Perhaps she should telephone Daisy again soon? She half-thought Daisy might be here today, but her absence is hardly surprising. Even after all this time, the awful taste of what she did, of what almost happened, hasn't entirely gone away.

As Fran gazes at the photograph, her focus sharpens. Unexpectedly, her wrist begins to tremble and a wave of champagne slops over the rim of the flute. In one swift move she drains the glass and claps her free hand over her mouth. In the truck parked behind Toby, two prisoners are loading equipment. Although the figures are small and rather blurred, one of them is nonetheless recognisable. The shape of his shoulders, the intensity of his gaze is as striking to her now as it was all that time ago, and if the photograph were not in monochrome the blue of his eyes would be the brightest colour in the room. The quaking moves from her wrist to her arm. Soon the whole of her body is trembling. How can glimpsing him now have such an effect? When they haven't laid eyes on each other for more than forty-two years.

And for forty-one of them she never even knew why he had left.

She found the envelope, his envelope, in the file containing Martin's will, along with a second envelope that had her name printed across the front in Martin's handwriting.

She opened that one first.

18 May 1984

My darling Fran,

I hope you find it in your heart to forgive me for not giving you the enclosed as I was asked, as indeed I promised, to do. If I was able to make you even half as happy as you have made me, then I go to my grave daring to hope that you might.

Yours, eternally,
Martin

She began to rip the smaller, yellowed envelope, then stopped. She knew what must be lying inside and for a long while she simply sat holding the letter in her lap. Her life, her married life, had been built on the fact of Thomas leaving without a word, without, perhaps, ever loving her at all. If the reality were different, did she really want to know that now? She fancied she could almost sense Martin, waiting, watching to see what she would do.

Eventually, slowly, she extracted a piece of paper as fine and as thin as baking parchment.

9 March 1947

Meine Liebste

If you are reading these words, it means I am on my way back to Germany. You will think that I do not love you, when the truth is I am more in love with you now than ever. I leave because I have no choice, because I cannot stay and also remain a man who is deserving of you.

My sister is alive.

The letter Daisy spoke of came from the nurse, the English nurse, who used to care for Gisela. After Eisenach was bombed she worried for my family and tried to contact my parents. They did not reply, so next she wrote to many hospitals. She found Gisela without difficulty, but it took her longer to locate me. I should be grateful for her service. Instead I am wretched with despair.

Gisela is in a convalescent hospital near Gotha. Her injuries are many and being frail I think she will not have the strength to sustain them for very long. Dearest Fran, I break my heart to leave you, but I cannot allow my sister to live what remaining life she has alone. I am writing my address in Germany. If one day I receive from you a letter, my unhappiness will be made a little less knowing that you understand.

Although I am returning to my country, to my village, I ask that you do not think of me as going home. My home is by your side and the finest minutes of my life will always be the ones I shared with you.

Ich liebe dich

Thomas

'Frances!' Alice touches her arm. 'You look miles away. Mum and Dad will be here any moment, so we're all going to line up on either side of the door…' She stops. 'Are you all right?'

'Of course.'

She finds herself beside a couple about the same age as Alice and Ben. The woman has very pale skin with a smattering of very dark freckles. Turning to Fran, she smiles. 'Do tell me, what's your connection with Toby and Vivien?'

'I worked for Toby shortly after the war ended. At the prisoner-of-war camp in the village.'

'Goodness, how interesting!' The woman looks surprised, as if she was expecting Fran to mention bridge or a book club. 'You've known them for ever – that was such a long time ago!'

Fran smiles back brightly. 'Yes, wasn't it?' She doesn't mention that her months at the camp don't feel long ago at all. That in fact they seem to be pressing upon her now more keenly than ever.

'Shh… everyone.' Alice raises her hands. 'Ben's car has just arrived and they're getting out. On the count of three we'll sing Happy Anniversary to the tune of Happy Birthday. Are you all ready? One, two, three…'

Almost three o'clock, Fran thinks, is a reasonable time to go home. The food has been eaten, the cake cut, and the anniversary banner has become detached at one end so that the message hangs vertically over the left-hand end of the stage like a kite tail. She glances around the room. She ought at least to say goodbye to Toby and Viv, but they are engrossed in conversation, pointing out one of the photographs on the board to another white-haired couple. Besides, she feels exhausted, exhausted by the chatter and warmth and company of other people, which all at once seems to have acquired the claustrophobic nature of a too-hot jumper.

Collecting her coat, she slips out of the door. The rain has stopped and in its place snow is falling in a gentle, wayward, flurry. She walks across the grass towards the coast road, inhaling the cold shock of the December air and the wide, still silence. To the west the sky is a firepit of pink and orange, while over the marsh the geese sketch ever-changing shapes amongst the clouds. The end of the war might seem a long time ago to the woman with the freckles, but to her the years seem to have lasted merely a couple of weeks, and to the wild expanse of water-logged land, she thinks, are nothing but the quickest, briefest, blink of an eye.

She halts. The snow is becoming heavier and she has left her umbrella in the cloakroom. Even though one of the spokes is broken and retrieving the wretched thing means venturing once again into the party, the alternative is a wet journey home and another trip to the village hall tomorrow. And she has had quite enough of the village hall for a while. With a sigh she begins to retrace her steps.

She almost reaches the side door before she sees him. At first she assumes her sight is playing tricks and then that she must be dreaming or has drunk too much champagne. She wants to walk faster but her feet refuse to cooperate, moving more and more slowly until she's afraid they might stop altogether.

'Fran?' He sounds incredulous.

Although it is she, surely, who should be amazed. She swallows and stares at the face, the exact same face, imprinted on her memory from forty-two years ago.

Or from last week.

'It's Thomas. Do you remember me, do you know who I am?'

She blinks away snowflakes. She wants to reach out to touch him, but if she does he will undoubtedly disappear. Besides she's unable to move. Perhaps unable to breathe.

'Did you think I could possibly forget?' Bizarrely her voice sounds strong. Strong and entirely certain.

She sees his eyes, those extraordinary eyes, fill with tears. 'I thought perhaps…'

She shakes her head. Snow is falling on her cheeks, on her lashes, yet she has never felt so oblivious to the cold, to anything except the person standing directly in front of her. 'But how?' she manages, then stops.

'I came to the village hall because I saw the lights. Because this is where I should have been. Forty-two years ago. Because you were not at home and I needed to find you.'

She steps close to him, inhales the scent of his skin and takes hold of the lapels of his coat. Flakes are melting on his neck, on the wool, magical little crystals dissolving into nothing.

'I was here,' she says. 'I've been waiting for you.'

He reaches inside his coat. 'I have something. Something I kept.'

She sees a soft, white square in the palm of his hand, watches the cotton soaking up the snow. 'My handkerchief. The one that I dropped.' For a split second, she is back before the marching prisoners. Falling, tumbling into the gaze of a stranger.

Closing his fingers, his arms encircle her back. Gently at first and then with a steel-like grip.

'Fran, do you mind, do you mind that I kiss you?'

She hesitates.

From inside the hall comes music. A peal of laughter, the start of a tune, before someone selects another in its place. A jazzy, crooning number, this time. One she has heard before, many years ago. Frank Sinatra, she remembers, Martin's favourite, and all at once it feels as if the sun is rising, the birds are singing, and she knows without a doubt that Tiffany was right.

'Fran, talk to me' – his eyes hold hers – 'is it too late?'

For answer, she reaches forwards, cups her hands around his face and tugs him towards her.

A Letter from Sarah

Dear reader,

I want to say a huge thank you for choosing to read *The English Girl*. If you did enjoy it, and want to keep up to date with all my latest releases, just sign up at the following link. Your email address will never be shared and you can unsubscribe at any time.

www.bookouture.com/sarah-mitchell

The English Girl is inspired by a true story. When I was researching my first book, *The Lost Letters*, I came across a newspaper cutting of an interview with a woman who lived locally to me. She spoke about a camp for German prisoners of war at a village called Salthouse on the Norfolk coast, and how in the winter of 1946 the villagers had been asked if they might invite a prisoner into their homes for Christmas. Her parents did just that and, she, their youngest daughter, fell in love with that prisoner and – eventually – married him. Although the couple were accepted by many, she describes how some of her neighbours never came to terms with what she had done and how, for many years, one particular old lady would spit at her feet every time they passed each other. I kept that cutting, knowing that one day I would like to tell, if not that exact story, a story born of the same spirit. Of course, so much has changed since the 1940s, but it never ceases to amaze me how quickly the history of a place reveals itself if you scrape the surface. A feeling that I think the landscape in this part of Norfolk exacerbates with its beauty and sense of timelessness.

Over the course of writing *The English Girl* I became very fond of the main characters. This was just as well because most of the novel was written in 2020, during those interminable periods of lockdown when, apart from my family, they were my main source of company. During that time, I was incredibly thankful to have such an enjoyable and fulfilling job that I would normally carry out from home, regardless of any pandemic. I was also very grateful to be writing about another challenging time in history. The winter of 1946/1947 is, I believe, the snowiest and one of the coldest on record in the UK. One can only imagine the strength of character that people must have shown during those months, dealing with such extremes of weather in the aftermath of war when shortages were rife, and most families would have been coping under a heavy burden of grief. Even from the remove of my desk I found their courage inspiring. And a welcome reminder that even the darkest days pass eventually.

If you enjoyed *The English Girl*, I would be very grateful if you could write a review. I really appreciate hearing what my readers think, and it makes such a difference helping new readers to discover one of my books for the first time. Also, I love to hear from my readers – you can get in touch through Twitter – whether you have any comments or thoughts about the book or would just like to say hello. It means a great deal to know that I am not writing in isolation and that there are readers out there actually reading and enjoying my work.

With thanks,
Sarah Mitchell

 @SarahM_writer

Acknowledgements

My first thanks must be to the parents of Janette Dams of North Norfolk, who by inviting a German prisoner of war into their home on Christmas Day 1946, sowed the seed for this novel (and for their daughter, of course, a whole lot more besides). Also invaluable was a little book called *Divided City: The Berlin Wall*, by Christian Bahr, that I found on a visit to Berlin in 2019. It contains first-hand accounts by West Berliners of the events of 9 November 1989, and the description by Herr Eckard Löhde was particularly inspiring. Another book I relied upon to try to capture that historical watershed was *1989: The Year that Changed the World*, by Michael Meyer. I would also like to thank my lovely agent and editor, Veronique Baxter and Cara Chimirri, who are wonderfully supportive and who provided me with expert feedback to make this book the very best version of itself. I also owe a huge debt of gratitude to my friend Clare Barter, who reads for me with such enthusiasm and insight that I'm sure she must have been an editor in another life. Finally, as always, thank you to my husband, Peter, who had to deal with everything from crashed computers to plot holes with – during lockdown – no escape.

Lightning Source UK Ltd.
Milton Keynes UK
UKHW011820050821
388367UK00002B/168